Aisling's Cravings

O'Sheeran's Mafia Book 4

Ciara St James

Copyright

ISBN: 9781955751674

Printed in the United States of America
Editing by Mary Kern @ Ms. K Edits
Book cover by Kiwi Kreations

Blurb:

Aisling O'Sheeran has known for years who her soulmate is. The only reason she isn't with him is because he doesn't feel the same way about her as she does him. She's a sister to him. After years of secretly yearning to have him see her in a different light, she's done. She's determined to find a tiny bit of happiness with someone else. And the way to do it, she believes, is to arrange a marriage of convenience. Something her family will strenuously object to, but she's determined. Her trip to California is for more than her work at Maeve's Cellars, the family winery. She's there to see if a family friend may be the man for her. She'll never love him, but she thinks she can care for him.

Alistair has known Aisling since birth. He's hidden his love for her since she came of age. He knows he's too old, has too much blood on his hands, and he's not good enough for her. Her family may treat him like family, and his friendship with her brothers and cousins is tight, but there's no way they want him with her. Even if they do, she doesn't feel the same way. He's merely another brother or cousin in her eyes. He's determined to hide his love forever.

Only fate has another plan, and when Aisling is seriously hurt and possibly dying, the secret, which Alistair finds out isn't a secret, is revealed. As it is, he finds out she's planning something else, and he has competition, even if her family tells him she loves him too. As Alistair waits for her to heal to reveal his love, there's no guarantee he'll win her. His competition turns into more than a simple rival. There's someone after her, and they aren't out to love her. A request to the Hounds of Justice may bring war down on the O'Sheerans and the other Irish families' heads.

The journey to becoming soulmates may not end the way they both hope. If it does, what will they lose along the way? In the end, more than Aisling and Alistair win and lose things. The whole family is affected. See how these long-suffering lovers find their happily ever after with their soulmate.

Dedication

This is dedicated to those who feel they've lost their chance with their soulmate. Never give up. You never know when the tiniest thing can change your life. That person you've loved from afar may be seeing you the same way. Or they might suddenly see you in a whole new light. While Insta-love scenarios are great, there's something to be said for a slow burn.

My husband, Trident, and I were the latter. From the moment we first met until we married was about eight and a half years. The tricky part was that we saw each other, and then it was five years before we laid eyes on each other again. At least by then, I was legal, LOL. There are eight years between us, and I didn't look my age. From there, we became pen pals. He was in the military and lived in another state and, for a few years, another country. By the time we married, we'd spent a total of about five weeks total physically around each other. January 2025 will be our thirtieth anniversary. Even as crazy and frustrating as he or I can be at times, he's my best friend and soulmate.

O'Sheerans / Soulmates:

Darragh w/ Ashlynn
Rian w/ TBD
Rory w/ TBD
Siobhan (Siv) w/ TBD
Declan w/ TBD
Cian w/ Miranda
Cillian w/ TBD
Ciaran w/ TBD
Cara w/ TBD
Fallon w/ TBD
Aidan w/ Karizma
Shane w/ TBD
Tiernan w/ TBD
Aisling (Ais) w/ Alistair
Cathal w/ TBD

Reading Order

For Dublin Falls Archangel's Warriors MC (DFAW), Hunters Creek Archangel's Warriors MC (HCAW), Iron Punishers MC (IPMC), Dark Patriots (DP), & Pagan Souls of Cherokee MC (PSCMC)

Terror's Temptress DFAW 1
Savage's Princess DFAW 2
Steel & Hammer's Hellcat DFAW 3
Menace's Siren DFAW 4
Ranger's Enchantress DFAW 5
Ghost's Beauty DFAW 6
Viper's Vixen DFAW 7
Devil Dog's Precious DFAW 8
Blaze's Spitfire DFAW 9
Smoke's Tigress DFAW 10
Hawk's Huntress DFAW 11
Bull's Duchess HCAW 1
Storm's Flame DFAW 12
Rebel's Firecracker HCAW 2
Ajax's Nymph HCAW 3
Razor's Wildcat DFAW 13
Capone's Wild Thing DFAW 14
Falcon's She-Devil DFAW 15
Demon's Hellion HCAW 4
Torch's Tornado DFAW 16
Voodoo's Sorceress DFAW 17

Reaper's Banshee IPMC 1
Bear's Beloved HCAW 5
Outlaw's Jewel HVAW 6
Undertaker's Resurrection DP 1
Agony's Medicine Woman PSCMC 1
Ink's Whirlwind IP 2
Payne's Goddess HCAW 7
Maverick's Kitten HCAW 8
Tiger & Thorn's Tempest DFAW 18
Dare's Doll PSC 2
Maniac's Imp IP 3
Tank's Treasure HCAW 9
Blade's Boo DFAW 19
Law's Valkyrie DFAW 20
Gabriel's Retaliation DP 2
Knight's Bright Eyes PSC 3
Joker's Queen HCAW 10
Bandit & Coyote's Passion DFAW 21
Sniper's Dynamo & Gunner's Diamond DFAW 22
Slash's Dove HCAW 11
Lash's Hurricane IP 4
Spawn's She-Wolf IP 5
Griffin's Revelation DP 3

For Ares Infidels MC

Sin's Enticement AIMC 1
Executioner's Enthrallment AIMC 2
Pitbull's Enslavement AIMC 3
Omen's Entrapment AIMC 4
Cuffs' Enchainment AIMC 5
Rampage's Enchantment AIMC 6
Wrecker's Ensnarement AIMC 7
Trident's Enjoyment AIMC 8

Fang's Enlightenment AIMC 9
Talon's Enamorment AIMC 10
Ares Infidels in NY AIMC 11
Phantom's Emblazonment AIMC 12
Saint's Enrapturement AIMC 13
Phalanx & Bullet's Entwinement AIMC 14
Torpedo's Entrancement AIMC 15
Boomer's Embroilment AIMC 16
Daredevil's Engulfment AIMC 17

For O'Sheerans Mafia

Darragh's Dilemma
Cian's Complication
Aidan's Ardor
Aisling's Craving

House of Lustz

Mikhail's Playhouse

Please follow Ciara on Facebook. For information on new releases & to catch up with Ciara, go to www.ciara-st-james.com or www.facebook.com/ciara.stjames.1 or https://www.facebook.com/groups/342893626927134 (Ciara St James Angels) or https://www.facebook.com/groups/923322252903958 (House of Lustz by Ciara St James) or https://www.facebook.com/groups/1404894160210851 (O'Sheeran Mafia by Ciara St James)

Irish/ Scottish Dictionary:

Angel/ angels= aingeal/aingil
Aunt/ aunts= aintín/ aintíni
Baby= leanbh
Baby (Scottish)= leanabh
Baby girl= cailín leanbh
Beautiful= álainn
Beautiful (Scottish)= bòidheach
Bastard= tuílí
Beast= ainmhí
Bitch= soith
Boss= ceann mi urra
Boy/Boys=buachaill /buachaillí
bride= brídeach
Brother/ brothers= deartháir/deartháireacha
Brother (Scottish)= bràthair
Bullshit= cac tarbh
Clan chief= ceannaire clan
Chief= taoiseach
Christ sake= son Chríost
Cock= coileach
Cocksucker= sucker coileach
Cousin/ cousins= col ceathrar/ col ceathracha
Crazy= craiceáilte
Dad= daid
Dad (Scottish)= *athair*
Daddy= daidí

Damn= diabhal
Darling (Irish & Scottish)= a stór
Daughter= iníon
Elder Elders = sine/ sinsir
Family= teaghlach
Father= athair
Fathers/dads= aithreacha
Fiancée= fiana
Firebrand= branda dóiteáin
Fuck (interjection)= foc
Fucker= fíochmhar
Fuck no= fuck uimh
Girls= cailíní
God= Dia
God= (Scottish) Dhia
Goddamn= diabhal
Grandbabies= *gariníonacha*
Grandmother= seanmháthair
Granny= mamó
Grandpa= daideo
Grandson/ My grandson= garmhac/ mo
gharmhac
Head of Clan= ceann fine
Healer= *bean leighis (medicine woman)*
Health!= Sláinte (drinking toast)
Hell= ifreann
Honey= mil
Hounds of Justice= Cúnna Ceartais
Idiot= amadán
I Love You= Is brea liom tú
Ireland= Éireann
Irish= *Gaeilge*
Jesus Christ= Íosa Chíost

Leader= ceannaire
Leader of the family= ceannaire an teagh laigh
Leader of the Hounds of Justice= *Ceannaire Cúirt an Cheartais*
Little Angel= aingeal beag
Little Brother- deartháir beag
Little girl= cailín beag
Little sister= deirfiúr beag
Lord= Tiarna
Love of my life and keeper of my soul= Grá mo shoal agus coimeádaí m'anama
Love you= mo ghráthu
Mom= mam
Moms= *mamaí*
Moron/s= moróin
Mother= màthair
My Angel= m'aingeal
My Beauty= *mo áilleacht*
My Love= *mo gra*
My Love (Scottish)= Mo ghràdh
My Darling= *mo stór*
My Defender= *mo chosantóir*
My Defender (Scottish)= mo neach-dìon
My sweetheart= mo leannan
My Heart= mo chroí
My One True Love= *mo ghrá amháin fíor*
My queen= mo banríon
My king= mo rí
My Beautiful Vision= m'fhís álainn
My Beautiful Vision (Scottish)= mo shealladh àlainn
No= nil
Our family= ár muintir

Piece of shit= píosa cac
Princess= banphrionsa
Pussy= púicín
Sack of shit=sac cac
Scottish trickery= cleasíocht Albananch
Sexy Goddess=bandie sexy
Shithead= ceann cac
Siblings= deartháireacha
Sister= deirfiúr
Son/ sons= mac/clann mhac
Son of a bitch= mac soith
Son of a bitch (Scottish)= *mac galla*
Sons of a bitches= mac bitches
Soulmate/ Soulmates= anamchara/ comhghlea
    caithe anam
Sweetheart= muirnín
Tempest= aimsir
Thank God= Buíochas le Dia
Thank you= go raibh maith agat
Thank you, God= Go raibh mait agat Dia
The   Family   always   protects   the   family=
cosnaíonn
    an teacghlach an teaghlach i gcónaí
Three terrors= tri sceimhle
Uncle/ uncles= uncail/ uncaili
Welcome= *Céad mile fáilte*
Whore= fraochÚn
Wife= *bean chéile*
Wife= (Scottish) *bhean*
Wildcat= cat fiáin
Witch= *cailleach*
woman= bean

Collins   Irish   Dictionary,   2019   and   Google

Translate: Irish and Italian translations

Aisling: Chapter 1

Another year had come and gone, and I wondered what this year would bring my family. Last year was a momentous one with three weddings. I enjoyed seeing both of my cousins and my oldest brother find their *comhghleacaithe anam*, soulmates. The happiness those women brought to them and the rest of our family was unbelievable. They were already like sisters, and they weren't the only ones we added to our family.

Alexis, Ashlynn's little sister, had been adopted as everyone's baby sister. She left her unfeeling, cold, and judgmental parents and now resided at the compound with all of us. Rather than live with Darragh and Ashlynn, even though they asked her to, she settled after a while at the main house. Lord knows it had more than enough room. She could wander around and never see anyone if she didn't want to. She had her own private quarters and was spoiled by all our parents as well as our *mamó,* granny.

Alexis was attending college and getting her life back on track after her horrible ordeal with the illegal underage porn makers who had trapped her, then forced her to work for them or risk them killing her family. It was Ashlynn's desire to free her sister and to stop those predators, which led her to come to us seeking assistance when the police weren't able to help her. One look at her and Darragh was a goner. It was hard to believe it had just been a year since they met. Now they are not only married but expecting their first baby, a son, next month. We couldn't wait to meet him.

Cian and Miranda had met not long after Darragh and Ashlynn. We loved to tease him about how he was actually working for once, and going to the bank himself was what brought him Randi. She was the right person to balance him. Of course, it hadn't been smooth sailing for them with her crazy admirers and her father. Only Cian would fall for the daughter of St. Augustine's police chief. A guy who'd disliked all of us and wanted nothing more than to see us put in prison for the rest of our lives. Thankfully, he changed his tune and now saw us in a different light. He wasn't naïve. He knew we weren't squeaky clean, but he could live with why we got our hands dirty or the part he knew. Cian and Miranda's wedding was three months ago, and they were due to have their first baby in June. They hadn't told anyone what they were having. They said they wanted it to be a surprise.

The last one to fall was my brother Aidan. His fall wasn't exactly perfect. The knucklehead jumped to the wrong conclusions about the new bartender at Sirens, our nightclub, and he fired her. When he found out he was wrong, and before he could make it right, she was hurt in a mugging. Somehow, he worked his charm on her and gained her forgiveness. It made me wonder who would find their one and only this year. Karizma brought even more than herself to our family. Her five-year-old daughter, Khloe, was an angel we all adored. She had everyone twisted around her little finger, especially my brother.

In addition, Karizma's mom, Carmen, and her

boyfriend, Bax, came along with those two. They hadn't trusted Aidan not to hurt Riza and Khloe at first, and it caused hard feelings between mother and daughter. But since their wedding, those feelings had mostly been repaired. Helping it along, I believed, was the fact Riza and Aidan were giving Carmen another grandchild. Their baby was due two months after Cian and Randi's. Three babies in seven months had to be a record.

With all the love in the air and new family members, you'd think I'd be over the moon about this new year, and on one level, I was. I was happy for them and wanted to get my hands on those babies. I wanted my other siblings and cousins to find their forever love. On the other hand, it only showed me what I didn't have and would never have. Everyone else who was single saw these three as the beginning of us all finding our *anamchara*, soulmate. And I thought it was too, for them. As for me, I already knew who mine was and he and I would never be together.

Hence, I was taking this extended trip to California, to Temecula, where our winery, Maeve's Cellars, was located in the States. No one thought anything of it since I was the one who managed the winery business for our family. We had one there and one in Italy, which was a new venture. This trip was for more than work. I needed to escape. Watching them all so happy and then seeing him was too much. I felt raw inside. There were times I would look down, swearing my heart was ripped out of my chest. I couldn't take it any longer.

As much as I loved my family, I was considering the possibility of doing two things that they wouldn't understand or support. One was to move away from the compound in Florida, where we all lived, and move to California. Even though I oversaw Maeve's and the work could be done remotely, I liked being more hands-on. The second thing they would object to strenuously was my marriage, a marriage of convenience. This would disappoint and probably infuriate them. They'd object loudly and long if I chose to do it.

In our family, the stance was we would only marry for love and when we met our *anamchara*. Our grandparents and parents had done it and now three of the current generation had. For the guys, they'd been waiting longer than us girls. Darragh was forty before meeting Ashlynn. Cian was thirty-nine, and Aidan was thirty-seven. I would be twenty-seven in two months, and many would say I had plenty of time. The reality was time didn't matter. My *anamchara* didn't want me and if I couldn't have him, it didn't matter who I married. So why wait?

This was why I was considering a marriage of convenience with someone I liked and would at least not want to kill. I would never lie and tell him I loved him when I didn't. He would know from the start what I was able to give and not give him. It would be a real marriage with expected fidelity on both sides and children. I had no doubt I would grow to feel affection for him, just never love.

If my family knew I was considering this, they would've never let me leave Florida. I'd be locked up at the compound with them trying to talk me out of it night and day. So, the trip here was for more than work. It was to escape my pain, too. It was to decide if I would go down this path, and if I did, who would I marry? I had a possible candidate in mind. I just needed to see if we got along in the long term and then if he'd agree.

That was enough thinking about the depressing part of my life. I was expected at the winery. And I enjoyed my job as a vintner. I'd studied hard to learn the craft. One of my favorite parts was working with the viticulturists, the scientists who knew everything about cultivating and harvesting grapes. Make no mistake, winemaking was a science, and competition was steep. You had to know what you were doing. Grabbing my purse and briefcase, I went to the door. When I opened it, Creed was standing there waiting for me.

I smiled at him as he escorted me to the waiting car. Creed was my bodyguard, and he went just about everywhere with me. The family wouldn't have it any other way. We all had bodyguards, even though were well-versed in personal protection. It was an unavoidable cost of being who we were. As we pulled away, I opened my briefcase to make one final review of the report I was sent on the new wines we were working on. I wanted to be prepared inside and out for my meeting. My dismal love life could wait.

Alistair:

The meeting of the *Cúnna Ceartais,* Hounds of Justice, had just wrapped up. It had been an extra-long one this time. We'd received not one but four requests for our services. Of course, the requesters had no idea they were asking the notorious O'Sheeran family to help them. What they asked to have done wasn't legal, no matter where you were. Being assassins-for-hire wasn't a typical job, nor was it ignored by the authorities. Anonymity was key.

I found it somewhat ironic. The O'Sheerans were technically a retired Irish Mafia family. Many law enforcement agencies still thought they were involved in the mobster lifestyle and would love nothing more than to be able to get something on them. If only they knew. The family created the Hounds back during Patrick's time as the head of the clan. It was their way of continuing to eliminate those who they knew were the truly evil ones in the world. Rapists, murderers of the innocent, pedophiles, and such. The type of people they protected their territories from when they were indeed the Mafia.

My father had been one of the original Hounds, and I grew up with the current generation of kids. We'd been wild and had a lot of fun. As we got older, I knew I wanted nothing more than to be a part of the Hounds. When I was eighteen, I went off to the Marines and spent the next ten years perfecting my skills in hot spots all over the world. In the beginning, it was as a regular Marine, but later as part of the MARSOC Raiders. The Raiders were a Marine Corps group specially trained to be a part of the US Special Operations Command. We were the ones who were dropped into complex and remote locations and had to operate in fast-paced and extremely dangerous situations. We conducted special reconnaissance, direct action, counter-terrorism, information ops, foreign internal defense, and unconventional warfare. I came back well-versed to perform the duties of the Hounds.

My father retired a couple of years after I joined then passed away a year later. That was ten years ago. As time passed, I was put in command of the team, with only Darragh as our ultimate boss. We did confer with a core group of our people on what assignments to take, but the ultimate decision-makers were him and me. Before anything was agreed to, a thorough investigation was launched. Our tech people, led by Cody, would dig through the lives of those involved. Not just the person or persons to be eliminated but also the people asking for the job to be done. No way did we want to be used to exact revenge or to get retribution of any kind on anyone who didn't deserve it.

If all parties checked out, the payment was made through layers of protection to an account that couldn't be traced back to the O'Sheerans. Sometimes, it wasn't money but a favor or some other promise paid in lieu of money. Not everyone had to be rich to benefit from our service. Besides, we didn't do it for the money. All communication was through a secure server, which again wasn't traceable. I loved what I did.

I listened with half an ear to Darragh and a few of his cousins talking. With the meeting over and the rest of the team dismissed, we were kicked back in CC, Command Center, underneath the main house on their family compound. It was the nexus point where all the various tunnels that ran underneath the compound and the houses on it met. It was not only a communication center but a massive safety bunker. Enemies coming for them would get more than a few surprises.

I jerked to attention when I heard them say her name, Aisling. I leaned forward in my chair so I could hear better. Aidan was the one who said her name, and he was saying it to Dar and Tiernan, one of his brothers.

"You think?" Tiernan asked. He was frowning.

"I do. Aisling has been gone for almost a month. She left right after New Year's and claimed she would only be gone for a week, maybe two max. I asked *Uncail* Patrick if there was trouble at Maeve's Cellars we should know about. He said no. I didn't think anything about it until I saw the news reports. Now, I'm not sure if work is the reason she's staying in Cali," Aidan explained with a bigger frown.

News reports? What news reports? What had I missed? I'd been out of things, on a mission for most of the month, but surely, if something had happened, someone would've told me when I got back.

"Surely not. I mean, sure, we know how he is, but so does Ais. We've always been friendly with him and his family, but I can't see her having a relationship with him." Tiernan scoffed.

My heart leaped. Aisling was seeing a man? Someone they appeared to think wasn't right for her. I had to hold myself in tight control not to come to my feet and shout she wasn't to be with any man. To do so would expose my deepest yearning. One I didn't see them appreciating or blessing. Aisling was one of the three princesses of the family. Her family would only want the best for her. I had too much blood on my hands to ever be good enough for her.

"They've been seen out together multiple times since she went to Temecula. He's been out to the house and even the winery. I don't know if we can assume anything," Dar cautioned them.

"You think she'd get serious about Christopher? I mean, sure, he's flirted with her over the years, but I never got the feeling it was anything more on either side. She's waiting for her *anamchara*. I can't believe suddenly, after all these years, he's turned into that," Tiernan objected.

The only Christopher I knew of who'd been around for years and was a major flirt was Christopher Brynes. He was part of the Brynes family, one of the other top Irish Mafia families in the States. There used to be six, with the O'Sheerans at the top, but now there were five after the elimination of the Doyles. They came after the women in this family one time too many. The few members left had bigger things to worry about than plotting revenge on us. They were trying merely to eke out a living. The other three families were the Kilkennys, the Connallys, and the Bragans.

My mouth tightened at the thought of it being Christopher. He was a manwhore and had been trying to charm Aisling, Cara, and Siobhan since they were teenagers. Every time I saw him, I gritted my teeth because I had the urge to punch him in his pretty face.

Hearing he was now spending time with her, and it didn't sound like just at special functions where they were both guests, made my ire rise more.

"What does Creed have to say about it?" Aidan asked, directing his question to Darragh.

"Why're you asking me? Do you think I asked her bodyguard to report back to me?" he asked innocently.

"Yeah, you fucking have them all reporting anything they find suspicious or worrisome to you. Don't lie. We know. You controlling *tuílí*, bastard," Aidan said with a smirk. Tiernan laughed and nodded his head in agreement. They weren't wrong. Dar took the protection of everyone in his family extremely seriously.

Darragh grinned and didn't answer them for a few moments, then he put them out of their misery. "Alright, I might've heard something. It seems Chrisopher has been spending a lot of time with her at the house. He hasn't stayed the night, but he's there for hours, and Ais dismisses Creed to stay outside or in his section of the house."

"*Mac soith*, son of a bitch! No, Dar, we can't let her end up with him. You know how he is. He makes chasing women look like an Olympic sport. People think we're playboys, but he is one. Hell no, he's not using our sister. I'm going out there and having a talk with him," Tiernan said angrily.

"If you do that, she'll lose her fucking mind and probably date him just to spite you. No, we have to be smart about this. We might be overreacting," Dar warned him.

I knew I should keep my mouth shut, but I wasn't able to. "I can go. You can make up an excuse that I'm out there doing work for the Hounds and you asked me to check and see how things are going with her. I'll keep an eye out for a few days and see what I find out."

Three sets of eyes landed on me and studied me thoroughly. I made sure my face only showed a calm facade. No need to let them know I wanted to go, and if I caught Christopher up to something, I'd be more than happy to beat the shit out of him and send him on his way. Finally, it was Darragh who responded to my offer.

"It's an idea. We could make it work. Why don't you hold on to that thought, Alistair? First, let me see if Creed can find out anything. Give it another week and if there's no news or they continue to be seen together, then we'll send you out."

"Should we wait, though? It sounds like the news reporters and paparazzi are speculating on the two of them being a couple," Aidan reminded him.

"Let 'em. They speculate about us no matter what. Another week shouldn't hurt. I don't believe they're honestly getting serious, but if they are, we need to know what his intentions are," Dar added.

"What do you mean?" Tiernan asked.

"Yes, Christopher is a lady's man, but even they can be reformed by the right woman. It's possible he may have fallen for Aisling, and she fell for him. If it's true love, no way can we stand in their way. We'll have to be sure he knows to be positive about his feelings and what'll happen if he hurts her in any way. She deserves happiness and a family of her own. It's gonna happen one day. We have to face the inevitable day when a man comes along and makes her his for the rest of their lives," he responded.

I couldn't stand here and listen anymore. I was

about to lose it. My stomach had a tight knot in it, and I felt nauseous. I stood up. "Well, if you don't need me, then I have some things I gotta do. I'll talk to you all later. Let me know if I need to go to California," I said to them as a whole.

"Sure will. See you later," Aidan said. The others called out and I waved as I walked out.

It took everything I had to walk casually out rather than storm away. I maintained my calm until I was in my car, and then I tore out of the compound as if the actual hounds of hell were after me. I didn't head into town. Instead, I headed away. As I drove, images of Aisling assailed me. I remembered back to the first time I saw her as something more than a child. It was the summer she turned sixteen. I was twenty-nine and had returned home from the Marines for good. Over the years, I made trips home, but I didn't always see the younger O'Sheerans.

Everyone was gathered at the pool that day. I was asked to join them for a day of relaxation. When she walked out in her bathing suit, it struck me she was growing up. She was a young lady, not a child. At the time, I only watched her as a friend. But over the next two years, she grew into an even more beautiful woman. When she turned eighteen, I had to admit I found her attractive in a sexual way. It made me feel like a dirty old man when she was only eighteen and I was thirty-one. I chose to ignore it and assumed those thoughts would go away.

They didn't. For the past eight-and-a-half years, they'd steadily grown. I tried to stay away as much as possible but the temptation to see her would grow to be too much and I'd cave and find an excuse to come to the main office when I knew she would be there or to drop by the compound on some pretext. Every glimpse only made me want her more. I'd wondered several times what the family would say if I told any of them I loved her and wanted her as my wife. Would they threaten me? Kick me out of the Hounds? Have my ass put in the ground? Maybe not the last one, but who knew?

However, to tell them would be senseless since she didn't see me the same way. Sure, she would flirt and tease sometimes. I did it too. She thought when I called her my love, I was joking. They all did. They had no clue I meant it. It killed me over the years to watch her date other men and to know she was sleeping with them, but I kept my mouth shut. It wouldn't be fair to burden her with my unrequited feelings. Even if she did return them, I was too old for her and I had too much blood on my hands to ever be good enough for her.

I tried to forget her. I dated other women. I took them to my bed, but they weren't Aisling and never lasted. Not once was I tempted to make one of them my girlfriend or wife. I know now that if I didn't marry Aisling, I'd never marry.

As the miles flew by, I made myself a deal. If Darragh or one of the others didn't give me permission to go to California to see what the hell was going on by the end of the week, I'd go on my own. I may have to let her be with someone, but not him. For sure, if I wasn't good enough for her, Christopher Brynes sure the hell wasn't.

Needing to work off my tension, I made the decision to go to the property most of the Hounds lived on and go out to our shooting range for target practice. I'd be able to imagine it was his face every time I put a bullet through the target. With this plan, I did a U-turn in the middle of the road. There was no one coming, so it wasn't endangering anyone. There was a smaller property owned by the family not too far from the family compound. The Hounds trained, and many of them lived there. It wasn't a requirement you had to live there, but you did have to live within twenty miles of St. Augustine. Sometimes, we had to deploy without notice, and this way, we didn't have to wait hours for members to get there. We were further out in the swampier area. The fewer people that came around to see what we were doing, the better. Prying eyes was the last thing any of us needed or wanted.

I hadn't realized how far I'd driven while I was lost in my head. It wasn't the most brilliant move to make, but since when had I been smart when it came to her? Other than keeping my feelings to myself, I wasn't able to protect my heart. As each year passed, my yearning got worse. I knew I'd have to take drastic measures soon before I broke. Leaving the Hounds was the last thing I wanted to do, but if they wouldn't let me work for them and be further away, I'd never be able to take it.

Aisling: Chapter 2

Four weeks. I found it hard to believe I'd been here four weeks already. In some ways, it seemed shorter. Maybe it was due to how busy I'd been. During the day, most days I spent hours at the winery, meeting and working with our employees or talking to people who came to our tasting rooms. When I wasn't doing those, I was in other meetings and talking to prospective clients interested in having Maeve's Cellars' wines sold in their establishments. Those ranged from restaurants and wine bars to actual higher end wine stores and merchants. We were making a more significant mark on the wine scene, and it wasn't just in California. Our wines were winning awards and this kind of recognition brought more interest in doing business with us. I was incredibly proud of what the staff and I had accomplished since I took over five years ago.

In addition to my work, I'd been spending several nights a week out. Sometimes, they were dinners and charity events where the O'Sheeran name brought attention and donors, in addition to what we personally donated to the causes we believed in. If they weren't those kinds of nights, I would go to dinner with friends or out with Christopher Brynes, the one I was trying to decide if we would be able to tolerate each other enough to be married.

Christopher, or Chris as I called him, had been a

part of my life for as long as I was able to remember. Although his family and mine were considered technically enemies, in reality, we weren't. My family was much cleaner than his these days, which was a significant consideration for me. Would I be able to be a part of his family's dealings? I wasn't sure. Admittedly, his family was nothing like the Doyles. That family's various businesses consisted of so many things I hated: prostitution, drugs, and gun smuggling. If Chris wanted this marriage, would he be willing to make changes in his family's business dealings? He was the oldest, and he'd taken over as head of the family like Darragh had ours. It would take hard work, but it was possible. I could help him do it.

I hadn't asked him if he would consider us joining our families. I wasn't broaching it unless I was positive I'd be able to do it. From a desirability standpoint, Chris was a very attractive man. Some might call him a bit pretty, but he was still manly and fit. Chris had no difficulty finding women. It was his ability to get them and how many he'd been with over the years, which was one of the factors that made me hesitate. I didn't want to tie myself to someone who would cheat on me and expect me to live with it. Even if we didn't love each other, fidelity was a must.

Sexually, I thought I'd have no trouble having sex with him. He was very sexually appealing. Intellectually, he was an intelligent guy, and he and I had many interesting conversations over the years once you got him past the flirting stage. When I called him to say I was in California and asked if he would like to have dinner, he jumped at the chance. For the past four weeks, we'd been seeing each other a few times a week, and not all were at social or charity events. He hung out with me at the house, or I went to his.

We hadn't slept together, but he'd kissed me the last few times, and it was kinda intense and enjoyable. So why hadn't I pulled the trigger and asked him if he had ever considered a marriage of convenience? And if he had, what about us? I didn't want to admit the reason, but I knew why. It was because of him, Alistair. The man I loved and had no hope of having.

I was pathetic. I'd formed a crush on Alistair when I was fourteen and he was twenty-seven. He was home on leave, and I lucked out and saw him. My heart had gone crazy. From that day forward, I listened for any word of him and prayed for him to come home safe and sound. When I was sixteen, I got my wish. I wanted to cry the day I saw him at our outdoor pool with my brothers and cousins. He was even better than I remembered. I hoped he'd see I was no longer a little girl. He hadn't. Alistair continued to treat me like he always had, as a younger sister or cousin. I hated it.

I held out hope because I was underage, he was holding back, and when I was legal, he'd confess his feelings, and we'd go on to marry and have a family. Again, I was disappointed. At that point, I tried to move on and give my heart to someone else. I dated, and I had lovers, but none of them ever lasted. They weren't him. As the years passed, I grew more and more depressed, especially when I saw the women he was with. I gave up hoping. It was the death of this hope and my inability to forget him which had me contemplating doing the one thing I never wanted to do and something my family would hate.

It was time to stop this nonsense. Tonight, when

Chris and I got back to the house, I'd see if he wanted to stay the night. If we were compatible in bed, then I'd see what he thought of my idea. The worst he could say was no. I was anxious to see what he'd say.

❧❧❧

Hours later after we'd gone to dinner, we were on our way back to my house. I found I was nervous about what might come when we got there. Creed and Chris's bodyguard Scotty were riding in the car behind ours. I'd convinced Creed to let us be alone. I knew he wasn't happy, but it wasn't as if this had never been done before.

We weren't far from the house, and we were laughing about the couple who came over to our table wanting to have their pictures taken with real-life mobsters—their words, not ours. I told them I wasn't one, and Chris denied it even though technically he was one. They'd been disappointed and spent the rest of dinner staring at us and taking sly photos of us on their phones. People truly baffled me.

"Did you see her face when you caught her sneaking the first picture?" I asked him.

"Yeah, she looked so—" he was cut off by the loud honking of a horn and the squeal of brakes. I whipped around in my seat to look behind us since that seemed to be where the sound came from. I gasped. A car had come out of somewhere and blocked the road for Scotty and Creed. Their vehicle was stopped.

"Oh my God, stop!" I hollered.

"Why?" Chris yelled as he eased off the gas.

"Creed and Scotty were just stopped by another car. We have to go back. We need to stay close to them."

"Fuck," he muttered.

Abruptly, he spun the wheel, and we were turning around. I was so busy trying to see if either of the men was getting out of the car that I didn't see the second car until its lights hit me in the eyes. I screamed, and automatically my hands went up in front of my face. "Chris, watch out!"

"Christ," he yelled, then there was a tremendous jolt. The screech of metal on metal was deafening. I snapped back and forth in the seatbelt. Pain shot across my chest. Glass went flying and then I felt us rolling. I couldn't seem to stop screaming. *Please don't let me die*, I pleaded to God. Chris was swearing and grunting. The car had hit my side of his car. When we stopped moving, we were hanging upside down. Pain was throbbing throughout my whole body.

"Aisling, are you alright?" I heard him asking urgently. Hands were running down my arm and face. I opened my mouth to answer him but nothing came out. I panicked as my vision began to fade. I tried to move or speak but nothing happened. His anxious gaze met mine as darkness completely overtook me.

Alistair:

Another boring night at home. I knew I didn't have to sit here and do nothing. I could be hanging with the other Hounds or out on the town. If I wanted companionship for the night, finding some wouldn't be hard. The problem was none of those things tempted me. This funk I was in lately wouldn't go away. I needed to find a way to get rid of it.

It didn't help that I was waiting for two more days to pass. Once they did, I'd be on a plane to California to see what the hell was going on between Aisling and fucking Christopher Brynes. The thought of them together had been eating at me since I overheard Darragh and them talking about it. Images of the two of them together haunted me, especially the ones of them in bed together. If I went there like this and he was sleeping with her, I wasn't sure I'd be able to resist killing the bastard.

Snapping off the television with the remote, I got to my feet. I had to get out of here even though it was almost midnight. The walls were beginning to make it hard to breathe. I got halfway to the door where my boots and stuff were when my cell phone rang. Sliding it out of my pocket I saw it was Darragh. My heart sped up. Maybe we had an assignment. That would be perfect to occupy my mind.

"Hey, Dar, good evening. What's up?"

"Alistair, I need you to get to the Command Center ASAP. Where are you?" was his urgent reply. My whole body snapped to attention. Adrenaline began to flow. Something was wrong, and based on the edge I heard in his voice, it was something terrible.

"I'm at home. I can be there in ten," I told him.

I lived on my own property not far from the family compound. As I was talking, I was slipping on my boots and shoving my other shit into my pockets and putting my gun in its holster. Anything else I might need was in my vehicle or at CC.

"Hurry," was all he said before he hung up.

Mere minutes later, I was flying down the road toward the compound. My mind was racing with thoughts of everything that could be wrong. The list was long. Was an enemy making a move against us? Or had one of the possible missions we were investigating taken an unexpected turn, requiring us to head out now? But if it was that, why didn't he just say so? No, it had to be something not related to an upcoming mission. Maybe an old one. Or had someone connected us to the work, although I didn't believe it was possible, not with all the precautions and things Cody had implemented to prevent it from happening?

Usually, I'd take one of the underground tunnels into the CC. We did this so as not to attract attention as to why multiple vehicles were coming and going to the compound all the time or at odd hours. Paparazzi were constantly popping up trying to get photographs. Tonight, I didn't bother. I went through the main gate. The guards waved me through. As I parked in front of the main house, I barely remembered to turn off the engine before bounding out of the car and up the stairs.

I knocked and rang the doorbell impatiently.

The thing with the O'Sheerans was that despite their extreme wealth, they weren't catered to by an army of servants. Sure, they had Agatha as their cook, but she was more like family, and she didn't work all the time. The ladies liked to cook for the family themselves a lot. They had gardeners and guards but no butler or anything fancy like that, which meant I had to wait for someone in the family to open the door.

When it opened, I saw an upset Cyndi standing there. I walked in. "What's wrong?" I asked. If she was upset then it wasn't work-related or not in the sense it was an assignment.

"Darragh will explain. They're all down in the Center. Hurry, Alistair." Tears gathered in her eyes.

A quick nod and I left her to get to the closest entrance to the tunnels. As I got closer to the center, I heard the loud murmur of voices. They all sounded upset. Bursting into the room, over a dozen sets of eyes landed on me, and the talk died down. I saw all the O'Sheeran men were present. The women were not. I went straight to Darragh, who was talking to Shane —Aidan and Tiernan's other brother, and their dad, Cormac. The rest of the family was gathered around them in a circle.

"I'm here. What the fuck is wrong? Cyndi looked upset as hell."

"Alistair, we need you to keep yourself locked down," Darragh said cautiously.

What the hell? Why would he tell me something like that? I had no issues keeping myself under control. I scanned the faces of the others. They were filled with worry, pain, and anger. I waited. If only I'd had a clue what was about to be said next. If I had, I would've told them to lock my ass down first.

"We just got a call from Creed. Aisling was in an accident," Darragh started out. As soon as I heard her name and accident, I let out a rumbling growl.

"Dar, it was more than that," Aidan said in a protesting tone.

"Is she alright? What does Aidan mean it was more than that?" I barked.

"Apparently, she was out with Christopher." As soon as Dar said Christopher, I growled again, only louder. He continued, "They were on their way back to our house when a car cut off Creed and Christopher's bodyguard in their car. While they tried to get around it, another vehicle T-boned the one Aisling and Christopher were in. It flipped their car—"

I cut him off before he went further. "Is she alive?"

"She's been taken to the nearest level one trauma center, which is Loma Linda University Medical Center. Creed has no other information. He's there with her."

A howl of pure anguish ripped from me. I wasn't any more able to hide my feelings than I was able to stop myself from loving her. Any thought of hiding how I felt about her washed away. I slammed both fists down on the table near me as I sank to my knees. I felt hands on my back and shoulders, but I was numb and blind to who they belonged to or what was being said. All I was able to do was think of her and the fact I might be losing her forever. If it happened, they might as well put me in the ground with her.

I had no idea how long I was lost in my head before I snapped out of it. When I did, the others were moving. Cormac was still beside me. As I looked up at him, he gave me a grim look. His hand squeezed my left shoulder tightly, painfully.

"We need you. Get up. We're going to California. The plane is gassed and ready. Let's go." His gruff command got me to my feet.

I'd like to say I started to fully function and think at that point but it would be a lie. I was on autopilot as those going loaded up, and we left for the airstrip, where they kept their private planes. As we boarded and began to taxi down the runway, not too much later, it finally registered who was going. Darragh was there, as well as Cormac, Cyndi, Aidan, Shane, Tiernan, and Cathal which made sense since they were her brothers and parents. Darragh made sense as the head of the family, and I understood why Patrick and Maeve came, too. The rest were their personal bodyguards. They were gathered in the far back, giving the family a semblance of privacy. I knew it must be killing the others to stay behind.

"The rest of the family is on standby. They'll come as soon as we have news. I didn't think we'd get out of there without all of them but time was of the essence," Darragh was saying when I tuned back in.

"Why the hell was Creed in a different car?" I barked out.

He sighed. "Aisling wanted privacy. We all do it, Alistair. There was no indication anything was wrong or that she was in danger. They were lucky Creed wasn't. It allowed him to get to her and run off the assailants before they finished the job."

"Finished it? What?" I snapped.

"It wasn't an accident. It was intentional, and the people who caused it aggressively converged on the car, Creed said. They acted like they were there to kill someone. The only thing we don't know is, was Christopher the target or her?" Cormac added. He was holding Cyndi tucked against his chest. Her red-rimmed eyes attested to her crying even if I hadn't been able to see the tear tracks on her face. Maeve was on the other side of her, rubbing her back.

This news shifted me into warrior mode. We were in the air, so I got up to move around the cabin. "What's Cody got so far? Any threats online, on the dark web? Who's there we can add to be on her protection detail? Creed alone isn't enough. We need to lock down the premises so whoever did this can't get another chance." I didn't give a damn about Brynes but it would satisfy me if he was in bad shape or even dead. The monster inside of me would relish it.

"Cody hasn't found anything but he's on it. As for security, we called Aegis and they have people out there. They're on their way now. We'll get some of our own on it too. Right now we just need to get to the hospital. Cormac had a call already, and he granted the doctor caring for her permission to do anything they needed to save her life. She's in surgery," Darragh informed me.

My brain shied away from the "save her life" part. I couldn't deal with it right now. Instead, I latched onto something else. "So I'm here as added security for you or her? Or do you need me to hunt down the culprits?"

"Believe me, we'll be hunting as soon as we can, and yes, when the time comes, I want you there for it, but that's not why we brought you. Nor is it to be additional security," Darragh stated.

"Then why? I'm confused."

I heard a throat clear. It was Cormac. He was

staring intently at me. "*Mac*, son, we told you and brought you because we know how you feel about my daughter. We've watched and waited and it's gone on long enough. It's time to confess those feelings. That's why we brought you."

A sense of panic filled me. Shit, how had they guessed before my outburst in the Center? I was sure I kept it well hidden. I decided to play it off.

"Cormac, I do care for Aisling. She's been like a little sister to me since the day she was born. I remember the day you and Cyndi brought her home from the hospital. Us boys were hanging out at the house. Of course I care about her but so do a lot of others. I'll gladly help do anything she needs."

Aidan snorted and rolled his eyes. "Come on, cut the crap. You don't see her as a sister. You haven't for a long time, I expect. Admit it."

"I have no idea where you got that idea."

"If he can't admit it, even when she might be dying, then fuck him," Tiernan snarled. He was on his feet, glaring at me.

"She's not gonna die!" I yelled.

"She might. Face it. She might die and you wanna hold on to your pride or whatever the fuck it is which keeps you from admitting you love our sister!" he shouted back.

We were close now, and I shoved him on the chest. He didn't rock back far as he stood his ground. I was fuming. "I'm not being prideful, dumbass."

Over the years, we'd all gotten into our fair share of scraps with each other. We were all strong, alpha men, and we had tempers. Sometimes, those would get out of control. More than one fistfight had occurred.

Another was about to if he didn't get out of my face.

"Stop!" came the alarmed voice of Cyndi. I paused. I glanced over at her.

She was crying again. Shit, I hated to see a woman cry, especially one I cared about. Cyndi was like a mom to me. All the older O'Sheeran women were. I took two steps back and Tiernan did the same. He cast his mom an apologetic look.

"*Mam*, I'm sorry," he said quietly.

"Don't be sorry. Settle down," Cyndi told him. He retook his seat, and I did the same. Once we were back in them, she turned to me again.

"Alistair, honey, I need you to be honest with me. We know you care for Aisling, and it's more than as a brother. Why won't you admit it? The time for hiding is over. We might lose her." She whispered the last part.

As I watched the misery and pain swamp her, I gave up. It didn't matter if they knew or not. They were right. If she was dying, this would be my last chance to see and tell her how I felt about her. The fact she didn't feel the same was no longer important. All of them were watching me.

"What good does it do to admit it, Cyndi? There's nothing I can do about it. I don't want anyone to pity me," I told her reluctantly.

"Why would we pity you? And it's good to admit the truth," was her response.

"Because I'm a fool for having these feelings. It's not like I can do anything about them."

"Why not?" Cormac interjected.

"Come on, even if Aisling had those kinds of feelings for me, which she doesn't, there's no way you'd want her to be with a man like me," I scoffed. Why were they forcing me to confess this shit? Did they want to make it more painful as they rubbed it in how I was never someone good enough for Aisling? I knew I wasn't, damn it.

"What kind of man are you?" Patrick asked suddenly. Up until then, he'd been silent and watchful.

"You know what kind I am. Come on, do you really want me to say it?" As I glanced around, I saw none of them were responding, but they were all watching me. Even the guards in the back had gotten quiet and were observing us. Finnigan and Seamus were Darragh's guards. Madden protected Cormac and Cyndi. Shane was shadowed by Niall while Gael oversaw Aidan's protection. Milo was here for Tiernan, while Troi and Riggs were guards for Cathal, Patrick, and Maeve. I continued.

"A killer who has blood on his hands he can never wash off. I've defended my country, the innocents we protect, and this family, and I don't regret it, but the things I've done have damned my soul. Even if I didn't have those things, I'm not the same as all of you. I'll never be the man Aisling deserves. She needs and deserves someone who'll be able to support her and help her navigate the world while loving and protecting her. A man who is her equal in every way. That's what I mean."

"Whether your soul is damned, we can debate, but if it is, it's not any different from our souls. We've killed, and it was in defense of our family and others as well as, in some cases, our country too. We'll never get the blood off ours either. Like you, we don't regret it for a second," Darragh stated.

"You say our daughter deserves a man who can

support and help her navigate the world and, on top of that, protect and love her. A man who's her equal in every way, right?" Cormac asked.

"Yes." What more did he want me to say? Why were we hashing through this?

"She knows a man who's all of those things and more," Cyndi declared.

"You think Christopher Brynes is the man to do all those? Are you joking? What did he do to protect her when their car was hit? Why didn't he have more men with them to prevent this? Do you honestly think he'll love her and give her everything she needs? Hell, I doubt he can keep it in his pants for more than a month," I snapped. My anger over Aisling being with him bubbled over. It was the only excuse for me speaking this way to Cyndi. Remorse was quick on the heels of my words.

"Cyndi, Mrs. O'Sheeran, I'm sorry. I didn't mean to be disrespectful."

"Hush. Enough. I don't want to hear another word. And enough of the Mrs. O shit. I wasn't talking about Christopher! He's a nice enough man, but he's not the one for my daughter. The man I'm referring to is the one sitting in front of me. The one who has loved her for a lot of years, I'm willing to bet." She stared hard at me.

I didn't know what to say. My biggest secret was out. If I weren't on a plane, thousands of feet in the air, I'd probably be trying to leave.

The silence stretched and stretched until, finally, Darragh broke it. "Well, have you nothing to say, brother? Do you love Aisling or not? Do you want to fight for her or let another man claim her?"

"Of course, I don't want another man to claim her! I fucking love her!" I roared as I got to my feet again.

"About fucking time. Jeez, I thought he'd never confess, the stubborn Scottish *tuílí*," Aidan muttered. The others were all nodding.

"I thought for sure he'd say something the day we were talking about her and Christopher seeing each other, but he didn't. He had me worried," Tiernan added.

"Worried? About what?" I asked. None of them were making sense. They should be yelling and telling me how stupid I was and how they'd never let me near her. Had I fallen into a parallel universe, or was I dreaming?

"That we had it all wrong, and you didn't love her, not as a man loves a woman, anyway. We thought for sure you'd confess your feelings that day," he explained.

"So you talked in front of me on purpose."

"Now he's getting it. Keep up. It hasn't escaped our notice over the last couple of years that you have over-the-top protective instincts when it comes to Ais. And we've seen some looks which you didn't know we saw. We talked and agreed it had to mean you love her, romantically love her. We've been waiting for you to tell her—to do something about it. We got tired of waiting, so we staged the conversation where you would hear it," Aidan told me.

"So she's not really seeing Christopher? So why were they out together?"

"Oh, she's been seeing him, and we're afraid it might mean she's considering him. Everything they said was true," Cathal popped in to add.

"Well, then what good does it do for you all to know I'm a fool?" I scowled.

"It frees you to go after her. To tell her how you

feel. I refuse to believe this is the end of her. She will get through this, and she'll need all the love and support she can get," Shane added.

"I'll support her no matter what, but confessing my feelings isn't the way to do it. She doesn't need the burden of knowing I have these feelings for her. It'll only make her feel guilty that she doesn't return them. No, this stays a secret between us."

"Alistair, for such a smart man, you're sure dense. Our daughter loves you so much. I venture to say she has since she was a teenager. Confess what you feel to her, and I promise you, she'll return your feelings," Cyndi said softly with a sweet smile.

I tried not to let myself get hopeful even though my heart jumped and began to race. They had to be wrong.

"And your nonsense about you not being good enough. It's *cac tarbh*, bullshit. Other than our sons and nephews, there's no other man we know who's as good as you. You're already family. We'd love for you to become our son-in-law," Cormac said gruffly.

Everyone's beaming smiles and nods made me choke. I was scared yet heartened by them. I slyly pinched myself to see if I was dreaming. Nope, it hurts. I was awake. Joy began to surge through me. Here was my greatest wish: acceptance by the O'Sheeran family and their blessing to be with Aisling. I only had two more things I had to know.

"The whole family agrees? They all know how I feel?"

"Yep, every damn one of them. Hell, I bet Khloe even does the little minx. *Mamó* told me before we left that if you didn't confess your love and tie Aisling down soon, she was gonna have to do something drastic. Be more afraid of her than those crazy what-ifs in your head," Darragh warned me with a grin.

"You think she really does love me in a romantic way?"

"Hell yeah. Now, can we stop talking about love and our baby sister? It's giving me hives. The mental image is making me want to kill this asshole, and then we don't have to worry," Cathal said with a grumble.

"It goes without saying if you hurt her in any way, we love ya, but we will hurt you, aka kill you if you do," Aidan warned.

"I second that," Shane called out.

"Third," Tiernan chimed in.

From the back, I heard someone mutter, "Fourth."

I saw the steely resolve in Darragh, Patrick, and Cormac's faces, telling me they would do the same.

"You don't ever have to worry about me hurting her. I do love her. I've tried not to, but I can't help it. I don't know what to say. I never imagined you'd all be okay with me and her."

"*Amadán*, idiot," Darragh said with a roll of his eyes.

With this major obstacle out of the way, my mind went to her and the unknown. I had no idea if she would make it. My gut churned at the thought. I knew they could see my fear as I looked at them and voiced the question. "What if she doesn't pull through?"

"She will. All we have to do is pray," Maeve declared.

It was this that brought all of us, even the bodyguards, together to bow our heads and pray. Even after we were done, I kept praying the whole way to

California. Heads were gonna roll, and bodies would be piling up once I found out who'd dared to harm her. Even if Brynes were the intended target, it wouldn't save them from my wrath or that of the O'Sheerans. I had no doubt this hound would soon be baying for blood.

Alistair: Chapter 3

The non-stop flight from St. Augustine Airport to the nearest airport to Loma Linda, which was Ontario-San Bernardino Airport, took almost five hours. Once we got there, it was a half hour drive to San Bernardino proper where the hospital was located. I was impatient to be there and hated the drive. Cormac had stayed in contact with the hospital and Creed. All we knew was she was alive and in surgery for most of the time we were traveling. When we landed, the latest report was that she was in recovery and the doctor was waiting for the family's arrival to update them.

With there being eighteen of us, arrangements had been made for two large limos to be waiting for us at the airport. Lucky for us, the family owned a limo company, Opulent Limos, which had offices in numerous major cities where those with extreme wealth lived and worked. Los Angeles was one of them. We were off the plane and into the limos much faster than if we'd flown commercial. Even so, it was too slow for me and I assumed the rest felt the same way. We were swept away to Loma Linda. We split both groups in half and got into the two cars.

When we arrived at the entrance of the hospital, we were dropped off and the drivers were given instructions to wait for one of us to contact them. Until then, they were on the clock and would stay in the parking lot, but they could relax and do whatever. Cushy gig if you asked me. We had all eyes on us as we got out then marched into the hospital. We were a wave of grim faces. People stopped and stared at us, nothing new when you were with the O'Sheerans. People were snapping pictures with their phones. The bodyguards and I surrounded the family.

The hospital was part of the Loma Linda University campus and, I'd been told, a big teaching hospital. We had the information on where to go, so we bypassed the front desk and went straight to the waiting area on the surgical floor. We saw Creed standing outside a room down the hall. His look of relief was visible as he saw us and then came toward us.

When we reached each other, I could see how tired and wrecked he was. His clothes were disheveled and wrinkled. His face was drawn with fatigue. He shook hands with the O'Sheeran men then me. He smiled and greeted Cyndi and Maeve. The other guards merely gave him nods or chin lifts.

"Creed, how is she? Any more news?" Darragh asked before his uncle could.

"No Darragh, nothing. She's out of surgery and in recovery. When you texted you were here, I told one of the nurses so they would go get her surgeon. I have no idea how long it'll take him to get to you. I'm so sorry. I should've been in the car with her." Remorse and disgust was evident in his voice.

"Creed, we'll talk about that later, but remember, if you had been, most likely you would've been seriously injured too and unable to do anything to protect her. You being in the other car probably saved her life," Dar told him. As mad as I was, he had a point. Creed nodded, but I knew he wasn't ready to accept it. For a man like him, it would weigh heavily on him for a while.

"What about Christopher? How badly is he hurt? I assume he had surgery too. Oh *Dia*, God, I feel awful. We haven't even thought to ask about him. I'm such a terrible person," Cyndi said shamefully. I didn't say what I thought, which was who gave a damn. He wasn't my worry, Aisling was.

"*Muirnín*, sweetheart, I'm sorry. I forgot to mention it. Creed did tell me how he was in one of his updates. Christopher was brought here, too, since he was with her and had some injuries. I'm not sure what they found out, but he was alive and talking to them, and from what Creed said, he appeared in better shape than her," Cormac said to his wife as he glanced over at Creed.

"He was brought here, and they checked him out thoroughly. He wasn't hurt nearly as badly as Aisling was. He didn't require surgery. He did break a leg and has other cuts and injuries, but nothing he won't recover from, thankfully," came the answer from a deep voice behind us. I swung around to face a stranger. He was a tall, somewhat imposing guy. Everything about him screamed bodyguard to me.

"And who are you?" I asked, not wanting to assume. He barely glanced at me. Instead, he addressed the family.

"Hello, Mr. O'Sheeran, ladies and gentlemen. It's a pleasure to meet you, although not under these circumstances. Let me introduce myself. I'm Scotty. I'm Mr. Byrnes' bodyguard." He held out his hand to shake the hands of Darragh and the family. When it came to him having to address me after ignoring my question, he paused.

"And you are?" he asked me as he examined me from head to toe.

I was opening my mouth to tell him when I was beaten to it by Darragh. "This is Alistair Graeme. He's a close and personal friend of the family and of Aisling. We're glad to hear Christopher isn't badly hurt. He was fortunate. I wonder how he got off so lucky? If you'll excuse us, Scotty, I believe the gentleman coming this way is the doctor. We need an update on Aisling then I'd like to ask you a few questions as well as Creed."

"Of course," he said before moving away.

I noticed that even though he did, he stayed close enough to hear what the doctor had to say. This irritated me. There was something about him I didn't like. I couldn't say exactly why, but he was pushed to the back of my mind as we surrounded the man in the white lab coat. He seemed distracted when Creed spoke to him.

"Dr. Case, this is Aisling's family. They'd like an update on how she's doing and what all you had to do, please," Creed explained.

"Hello. I know you have to be anxious to know where she stands. I spoke on the phone to a Mr. Cormac O'Sheeran. Would one of you happen to be him?"

"I am. You're the one I gave consent to for the surgery and any other treatments she required. I'm her father, and this is her mother."

"I am and thank you. We couldn't have waited for you to get here. I'll be honest with you. Even though she's out of surgery, she's still in critical condition. The next twenty-four to forty-eight hours are crucial. If she hangs in, then the likelihood of her pulling through is really good. There are no guarantees as you know. I wish I could make those. She was seriously injured and there are chances of complications which may arise unexpectedly no matter how well we try to prevent them."

"What exactly were her injuries and what did you do?" Darragh asked. I heard the note of impatience in his voice.

"May I ask whom I'm speaking to? I don't want to share information with just anyone. Patient confidentiality and HIPAA and all that, you know. I can't share information unless Mr. O'Sheeran gives permission," Dr. Case said, and the way he did, implied he was possibly being condescending. Did he not know who he was messing with? If he did, then he must have a death wish. I'd seen grown men a helluva lot tougher than this doctor pissing themselves after one look from Dar when he was angry.

"Everyone in this group is free to ask and receive any and all information about our daughter. We'll soon have a lot more of our family joining us. I'll be sure the staff have all their names as well. The same goes for them. This is my oldest nephew, Darragh, and he's the head of the family. Surely you've heard of Darragh O'Sheeran," Cormac informed him with a raise of his eyebrow. I knew the second it registered who they were. What a dumbass? They were always in the news and papers for one reason or another. Did the guy live under a rock?

"I-I'm sorry, I didn't recognize you, Mr. O'Sheeran. I had no idea Aisling O'Sheeran was part of that O'Sheeran family. Yes, well, uhm, her injuries as I said were severe. The paramedics who brought her in reported her side of the car took the majority of the impact and it rolled a few times, ultimately suspending her upside down from her seatbelt. Due to this, she has a concussion and multiple cuts all over her body. There was a piercing injury from a piece of metal which lacerated her liver, causing internal bleeding. We had to take her in and surgically repair it. A few bruised ribs, a contusion to her spleen, a broken arm, a dislocated shoulder, and a sprained ankle round out the list. Luckily, the break didn't require surgical repair. I saw the pictures the officers took at the scene. She's lucky to be alive. She's weak and we have to see if she can avoid blood clots or an infection, which are two of the biggest complications at this stage. If she were to get those, her recovery might be in jeopardy."

As he listed everything that was wrong with her, I wanted to pound the wall. He was right, she was badly injured and those things and more were a definite risk. I was practically ready to jump out of my skin if I didn't get to see her soon. I had to see with my own two eyes that she was alive. I had to touch her and feel her warmth and listen to her breath.

"When can we see her?" Cormac asked.

"She should be moved to a room shortly. We're waiting for her to come out from under the anesthesia. Until we know she's off the critical list, she'll be in the ICU. The hours are posted and no more than two people at a time with her," Dr. Case stated.

"Unfortunately, that won't be possible. She has a lot of family who'll be here to see her. There will always be someone here regardless of the hours. Which in case you aren't aware, will include bodyguards. One will be in the room with her at all times and then one more minimum outside the room. As soon as she's stable, she'll need to be moved to a private room. I assume you have ones for VIPs. We'll need one," Darragh informed him.

Dr. Case stared at him aghast. He was speechless. I waited to see if he'd go with it or argue. I had news for him, arguing would get him nowhere with this family, especially Darragh. They weren't doing it to be a pain in the ass or to throw around their weight. It was to ensure her safety and privacy. While she was here, she would be vulnerable. End of story. It took Dr. Case several seconds to regain his voice.

"Mr. O'Sheeran I'm afraid it's not possible. The staff need to be able to perform their duties. Aisling needs to be able to rest so she can recover. Having people with her twenty-four seven and more than two will be too much. As for the private accommodations, we'll do our best."

"I expect nothing but your best. And we know how to stay out of the way so the staff can do their jobs. She won't be comfortable or able to relax in order to heal if her family isn't here. We'll also need to vet the staff taking care of her. We'll need their names. Also, our personal physician, Dr. Keim, will be contacting your medical director. All her care will be approved through him," Darragh added.

"Sir, our physicians are more than capable of taking care of her. Is this Dr. Keim local? I don't know him." His face was twisted up like he'd tasted a sour lemon.

"No, he's based in Florida, where we live, but I find it hard to believe you haven't heard of Dr. Gregory Keim. He's well known in most circles, especially trauma medicine."

Dr. Case grew pale. I wondered why. If he was doing everything right for Aisling, why would he be worried about Dr. Keim? Or was he merely upset because he thought Dr. K would be stepping on his toes. Well, if so, too bad. She would get the best care possible no matter what we had to do. If Dr. K couldn't handle it, he knew the people to call who could.

"I-I-I didn't realize you meant that Dr. Keim. Of course I know of him. I've never had the pleasure of meeting him. As much as we'd love to accommodate him, he's licensed in Florida and our medical licenses do not allow us to practice across state lines. He'd have to have a license here and by the time he would get his endorsement approved, she would be long healed and discharged."

"Oh, it's not a problem. He maintains his license in several states and California is one of them. I'm sure he'll have no problem getting privileges here to take care of Aisling. I'll have a word with the hospital administrator and the medical director just to be sure. Now, if that's all, will someone tell us as soon as she's moved to her room? We're anxious to see her as you can imagine," Darragh informed him.

I knew the way he was talking to the doctor, he didn't like him. If he did, he wouldn't be so overbearing. He would've still insisted on Dr. K and all the other things but the wording would've been nicer, more politically correct.

"I need to get to my other patients. I'll tell the nurses to come get you when she's moved. She'll likely sleep a lot so don't be surprised if she doesn't talk much. Excuse me," Case said before scurrying off.

"Christ, can you believe what he said was wrong with her? I want Dr. K to double check shit. I'm not totally confident in that one for some reason. Okay, let's talk to Creed and Scotty and find out exactly what happened," Darragh suggested.

He caught Creed's attention and waved him over. Scotty was pretending not to have been listening until Dar called his name. As Creed came to us, Finnigan left and went to take his spot outside of the recovery room door. We all moved off into a room nearby which ended up being the waiting room for surgical patients. We were in luck and no one was in there at the moment. I closed the door and the other guards spread out to cover the room. Seamus blocked the door so no one could disturb us.

"Tell us exactly what happened last night. Where did they go? Was there anyone suspicious who caught your attention before the accident? What happened to cause the accident? All of it," Darragh demanded.

I listened to them explain the dinner they went to. I hated the thought she'd been with him and they were on a date. I wanted to howl and tell everyone who was within hearing distance she was mine. I hoped I wasn't too late. The family insisted she loved me. What if they were wrong? Or what if her love had died because I held back and she was now in love with fucking Brynes? Either option would gut me but the latter would do it even more painfully. If my own stupidity lost me my chance with her, I didn't know what I'd do. My scattered thoughts settled when Creed began describing what happened on the drive home.

"Aisling insisted she and Mr. Byrnes take his car and we should ride in a second one. I've done it in the past, so I didn't think too much about it. We had no issues on the way to the restaurant or any at all the entire time we were there. Our whole stay here in California has been without issue. It wasn't until we were headed home and we were about twenty minutes away that it happened. They were a couple of car lengths ahead of us. Traffic wasn't terribly heavy. Suddenly, this car came barreling out of a side street and cut us off. Scotty slammed on the brakes. We barely missed hitting them. While we were yelling and waving for the driver to get out of the way, Ais and Brynes kept going, but I knew she saw what happened to us because they were slowing down and turning to come back to us. That's when another vehicle came out of nowhere and slammed into the passenger side of their car, going at least fifty miles an hour. It flipped their car, and it rolled three times.

"By then, I was out of our vehicle and running up toward them. The other one still hadn't moved. Thank God I did because two men jumped out of the one that hit her car and were headed for them. When they saw me coming, they ran to the first car, jumped in it, then took off. It was this odd behavior that proved they were working together, although I suspected it. When I got to them, Brynes was awake, trying to get her to respond to him. They were hanging upside down, and Ais was out cold and bleeding from a cut on her head and other ones. I called nine-one-one and worked to stanch the bleeding and to wake her up. At first, I was scared to death that she was dead. I didn't release her from the belt because I didn't want to cause her more injuries or make what she had worse." He inhaled a shaky breath. He'd been her personal bodyguard for three years, so they were close.

"Thank *Dia,* you were there," Cyndi whispered. She cried as Cormac held her.

"Did you get a look at their faces? What about the vehicles? What can you tell me about them? What have the cops had to say?" I asked, not to belittle how upset her mom was but to get all the pertinent details. Everything I could get to hunt these dead men.

"I did give the information on the car they got away in to Cody. The wrecked one the police had towed away. As for their faces, no. It was dark. The one who cut us off had dark tinted windows and the ones who got out after hitting them were in the shadows and backlit by other cars' headlights. But there's no doubt they were there to either kidnap or kill them. It's the only thing that makes sense. If the one car had T-boned them alone, we might've thought it was an accident and they got scared when they saw me, but no way."

"I need the information you sent Cody. I'll work on those, too. Jot down anything like clothing, approximate heights, and builds. Did they say anything? If so, did they have accents? Did you see guns on them?" I fired off.

"I did those and it'll be with the car information. No, I didn't see any guns but I highly doubt they weren't armed. There were other cars stopping and me coming toward them. That was what made them leave before completing whatever they were there to do."

The whole time he was telling us everything he recalled, Scotty stood there, not saying a word. When Creed was done, I turned to him. "You got anything to add? What were you doing while he was running to help them?"

"I was getting our car around the other one blocking the street so I could get there and help cover them."

"Why not get out and run like he did? The car wasn't important at that point. The lives of your charge and his date were," I snapped.

His laid-back attitude grated on me. He almost had what I would call a bored expression on his face. I wanted to punch it off. No way would I have someone like him as a guard or anything else. He'd never make it on the O'Sheeran protection details and he sure as fuck wouldn't make it as a Hound. In addition to training the Hounds, I often worked with the regular bodyguards and enforcers to improve their skills.

He gave me an offended look. "I didn't believe two of us on foot was the answer. The car would provide us with cover if it became a gun battle. Listen, I don't have any other details other than what he told you. I need to get back to my boss."

"Speaking of your boss, where is he?" I asked. I wanted to set eyes on the bastard.

He stiffened but I think he knew by my expression he wasn't going anywhere until he told me. "He's in room three twenty."

"Is that an ICU room too?" Aidan asked. Up until then, the others had remained quiet and let me or Darragh ask them questions.

He shook his head. "No, it's a regular room as far as I know. They didn't think he needed to be in the ICU. I need to go relieve my partner."

"So you brought in backup for you. It appears to me you slept. Your clothes are fresh. Did someone do the same for Creed?" I questioned. I knew they hadn't.

Creed was dog-tired.

"No, he didn't ask," was his lame-ass excuse.

I snorted. "I see. Well, we're here and we'll make sure he gets what he needs as well as Aisling. Don't go far. I may have questions for you."

"Why're you asking all these questions? Shouldn't it be one of the family or better yet, the police who're trained to do this kind of work? As a family friend, I'm not sure why you need to know." He gave me a condescending glance.

"Alistair is more than a close family friend, and he's more than qualified to investigate with his background. He's in security work," Aidan stated.

"Oh, so you're a bodyguard too."

"No, I'm much more than that and way more deadly. The men responsible will be found and when they are, they'll wish they never tried what they did. No one touches a hair on Aisling's head or anyone else in this family." I let him see the killer crouched inside of me. If let off the chain, I became a savage bent on justice and at times retribution.

He blanched then with a quick nod to the group he went to the door. Seamus didn't move aside. He looked over at me. Dar gave me a nod so I gave Seamus a chin lift and to be a dick I called out. "You can let him leave, Seamus. I'm done with him for now."

I saw Seamus trying not to grin as he moved and Scotty went tearing out of the room. When he was gone, we got down to business.

"We need to get the names of the cops on the case and their contact information. Get Malone out here. I don't want the cops talking to Ais or Creed without him. If he can't come for some reason, then we'll call Donal.

Creed, have you given a statement yet to the police?" Darragh asked.

"No, they left us alone since Ais was in such serious condition, and I think they were afraid to do anything to piss off the family. They're waiting for her to get out of surgery. They won't hold off for much longer, though. I've seen them creeping around and watching. Here are the cards for the two who introduced themselves." He took two business cards out of his pocket and handed them over. Cormac was the one to take them.

"I hope I didn't overstep with the questions. There's something about that Scotty guy I don't like. No way would I trust him to be a bodyguard for any of you. It sounds like he sat back and let Creed take all the risks while he stayed safely in the damn car. Speaking of the car, were either of them reinforced like yours are?" I asked Creed.

He shook his head. "No, not that I could tell. The way the one Brynes was driving crumpled when it was hit and how easily the windows shattered, they aren't bulletproof, reinforced, or anything. Scotty seemed to be less concerned about the attackers' cars than I was. I thought for sure he'd get out and follow me. I yelled for him to do it."

"We'll talk more about this later. Right now, let me make the call to get Malone or Donal and see what Cody has discovered," Darragh stated.

"I'll call Malone. You take care of Cody, and while we do that, Cormac, why don't you go let the nurses out there know we're here and waiting? I don't think Dr. Case will emphasize the urgency of our need to see Ais," Patrick said.

This was what occupied us for several minutes while the rest paced or sat waiting. I was about to go out and demand we be taken to see her, the hell with waiting for her to get to a room, when there was a knock on the waiting room door. Madden had taken over there, so he answered it. He only cracked the door open and then stepped back to open it further. A nervous nurse reluctantly came into the room. We smiled, wanting to put her at ease.

"Hello, has she been moved? Can we see her?" Cyndi asked quickly and hopefully.

"Yes, she's in ICU bed number one. The visiting hours start in a half hour. You can go there and ring the button, and someone will let you in. She's allowed two visitors at a time."

Not bothering to argue, she was thanked and allowed to leave, and then the mass of us headed to the ICU. When we got to the door that the nurse mentioned, most of us hung back. It should be Cormac, Cyndi, and her brothers who saw her first, even if I was dying to. They were gathered at the door, and the rest of us lined the walls in the hallway near them.

When the doors buzzed and unlocked, Cormac opened them. Creed tried to go with us when we came up, but he was ordered to rest. Niall and Gael were to take over for a while. The others would assume responsibility for watching over them. I had no doubt more guards would be sent to help. No one could stay on duty twenty-four seven.

At home it wasn't a problem inside the compound where most were every night. Out here, the family would be at a nearby hotel no doubt rather than their Temecula home so they were close to the hospital. I was walking over to talk to Darragh about me coordinating with Brayden, the technical head of security for the family, when my name was called by Cyndi. I changed course and went to her.

"Yes? What can I do for you, Cyndi?" Growing up with them, I was long ago repeatedly admonished to call them by their first names. I heard it enough that I eventually did it. They didn't like to stand on ceremony with those close to them.

"Honey, aren't you coming with us?"

"I-well, I figured you, Cormac, and your boys would go first then the rest of the family would want to check on her."

"They will, but I think you need to come too for this round. She needs to see you. She needs to know how you feel, even if now isn't the time to hash it out. Come." She held out her hand.

I glanced at Cormac. He nodded. Taking her hand, I let her lead me. I was nervous. Would Ais think I was being presumptuous? What if she didn't want to see me? I didn't get to debate long because room one was the first room right across from the nurses' station. The nurses at the desk were staring. An older one got up and marched over to us.

"I'm sorry but only two people at a time. Didn't you read the sign?" she asked snappishly.

"We did and as we told Dr. Case, we won't be complying. My daughter must have her bodyguards which automatically puts her over two. We're her parents, her brothers and her *anamchara*. There's no way any of us are staying in the hallway. I'll warn you, there's a bunch more to come. If you need to, call the administrator and see if he or she wants to throw out the O'Sheeran family," Cormac told her sternly.

He was tired of the nonsense. He tended to be quiet until you pushed him too far. I'd seen it more than a few times over the years. His sons were much more like me and would have no trouble pushing their way in if charm didn't work.

"If you don't have everyone else leave but the two of you, I'll have no choice but to call hospital security," was her comeback.

All of our shoulders went back. Here it went. Aidan was opening his mouth, only he didn't get a chance to say anything because we were joined by a huffing portly man in a suit. He was pale and sweating.

"Nurse Walker, the O'Sheeran family will be given unrestricted access to their family member. This includes the guards who will be posted in her room and in the hall. They are aware to stay out of your way so you can perform your duties. They'll only be here as long as it takes for Ms. O'Sheeran to be moved to a VIP suite. The visiting hours do not apply to them either."

"Mr. Rutledge, this isn't how we do things in the ICU! The patients need peace and quiet. A bunch of visitors at all hours of the day and night won't allow her to heal. I'm afraid I can't allow it. Dr. Case said nothing about this to me," she partially growled.

"Dr. Case and I spoke. Yes, you can." Rutledge turned his back on her, dismissing her. She stood there fuming as he introduced himself. "Sorry, I was detained. I meant to be here to greet you. I'm John Rutledge, the hospital administrator. Please, if you need anything while your daughter is here, just let me know."

"Mr. Rutledge, we appreciate it. We promise not to get in the way but Aisling must be protected and she won't heal if her family isn't close by with her. We're a very close-knit bunch. I'm Cormac and this is my wife, Cyndi. We're her parents." Cormac went on to introduce Shane, Tiernan, Cathal, and Aidan. When he got to me, I was taken back by his introduction of me.

"This is Alistair Graeme. He's our daughter's heart. He'll be here constantly, I have no doubt. He's authorized to make decisions on her behalf as well as any of the family members. We'll give the nurses a list of names. Aisling is to have no visitors except those on the list and we must have the information on everyone caring for her so we may vet them. I hope you understand our need for caution. Our name and the car wreck have made it necessary," Cormac explained.

"Of course, of course. I'll have our security come up to assist."

"No need to take them away from their other duties. We'll be more than capable of doing it. Now, if you don't mind, we need to see her."

"I do understand. Please, go right ahead." He waved us toward the door.

As we walked toward it, I saw the outraged look on Nurse Walker's face. As the door swung open, we quietly entered. The only sound in the room besides us was the beep of a machine. As I got close to her bed and caught sight of her for the first time, I stumbled. I heard Cyndi cry out. Rage along with fear consumed me again. Angry murmurs came from her brothers and a hiss from her dad. Whoever did this would suffer.

Alistair: Chapter 4

Her eyes were closed. Her beautiful face was swollen black and blue and she had cuts on it. Around her forehead close to the hairline was a white bandage. Her arms were covered in cuts and bruises as well with IVs inserted into both of them. She had oxygen prongs in her nose and the machine making the noise was monitoring her vitals. The rest of her I couldn't see under the covers. I wanted to cry and scream in outrage at the same time.

"Oh *Dia*, no. My poor *cailín leanbh*, baby girl. Oh Cormac, look at her. Look," Cyndi sobbed.

She laid her hand on top of Aisling's. They were both bent over one side of the bed while the guys were on the other. I stood at the foot. I didn't know what to do. I was afraid to touch her anywhere and cause her more pain. As her mom sobbed against her husband's chest, I scanned her brothers' faces. They were clenching their jaws and their tempers were burning in their eyes. One by one they leaned over and pressed their lips to her face. When they were done, they stepped back and Aidan gestured toward me.

"Don't stand there. Come up here. You know you want to. No more hiding, Alistair," he said gruffly.

I moved up, as I did I saw her parents watching me. Cyndi was smiling and Cormac gave me a chin lift. Taking a deep breath I stopped and gazed down at

was under an hour to get from the house to here. With traffic, which was a nightmare most of the time, it could be two hours or more.

Along with the family, there were their guards and a few which they got from Aegis security. They were a top-notch company we dealt with when we needed more than our guards and enforcers. I thought they might just be going overboard but my protestations were ignored.

I was exhausted but not from all my visitors, or at least not much by them. It was my conversation late yesterday with the police. They showed up around dinner time. The thing with cops and our family was, although we're mostly on the up-and-up, we didn't trust them, and they sure didn't trust us. This meant when it came to the men who tried to kidnap or kill us, we'd give the appearance of cooperating while not really doing it. Why? So the family could find them and take care of the problem themselves. No one messed with our family or friends and got away with it. Conventional justice was usually a joke so they didn't bother with it in most cases.

When the detectives arrived to insist on speaking to me, Malone Kelly, our lawyer, had already made the trip from Florida. He was an intimidating adversary to go up against. Hence why, we employed him as our lead legal counsel. The other reason was he was a distant cousin to Maeve. This made him family.

It soon became obvious during the interview they were positive I knew who had run into us. They kept pushing and insinuating it was a rival family in the same business as us. They were more cops who thought we were the old guard mafia. It did get old. After a while,

I stopped talking. Malone was a tiger, and he soon sent them on their way with the admonishment to find the culprits who were the real bad guys and stop trying to make it the victims' faults.

We did learn they talked to Chris before me, but they wouldn't say what he told them. When they left, Darragh, Malone and to my shock, Alistair left to go question Chris. I was anxious the whole time they were gone. When they returned and I asked what he told the cops, they said essentially the same thing me and Creed did and they treated him the same. I had no confidence the police would find the men responsible.

At present, I was in my hospital bed trying to get comfortable. I kept wiggling. I didn't want to take the pain medication but lord did I hurt. I was waiting to see if I would be moved to a regular room today or not. The guys were having a meeting somewhere in the hospital. I had no doubt it was about the situation and anything they might've found out. I knew they'd have Cody and all our other resources working on it. My guards were two Aegis employees. *Mam*, Cara, and Siobhan were sitting with me. I wiggled again.

"I swear if you don't take the medicine I'm gonna inject it myself. You're miserable, Ais," Siobhan threatened.

"It makes me feel all loopy and exhausted, Siv. I don't like that feeling."

She snorted. "Better that than in pain. You have broken bones, contusions and had a damn piece of metal stab into your body then surgery. You're not gonna heal if you can't rest. Are you going to call the nurse or should I?" she raised her brow at me.

We girls had been close growing up. It was a weird

fact in each of the three branches of the family the last child was a girl. The three of us were only three years apart. Siv was the oldest by a year then me and Cara was the baby. Siv was bossier as the eldest. She thought it meant she could tell us what to do. We were all the best of friends, but it didn't mean we never fought or had disagreements. We'd been known to throw hands just like our brothers. When we did, our *mams* would roll their eyes and sit back to see the outcome.

"You can call her but it doesn't mean I'll take it."

"You will if I knock your ass out before she comes and you can't say no," was her quick comeback. Knowing the *cailleach,* witch, she'd do it too. Seeing the humor in it, I decided to play it out.

"*Mam*, Siv is picking on me. Make her stop. She's mean," I pretended to pout.

Mam had been stressed since her arrival yesterday. I wanted to lighten her mood. This did it. She started to laugh and shook her head. "I swear you girls are still preteens sometimes. *Dia*, the way you'd fight. Okay, let me see. Siv, stop being such a bossy pants. Ais, don't be a whiner. Cara, don't encourage them."

"Hey, I didn't say anything," Cara protested.

"I know but I can't leave you out. It doesn't feel complete if I do."

My bodyguard in the room was trying not to grin. He was studying the far wall and wouldn't make eye contact. We were all giggling when the door opened. My guards from outside gave us an apologetic look.

"Ms. O'Sheeran there's a gentleman out here who is insisting he has to speak to you."

"Did he give you his name?" I asked.

"He said he's Christopher Brynes. He claims he

was in the accident with you and wants to check on you."

I relaxed. "He was. Please let him in. I've been meaning to go see him so this will be perfect. Thank you."

He nodded and his head disappeared. Not even a minute later the door opened further and in came Chris. He was on crutches and moving slowly. I caught a glimpse of Scotty in the hallway. He didn't appear happy. The door closed behind Chris. He was giving me the once-over as he approached my bed. I caught a look pass between *Mam* and the girls but I had no idea what it was about. Chris smiled at them.

"Look here. I have the four most beautiful women in the whole place right here. Hello ladies," he greeted them. They smiled, and he leaned over to give them each a kiss on the cheek, even *Mam*. I knew if *Daid* was here he wouldn't have.

"Hello Christopher, how're you feeling? I was planning to come see you today. I'm sorry I didn't come yesterday. It was rather hectic as you can imagine," *Mam* informed him.

"No worries, I don't blame you. Aisling, God, I'm sorry, sweetheart. Please tell me they're controlling your pain and you'll be moved out of here soon," he said as he came closer to the bed.

He reached out and ran a finger down my cheek. Instead of feeling comforted or even excited by his touch, I was uncomfortable. It grew worse as he leaned over to kiss my mouth. I turned my head at the last second and it landed on my cheek. When he lifted his head, he gave me a quizzical look. I pretended not to notice as I smiled at him.

"I'm hoping they'll move me today sometime. The pain is tolerable."

Siv snorted. He glanced over at her.

"Don't believe her, Christopher. She's lying. She won't take the pain meds because she hates how they make her feel. We were arguing about it right before you came in. I'm calling the nurse, and if you give her trouble when she brings it, I'll have your guards, your mam, Cara, and Christopher help me sit on you so you take it," she glared at me.

This made Chris laugh and my guard let a smile slip before he wiped it away. "I saw that, traitor," I called over to him. His eyes were twinkling. He didn't say much but I liked him. He was serene and not hard on the eyes.

"Fine, since you're all ganging up on me, call her," I grumbled. In reality, I was glad to take something. The pain was ramping up to a very painful stage.

"Good. I'll go find one of the nurses. Why don't we leave you two to talk?" *Mam* said out of the blue. Before I was able to protest, the three of them were up and making tracks for the door. With them gone, Chris moved around and sat in the chair next to my bed. He was scanning me. He grimaced.

"I hate to see you like this."

"You got beat up too."

"Yeah, but not like you. Shit, why didn't I see that car coming? I could've prevented all this."

"Neither of us saw it until it was too late. They had it perfectly planned. Too bad for them, they didn't count on Creed coming to us on foot. I heard you broke your leg. How's it feeling?"

"Not too bad. What about your arm and your

incision, cuts and bruises? I can't believe a piece of metal pierced you. When I saw you bleeding and then you closed your eyes, I was scared to death, Aisling. I thought you were dead. I've been meaning to talk to you about something since before the wreck. Could we have some privacy?" he asked my guard.

Panic began to creep in when he said it. I thought I might know what he wanted to talk about, but I wasn't ready. The confidence I felt before the accident about progressing to a new stage was gone. I floundered to find a way to stop this. I lucked out when my guard shook his head.

"I'm sorry, sir, but I have strict orders not to take my eyes off Ms. O'Sheeran."

"She's safe with me. My bodyguard and your partner are outside. There's no reason to not let us have a private conversation," Chris told him impatiently.

"Sir, I work for Mr. Darragh O'Sheeran. I take my orders from him, and he was very clear. She isn't to be left alone, ever. No matter who is with her. Mr. Graeme was clear about his orders as well. I'm sorry, but no." He folded his arms across his massive chest. I was taken aback to hear Alistair was giving the bodyguards orders. Chris stiffened, and a pissed expression spread over his face.

"Mr. Graeme has no damn right to give orders when it comes to her. If you don't give us—" Whatever else he was about to say was cut short by the door swinging open abruptly, and in walked Darragh and Alistair. My heart skipped a beat seeing him. Even though I saw him this morning, it never got old, even though I tried to control my body's response to him. His gaze zeroed in on Chris. What I saw there was anger and dislike. Darragh didn't appear very happy either. What in the world?

"Chris, I thought I was clear yesterday," my cousin said without bothering to greet him.

"Dar, what's wrong? What about yesterday?" I asked.

"Drake, would you mind giving us some privacy?" Dar asked my guard. Without a word, Drake nodded and went to the door. When he opened it, Scotty came bounding inside. He looked panicked.

"Scotty, we're having a private talk. Wait in the hallway with the other guards. Drake, please make sure no one disturbs us," Dar added.

"Mr. Byrnes, I need..." Scotty let the words die away when Alistair looked at him.

"You heard him," Alistair said.

Scotty didn't like being spoken to by either of them that way. On the one hand, I understood it, but on the other, I wasn't very sympathetic. I knew Chris relied on him, and they'd been together a while, but he wasn't someone I liked. I felt as if he was secretly judging me every time I was around him.

"I give the orders to my people, not you," Chris snapped at Alistair. I was taken aback.

"And I give orders I expect to be followed when it comes to my family. He can leave, and we talk, or you both can go," Darragh snapped at Chris.

The tension was mounting, and I had no idea why. What happened yesterday when they met? Whatever it was, they weren't acting as if they were friends. I wouldn't have called Chris and my family the best of friends, but they were always courteous and got along. The four of them stared at each other for a whole minute or so. I was about to tell them enough when there was a timid knock. Glancing over, I saw a nurse. She gave me a hesitant smile.

"Sorry to interrupt, but I have your medication, Ms. O'Sheeran. Your mother said you were in a lot of pain." she came scuttling over as she explained.

Alistair was next to me in a blink. He was frowning. "Ais, what's wrong? Why are you hurting more?"

"Stair, don't get excited. Nothing is wrong."

She injected it into my IV so it would go into effect right away. "There, you should feel better in a jiffy. Anything else I can do for you?"

"No, thank you," I told her with a smile. She nodded at the men before leaving.

"What's it gonna be, Chris?" Dar was right back at it.

Chris waited several heart beats before he responded. "Scotty, wait for me outside. I'll be fine." He scowled. Scotty left reluctantly and unhappily. As soon as the door closed, I jumped in.

"What in the world has gotten into you guys?"

"He knows," Darragh said. Alistair grunted in what I thought was agreement. I looked at Chris.

"Would you care to explain?"

"Your cousin and his friend seem to think I should stay away from you since they're convinced the attack on us is my fault. I recently had someone send me threats, nothing I haven't heard a thousand times before in one version or another. Until whoever it is, is caught and dealt with, they said to stay away from you."

Even if I didn't want to get into a private conversation with him, I didn't like Darragh or Alistair making decisions for me. I narrowed my gaze on them. "Would you two like to explain yourselves?"

"I think he explained it. He's at fault for your pain and injuries and he almost got you killed. There's no way we want you to continue to be a target so it means he stays away from you," Alistair said gruffly.

"Yeah, you'd love that, wouldn't you?" Chris said with a sneer.

"I want her safe!" Alistair snapped.

"Agreed," Dar added.

They began to argue with each other, totally ignoring me. As they did and they got louder, the angrier and worse I felt. They were causing me to tense up more, and it was pushing my pain rather than letting the medicine do its job. After a couple minutes of it, I had enough. Placing my fingers in my mouth, I let out a shrill whistle. They flinched, and the yelling died off as they all faced me.

"Enough! Do you hear yourselves? Even if whoever did this is someone after Chris, it's not your place to dictate who I may or may not see." This earned them a flash of a smirk from Chris.

"And you, how dare you order anyone who works for us around? Drake isn't one of your people. Plus, you have no right to order Alistair to leave," It was one of the things he'd been yelling. I might ache to my soul with him near, but it was my right to send him away, not Chris's.

"Darragh, I love you, but you have to tone down the overbearing overlord shit. We don't know who targeted us or why. I agree we need to be cautious but to outright declare someone as not allowed near me isn't your place. I'll decide who I spend time with and when and where. Now, since the three of you can't seem to be civilized, I want you all to leave. The only ones I want to see besides Drake or his replacement are *Mam*, the girls, and *Daid*. Later, the others can come in. If you settle down, I might let you back this evening. Chris, thank you for your concern. I'm on the mend. You should go get some rest. We'll talk soon."

They tried to get me to change my mind but I closed my eyes and ignored them. My head was pounding again. I just needed peace and quiet and sleep. Eventually, Chris left. Dar promised he'd see me later and so did Alistair. When the door closed, I sighed. I felt eyes on me so I knew Drake must be back. I drifted off.

Aisling: Chapter 5

When I surfaced, I had no idea how much later it was, but I knew something was wrong. My head was still pounding, I felt so hot, and my side was throbbing like a deep, persistent pain. I hissed as I opened my eyes and pressed my hand to my incision. I moaned as my pain increased. I heard a rustling sound then Christian, the other Aegis employee, was bending over me. He appeared worried.

"Ms. O'Sheeran, what's wrong?"

"I don't know. Something's not right. I feel terrible and my side hurts so much," I moaned.

"May I?" he asked, raising his hand. I nodded, having no idea what he was about to do, but I didn't care. First, he pressed gently on my side, and I cried out, then the back of his hand pressed to my forehead. He swore.

"Christ, you're burning up. I'm calling the nurse and your family. You lie there and rest."

I did as he said as I heard him at the door talking. I assumed it was to Drake or whoever might've relieved him. I wasn't sure how long it was before the door opened, and a nurse rushed in. On her heels were half my family and Alistair. Anxiety was coming off them in waves.

"I need you all to step outside and let me examine her. You can come in when I'm done," my nurse ordered.

CIARAST JAMES

To my amazement, they did it.

"I'm going to lift your gown and look at your incision, and then we'll check your temperature," she said calmly.

"Okay."

Moments later, the bandage on my side was peeled back, and she pressed around it with a gloved hand. I hissed. She frowned. When she was done, she didn't bother to cover the wound with the dressing; she just pulled down my gown and took my temperature. When she finished, I had to ask, "So?"

"It looks like you have an infection in your incision. Your temp is one hundred and two. I need to call your doctor. He put you on prophylactic antibiotics after surgery and it should've kept you from developing an infection. He may need to change your antibiotic. Hang tight. I'll be back." She patted my hand before hurrying out.

As she left, my family came in. They were asking me what was wrong. I told them what my nurse said. They continued to fuss and talk but I remained quiet. I was too miserable to speak or care about much of anything. In fact, the longer I lay there the more nauseous I became. I grabbed my *mam's* hand.

"I need something to throw up in," I whispered to her.

She barely grabbed the small trash can beside the bed and gave it to me before I was throwing up. Talk about humiliating. Who wanted anyone to see them puke? No one, that was who. The chatter became more anxious. When I was done, I fell back against the pillows. My mouth tasted foul. The trash can was taken from me then a cool cloth was pressed to my forehead. I

90

sighed in relief.

"*Mil*, here, rinse your mouth out," *Mam's* soft voice had me opening my eyes. She was holding a cup up for me and had the trash can in the other hand. Taking the cup I took a mouthful and the fresh mint taste was wonderful. I swished it around and spit then did it a couple more times until my mouth felt fresh and clean again. She took them away. The others were all quietly watching me.

"Will you stop looking at me like that? I feel like a lab experiment. Can't a girl puke without an audience?" I grumbled.

"Maybe, but we want to know what caused it. Christian told Drake you have a fever and your side is hurting more. The nurse confirmed it. They better get their asses in here and do something about it," Aidan muttered.

"Big brother, give them time. Jeez, I'm not their only patient. They need to talk to Dr. Case and see if he wants to change my antibiotic."

"Dr. Case my ass, Dr. K is here. He just got in. He'll tell us what's up," Darragh said confidently.

"Why is Dr. K here? There was no reason for him to come all this way," I protested.

"Really? You were seriously injured. You think we wouldn't have him consulting? He tried to get here yesterday but he couldn't," *Daid* added.

"You're unbelievable," I muttered.

They smiled like it was a compliment. I stopped arguing with them and let *Mam* fuss over me. I wasn't too proud to say when I felt this badly, I wanted my *mam* like I did when I was a little kid. It was about ten minutes later when my nurse was back.

"Excuse me, but we're taking her for an ultrasound. I'll bring her back when she's done." As she said it, there was a knock, and then a man strolled in. The guys all straightened. I noted that when he got to me, his name badge identified him as an orderly.

"She can't go alone. Drake, you and Alistair go with her," *Daid* ordered.

"Alistair? Why him?" I asked.

"Just to give Christian a break. That's all. See you when you get back," he told me with a smile.

He kissed my forehead, *Mam* my cheek. Then I was pushed in my bed out of the room and to another room on a different floor. It was a whirl of activity, and the ultrasound, though not too lengthy, hurt significantly when the wand thingy they used was pressed close to my incision. By the time they were done, I was drained. Back in my room, I found it was a smidge less crowded, although my parents, brothers, Darragh, and Karizma were there.

"I can't believe you had her fly her pregnant butt out here for this," I chided Aidan.

"I didn't make her do anything. She wanted to come. Do you think I could keep her away?" he asked.

I wanted to say yes. I knew if he was truly worried she'd be locked down tight. It would be with every comfort and luxury but she would've stayed in Florida. Dr. K and her baby doctor must've given them the green light.

"Ashlynn and Alexis would be here, except I didn't want her to fly or travel this close to her due date. Carmen and Bax are keeping an eye on her for me," Darragh explained.

Guilt assailed me. He should be at home with

his pregnant wife, not hovering over me. "Dar, you should go home. Ash needs you. I have plenty of people here. Promise me, as soon as the doctor changes my medicine, you'll go home. In fact, as much as I love you all for caring so much, you don't need to be taking time off to come sit here doing nothing. I'll be fine and as soon as they let me out of this place, I'll be even better."

"You let us worry about what we're taking time off for. We'll see what the doctor has to say," Cathal informed me.

I was still very hot and sweaty. The cool cloth kept being changed out which eased it a tiny bit. They talked quietly and I let their voices wash over and through me. I had my eyes closed until a slightly rough, large hand engulfed mine. I opened them to find myself staring up into Alistair's light blue eyes. They always fascinated me. They reminded me of denim after it had been washed a thousand times.

His square jaw had a faint shadow to it. He hadn't shaved today. His goatee was trimmed. I was always fascinated by how it was slightly more reddish in color than the hair on his head. His hair was shaved close on the sides and the top was ever so slightly spiked in an artfully messy way. It begged you to run your hands through it and mess it up more and it had a slight reddish cast to it but it was really a dark natural brown color. His masculine face combined with his tall and muscular build, tattoos and his whole physique made him so handsome and irresistible. I could get lost in him if I wasn't careful.

"Can I get you anything, my love?" he whispered.

I wanted to cry. When he called me my love or my vision, I wanted it to be because he loved me and he believed those words. I had to swallow twice before I was able to answer him. "I'm fine. I don't need anything."

"Are you sure?"

I nodded.

A hard swift knock at the door silenced everyone. It cracked open and Drake peeked his head inside. "There's a doctor here who says he needs to speak to you."

"Let him in. Thank you," Shane said. He was the closest to him. When the door widened, I saw it was Dr. Keim, or Dr. K, as we called him. He was greeted and returned their handshakes and smiles. Eventually, he got to me.

"Hello young lady, I hear you've been having a hard time the past few days. Don't worry, we'll have you right as rain in no time," he informed me with a wink.

"Do you know what the ultrasound showed, Dr. K?" *Daid* asked.

"I do. It seems an abscess has formed where the penetrating wound was which they surgically repaired along with the injury to your liver."

"So just change up the antibiotics and she should be good to go?" Tiernan asked.

Dr. K shook his head. "Regrettably no it won't be that simple. I'm afraid we need to take you back into surgery, Aisling. I need to drain the abscess and see if there's anything else going on in there. I hate to do it, but it's necessary. I'd like to do it as soon as possible. You'll only get sicker and we don't want it to run rampant and cause sepsis throughout your body. Right now, it appears to be walled off. When was the last time you ate or drank anything other than a few sips of water?"

I wanted to cry. Another surgery? Jesus, I had no luck it seemed. I had to think back. "I threw up not long ago. I haven't drank anything significant in six hours at least and as for food, nothing since breakfast, so eight hours."

"Good. That means we can do it soon. I'm going to get the OR set up and then we'll be taking you in. There should be nothing to worry about. Once it's drained and I'm sure it's good to go, we'll change up the antibiotics and make it a cocktail. We'll hit it hard and with different types of antibiotics. Now, let me listen to your heart and lungs," he said. I did as he asked. When he was done, the questions began to fly from my family.

"What caused the abscess?"

"How long do you think surgery will take?"

"Is she at risk?"

"How far back will this set her recovery and ability to get out of the ICU and the hospital overall?"

"Why didn't the antibiotic she's on now help?"

He was at ease answering them despite them coming at him like bullets. The poor man deserved a raise for putting up with us. I let them do all the asking. I was too tired and depressed.

"She was punctured by a dirty piece of metal. Even the minutest speck of dirt from it could've caused the infection. Not every antibiotic works on every organism that can infect your body. This appears to be the case with Aisling. Surgery, if all goes as planned, should be an hour, but add on getting her sedated and then fully awake, say three hours, to be safe. There are always risks in surgery, but I swear she'll be in good hands. Once I drain the exudate and assume it doesn't reform, and she has no more complications, plus the new antibiotic starts to clear up anything left, she should only be in the ICU a couple of extra days, and her stay won't be extended more than a few days. I'll do everything I can to have her healed and back to her old self ASAP."

"Thank you, doctor. You have no idea how much we appreciate you coming and for taking over her care," *Daid* told him.

"Yes, thank you, Dr. K," I told him.

"You're more than welcome, Cormac, Aisling. Okay, I'm off to get us on the schedule. Hang here and someone will come get you when we're ready. When we go in, the rest of you can hang out in the waiting area outside the OR. I need to confer with Dr. Case."

"Will he be in there too?" Cathal asked.

"He will be assisting, yes, but I'll do the surgery."

"Good."

As he left I tried to act normal and talk to my family but deep down I was wondering if more was yet to come. Who knew a simple night out for dinner would end in such a mess. Although, if the surgery got rid of the aching, sweating, nausea, and pain, or at least the pain in my side, which was growing by the minute, I'd gladly do it. I already hated feeling weak, helpless, and useless.

Alistair:

Hearing she was feverish had made me anxious. Watching her puke and being miserable made me want to scoop her up and rock her in my arms. When Dr. K. informed us she had an abscess and had to go back into surgery, I grew more anxious and fearful. Every time you went under there was no guarantee you had to wake up. What if something went wrong?

I knew Dr. Keim was one of the best doctors in the world. If he wasn't, he wouldn't be the personal physician and surgeon to the O'Sheeran family. I was thrilled she was in his hands, but it was still a worry. I detested seeing her in pain or feeling badly. What rotten luck.

We were all gathered in the OR waiting area as Dr. K suggested, waiting for her to be done and back on her journey on the road to recovery. There were murmurs all around the room. Only a couple of other people were in there with us who weren't part of our group. Suffice it to say they were casting looks at us, which were a combination of intrigued and frightened. They recognized the family. It was rare for people not to.

When it occurred, there were several ways they would act. Curious was one way, along with scared, nervous, excited, and some outright cagy. The O'Sheeran's wealth, and the rumors of who they were, were factors in those responses. Many had an angle they wanted to play. It was due to those angles they had bodyguards.

I wasn't able to sit still and wait. I was a man of action. When there was a problem, I was the solution the majority of the time. I'd come up with the strategies and then execute the plan. Yeah, I had help, but most of the time, I was the one coming up with a good chunk of the game plan. In this instance, I had no role to play other than as a bystander who could do absolutely nothing other than pray.

The others were giving me distance, which I appreciated. I was deep in thought and prayer when the door opened and in came the last person I wanted to see. Being pushed in a wheelchair was Christopher. He was flanked by Scotty and two other bodyguards. They mean-mugged the room. I wanted to snicker. If they thought that would work here with this crowd they were stupid. Examining them, they came nowhere close to the caliber of the family's men.

However, my amusement over the guards was far outstripped by my anger over Brynes' audacity to come in here. He'd been warned to stay the hell away. It was most likely the threat to him that caused her to be hurt in the first place. My fury, which I'd been stamping down, bubbled up, and I was marching across the room without a thought. I was intercepted before I made it to the bastard. It was her brothers and Darragh who stopped me.

"We know you want to beat his ass into the ground, but this isn't the time or place. You have to keep your cool," Darragh warned me softly.

"We told him to stay the fuck away from her. Doesn't he understand English? Maybe I need to translate it for him," I snapped as I clenched my fists. In my experience, a good ass whooping translated across all languages.

I heard Tiernan snicker, and then he coughed to cover it up. The others, including Dar, were fighting not to grin. They knew I was right. How they were keeping in control, I didn't know. They had to be just as angry as I was.

"How can you stand to look at him? Are you really going to allow him to stay here? It's his fault she's in surgery."

"It may be and no, I'm not happy he chose to ignore the possible danger to her but I won't deal with him here. There are too many eyes and ears. He's not actually near her at the moment and we won't let him when she comes out. What we can't afford is for you to go all berserk like a Highlander and pull out your halberd and go to town on him," Dar said with a smirk. I knew he was trying to ease my anger.

"You're just jealous we Scots had the cool weapons, and you Irish had shit ones," I shot back.

"Fuck you, we had the same ones, asshole," Cathal snorted back.

"Well, it didn't seem like it. You don't know how to use them worth shit. The Scots do." I smirked.

"You're full of shit we didn't. Keep telling yourself that," Shane said.

They were so successful in diverting my attention away from Brynes and his men that they made it over to us. The rest of the family was watching and murmuring. When I noticed the four intruders had gotten to us, I scowled and folded my arms to glare at them. I'd let Darragh and the others take the lead until

I had to step in. Even if Aisling didn't want me the way I wanted her, I would protect her no matter what I had to do. Out of the corner of my eye, I saw the few other people waiting with us get up and make their way out the door. I wondered why the guards outside hadn't warned us Brynes and his men were coming or tried to prevent them from entering. I'd have to see why later. The other O'Sheeran men got up and came over to join us.

"Chris, what're you doing here?" Darragh asked.

"I came to wait for word on Aisling. I heard she was going back into surgery."

"And how did you hear that? Paying staff to talk about her or was one of your guys lurking around listening to private conversations?" Cian chimed in to ask.

"I can't help it if the staff talk loudly and my men overhear things. I don't need to pay anyone to tell me. What's with all this hostility all of a sudden? We don't know if this incident has anything to do with me. It could've been something you O'Sheerans have gotten yourselves mixed up in and I'm the victim," was his comeback.

"I highly doubt it, but even if it is, you should be worried about yourself and stay away so it doesn't happen again," Ciaran suggested.

"Whether you like it or not, Aisling has asked me to be part of her life, and I intend to stay in it unless she tells me to leave."

"And exactly how did she ask you to be a part of her life?" I asked. I couldn't keep my mouth shut a second longer. Scotty was eyeing me and I was ready to punch him in the mouth. His dislike of me was oozing out of him.

"She approached me when she came to California and asked if I would like to go out to dinner. Since then we've grown extremely close and have spent hours and hours together. Once she's feeling more herself, I don't see her asking me to go away. We have a connection," he said with a smirk and his voice full of innuendo.

I didn't know if they were sleeping together or not. I wouldn't allow myself to think about it because if I did, I'd kill him on the spot. What I did know was if they were, I'd do everything in my power to make sure it never happened again. If she didn't love him and only turned to him because I drove her to it, I'd have to live with it just like anyone else she had been with over the years. I'd been a fool to fight what I felt for her. As soon as she turned eighteen, I should've confessed my feelings and claimed her if she was in agreement like her family thought.

"When my daughter is fully healed, she can make her own decisions about who to spend time with. However, until the threat is neutralized, I don't care if she is healed or not. She won't be exposed to unnecessary danger, which means you need to stay away, Christopher," Cormac informed him sternly.

"Mr. O'Sheeran, I don't want to expose her to danger, but if I can't see her, how will I know if she's being unfairly pressured to accept something she doesn't want?" He was staring at me as he said the last part.

"What the hell does that mean?" I asked with a snap.

"I can see you have a thing for her. I'm not sure if the family agrees with it or not, but I won't have you pressuring her to accept your suit."

"You won't have it? Who the fuck are you to say anything about things pertaining to Aisling? And if you think for a moment anyone can pressure her into doing anything she doesn't want, then you don't know a goddamn thing about her. Ais would never allow herself to be backed into a corner," I told him.

"Do you condone this? An employee in a relationship with your daughter? She's a princess of the family. She deserves someone who's of her social standing who can relate to her. Give her the life she's accustomed to." He directed this to Cormac and her brothers.

I seethed inside. It was taking all my control not to snap his neck. Stuck up bastard thought he knew her. There was no way he did, not like me. He may have popped in and out over the years for a moment here and there, but that didn't make him an expert on her. I knew so many things about her. I might not have claimed her but I made it a point to study and know her. Creepy? Maybe in some people's books, but in mine, it was to ensure she was safe and happy even if she was never mine.

"I'd change my tune if I were you. Yes, she's a princess and she deserves many things, but there's more to life than social standing. And no matter who she ends up with, her having the life she's been accustomed to is guaranteed," Darragh told him through narrowed eyes.

Cormac and her brothers were fuming. Their faces might not show it, but I knew them so well that I saw it. It was true. I wasn't a billionaire like them, but I was far from a poor man. Just because I chose to work for a living didn't mean I didn't have the means to take care of her needs, assuming we got together.

"Of course she'll always be an O'Sheeran but shouldn't the man she's with add to her standing and ability to leverage it? Aisling and I would join two very powerful families together. You have to see it just as I do. As she does," he argued.

"You seem to be under the impression she plans to spend her life with you. I haven't heard a word from her to support that. Spending time together and having some dinners and going to a few parties isn't a lifelong commitment," Aidan added to the argument.

"If this hadn't happened, we would be there soon. All I'm saying is I want to continue to press my suit with her. She'll make me the perfect wife. I have more to bring to the table than he does," he sneered when he glanced over at me.

"I suggest you take your friends and leave before I show you what I bring to the table. You've been asked to stay away. I promise if you force me to make you, I'll be the only one smiling about it," I told him with a smile. It wasn't a nice one.

Scotty's chest puffed out, and I knew he was about to try and prove he was a badass. Something he had no hope of doing in this group. I knew Brynes had no true concept of the training Darragh and the others had. It wasn't something advertised outside the family and closest friends. And none of them sure had a clue about the Hounds. They were an even closer guarded secret. Having a technical rival know about something of that magnitude was asking for trouble in the worst way.

"Enough! My daughter is in surgery. This isn't the

time or place for any of this. Christopher, I'm asking you to leave and to keep your distance as requested. When she's feeling better, I'll ask Aisling to call you so you can speak to her. Until then, there will be no contact. Understood?" This came from all people, Cyndi. Immediately, the O'Sheeran men and I nodded our heads. The other women were almost as upset by the expressions they wore.

I was surprised when Brynes didn't argue. "Of course, I'm sorry. Please let Aisling know I was here and I can't wait to talk to her. I'll be praying for her speedy recovery." As soon as he said this to Cyndi and he nodded to Cormac, he turned his wheelchair around to face the door. "Let's go," he told his men. As they left, I knew it was only the beginning of a mess.

Aisling: Chapter 6

I'd been in the hospital for seven days total and I was beyond ready to climb the walls by my fingernails and scream. The first couple of days after my second surgery I was in and out of it and did a lot of sleeping as the new antibiotics started to clear out the rest of the infection. Dr. Keim thought he'd cleared out ninety-nine percent of the infection when he drained the abscess, but he was keeping a close eye on me. When I got past those few days, it was the boredom which was making me crazy. I was used to staying busy.

It would've been easier to tolerate if I had work to occupy my mind with, but my family refused to let me do any. I tried to have my laptop and cell phone smuggled into me by one of the employees at the winery when she came to visit but they confiscated it. Anyone connected to Maeve's Cellars who came to visit was watched closely and if they began to talk shop, they were told I was on strict doctor's order not to work. If they kept trying, they were politely asked to leave. I argued, threatened, and pleaded but it got me nowhere.

It wasn't just my family who were doing the warning and running off. The bodyguards did it and an infuriating Alistair did too. I resorted to threatening to castrate him. He'd laugh and tell me I was welcome to try when I healed. I tried not to admit to myself my frustration with him went deeper than denial of work.

He had me confused and off-kilter.

As I healed and worked on my therapy to learn to cope with my broken arm, messed-up shoulder, and ankle, he spent most of his time with me. The man wouldn't listen when I ordered him to go back to Florida. He told me he didn't answer to me and would stay until I was ready to go back. I asserted I knew there was work to be done with the Hounds. He claimed they were good.

Finally, I had what I hoped was a reprieve coming. Dr. K agreed I was well enough to finish my convalescence at home. Since home was Florida for him and he wanted to check on me a few times a week, I was headed back there. I tried to stay in California at our house in Temecula, but it was shot down, so I was on one of our planes headed home. Most of the family had returned a few days ago since I was out of the woods and they needed to go check in on their various businesses. The only ones who stayed were assigned bodyguards, *Daid*, *Mam*, Tiernan, and Alistair.

As the flight got in the air, I was determined not to say a peep about feeling tired on the flight. I was determined to have them stop treating me like I was dying or something. We were sitting in various seats scattered around the main cabin. This plane had a bedroom too. I told them when we boarded I didn't need to lie down. A part of me wished I had done it. How in the hell could I be so tired when ninety-five percent of my time for the past week was spent sitting or lying down?

I thought I'd hidden my yawn. I discovered I hadn't when a pair of denim-clad muscular thighs appeared in my line of sight. I ran my gaze up them, deliberately skipping over the bulge which couldn't be disguised. If he was this big soft what would he be like when he was fully hard popped into my brain. *Dia, don't think shit like that, Ais! You know you'll get yourself in trouble thinking anything sexual about him. When will you ever learn?* I warned myself.

When I reached his eyes, I saw a flash of something but it was gone too quickly to know what it was. "Yes? May I help you?" I asked him, sounding bored.

"Yeah, you can get your ass back there and in the bed. Why're you fighting it? You need to rest. We have four more hours to go, Ais."

"Stair, I don't need to lie down. That's all I've been doing. I'm fine." I prayed I sounded confident.

He shook his head. "Cormac, I'm taking over," he called over to my *daid*. All *Daid* did was glance over, smile and nod.

"Taking over what?" I asked, mystified.

"Keeping your sweet ass in line. Remember, you asked for it," he said softly a moment before he unlatched my belt.

The next thing I knew, I was swept up out of my seat and into his arms. He had me held bridal-style. His long legs ate up the length of the aisle as he headed for the back of the plane where the bedroom was. As much as I might want to fault him and say he was too rough or didn't look out for my bad arm, ribs, shoulder, or anything else, I wasn't able to because it would've been a lie. He cradled me close to his chest and held me as if I was a delicate flower or something beyond precious. I fought down the wave of heat that washed through me at his delicious smell and the feel of his strong arms and incredible chest against my body. I did kick my legs a bit in an attempt to get him to put me down.

"Alistair, put me down right this instant! I'm not a child you can do anything with. I'm a grown-ass woman!" I shrieked shrilly.

"Then act like a woman and stop being childish and stubborn. You're exhausted. We can see it. You're lying down."

He gently pushed the door to the bedroom open with his foot. When we were inside, he kicked it shut behind us and took me over to the bed. Even if it was a plane, the bed was a king-size one. He gently eased me onto the mattress. I knew there was no way I could get off the bed in the shape I was in, so I carefully folded my arms and glared at him.

"Fine, I'm in bed. You got what you wanted. Now leave and let me rest."

He shook his head. As I stared at him, he took off his jacket and placed it on the back of the chair off to the side of the bed. When he took off his shoes, I wiggled into a semi-sitting position. "What are you doing?" Shit, he was planning to sit in here and make sure I remained in bed.

He flashed me one of those sexy grins of his I had found scrambled my brains since I was thirteen. "What does it look like I'm doing? I'm making sure you get the rest you need. You don't have to sleep but you will rest. You keep pushing yourself, Aisling. Why? You can take time to heal. The winery will be more than fine."

"The point is I'm bored. I'm used to keeping my brain and body active. Just lying around like a useless lump isn't me. Besides, if I don't work then it means someone else has extra work falling on them. It's not fair."

"Is it fair to push yourself too much too soon and have a relapse? No one begrudges a bit of extra work. All we want is for you to get better, *bòidheach*."

I had to fight not to shiver at hearing him call me beautiful in Scottish. After growing up around him all my life, I'd picked up words here and there even if they weren't always the same as they were in Irish. I reminded myself he didn't mean anything by it. It was just his way. I'd be an idiot of the first order if I read more into it.

I sighed, sank back, and closed my eyes. I had to block out the sight of him. I was in a weakened state and the last thing I wanted to do was slip up and confess my feelings to him or do something to reveal them. I'd be humiliated if that were to happen. This freaking wreck had happened at the worst possible time. If only it hadn't or held off until after I had a chance to sleep with Chris. Maybe he would've wiped my foolish love for Alistair out of my heart. I was lost in thinking of this so I was startled when the bed dipped. As I opened my eyes, I was engulfed in his arms.

"Alistair! What the hell are you doing!?" I cried out. I tried to wiggle away but between all my injuries and his strength it didn't work. He carefully eased me over so my back was to his front.

"Hush, rest. I'm just making sure you stay. I'm tired. I need a nap. Yell if you want, but no one will come rescue you. They know I'm not hurting you."

I tried to argue with him but he refused to engage. In the end I gave up and I'll be damned, I fell asleep in his arms. A place I'd wanted to be for half my life.

❦❦❦

Things at home were weird. I'd been back for

five days. Everyone should've been back to their normal activities even if I wasn't. I'd finished off my antibiotics and Dr. K. was very happy with how my wounds and incision were healing. I hated the sight of the incision. It was an ugly scar in my mind. Once it was healed enough, I'd be having it covered with a tattoo. I knew Judge could come up with something awesome over at Wrath Tattoo. Yeah, call me vain but no one wanted to have a scar, especially a woman. Men could have them and be seen as tough and even sexy. Women were just seen as flawed and less desirable.

The weird factor was the fact that while most of the family seemed to be back to work, which I was grateful for, Alistair was around constantly. There wasn't a day he wasn't here and made sure to come see me and talk. Since I was healing and limited in my mobility, all three sets of parents insisted I stay at the main house in my old room. I knew if I didn't, they'd go out of their way to come to mine and I didn't want them taxing themselves. Yeah, they were healthy and even at seventy, Patrick as the oldest was strong and active. It was the idea of them doing it. And I knew *Mamó* would be trotting over every day and she was gonna be ninety at the end of this year.

I was moping around my room. Today was a day I wish I could sleep through. I would be surrounded by the day and it made my heart hurt. It was Valentine's Day, and I knew our parents and the three newly married couples would be going all out for it. I didn't begrudge them their happiness. I wanted them to show each other how much they loved one another. The issue was I was envious and green wasn't my color.

I hobbled into the kitchen. I was hungry, so I left

the safety of my room to find some food. I'd waited as long as possible, but my stomach was loud and trying to eat itself. Agatha was there puttering around. As soon as she saw me, she began to fuss. She hurried over to me and took my good arm.

"Ms. Ais, you sit right here and tell me what you want. What're you hungry for?"

"Agatha, you don't need to cook me anything. I can find something to eat in the fridge. Go back to whatever you have cooking. It smells delicious by the way."

"It's no trouble. And what I'm cooking right now is for tonight. Your parents along with Mr. Patrick, Ms. Maeve, Mr. Sean, and Ms. Brenda are having dinner here tonight. The others have all made arrangements elsewhere. You can eat this with them when it's done."

"No way. I'm not horning in on their Valentine's dinners. No way. I'll make something later and have it in my room."

"Nonsense," she scolded me.

I stopped arguing, but I would be sure to be well out of the way when the time came. As a way to get her off the subject, I allowed her to gather leftovers for me. As they heated up, we were chatting. I wasn't too surprised when my parents came wandering in. Both gave me a kiss and then sat to visit with me. The house phone rang, and Agatha answered it.

I wasn't paying attention to what she said so several minutes later when Creed came in, I didn't think anything of it. It wasn't unusual for the guards and enforcers to come and go. I assumed the call must've been from him. His arms were full. In them was a huge bouquet of gorgeous flowers. It was an explosion of colors. In addition to those, there were two wrapped boxes. I was eager to see what *Daid* had gotten *Mam*. I perked up and smiled. I was so busy checking out her face to see how she was reacting I didn't notice until he came to stand next to me, that Creed hadn't handed them to *Mam*. I squinted up at him. He was studying me hard.

"Why're you still holding those? Do you want *Daid* to kick your ass for not giving them to his *anamchara*?" I joked. He was taking his daily check-in on my health too far. Sure, he'd said hello to them but to come check on me first wasn't necessary.

"These aren't for Ms. Cyndi. These are for you." he held them out to me. I sat there frozen.

Daid came over. He was frowning. "Creed, have these been checked?"

"Yes, they have. There's no indication of anything harmful, sir. I double checked myself."

Our mail and anything delivered to us was checked to ensure it didn't contain bombs or anything else harmful. At the compound, we had equipment that allowed them to test for indications of a bomb, and we had dogs. A few were trained to sniff out bombing components. It sounded like overkill, but not in the world we lived in. Even if there wasn't the family history to contend with, our wealth was enough to make us targets.

"There has to be some mistake. Are you sure these are addressed to me?" As I asked, the kitchen began to fill up. What the hell? Why were so many home from work and what brought them here of all places? As I thought about the last part, it dawned on me. Creed must've alerted them. All six couples in the family were there as well as a few of the single ones. I narrowed my gaze to Creed.

"Those have to belong to one of the others, not me."

He shook his head. "No, the delivery man clearly stated these were to be given to Aisling O'Sheeran and were to be delivered as soon as possible."

"And all these curious bystanders just happened to arrive at the same time."

"Nope. I messaged them. I knew your parents were already here." He didn't show an ounce of contrition.

"Well, hand them over then if they're mine."

He slowly put them on the table next to me. He took a step back but he didn't leave. Everyone else was intently watching me. There was no way I planned to open the boxes or read the card attached to the flowers in front of them. Ignoring them, I went back to eating. I only got a couple of bites down before I was interrupted.

"Aren't you gonna see what's in those boxes and who sent them?" Aidan asked impatiently.

"I am when I get back to my room. Why?" I loved fooling with them.

"Your room? Hell no, we need to know who the hell is sending you stuff and what it is," he objected.

"No, you don't. It's my business. Why don't you all run along and let me finish my lunch? You have to have things to do before tonight. I assume you all have big plans."

"Ais, we just want to be sure it's nothing harmful. Even with all our efforts, it could be." Darragh stated as the voice of reason I suppose.

"But highly unlikely. Dar, since when do we open

our mail in front of others?"

"We don't, but then again, none of our sisters have been receiving gifts. We can stay here all day if you like," Shane said.

The room had gotten fuller. I was about to tell them to go to hell when Alistair came striding in. From the expression on his face, I knew he wasn't here by accident. He'd been told I had a delivery. He made his way to stand next to me. When he saw what was next to me, his face tightened.

"Who sent these?"

"That's what we're trying to find out. She's being a pain and refusing to open the boxes or the note," Shane tattled.

"*Mam*, tell them to stop and go away," I pleaded.

"*Mil*, you know them. I might as well save my breath."

"It's not fair."

"You were almost killed. Someone obviously intended to kill or kidnap you. There's no damn way we're allowing anything to harm you," Cathal said calmly.

"Fine, then Creed can stay and make sure it's safe. The rest of you can go."

This was an example of me feeling suffocated, and it was one of the times I wished I lived thousands of miles from them. There was such a thing as people being too much in your business. Cara, Siobhan, and I had dealt with it all our lives. The men in our family took being protective, as they called it, to the extreme. They all crossed their arms.

I threw up my hands in defeat. I was sure it was a mistake anyway. Dropping my half-eaten sandwich on my plate, I grabbed the envelope nestled in the flowers. The flap was sealed. I gently tore it open, then pulled out the note. At first glance, I saw it was a long one. Focusing on the words, my heart skipped a beat.

Aisling, you have no idea how much I wish I could be there with you right now. I want you to know I'm thinking of you day and night, and once this craziness is over, I'll be at your side. We have so much to discuss, and I have something important to ask you. I can't forget how close we've become. I miss it. Until then, these are just a token to remember me by. Love, Chris.

I was rather speechless. Chris was the last one I thought would do this. My heart sped up as I began to wonder what was in the boxes. His note hinted he was more serious than I knew, which would be a good thing if I were to go through with my plan to ask him if he wanted a marriage of convenience.

"So, who're they from?" Tiernan asked.

"They're for me, and I can promise you, it's nothing to be worried about. I'm not in any danger." I stood up. I was going to take these somehow and get them to my room, so I was alone to open the rest. Alistair gently pushed me back into my chair.

"Who sent them?" he asked softly.

"It's none of your business," I told him. I barely had the words out of my mouth before he snatched the card out of my hand. I tried to take it back, but he was too tall for me to get it.

"Give it back!" I shouted.

My brothers' and cousins' voices were all calling out encouragement for him to tell them who it was. I kicked Alistair in the leg, and he barely glanced at me. His frown turned to a thunderous look after he read it.

He threw the card on the table.

"It's from goddamn Brynes. He was told to stay away from her," he snapped.

I knew their reasoning for him keeping his distance, but they had no right to dictate he had no contact at all with me. "He is staying away. Do you see him here? No. Just because he should stay away doesn't mean we can't have contact," I snapped back.

"Yes, it does," Aidan immediately added.

"Open the boxes," Alistair ordered.

"Go to hell," I snarled.

"*Buachailli*, that's enough," Mam finally told them. She knew I was about to lose it. It was a race to see if I'd hit someone or cry.

Before I could stop him, Alistair snatched the boxes away from me. I screamed, but he ignored me as he tore them open. Inside one was a box of some of the most expensive chocolates in the world. In the other was a gorgeous diamond necklace. Tears filled my eyes. They were all quiet as I shoved my chair back and stood. I didn't say a word as I walked off. There were feet hurrying after me. Hands tried to stop me, and they were all talking at once, but I ignored them. I kept slapping them away. They dogged me all the way to my room. As I opened my door, I faced all of them. I did see worry and remorse on most faces.

"When I'm healed, I'm leaving. I'm moving, and there's not a damn thing any of you can do about it. I'm over this. I'll never be happy as long as I live here." I slammed the door in their faces and locked it. The pounding, pleading for me to talk to them and open up, went on for a long time. I blocked it out with my pillow as I sobbed into it.

The real reason I cried wasn't that they opened my stuff or even pushed me to know who it was from. It was my heartache over the fact that the gifts weren't from the man I loved and never would be. This was the final straw. When I was healed, I'd ask Chris if he would marry me—anything to escape this.

Alistair:

I was half numb. It was hours after the altercation in the kitchen over the Valentine's gifts sent to Ais by that fucker Brynes. Afterward, I felt bad for making her cry, but at the time, I had to know who was sending her presents even if my gut told me who. I'd wished it wasn't him and was a mistake. So much for wishing.

Her declaration she was moving away when she was healed terrified the hell out of me. There was no way I could allow it. Even if she didn't love me or want to be with me, there was no way I'd survive her being far away where I didn't know if she was safe and I couldn't at least see her from afar, which was why I was now in the CC, and the entire clan of O'Sheeran men was gathered with me. We had to figure out what to do and fast. After she refused to talk to us or open her door, we all dispersed. It was Cormac who'd sent out the text asking those who could to gather hours later.

He was there, flanked on both sides by Patrick and Sean. Her brothers were sitting around the huge conference table with troubled visages. The rest of the family was seated and eyeing the rest. As I sat, their gazes landed on me. Cormac rapping his knuckles on the table drew all the attention to him. His face looked almost haggard.

"Today went too far, and I was just as guilty as

anyone else. I should've put a stop to it before it got out of control. My only excuse is I, too, wanted to know who sent those things and why. We fucked up. I read the note from the flowers afterward..." he paused.

Reading it had gutted me more. I knew, without a doubt, that Brynes was shaping up to ask her to marry him. I just knew it. And even if she never married me, he was the last man I saw her with. I didn't see him as able to make her happy.

"What did it say, *Daid*?" Cathal asked.

"They were from Christopher, and he's thinking of her all the time, and he has something important he wants to ask her once this threat is past. I'm pretty sure he'll ask her to marry him." As he said it, he watched me. Since I'd come to the same conclusion, I didn't flinch.

Groans, swearing, and muttering broke out. He let it go for about a minute before he interrupted. "I know we all have strong feelings about the idea but what we have to remember is all we ultimately want is Aisling's happiness."

"But she doesn't love him. She loves Alistair," Cian objected.

"She's been in love with him since she was a teenager. However, we don't know what happened that month she spent in California with Christopher. She might've begun to have feelings for him," Cormac told him. He gave me a sympathetic look.

"There's no way she loves Chris," Fallon muttered. There were more murmurs of agreement.

"My brother is right. We don't know. And Aisling's response tells me we have to tread carefully. If she's on the fence about him, we might very well drive her into his arms if we keep pushing her. That's the last thing we want to do," Patrick interjected.

"What do you suggest we do? Just let him call her, send her gifts, and we say nothing?" Cillian asked.

"We can't prevent those but we can temper how we respond to them. No outright objecting to them or making scathing remarks about him. We need to show her she can have a life without moving away. I can't have my daughter on the other side of the country or, worse, the world. I can't. It'll kill me and her *mam*. Cyndi has been crying most of the afternoon in fear we'll lose Aisling."

"What about Alistair having a talk with her and letting her know how he feels? It was the plan when we flew to Cali," Rory added.

All three of the older O'Sheeran men shook their heads. It was Sean who answered him. "After this today, I don't think it's the right time. She might see it as an attempt to get her to stay here under false pretenses. There's no guarantee she'll believe his feelings are real. She'll wonder why now."

As much as I hated it, I agreed with him. I'd fucked around and waited far too long, and adding this on top of all the time I wasted might be what drove her into his arms.

"Then what would you have us do? There's no way I want her moving or marrying him," Declan declared.

"We show her she has a say in her life. We can't smother her. Demonstrate how lonely she'd be without us. As for Alistair, I know you won't like this *Mac*, but you need to keep your feelings to yourself just until she's better. Once she is, then pull out all the stops," Cormac advised.

"You're right. I was already thinking the same thing. It'll be hard, I won't lie, but I'll do whatever I must to ensure she's not pushed into his arms. She might not love me anymore, but she won't be happy with him."

There were plenty of muttered curses and conversations, but in the end, we all nodded our heads in agreement.

"Good. Since we're all here, any success in figuring out who targeted them and why?" Patrick asked.

"I wish. Cody is digging, and he admits that, like us, the Brynes get a fair share of threats. Most are like ours, but then you have to take into consideration those tied to the family business. They aren't as dirty as most, but they're not clean either. Cody is still working on it and refuses to give up until he uncovers who did it," Darragh informed all of us.

"I know we're confident it ties back to Chris and his family. What if we're wrong? What if it is our threat?" Rian asked.

"It's being considered too. Cody has others working to look into anyone who has made a threat, even an insignificant one, against our family in the past five years. The reason I believe it's more likely due to Chris is the fact no one has made any kind of move against any of us. If you were coming after our family, why pick Aisling? Most people would go for us men. We're the ones they see as in charge and we go around without a protection detail at times. If they wanted to hit us hard, then why not also go after the other women? Surely Aisling wasn't the opening strike." Dar explained.

There was logic to what he was saying. Pity there

was no way to know for sure. As it was, their enemies wouldn't be given an opportunity to strike at her or any of the women. They were covered any time they left the compound, although they'd been asked to limit those trips unless it was work or they had to go to something that absolutely had to be in person and not postponed. As for the men, while they had their typical security, they weren't adding more men. I knew it was to tempt whoever it might be to make a move if this was about them and not Brynes.

"Then we're just in a holding pattern on both fronts. I hate doing nothing, but I guess we don't have a choice," Fallon muttered darkly.

"We all hate it. If there's nothing else, I suggest those with wives get out of here and make sure you don't piss them off too. One angry and upset woman is more than enough for all of us," Rory jokes. I knew he was partially doing it to break the tension. As they all got up and started to leave, I knew I had my work cut out for me. The next four-and-a-half or so weeks couldn't pass fast enough for me. *God, please don't let me lose this chance with her.*

Aisling: Chapter 7

Looking at the bags open on my bed, I tried to generate some enthusiasm for what I was about to do. You'd think I'd be excited at freedom being hours away, but I couldn't seem to generate any. The past six weeks since the wreck had been tough, but the weeks since the blow-up on Valentine's Day had been trying in more ways.

After the abscess was drained, my healing was uncomplicated overall. Dr. K made sure to keep checking on me. He signed off on me being back to one hundred percent yesterday. My broken arm healed without delay. I was lucky it was a simple break overall. The weeks of recovery were more painful because I couldn't do things the same way as a person with two functioning arms. I was frustrated when I had to accept help with everyday tasks.

I was working to get the strength back to full functioning, but it was healed. My ankle was good after two weeks. My shoulder ached at times if I overused it, but it was fine as well. My various cuts and contusions were gone, and my incision was scarred over. I knew I had to wait until it was a year old before Judge would tattoo something pretty over it for me. I called and asked him what he suggested for a wait time. I hated the idea, but it wasn't a huge deal.

It was the rest that had me not only confused but

anxious for a change. Only the change I had intended to make wasn't what I really wanted. Things had been rather uncomfortable for me and the whole family. I received a group apology from those present who'd been a part of the gift snooping debacle. Alistair had come and spoken to me alone and made his apology.

I didn't just automatically accept them, though. I informed them how they had disrespected and hurt me. I left it with all of them that I would have to get over my hurt. With Alistair, it was different. Although I didn't tell him this, I was hurt on two fronts by him. My response over these past weeks had been to distance myself from him as much as I was able, which was surprisingly hard to do. The man wouldn't stay away or leave me in peace.

He was constantly dropping in and cornering me. Sometimes, he'd want to watch television with me or talk about anything and everything. He was always asking how I was feeling and if I needed anything. He didn't let a thing like a locked door keep him away, either. If I locked myself in my house or room, he'd sit on the front porch or in the hallway and talk through the door.

Our conversations were never dull. He didn't just ask me about myself and my day, he seemed to want to know how work was going with the winery. After the first two weeks, everyone backed off about me working. In addition to wanting to know about my day, he would share about his work or the parts he could. I was shocked he hadn't been sent out on a mission. There must've been an unprecedented lull in requests for the Hounds' aid.

I'd been in contact with Chris as well. He kept me

entertained with his anecdotes and tales about what he was doing. No one on his end or ours had been able to determine who was behind the attempt. There had been no new incidents, though, which made everyone nervous. I knew my family was, even if they worked hard not to show it. All the women were covered by double guards whenever they left the compound. Cara and Siv complained to me about it. *Mam* and my *aintíni*, aunts, had less to complain about. They tended to go out to do things with their husbands or in groups, so it wasn't as big of a deal to them. Plus, they recalled the old days and how much security went with them.

Chris had been eager for me to get the green light from Dr. Keim. He was pushing for me to come back to California as soon as I did. He swore he'd have more than enough men to watch over me when I arrived. He kept hinting at a talk we needed to have. It was the talk I knew deep down I wanted to avoid. As much as I thought I wanted to ask him to marry me so I'd be able to move on, I didn't want to. My stupid heart was holding onto the idiotic hope that Alistair would suddenly declare his undying love for me and beg me not to leave. Stupid, I know, but no matter how many times I told myself I was a fool, it didn't seem to sink in.

It was my last pep talk with myself, which had me packing my bags. I knew I'd never get out of here with them and to the airport without being seen or stopped, so I was working up my courage to speak to the family tonight. I would lay out my intentions and let them know there was nothing they could say or do to stop me. When I got to California, I'd decide how to broach the talk Chris wanted to have. Maybe if I were away from Alistair, it would make it easier for me to do it.

Everyone planned to be at the main house to have dinner together. I would go over there and have it, then tell them my decision. Thankfully, I moved back to my house three weeks ago. When I was done telling them, I'd be able to escape back here. Checking the clock, I saw I needed to get my butt over to the house. Leaving the bags open on the bed in case I had any last-minute things to throw in them when I got back, I went downstairs and headed over to the main house. My house, along with Cathal's, were the farthest ones back on the compound. It was a hike to the main one so I took my car rather than walk. It was nice outside, but I thought I might have to make a hasty retreat later, and walking wouldn't make it possible.

Parking outside in front, I went up the steps and walked in. No one bothered to knock. This was our family home, and despite having our individual ones, it would always be that. Our parents encouraged us to treat it as if we all still lived there. The loud chatter of voices led me to the main living room. It was the one we used for family, not guests. The fancier one for those times was in another section of the house.

Despite how big the room was, with everyone there, seating was scarce. We had several large sectionals and chairs scattered everywhere but several people wound up sitting on the floor or the arm of a chair or couch or even on large pillows they tossed on the floor. I noticed some had a pre-dinner drink in their hands. Along one of the walls was the bar, which held a wide selection of alcohol for those inclined to have one. I wish I could, but I had to keep my wits.

"There she is. Can I get you a drink, sis?" Shane asked as soon as he spotted me.

"No, I'm good."

I went to sit on the floor, but Rory got up. "Sit here."

"Ror, I can sit on the floor. I can get up and down just fine now," I assured him.

"I know you can, but still take it."

"Agatha said dinner will be ready in about ten minutes," Maeve announced. The groans of appreciation were loud. It appeared everyone was hungry tonight. My stomach was flipping too much to be hungry. I sat back and let the conversations flow around me.

I was deep in thought when I was jerked out of it by the arrival of Alistair. I thought for sure he wouldn't be here tonight. He'd make my announcement harder if he hung around after dinner, but it couldn't be helped.

"Agatha said dinner is ready and to come to the table," he announced with a smile.

This caused a mass exodus to the dining room. I brought up the rear. Somehow, Alistair ended up next to me. He gave me a probing glance.

"Are you okay, Ais?"

"I'm good, just have nothing to say."

"Hmm," was all he said.

When we reached the table, he paused to pull out my chair and then scooted me in. At the table, no one had assigned seating, really, but over the years, we'd all claimed what we saw as our spot, and we gravitated to those. Alistair had joined us enough times he, too, had one. It was just a couple of spots down from me on the other side of the table. In the past, I loved it because it meant I was able to sneak peeks at him. Now, I hated it because no matter how hard I tried not to, I would still do it.

Dinner was a loud affair with lots of chatter and everyone talking over each other as they talked about their week and asked questions. The food was wonderful as usual, but I wasn't able to enjoy it, which was a shame since I had no idea when I'd have one of Agatha's home-cooked meals again. By the time dinner was done and we all retired to the living room again, I was a ball of anxiety. My prayer, wishing Alistair would leave, wasn't answered. As soon as everyone was seated and those who wanted a drink had one, I knew there was no use waiting. If I didn't do it immediately, I'd chicken out. I stood up. Everyone's attention settled on me.

"Can I have everyone's attention, please? I need to talk to all of you about something important. It's a good thing we had dinner together tonight. This saves me time." I began to keep their attention and hopefully keep them silent. I saw some side glances while the rest were merely alert.

"Of course, *muirnín,* you have the floor," *Mam* said with a smile.

"Thank you, *Mam.* As you know, I went to see Dr. Keim yesterday."

I was interrupted by Aidan. "What's wrong? I thought he gave you a clean bill of health."

There he was, my impatient oldest brother. "Aidan, don't interrupt. I need all of you to listen without jumping in every two seconds."

He sighed but didn't say anything more. When no more comments were made, I continued. "As I was saying, I saw Dr. K yesterday. Yes, he gave me absolute clearance to resume all activities. Everything has healed as good as new. Now that there's nothing to stop me, I've made a decision." I paused to see if anyone would say something. No one did but they were exchanging looks.

"Tomorrow, I'm taking the plane back to California. I'll be staying there for the foreseeable future while I decide if moving there is the best decision for me. Who knows, I may end up settling somewhere else. I know this isn't likely to be something you like but it's my decision to make. I'm an adult. I want to focus my attention on my work and life. I can do it better there than here. Before any of you object, know that nothing you say will change my mind. I'm not happy here. I need a change. I hope you'll support me, but if you can't, at least don't get in the way."

The protests and curses were loud and came from all directions. I knew it was gonna go over badly.

"What the fuck?"

"We need to talk about this."

"You can't mean this."

"Please don't go."

"I can't stand it."

"Like hell, you're moving."

The worst though was my *mam* and *daid*. *Daid* had such a dejected expression, and I saw him glancing around the room. *Mam* burst into tears. I'd tried to prepare them for this. I'd been talking openly about my plans for the winery and all the things I wanted to do in Temecula when I got back there. I hinted more than once that I was only waiting for my medical clearance. I knew if I told them outright beforehand, they would've had the whole family after me. My determination was shored up with shaky walls. Knowing it was a cowardly thing to do, I still did it.

"I'm sorry, but that's it. There's nothing more to say. Excuse me."

I beat a hasty retreat for the door. The loudness behind me grew louder. They were all talking and yelling at the same time. I was shocked when I made it to my car without being accosted by any of them. The drive back to my house was quick. I went inside, but instead of going to my room to finish packing, I wandered the house, trying to calm myself down and not go back and tell them I changed my mind. I had to do it. It was possibly my only chance at trying to grab a tiny bit of happiness for myself. Without it, I'd end up miserable and hateful.

Alistair:

It was fucking time to end this. No more waiting and holding back. She was leaving and didn't have plans to return. No goddamn way I'd let her do it, especially without telling her how much I loved her. Trying to picture my life without her in it was one of utter darkness. No one knew what kind of animal lived deep inside of me, and without her light, who knew what I might do? The room was in an uproar, after her hasty exit. The women were all in tears. The men were angry and threatened to force her to stay. A loud whistle cut through the loud din of voices. It was Cormac.

He resembled a man who'd received the worst news of his life. Cyndi was huddled in his arms as she cried into his chest. He was rubbing her back. His perusal of the room ended up focused on me. There was both fear and determination in his eyes.

"It's time. You go talk to my girl, and you tell her how you feel. You lay it all out and hold nothing back. It's the only way I see we have not to lose her. She's hurting and has been for a very long time. She's about to do something I know she'll regret. I can't have it. Alistair, if you have any doubts about how you feel about her, then tell me now so I can come up with another plan." His voice was rough with emotion.

"Cormac, I have not a single doubt about her. I love your daughter. I've been a damn fool. The only thing that held me back was waiting for her to heal. I'll do anything to stop her going to California or being with him." I sneered the last bit.

The thought of her with Brynes made me insane. Wild thoughts were racing through my head. I had places off the grid where it was possible to take her. No one would be able to find her and I'd have her all to myself to prove beyond a doubt I loved her and wanted to spend my life with her.

"It might take me doing some drastic things. Will you be able to let me do those? I'll never hurt her."

"I trust you with her life, and I'm trusting you with her happiness. Go," he ordered.

I didn't wait to hear anything from the others. For all we knew, she might've decided to leave tonight. Rushing out of the house with their chorus of good luck in my ears, I ran to my car. Jumping in, I hightailed it to her house. Pulling up outside, I saw there were a few lights on. Getting out, I ran to the door. Knowing they rarely locked their doors inside the compound, I didn't bother to knock or ring the doorbell. I just opened it and walked in. I headed toward the closest light, which was the kitchen.

Not finding her there, I went down the hall to the living room. She wasn't there either. Frowning, I began to wander the first floor, where I saw the lights on from outside. Eventually, I found her. She was in her office. I watched her from the doorway as she muttered under her breath and jammed papers and stuff into her briefcase.

"I'll need this. Maybe this, too. I'll take it just in case. Hmm, let me see. I can't forget anything because I won't be able to ask anyone to forward them to me, and

I can't come back," I heard her utter.

"And why the hell can't you come back? In fact, why are you so damn determined to leave?" I asked.

She jumped and swung around to face me. Her eyes were wide, and her face was pale. She gripped the edge of her desk and stood so it was between us. I had news for her. That desk wouldn't keep me from her. Nothing would.

"What're you doing here? Did they send you? Never mind. Go back and let them know there's nothing they can say or do that'll make me stay. I'm leaving."

"I'm not leaving until you and I talk. It's past time for us to do it. I want you to come sit with me." I held out my hand. I hoped she'd at least meet me this far. She shook her head no and didn't move an inch.

"We have nothing to talk about. Didn't you hear me? I don't want to hear any of your arguments. I'm an adult. It's my life. I'm doing what'll make me happy."

"And do you think living thousands of miles away from your family among mostly strangers will do it? Come on, you know it won't. You love your family too much."

"I do love them, but it doesn't mean I have to have them crammed up my ass all the time with their noses in my business. I'm tired of it. That's been the way of it my whole life. I have friends out there. I won't be alone."

I snorted. "And is one of those friends Christopher Brynes?"

She stiffened. "What if he is? Again, it's not anyone's business. However, yes, he's been asking me to come back. I've thought about it, and it's the best thing for me."

"Like fuck it is! Answer me this, and if you tell me

the truth, I'll walk out this door and let you go without a fight."

"Shoot," was her only response. She had her arms crossed over her chest now. I recognized the mutinous look she wore. The woman could be as stubborn as a mule. She'd been this way since she was a toddler.

"Look me in the eyes and tell me you love Brynes more than your own life and want to spend the rest of your life with him. That you want to grow old with him and have him be the father of your children. Tell me he makes you feel so much you can't breathe, and to continue to live without him will kill you. To be away from him is agony. Tell me the absence of his touch hurts and you burn for him and can't sleep at night because all you do is dream of him," I snarled. I was telling her all the things she made me feel only she had no clue, but she would.

A flush entered her face. I saw her swallow, but she maintained eye contact. "I refuse to discuss my feelings for Chris with you. It's none of your business, Alistair. Your brotherly concern is sweet but not necessary. I have more than enough real and extended brothers. Go back and tell them you tried. Now, if you'll excuse me, I have to finish packing. I plan an early flight tomorrow." She presented her back to me, dismissing me. Well, I had news for my princess. She wasn't getting rid of me that easily.

I darted around the desk and grasped her upper arms. I was careful so I wouldn't hurt the one she just broke or the dislocated shoulder. I twirled her around to face me. Her mouth was open, and I saw alarm on her face. It turned my stomach to think she might be afraid of me. I had no problem being a bloody monster when the situation called for it, but I'd never harm a hair on her head.

"Don't do that. You have to know I'd never hurt you, Ais. This is important. Tell me how you feel about him," I pleaded. I felt like I was drowning.

"What difference does it make how I feel about him?"

"Just tell me," I said louder.

"The things you want me to tell you, they're ridiculous."

"Why?"

"Because you don't need to feel that way in order to want to be with someone."

"You do if you want to be with your soulmate."

She snorted. "Soulmates, it's a nice dream but the reality is most of us don't get one of those. We have to learn to settle for what we can have."

"So you're settling for Brynes because you don't believe you have a chance at a soulmate? You don't love him?" I prodded. I had to hear her admit that much. It was tearing me apart inside, the slim possibility she did.

"Fine, no, I don't love him, but I like him, and we get along well. We're sexually compatible. He'll make a good husband."

The mention of their sexual compatibility pushed me to the edge. I growled and hauled her closer. "Have you slept with him?"

Her mouth gaped open. "That's none of your business! Let go of me." She tried to get away, but I held her firmly, still careful not to hurt her.

"Like hell, it's not. Tell me. Has he been inside of you? Has he made you scream from so much pleasure you almost can't stand it? If you don't love him, then it was just fucking," I snapped.

"So what if it was? A good fucking works for me."

That snapped the restraint I had been trying to hold on to. I let out a loud roar then I pushed her back until she was trapped against the wall. I made sure not to be too rough with her, but I crowded her.

"You deserve more than just a good fucking. You deserve a man who, even if he is fucking you, he loves you too. He desires only you and would do anything to have you and make you happy."

She gave me a humorless laugh. "Oh really, well, show me this wonderful man. Where is he?"

"Right in front of you. He's here trying his damndest to get you not to leave and to stay with him. He's dying because the thought of you being with anyone but him is driving him insane. He wants to go out and kill Brynes for being inside of you," I confessed.

To say she was stunned was an understatement. I saw disbelief warring with hope. I let what I said sink into her brain and heart. Her mouth opened and closed a few times before she was able to say something.

"A-Alistair, don't say that. Please. It's not fair. I never thought you'd stoop to lying. Christ, what did my family say to you?" There were tears in her eyes as she hoarsely asked.

"*Leanabh*, baby, I'm not lying. The only thing your family said was it was time I told you the truth. No lies or hiding."

"You don't love me. Not like that."

"Oh, you have no idea how I feel about you. I've been a damn fool, and I'm done. Do you hear me? Done. You accused me of trying to be another brother. I can promise you what I feel for you isn't brotherly love. I am full of passion, lust, desire, love, and so much more for you. I have been for years. Please, don't go to him. Stay here with me."

I wasn't able to stop myself as I lowered my head to kiss her. I did it slowly to give her time to say no, but she didn't. As our lips met, I swear sparks or something shot throughout my body. The fire inside of me, which always was there burning for her, flared into a bonfire. She whimpered and moaned. Her lips were so soft, and I had to nibble on them. I nipped her bottom lip and tugged on it. Letting go of it, I licked across where I bit. She gasped, and her lips parted. I took advantage without a bit of remorse. My tongue wiggled its way inside her mouth.

I'd kissed plenty of women over the years. Not a single one tasted like her or made me crave them even a tenth as much as tasting Aisling. I could easily continue kissing her for hours, I had no doubt. Her mouth was sweet, and she tasted like the apples we had in our dessert. I explored her mouth and teased her tongue with mine to get it to play. As they twined together, I fought not to tear her clothes off and take her against the wall. My cock was so hard and aching to be inside her, but this wasn't the time. I was here to convince her to stay, not to ravish her.

I have no idea how long I kissed her before I was able to tear myself away. We were both breathing hard. I knew I needed to tell her all of it, but I wondered if I'd blown it. God, I hoped not. I placed my forehead on hers as I stared deeply into her eyes. She was dazed.

"I love you, Aisling. I want you. I need you. Please, don't go. Stay here with me," I whispered. The big speech I'd rehearsed in my head was forgotten. I might be messing the whole thing up, but she had to hear my honesty. This wasn't something I'd lie about, no matter the reason.

Aisling: Chapter 8

I had to be dreaming. It was the only explanation for what was happening. There was no way Alistair had begged me to stay, all but confessed he loved me and then kissed the hell out of me. A kiss which erased all others I'd ever had. My body was aching. As I stared up at him, his words sank in.

"I love you, Aisling. I want you. I need you. Please, don't go. Stay here with me."

I swear I saw pain and desperation on his face. Afraid to break the spell, but hope was flickering in my heart. I opened my mouth to let it all come pouring out. If it were a dream, it wouldn't matter. If this were real, then he'd either finish breaking me, or I might get my biggest dream fulfilled. I was past caring. It had been festering inside of me like cancer for too long. I pushed on his chest. He reluctantly lifted his head off mine and took a few steps back. I slid along the wall until I reached the chair behind my desk. I dropped down in it. He moved and sat on the edge of my desk. I stared down at my hands. This was too difficult for me to say and do it with eye contact.

"Ais, look at me."

"I can't. This is so embarrassing, but here goes. Stair, I have been in love with you since I was thirteen years old. I've fought it and tried to make it go away. I knew you didn't feel the same way. However, no matter who I was with, they were never you, and it didn't last. This is my final attempt to find happiness. If it fails, I don't know what I'll do. I don't want to be alone anymore. Don't you see? You saying those things gives me hope and hope will only destroy me once and for all. Please, I need you to leave and let me go. I want a family of my own. I can't do that if I have to see you all the time."

The tears I'd been trying so hard to hold back spilled down my cheeks. I put my hands over my face and bawled. I was truly broken. The next thing I knew, I was airborne and moving across the room. He sat down on the small loveseat I had in my office. He cradled me on his lap. His lips were moving against my hair. Eventually, they made it to my cheek. My hands were pried away. Great, he got to see me looking like a raccoon. Would this nightmare ever end?

"*Mo ghràdh*, please stop crying. You're killing me. Tell me what to do. I can't stand to see you in so much pain," he whispered in my ear.

"I just wish you really did love me, and this wasn't some crazy scheme my family cooked up to get me to stay."

"Let me tell you a story. It's one which started a long time ago. I want you to listen to it, really listen, and don't interrupt. There was a grown man who came back to the one home he always had. He'd spent years learning to be a protector, and he was almost ready to put those skills to the test at home rather than abroad. While home on leave, he was invited to enjoy a day with his friends, the guys he grew up with and thought of as his brothers and their family was his, which included their sisters being his sisters."

I squirmed. I knew the day he meant. Jesus, I didn't need to hear him tell me more. A sister. His words about not being my brother were just words. His arms tightened when I tried to slide off his lap.

"I was by the pool when this absolute vision came striding out in her bathing suit. Standing there wasn't a girl anymore. She was a beautiful young lady. God, I didn't know what to think. One thing I knew was I had to protect her and others like her, so I went to work serving the world and her family. Then, two years later, I finally admitted there were more than brotherly feelings in me. I felt like I'd been hit with a lightning bolt or something. She was even more beautiful and so damn sexy. That's when I acknowledged I desired her, but I couldn't pursue her. There was no way she wanted me, and besides, her family would never see me as good enough for her."

I made a protesting sound, but he placed his fingers over my lips to stop me from talking.

"Shh, let me finish. I watched as the years passed and she got more gorgeous, smarter, and sexier and went on to be a successful businesswoman. I ached for her, and every time I saw her with another man, I wanted to tear their hearts out and scream she was mine, but I didn't. I kept quiet. It wasn't until your wreck that I found out there was hope." He gave me a faint smile. I raised a brow in question. What changed with my wreck? I was now hanging onto every word.

"When I heard what happened to you and that you were life-flighted to a hospital, I almost died. Fear and panic filled me. We couldn't leave soon enough to suit me. Your *daid* and the others got me in the Command Center and told me what happened. This was after I'd heard before how you were cozying up to Brynes, and they thought you might be getting serious with him. It gutted me. After they dropped the bomb about the wreck, they hit me with something else."

"What?" I said, despite his edict.

"How they all knew I loved you and had for years, and they were tired of waiting for me to make a move. They wanted to know why I didn't and if I was willing to stand back and let him have you. I confessed it all."

"If that's true, why did you say nothing until today after I told everyone I'm leaving?" I asked.

"Because I was waiting for you to heal, then I planned to tell you and beg you to give me a chance. They all swore you loved me too. I was afraid to hope. I know I'm not good enough for you. I have blood on my hands, and I've done terrible things to protect others, but no one in this world will love you or work to make you happy like I will. *Mo shealladh àlainn*, tell me if I've waited too long." He whispered the last part as he stared into my eyes.

I gave him his answer in the only way I knew how. As I did, I prayed I wasn't setting myself up to be devastated. I reached up and latched onto his neck, then drew his head down to mine. My mouth crashed into his, and I kissed him like a starving woman. He groaned then he gripped me tightly against him, and our mouths hungrily attacked each other. My body went up in flames as my pussy became slick with my cream, and my nipples became hard beads. I pressed my legs together, trying to get some kind of relief. I hadn't had sex in a long time. For me, the only sexual release I'd been getting was self-induced with my fingers or toys.

As I writhed on his lap, I ended up finding a

large bulge. I gasped. He pressed up into me, pressing it against my pussy. I slid back and forth over him. We both moaned. I kept riding him until he grabbed my hips and held me still. He lifted his mouth away from mine. I followed, trying to reconnect our mouths.

"Ais, you have to stop. If you don't, I'll either come in my pants, or I'll strip you naked and take you right here."

"Don't come in your pants. It's such a waste. Come inside of me," I begged. I found his bulge and squeezed him. He threw back his head and groaned long and hard.

"Fuck, you're making this so hard. I didn't come here to take advantage. I just wanted you to know how I feel. We need to take things slow."

"I don't want to go slow. We've been at a snail's pace for years. Either you love me and want me, or you don't. I want proof. Show me," I challenged him.

His face tightened as he fought to restrain himself. I kept rubbing along his bulge. *Dia*, I couldn't wait to see him. He felt so thick and long. My pussy ached to be filled. I hadn't had sex with a man in two years. His hand came up and grabbed my hair in the back.

"You have to be one hundred percent sure I'm what you want because once I've been inside of you, there'll be no going back. You'll be mine until the day I die. I'll be the only man who touches you. Only my seed will be inside of you. It'll be my babies growing in your womb. I don't share, and I don't give up what's mine," he snarled. He had this wild look. It excited and frightened me at the same time. More moisture flooded my panties.

"Please. I need you, Stair. I'll die if you don't show

me," I whimpered.

A loud growl came out of him, then I was up in his arms again, and he was striding for the door. It took no time for him to reach my bedroom upstairs. He had been here enough times to know the layout. He held me in one arm as he locked the bedroom door. When he was done, he brought me to the bed and laid me down. He straightened and scanned me. His look made me feel as if he'd stripped me naked with a look. I shivered. I watched as he began to unbutton his shirt. I'd seen him shirtless numerous times, but it never got old. He was a work of art, in my opinion. He should always go around bare-chested. As he took it off, I sat up enough to drag my sweater over my head.

Alistair:

I couldn't believe I was here with her and about to see her naked for the first time. To taste her and feel her pussy clamped tight around me. I fought not to lose my control. As my shirt fell to the floor, she shed her sweater. Underneath was a lacy hot pink bra. I'd seen her in bathing suits plenty of times, but I still stared in rapt bliss. Her full breasts were almost overflowing her cups. Her creamy skin made my hands shake with the need to touch her.

Toeing off my shoes, I undid my belt, then my button and zipper on my dress pants. She was wiggling out of her pants. She took her shoes off when she got home, so no need to get rid of them. I didn't want her to take off the rest. I wanted that pleasure for myself. I shoved my pants to my knees and let them drop to the floor. I heard her gasp and moan.

The thing about me was I hated to wear underwear. They always twisted around and made my cock and balls feel like they were being strangled, so I didn't wear them. My fully erect, dripping cock sprang up and bounced. I waited to see what she'd say or do.

"Don't take anything else off," I demanded. I couldn't stop myself from stroking up and down my length. She was raised up on her elbow as she lay on her side facing me. She licked her lips.

"I won't if you do something for me."

"Oh yeah, what?"

"Bring that gorgeous cock over here so I can taste it."

My whole body jerked in response. I wanted her mouth on me badly. Gripping myself tightly so I wouldn't come, I walked over to the edge of the bed. She wiggled closer. As we met, she reached out and ran her fingers over the head and down my length. As she did, she went over the two barbell piercings through the head of my cock. It formed what was called a magic cross. They crossed each other, and I had four beads poking out. I'd gotten it on a dare several years ago. It hurt like hell, but once it was healed, it stimulated nerves in the head when I penetrated, and women seemed to love it. If Aisling didn't like it, I'd take it out. I shuddered as she kept rubbing the head and those beads.

"*Leanabh*, fuck, that feels good."

"Good. I want to make you feel good. And I love this. Let me taste you, Stair. I want you in my mouth, please," she begged.

"I'm yours," I told her as I leaned over and gripped the back of her head with one hand, bringing her closer while using the other to hold myself for her. Her hand encircling the base made me hiss then I moaned as her tongue came out to flick back and forth and around the head. She was lapping up the precum oozing out of my slit. The whole head was covered in it. She hummed, and the way she kept going told me she liked not only the taste but giving head.

She sucked me inside of her hot mouth and thrashed my sensitive head with her tongue. Another moan was torn from me. I kept myself from thrusting it down her throat, but barely. The image of her deep-throating me and of me fucking her mouth played in my mind. Maybe one day, but not the first time. She might not like it, and I would never do something she didn't want or like.

As she took me deeper, her hand was wrapped around the base, and she was pumping up and down. Christ, she could suck cock. In no time, she was driving me toward an intense orgasm. I could feel it deep in my gut and balls. She was stroking me, fondling my balls, licking, sucking, and more. My head was whirling. I tried to stay quiet, but when she deep-throated me and hummed as she gagged on it and kept going, I had to say something. My hand tightened in her hair, but I didn't shove her further down, though *Dhia*, God, did I want to.

"Take me deep. That's it. Gag on it. *Dhia*, I love fucking your mouth and having you take me so deep, Ais. So pretty, so sexy," I told her gutturally.

She lifted off me. I wanted to protest, but this was a gift she was giving me. If she wanted to stop, she had the right. Her words made the breath inside of me catch.

"What I'd love is if you'd fuck my mouth and come down my throat. Make me really gag on your big cock. I love those piercings. They feel so good. Can't wait to find out how they feel in my pussy and ass." The heat in her gaze made me shake. Her words sank in, and when they did, I let the leash slip more.

"Are you sure?" I gave her a chance to change her mind.

She nodded. "Yes, fuck my mouth, Stair. Give it to me. I'm your little cum slut. Give me your cum."

How she knew a secret fantasy I had was to take

a woman like she was my sex toy to do with anything I wanted. I had no idea. I'd played with women but never found one I could do that with. And her admission of willingness to let me take her ass made me almost lose it. When I didn't say anything, she took the lead and sucked me back into her mouth. As she bobbed up and down on me like her life depended on it, I broke and began to fuck her mouth. I went deep, and I held my cock there until she'd start to struggle to breathe, then I'd ease back. I used her hair to control the speed. I wasn't pulling too hard, but there was a bite to it. Her moans vibrating up my length told me she was enjoying it.

Suddenly, she grabbed my other hand and tugged me closer to her. She pushed my hand underneath her panties and between her legs. I groaned as her slippery pussy lips parted, allowing me to slide up and down her slit. As I did, I got a surprise. I bumped a hard piece of metal. It seemed my woman had her clit pierced. I growled and focused on teasing it.

She went wild, and within a matter of a minute or less, I was wildly taking her mouth as well as fingering her pussy as if my life depended on it, and it did. She stiffened and clamped down on my cock. Her scream was garbled by my cock, and the vibrations sent me over the edge. I came shouting, and my hips jerked as I filled her mouth with my cum. Her cream gushed over my fingers as she came. By the time I was done orgasming, I had to sit. She let go of me and collapsed on her back. I eased onto the bed next to her, and she curled up against me. We were both breathing fast.

Cupping her face, I brought her mouth to mine. Before they could meet, she put her hand between us.

"Let me go rinse my mouth."

"If you don't like the taste of cum, you don't need to do what you just did."

"It's not that. I know guys don't like to taste themselves. It'll only take a minute." When she tried to scoot away, I held her fast.

"Ais, I don't give a fuck about that. Do you not want to kiss after I go down on you? If not, just let me know."

"I don't mind. It's just… You know what, forget it. I don't mind, and if you don't, then kiss me."

Not wanting to think about her with other men, I did as she suggested. The kiss was hot, and when we were done, I was ready for the next step. I reached behind her and undid the hooks on her bra. I eased it off. My first eyeful of her lush breasts made me ready to feast. Pressing her flat onto her back, I kissed and licked my way from her mouth down to her breasts, where I sucked a nipple into my mouth to make love to it while my hand fondled and teased the other. She squirmed and moaned over and over.

I spent time on both breasts until she pushed me further down her body. I chuckled and took her hint. Her rich scent filled my nose as I got closer to her pussy. Seeing her scar from her surgery made me pause. She tried to put her hand over it, but I shoved it away so I could place kisses along it.

"It's ugly. You don't need to kiss it," she protested.

"It's part of you. Nothing about you could ever be ugly."

"I'm covering it with a tattoo as soon as I can. I have to wait a year."

"If you want to, then do it, but not because of me

or thinking it's ugly. I'll love it either way," I told her before placing one more kiss on it.

Seeing her astonished look, I moved on. We could debate this later if she wanted. Hooking my fingers on each side of her delicate panties, I worked them down her hips and to her knees before shoving them to her ankles. She kicked them the rest of the way off. I maneuvered myself so I was able to spread her legs, and I was between them.

Her pussy lips were the same pale pink as her nipples. Everything about her was creamy and pink. Much paler than my skin, and I loved the contrast. She had the paleness of a redhead without the freckles. She was slick, and her pussy lips were engorged. The piercing through her clit shined up at me. Another time I'd take the time to kiss and taste every inch of her body, but today, I needed to know what her cum tasted like, and I'd waited long enough. Holding her lips spread wide, I dove in and fluttered my tongue all over her piercing, clit, then down her folds to her entrance, where I thrust it in and out of her tight hole. I was instantly in love with her flavor, and I wanted more. She was sweet with a slight hint of musk and a floral scent.

Nibbling up her outer lips, I made it back to her clit. I sucked it into my mouth and thrashed her barbell with my tongue. She cried out, and her legs tried to clamp shut around me, but I held her open.

"Oh God, Stair. Jesus, it's too good," she wailed.

I shook my head, rubbing my light beard over her sensitive folds. She wailed louder. I stopped eating her long enough to answer her.

"I'm not stopping until you come to my satisfaction. Give me everything you've got. Your scent is now my favorite perfume, and your taste is ambrosia. Come for me. Let me have your cum like I gave you mine," I ordered her.

"Alright," she whispered.

I went back to pleasuring her in every way I knew. I lost track of time as I worked her up and over the edge, but once wasn't enough for me. I kept going. No part of her was safe. My tongue and then my finger even teased her asshole. I didn't penetrate her, but I planned to, and soon. She was so sensitive just on the outer ring of her ass that she came. I held out until she orgasmed a third time then I was done. Eating her out had the effect of waking my cock back up. I was back to being full and hard. I wanted the ultimate intimacy, My cock inside of her pussy. I sat up on my knees and watched her come down from her last high. She blinked slowly as she met my gaze.

"We can stop if you want, but I hope to hell you don't. I want you, Ais. Let me finish one more part of this claim. I need to feel your tight, wet pussy clenching hard around my cock. Can I?"

She ran her hand over my pecs and then down my stomach to wrap around my cock. She pumped gently up and down. "Yes, do it. I need you inside of me, Stair."

"I'm clean. I want nothing between us. I want to take you bare. Are you on birth control?"

I wanted her answer to the birth control question to be no. It wouldn't change my desire to take her without a glove. In fact, it made me harder, thinking of her not being on anything and me filling her full of my cum and impregnating her. I'd imagined what our kids might look like if we ever had any for years.

She moaned. "I'm on birth control but right now,

as nuts as it sounds, I wish I wasn't. I'm clean, too. No condom. I want to feel all of you. This will be a first for me," she admitted.

Her voicing her wish not to be on anything made me shake then to know no one had ever had the privilege of being in her bare made me moan.

"Baby, we can be nuts together, and this will be a first for me, too," I told her right before I notched the head of my cock at her entrance.

Holding her gaze, I began to slowly press inside even though a part of me wanted to turn into a beast and slam my cock inside of her. She opened for me, but it was tight, and she resisted. It was so intense feeling her surrounding me. No condom, her tight wetness, and the rubbing of my piercings drove my sensitivity and pleasure through the roof. Based on the cries and the other sounds she was making, it was doing the same to her. Her nails bit into my forearms. When I was all the way inside, I paused to get control. A rutting animal wasn't what she wanted.

Her legs came around to circle my waist. She rocked her hips, causing us both to moan. She did it again. I wasn't able to hold back anymore. I withdrew and then slid home again. I set a slow pace even though I wanted to go fast and hard. She soon made me aware she wanted more.

"Harder. I want to feel you tomorrow. I've waited so long, Stair. I need to know I'm yours. Please!" she pleaded as she ground her pussy hard down on me.

I began to drill into her hard and fast. As I did, I made sure to hit her clit over and over. My thrusts built and built. Eventually, when I felt her tightening, I rubbed circles on her clit. She stiffened and then screamed as she came. I swear my eyes rolled into the back of my head. It felt that good, but somehow, I held onto my control and didn't join her.

When she relaxed, I went back to pounding her. She went wild on me. She scratched and pulled me down to kiss her. Her teeth even bit my lip as her nails sank into my ass cheeks. My baby seemed to like it wild and primitive in bed, so I gave it to her. I used my teeth to leave marks on her without breaking her skin. I knew I was on the right track when she started to talk dirty.

"That's it. Yes, Oh *Dia*, yes. Fuck me. Harder. Pound my pussy. Your little cum slut needs more."

All sense of finesse flew out the window as I growled and went crazy. The headboard was banging into the wall as I fucked her toward another orgasm. She was crying and begging. She was gushing so much cream it was insane. I saw her orgasm hit a second before she clamped down on me and came. She screamed long and hard as she beat the mattress with her fists. Seeing her in the middle of such an intense orgasm caused my own to peak. As it did, I grabbed her neck and squeezed. I swear she gripped me tighter with her pussy, and she grabbed my hand to hold it to her throat. I was aware enough not to hurt her or leave bruises. I roared as my cum was milked from me. I shuddered as I jerked and flexed. When I was done and drained, I had to catch myself before I crushed her. We were both breathing so hard it was as if we'd run a race.

It was with reluctance that I withdrew when I softened, and then I fell beside her on the bed. I dragged her into my arms. "That only showed you a tenth of the love and passion I feel for you, Aisling. If you still wonder if I love you, give me about twenty minutes, and

I'll show you again."

She rubbed my jaw and smiled. "I won't say no to more of that, but I believe you. I hope you know how much I love you."

I placed a gentle kiss on her lips. When we surfaced from that kiss, I knew it was time to get cleaned up so we could rest for the next round. One wouldn't be enough tonight. She wouldn't be catching a plane tomorrow or any time soon, not if I had anything to say about it.

Alistair: Chapter 9

I wasn't able to wipe the smile off my face even if someone had threatened me if I didn't. Last night was hands down the absolute best night of my damn life. From the scare of her leaving to this was night and day. I wanted to kick my own ass for waiting all these years to tell her how I felt. We wasted those. She could've been my wife, and we'd have a house full of kids by now. I would always regret that I hadn't said something sooner. She admitted this morning, she felt the same way.

I was grinning for another reason. My tough, confident, take-no-prisoners woman was embarrassed, and I loved seeing this side of her. I was practically dragging her into the main house. She kept trying to get away and run. Finally, I laughed out loud, and when she glared at me, I swept her up in my arms and strolled inside.

"Stair put me down this instant! Don't you dare," she hissed at me as she kicked her feet, trying to wiggle loose.

I stopped in the foyer and balanced her in one arm as I captured her face with the other hand. I held her still as I kissed her. It wasn't a peck on the lips either. It was full-on devouring with tongue. She went limp and returned it after a second or two of resistance. I greedily savored her. I would never get enough of kissing her. I lost track of how many I'd given her since last night. Being free to express my desire and love for her was incredible. What broke the kiss was a loud voice, no it was voices.

"What the hell is this?"

"I'm dreaming. Or is it a nightmare?"

"I knew we should've gone after them last night."

I raised my head to glare at the ones gathered around us. There stood half the family. The assholes who said something were Cian, Declan, and Tiernan. They were frowning, but I knew it was all an act. They wanted to give us a hard time.

"Put me down," she pleaded in my ear.

Reluctantly, I lowered her feet to the ground, but I didn't let her move away from me. I kept my arm around her with a hand resting on her hip. I hiked up a brow as I stared back at them. Among them were all three sets of parents. Cormac and Cyndi had smiles on their faces. Patrick, Maeve, Sean, and Brenda were all nodding their heads. I knew they'd all be gathered this morning for a family breakfast. Aidan pushed himself to the front of the crowd.

"Wanna explain why we just saw you mauling our sister?"

"Aidan, don't," Aisling warned him.

"I'm your big brother. It's my right to ensure you're taken care of. This big ugly Scotsman had his paws and lips on you. That's grounds for a beat down at a minimum."

"Hate to warn you, but there was more to it than that," I taunted him.

We were all adults here except Khloe, and she had no idea what I was talking about. Aisling gasped and elbowed me in the stomach. I leaned down and nipped her ear with the edge of my teeth. She shivered, and I heard her stop a moan. I was finding *mo shealladh àlainn* loved a degree of pain. Nothing too crazy, but it made her even wilder, and her response was out of this world. I was looking forward to exploring it more.

"That's it. He's defiled her. He must suffer the consequences," Aidan said with a mock growl.

The jackass was having fun with this. I knew none of them truly disliked me being with her from the prior conversations. I'd told her the whole family knew about our feelings and were all for us as a couple, but she still seemed hesitant when I made her come here. Her body stiffened. Enough of this. I wouldn't allow their teasing to upset her.

"Okay, enough joking around. She thinks you're serious. Don't make her reconsider. If she does, I'll be the one doing the killing."

His disapproving expression dropped, and a smile replaced it. The others were all openly smiling, too. "I'm just messing around, Ais. I take it you two have good news for us? You're not leaving and flying off to California, are you?"

As much as I wanted her to tell him no, the answer wasn't that simple. We'd talked about it this morning after we got up. I waited for her to answer first.

"We do have good news. Actually, it's wonderful news. Can we sit down so we can share it?" she asked.

Everyone began to disperse, and we found our way back into the family room. Spots were taken. They let me and her have the large, overstuffed chair. I held her on my lap. I wasn't able to let there be any distance between us. It would take time. My brain hadn't fully

CIARAST JAMES

processed and accepted she was mine at last. She was
staring at them and seemed not to know what to say, so
I got the ball rolling.

"As you know, last night, things got intense. I
went to see Aisling, and I did as you all have been telling
me. I told her how I felt about her. I laid it out for her. To
my amazement, she feels the same way. So the answer
is yes, we have wonderful news. Aisling has agreed to be
mine. I have my *anamchara,* and so does she." I had to
place a soft kiss on her delectable mouth. She was half-
turned to face me as I talked.

"Hey now, none of that. Tell us what your plans
are. You're not thinking of stealing her away to your
hideaway, are you?" Shane asked. He was referring to
my retreat, which was way out in the swamps, not far
away. No one bothered me when I was there.

"We haven't talked through all the details. Jeez,
give us time. We just decided this last night. We wanted
to let all of you know, and that's it. The details are
between us," she told him when she ended our kiss.

"But surely you won't go far if you do. I'm glad
this nonsense about going to California is over," Aidan
added.

She exchanged a worried look with me. I nodded.
I wasn't happy about the next part, but I understood it,
and I would support her.

"Well, the California part isn't off. I'm still going."

"What!?" was shouted from more than one
mouth.

"Let her finish!" I shouted over them. They slowly
quieted down, and when they were silent again, she
continued.

"I know this probably sounds stupid or

unnecessary to you, but it's not. There was more than one reason I planned to go to California. The biggest was I needed to personally check in to see how everything was going at the winery. We're on the cusp of rolling out a whole new line of wines. Ones I believe will be award-winning. I have to make sure it goes off without a hitch. This is going to put Maeve's Cellars on the map in a big way. Yes, I can do a lot remotely, but it's not the same as being there for the staff and them being able to come to me directly."

"Alistair, what do you think of this idea?" Declan asked.

"You know who'll come sniffing around if she goes out there," Shane muttered.

"How long will you be gone?" Ciaran asked.

They were all good questions, ones I'd already thought of and some I'd asked. The one I was the least happy about was it put her within Brynes' territory. Even when she informed him she was with me, I had no doubt he'd continue to push himself at her. He wasn't a man who liked to lose. And Aisling was a huge prize to give up, which was the main reason I had to talk to Darragh. No way in hell I was letting her go to California without me. Plus, there was still the possibility of a threat.

I caught Darragh's gaze. He had them narrowed on me. I gave him a subtle chin lift. He nodded back. He knew what I was thinking, no doubt, and we'd talk it out once she was done telling the rest of the family. At least I got her to agree not to fly out today. We'd be waiting a couple of days so I was able to get things in order. I'd need to take time off from work, and right now, we had nothing happening. The missions we'd been hit with when she was hurt had all been resolved. Of course, it could change with one email or phone call.

There was still a bunch of talk, and everyone was trying to talk over each other. If you weren't used to having a family like this, they were very overwhelming. I was always impressed by how Ashlynn, Miranda, and Karizma handled it. None of them came from families remotely like this one. If I hadn't grown up around them, I'd be in shock.

Finally, after five minutes or so of debate and no end in sight, Darragh yelled for their attention. "Alright, take a breath. You're not giving them a chance to answer us." This made them grow quiet. Being the focus of two dozen sets of eyes was intense, no matter who you were.

"I don't know exactly how long this trip will take. It won't be the last one. When we get ready to do the official launch, I'll have to go back and work for a period with them. This trip is the last part before the actual making of the new wines. The later trip will be to roll it out to the masses. This time, it might be anywhere from two weeks to a month. If you want to know what Alistair thinks of it, I'll let him answer that." She gestured to me.

We had a pretty in-depth talk about this. She knew why I wasn't thrilled, but I also knew why she had to do it.

"I don't want her anywhere that she isn't behind secure walls with lots of guards like she is here. But I do understand what her work means to her and why this is important. The sooner she goes, the sooner she can resolve the work and get home, so I support her need to go. Her security will be thoroughly vetted and precautions will be put in place before she does. She's agreed to give me this for my peace of mind."

"We can talk about her safety in a minute. How the hell can you let her go to Cali, knowing Chris will be at her doorstep the second he hears she's there? You know he'll know it. I wouldn't want my woman to be exposed to someone who wants her. And make no mistake, he does. I don't think he'll just back off once he hears about the two of you," Cian pointed out.

"I plan to meet with Chris and explain to him there is no us. His feelings and actions after that are his. He's not going to change my mind or anything," she protested.

"Are you letting her go without you?" Tiernan asked in outrage.

"I need to talk this over with Dar. No, ideally, I don't want her there and me here, but I have a job as well."

"We'll figure out the job situation, don't you worry. The teams know what they're doing. They can handle any work we get. Remote meetings aren't perfect, but they get the job done. We've done it before when we needed you, and you were on an assignment. I'd rather have you with her to ensure her protection than her out there and something pops off. You both need to be prepared for pushback from Chris. Cian's right. He won't just accept it graciously and leave her alone. He isn't one to give up easily," Dar warned us.

"He might not be, but I've waited an eternity to make Aisling mine. I don't give up what's mine, and make no mistake, she is. I'll fight to the death to keep her," I stated with a growl.

The mere thought of losing her made me want to go into a blind rage. After all these years of not having her, I foresaw a long stretch of me being at her side until I was able to relax. Her hand rubbed up and down my lower arm. I realized I was gripping her tighter. I eased up my grip.

"Well, if you have to kill him, make sure no one sees you or finds the body. They'll probably know it was you, but if they can't prove it, oh well," Rory added with a shrug.

"I won't go to that extreme unless he forces me by harming her in some way."

"You need to stop encouraging him, and you have to stop worrying about Chris. He'll get over it. It's not like he loves me or anything. We were going out on casual dates and hanging out, nothing more," she stressed.

She confessed this morning that they had never slept together. While it relieved the hell out of me, her confession that she had been thinking of a marriage of convenience didn't make me happy. She'd been so depressed and sure I would never see her as anything more than a sister that she'd been ready to marry without love. If I hadn't gotten my head out of my ass, the thought of her married to anyone but me made me want to howl and tear things to shreds.

"Okay, enough about Brynes and California. As long as Alistair is with you and we have security in place, go and get it done then come home. We have more important stuff to discuss," Fallon said.

"What is that?" Ais asked.

"When the hell is the wedding? I don't see a ring on your finger. Don't tell me he hasn't asked you yet. If he hasn't, then we need to go outside and have a conversation. He defiled you without the agreement to marry you. Oh no, we'll have none of that."

This caused the others to mutter in agreement. They were back to teasing but I knew it wasn't all in fun. They wanted to know how soon I'd make her my wife. If I had my way, it would be today, but I wanted her to have the wedding of her dreams. All women dreamed of their wedding day, didn't they?

"Oh my *Dia*, stop. You're not pushing him into asking me to marry him just to appease you," she cried.

"*Leanabh*, it's not pushing me, I assure you. I want you as my *bhean* wife, more than anything except as the mother of my children. It's happening. The when is for me to know and you to find out. It won't be here in front of the kangaroo court."

This set the guys off. They were booing and making threats, which I knew they would. That was why I said it. I loved riling them up. It wasn't until Seerie stood that everyone settled down. As the matriarch of the family, she was the final authority on family matters, even above Darragh. Everyone got quiet and gave her their undivided attention. She smiled at me and Aisling. Love shone from her face. I knew it wasn't just love for Ais. Seerie had been a grandmother to me for as long as I could recall. Neither of my grandparents lived to see me born.

"I can't tell you how happy it makes me to see the two of you together at last. It's been a hard road, but you've now found each other. Let nothing or no one divide you. Alistair, I'm so thrilled to make you an official part of the family, even though you've been a part of it forever. Know that when you do ask her to marry you, we're all ready and waiting to help her plan the wedding. Just don't wait too long. I'm not getting any younger. The rest of you jokers need to get a move on. I want to see all of you married and hopefully get to hold at least one of your children before I join my Conall. Now, who's ready to eat? I think these two have heard enough for today. You can recommence the teasing and torture tomorrow."

This earned her a bunch of laughs. She smiled bigger. This was how we were freed to enjoy a loud, boisterous family breakfast. As we sat around eating and talking, I couldn't help but picture what it would be like in a year or two. My hope was we'd have our firstborn at the table. Along with a ring and a wedding, I would be working to get her to ditch her birth control. I'd waited long enough to see her round with my baby.

My eyes landed on the newest member of the O'Sheeran clan. A month ago, not long after Aisling's wreck, Ashlynn and Darragh welcomed their son, Ronan, to the family. I wanted that. The happiness on Dar's face was evident. He loved Ashlynn and his son like no other. I wanted strong sons and at least one feisty daughter who hopefully would be the carbon copy of her mother. The sons were not to carry on the Graeme name so much as to protect their sister or sisters and mother.

🙵🙵🙵

The flight from home to California was a smooth one. Maybe the fact it was only us and a few guards or that Aisling and I spent most of it in the bedroom was the reason. At first, she refused to go in there with the guards out in the main cabin. I assured her they knew we had sex and they couldn't hear us. The family ensured the bedroom was soundproofed. They were all professional when we came out later and didn't indicate they even knew we were gone, but it was kinda sweet to see her blush at first. She was tense, but when they didn't say anything or give us funny looks, she relaxed.

On this trip, we had Creed with us, of course, and two of the men the family called foot soldiers. It was a term from the old days. Reggie and Dario were both well trained, and I trusted them to watch over her. I'd worked with both of them extensively. The family tried to say now that I was with Aisling, I needed a bodyguard, too. I told them there was no need. First, no one knew of my new connection to her and secondly, I was more than capable of protecting myself. They reluctantly agreed but stated once we were engaged I would have to get used to the idea. I was all for bodyguards for her and our future children, but didn't see the need for me. We'd have to debate it later.

Thank God, we weren't picked up at the Ontario airport by a limo. The winery manager had gotten a couple of staff members to come with two SUVs they used at the winery. It would do until I got the ones I had lined up delivered to her house. They would be more heavy-duty than these, but I appreciated the thought.

The two men driving them were a bit nervous when Dario and Reggie said they would drive. Both had been taught to watch for tails and were trained in offensive and defensive driving. They were both skilled men who I would love to add to the Hounds, but Dar threatened me if I stole them, so I had to leave them to work with the family. Maybe one day, I'd get him to change his mind.

The drive to Temecula was quick—barely an hour at this time of day. We timed it to avoid the rush hour at the end of the workday. We would be dropped off at the O'Sheeran house, which was outside the actual town. It sat in the country and was a large piece of land with a lake. It was at the intersection of Anza Road and De Portola Road, while the winery itself was on the De Portola Wine Trail not far away.

As with any of their homes, it was behind a high wall, and not just anyone could come and go. There weren't any staff who were here at all times, like in some rich families. They had people they used when necessary, but most of the time, if anyone was here, it was to relax, and they did things for themselves.

Due to what happened the last time she was here and the fact we had no idea if it was related to a threat against Brynes or her, Darragh and I had arranged for there to be some of the Aegis people at the house at all times. If I felt they needed to accompany us elsewhere, they would do so. As much as the family had their own security people, there were times more were needed, and Aegis was the go-to for them. Most were ex-military and highly trained men and women. They were patrolling the grounds, and two were at the gate when we came rolling through it. They didn't hide what they were either. Their guns were visible.

The winery employee in our car turned a bit pale when he saw them. I wondered if he was new. Those who had been around the family usually didn't react too much to guards. He had done the same when he saw Creed, Dario, and Reggie. As soon as we came to a stop, I got out and rounded the car to open her door. The three Aegis people came toward me. I'd been sent their dossiers and knew all of their history. I just needed to meet them in person. They waited quietly as I assisted Aisling out. When her feet hit the ground, she smiled at all of them.

"Hello, you must be the poor souls my family and Alistair hijacked into being bored to death watching over me. I'm sorry."

They didn't crack a smile. The one I knew was Marco responded. "Ms. O'Sheeran, we're happy to be here to help with your protection."

She shook her head. "Okay, we need to talk, but let's not stand out here and do it. Let me get these two off so they can get back to their real jobs, and then we'll talk. Excuse me," she said before walking over to talk to the two from the winery. I stayed with the Aegis crew. While she took care of the others, I introduced myself.

"Hello, I'm Alistair Graeme. I'm the one who will be overseeing Aisling's protection while she's here. Anything, and I mean anything, that sets off your alarms, no matter how small, I want to know about it. You've been briefed on what happened last time she was here in Cali. We will not have a repeat."

"Yes, we've been briefed and know who you are, Mr. Graeme. I'm Marco," he went first again. I wondered if he was their leader by default or had been assigned that way. I shook his outstretched hand.

"I'm Ezekiel, but everyone calls me Zeke," the next guy said as we shook hands. The last one was a woman. She nodded as she shook my hand. Her grip was fierce.

"Hello, I'm Remi, sir."

"No need to call me sir or Mr. Graeme. Alistair is fine."

"All done, let's go inside, shall we?" Ais said as she rejoined us. I wrapped my arm around her.

I saw the looks the Aegis crew exchanged before they blanked their faces. Her bodyguards fell in step. I knew when we got inside, they'd disperse to check out the area even though the Aegis people would've already done it. It was just the way they were.

I was right. As soon as we got inside and into the family room, which Creed and Dario cleared first, the two of them left. I knew Reggie would remain outside the door. "Can I get you something to drink first?" Aisling asked.

They all shook their heads no. I was seated next to her on the small loveseat. They were on the couch and one of the chairs. They sat back straight as if at attention.

"So let's get to know each other a little bit. I'm Aisling O'Sheeran, as you know. I don't stand on ceremony. Call me Aisling. I'll try my best not to cause you too much work, but I will be busy, and that means a lot of time at the winery, Maeve's Cellars, and other meetings and even social engagements. I'd love to keep those to a minimum, but I have to do a lot of marketing at those kinds of functions, so there will be some, I'm afraid. Now, tell me your name and something about yourself."

I saw they were surprised by her warmth and lack of snobbery. The family only pulled that with those who earned it or royally pissed them off. Again, Marco went first. In addition to sharing his name, he told her where he was from. The other two quickly did the same. It would take some work to get them to open up, but she'd make it happen. She knew who they were. I'd shared their files with her.

The next topic she brought up was one I planned to do myself. "You might be wondering why Alistair had his arm around me. Well, I can tell you, you'll see more than that."

Three sets of eyes flickered over at me. I took over. "Yes, you will. It's not common knowledge yet, but Aisling and I are together. If anyone asks you questions, refer them to us, and we'll handle them. No, we're not hiding it. We'd just like to stave off the media frenzy that'll come with it. Any time an O'Sheeran settles down, it's big news. You shouldn't have to deal with it more than your job requires. In addition, you need to be on the lookout for there to be backlash from another prominent member of the elite." I glanced at her. She sighed.

"You all know who Christopher Brynes is, right?" I asked. All three nodded yes. "Brynes has been pursuing more than friendship with Aisling. He doesn't know about us yet, and when he finds out, I doubt he'll take it well. I expect he'll keep trying to see her and press his suit. Under no circumstance is she to be left alone with him. If he gets too persistent, I'll handle him. All I want you to do is to protect her from him or anyone else. The last time she was here, someone targeted them in his car, and she was almost killed. We don't know if the culprits were after her or him, but we remain alert since no one was caught."

"We were briefed on the incident. We're ready," Marco said.

"Good. For now, that's all we have. Make yourselves comfortable. I'll take you to meet Dario, Creed, and Reggie officially. They can show you where you'll be sleeping and where everything is here at the house. If you need anything, you should already have my number. Call or text any time, night or day. I'll be with her at night, so other than roving patrols, you'll be able to get sleep."

We spent a few more minutes talking about logistics then we took them to meet the others. I was eager to see how they stacked up with our guys. I planned for them to join us in our workouts and training sessions. After all, a guy needed to stay in shape. I knew Aisling would be joining some of them, too. They were in for a shock.

Aisling: Chapter 10

On my first day back at the winery, the staff all seemed excited to see me. I knew they were just as revved up for the new wines as I was. They took a lot of pride in their work, and it showed. Today being the first day, I was just catching up with everyone before diving into the real work. They were all asking how I was doing and if I was fully healed. Many of them I kept in touch with via text or email while I was recuperating. I assured them I was back to my old self and ready to work.

They eyed Alistair when he arrived with me. They were used to Creed, but when they saw I had more than him with me, they raised a brow. When they saw Alistair remain at my side while the others spread out around the winery, they really looked. We hadn't explained ourselves, but I knew it was only a matter of time before they caught us kissing or holding each other, and then we'd tell them why.

At the moment, Alistair was out with Creed, checking out something Creed had found on his rounds. He wanted Alistair to see it. I was secure in my office with Reggie outside the door. I loved Stair to death but he could be over the top with safety. He told me when I mentioned it to him that I was the most important thing in his world. He made me melt when he said things like that. I was still getting used to the fact he really loved me, and he was determined to show me. Case in point: last night in our bed. The man was a sexual beast. I never orgasmed so much or so intensely in my life as I did with him. He was a very inventive lover I was finding. It made me look forward to our alone time every day.

The desk phone buzzed, causing me to jump. I laughed before picking it up. "Yes, Carrie," I said. She was my assistant and the one who had her desk outside my office. I tried to get her to take one of the better offices, but she refused.

"Aisling, just wanted to let you know that Donald saw a car coming this way. It appears to be Mr. Byrnes. I already let Reggie know." I heard the edge in her voice. The ones I spoke to this morning knew if he was seen to let me know. If Reggie knew, then my man and the others would soon know and be hot-footing it back to the office. I had my fingers figuratively crossed that Chris wouldn't cause a scene.

"Thanks, Carrie. When he gets here, offer him a drink and then ring me. I'll let you know when you can let him in."

"Of course."

Hanging up, I took a few deep breaths to prepare myself as I stood up. A part of me felt guilty. I'd led him to believe there might be more than friendship between us by spending so much time with him last time. No, I never said anything, but he would've read between the lines. He wouldn't be happy with the excuse that the man I really loved had finally stepped up and confessed his feelings. However, nothing he said would change it, and his becoming ugly or pushy would only lead to harder feelings and possibly repercussions if it went too far. Now that I had Alistair nothing would make me give him up.

The door swung open, making me squeak in alarm. I wasn't expecting it. It was Alistair. He was scowling as he hurried over to me. Before I was able to say a word, he tugged me against his chest and kissed me. It was an explosive kiss that lit off my desire. When he let go of me, I wanted to pull him over to the couch in my office and ravish him. I was panting.

"Perfect," he whispered with a smirk.

I had no idea what he meant. The phone buzzed, alerting me Chris was there. Hurrying to answer it, I spoke to Carrie in a haze and informed her to send him in in a minute. After hanging up, I tried to calm my racing heart and smoothed down my skirt and blouse. I didn't have time to check my makeup or hair. As I fidgeted, I became suspicious of why Stair kissed me. The sneaky devil wanted me to look freshly kissed. I narrowed my eyes on him. He merely grinned, then gestured for me to join him. I sat on the couch with him and then elbowed him. He chuckled and faced the door.

"Relax, I'm here," he told me softly as he rubbed the back of my neck. I nodded.

When the door opened, in came Dario and Creed, and behind them was Chris. He had a smile on his face, but it slid off when he saw I wasn't alone. His smile turned to a glower.

"Dario, Creed, you can wait outside. If we need you, we'll call," Alistair informed them.

They both nodded, and without a word or bit of hesitation, they left. When they did, I caught a glimpse of Scotty in the outer office. He saw us, scowled, and moved toward the open door. It was shut before he had time to enter. I settled my gaze on Chris as I rose to my feet. Alistair did the same. I forced a pleasant smile on my face.

"Chris, this is a surprise. What brings you here?"

"Aisling, really, do you think I wouldn't hear you were back in California? Why didn't you tell me you were coming?"

"I didn't really think of it. I was so eager to get back to work. I only got in late yesterday. Did you just drop in to say hello? That's a long drive from Newport Beach to here. I wish you'd called. I'm busy right now, and I don't have much time to talk."

"What's he doing here?" he asked instead of answering me as he glared at Alistair.

"It's none of your business why I'm here, Byrnes." The implied threat was clear in Alistair's voice. *Dia*, I'd be lucky if there wasn't an all-out brawl before this was done. Both men were giving off waves of aggression and alpha dominance.

Turning more toward Stair, I put a hand on his wrist. "I've got this," I told him softly.

"I know you do, but it doesn't hurt for him to know you're not alone," he replied just as softly. Chris wasn't able to hear us. He was still several feet away.

"Aisling, we need to talk in private. Send your guard dog outside. There's no need for him to be here. You're safe with me," Chris ordered crossly.

Alistair's mouth opened, but I beat him to the punch. "Chris, Alistair isn't my guard dog. He stays. Anything you have to say to me, you can say in front of him."

He moved to stand nearer to us. I decided to sit down. Alistair sat beside me, leaving the chair for Chris.

He took it, but I saw he wasn't happy. He was staring daggers at Alistair.

"We have private things to talk about. I've been waiting for you to heal and come back so we could. I don't think the help needs to hear our intimate conversation, babe." he smiled at me and sent a smirk toward Alistair.

I knew from what Alistair shared that Chris had been more or less told of Alistair's interest in me, and he hadn't been happy when I went home, and he wasn't allowed to see me, but Stair was.

"Let's get something straight, Brynes. She's not your babe, baby, darling, sweetheart, or anything else. Her name is Aisling. Use it. And there's nothing you have to say to her of an intimate nature," Alistair said menacingly.

"Wanna bet? It seems you think you have more than an employee relationship with her. Despite what was said the last time we met, I highly doubt the O'Sheerans want a man like you to be sniffing around her. Aisling is meant to be with a man who is her equal, not a nobody like you. I know Darragh, Cian, and Aidan have gone slumming, but I don't see Aisling or the others doing it. Those three seem to believe in this whole *anamchara* bullshit. Aisling is too smart for that."

Instantly, outrage and fury filled me. How dare he say such things and be so dismissive and horrible about the three happy marriages my cousins and brother had. It was ridiculous. He had no clue. If I had any doubts I'd picked the right man, which I didn't have for a second, these remarks would've cleared them up. I came to my feet. Alistair stayed seated as I faced off with Chris.

"How fucking dare you!? My cousins and my

brother have made love matches. You sneer at them finding their soulmates. You'd be so lucky if it happened to you. As for Ashlynn, Miranda, and Karizma not being worthy of them, I'd rethink those words. When I tell them what you said, you'll be lucky if Dar, Cian, and Aidan don't beat you into a coma. News alert: I believe in soulmates, and it's all I ever wanted."

He got up. "Aisling, okay, that was uncalled for. I'm sorry. I just hate the thought of you waiting for something that most likely won't happen. Why wait for some impossible soulmate to appear? I mean, how many people get that lucky? You and I are of the same background. We like each other, and I know we're compatible in other ways. I think you should consider marrying me. I know you were thinking about it when you were here last time. Nothing has to change."

"You're right. I was considering if a marriage of convenience might be the way to go. And you were one of the few men I thought I might be able to stand to be married to. I was depressed because I thought I'd never be with my *anamchara*."

He smiled. "I knew it. So let's do it. Marry me."

I shook my head. "I said I thought I'd never be with my soulmate. I thought he didn't love me the way I loved him. I was wrong."

"What the hell does that mean? You were wrong? Who is this supposed soulmate of yours?" he asked belligerently.

The moment Alistair took my hand, the light bulb went off. How he could've been so blind, I had no idea. Chris's face contorted with rage. I saw his fists clench at his sides. He scanned Alistair up and down with disgust. His mouth twisted into a sneer of disdain.

"Please tell me this is a joke. There's no way this fucker is the man you want. He's nothing but a common bodyguard. He works for your family! What's with you people and marrying the help instead of those of your own social standing? Jesus Christ, has someone brainwashed you or something? He can't make you happy. He can't give you the things I can. I'll increase your social and business standing. He'll hurt it. You want Maeve's Cellars to become a premier brand. It won't if you and your family insist on tying yourselves to lowlifes like him."

I was fighting to hold back from decking him. It was hard. I knew Alistair wanted to do the same. "No one we're marrying will hurt our reputations or anything else. Alistair is much more than a bodyguard but even if he weren't, it wouldn't make a difference to me or my family. What counts is love. I've been in love with this man since I was thirteen. He's been in love with me for years. Misunderstandings kept us apart, but not anymore. We're together, and it's not changing. One day, we'll marry. I'm sorry I led you to believe we were going to be more. It wasn't done maliciously. Now, I think it's time you leave. You've said enough."

I moved to head for the door. I wanted him out of here because if he said one more ugly thing about my family, I'd have to punch his ass.

"No, I haven't. Who knew you were a cock-teasing whore?" he spit out as he grabbed my wrist as I got near him. A roar came out of Alistair as he lunged for Chris, but I beat him to the punch, figuratively and literally. I pulled back my fist and let it fly.

Growing up with twelve older brothers and male cousins, I'd learned early how to defend myself. That was before I was professionally trained. I knew how to land a punch without breaking my hand or wrist. I knew how to put my shoulder behind it for more power. And I knew the best spots to punch. I aimed for his head, and I knew the spot I wanted. I connected with his jaw right at the hinge where it connected to his skull. It would cause him not only a lot of pain but with the force I put behind it, he'd be extremely lucky if I didn't dislocate his jaw, which was my goal. He'd mouthed off enough about my family. It was time for him to shut up. I didn't care too much about what he said about me, but my family and Stair were another matter.

His head snapped to the side, and he cried out in pain. He cupped the side of his face for a second then he let out a muffled roar. He made it one step before Alistair was on him. He punched him in the solar plexus. I winced.

This area was a network of nerve fibers halfway between the nipples and the belly button. I'd learned all about it during my martial arts training. The wind was audibly knocked out of him, and he doubled over. Having been hit here myself, I knew he was unable to breathe, was nauseous, and feeling searing pain. He was making these horrible wheezing sounds. The angle of his jaw told me I had dislocated it. The door came crashing open, and in ran Creed, Dario, and Reggie as well as Scotty. When he saw Chris bent over, he came running over and placed himself between Chris and the rest of us. I saw his hand go toward his back.

"Boy, I'd think twice before you bring your piece out to get involved in this. Before you can pull that gun. I'll break your fucking arm and have you on your way to the hospital before you can blink. This son of a bitch got what he deserved for what he said and for grabbing her," Alistair snapped.

"Four against one wouldn't be fair, but I guess I shouldn't expect anything less from the likes of you," Scotty sneered.

"Scotty, enough. Get Chris out of here before he really gets hurt. He's just had the wind knocked out of him, and his jaw isn't broken, just dislocated. It needs to be put back in place. He earned this. In case it's not clear, he's not welcome here anymore. Go before I'm forced to call the police and have you both removed for trespassing. Sorry it had to be this way, but he chose this with his words and actions."

Scotty glared at me as he put his arm around his boss. Chris was slowly straightening up. He gave me a look filled with so much anger bordering on hate. As Scotty maneuvered him to the door while keeping the guys in his sight, Chris finally spoke. His speech was somewhat garbled due to his jaw.

"You'll regret picking him and doing this."

"And if anything happens to Aisling or her family, you will have signed your death warrant," Alistair threatened.

As they exited my office, Reggie and Dario followed them. I knew they'd make sure they left the property. Creed stayed behind. I could see Carrie and a few others in the main area watching wide-eyed. Great, just what I needed. I was tired and just wanted to go home. Well, it wasn't possible, so I needed to talk to the staff and then get back to work on top of calming down my man.

"Creed, will you give me and Alistair a few minutes, please?"

"Sure thing. I'll be right outside."

Once he left and closed the door, I moved over to Alistair and wrapped my arms around him. He did the same back. His body was vibrating.

"You can calm down now, *mo chosantóir*," I told him.

This earned me a chuckle for calling him my defender, which was a form of the actual meaning of his name in Scottish, which was man's defender. Luckily for me, he knew a lot of Irish in addition to his native Scottish from growing up with my family. Unlike us, his dad came over when Stair was a boy, though he easily picked up the language. He still had traces of his Scottish accent, which I adored.

"That's right. I'll always be your defender, but you need to say it right, the Scottish way, *mo neach-dìon*," he teased.

I laughed. "Okay, I'll use that barbaric language, *mo neach-dìon*."

He gave me a mock growl and then kissed me. I forgot what I was supposed to be doing and kissed him back. Eventually, I'm not sure how much later he broke it.

"We need to talk about what just happened, Ais. Byrnes isn't a happy guy, and he's vindictive enough to cause trouble. What form? Who knows, but he won't forget we both hit him, and he lost you to a commoner as he thinks of me. He won't take it lightly," he warned.

"I know. I hate the way this went. And the things he said about the family and who we fall in love with. I feel sorry for him."

"Sorry? Why?"

"Because he'll let his prejudice blind him to the

potential he might find true love if he would just look outside the uber-rich crowd. It's a shame. His soulmate could be right under his nose, and he'll never know it."

"If so, it's his fault. Some people will only see what they want. What I want is to be sure while we're here, you're safe. Not only do we have to worry about the typical weirdos who target your family, but whoever caused the wreck and now Brynes. His family is powerful and not without resources. We need to talk to your family and let them know what happened. Be prepared for there to be more people out here to protect you."

I groaned and lay my head on his chest. He chuckled because he knew how I felt about guards. I knew I had no choice, but still. I'd be lucky if half my cousins and all my brothers wouldn't come. I needed to get things in order for the winery, then go back to Florida. So much for easy.

⚜⚜⚜

Soaking in the hot water filled with bubbles was slowly easing the knots in my muscles. After the fight with Chris this afternoon and then the call with my family earlier this evening after we got back to the house, suffice it to say I had stress knots all over my body. Stair insisted I soak in the tub and have a glass of wine. I had no idea what he was doing. I heard him a few times moving around in the bedroom, but he didn't come into the bathroom.

I was lying back with my eyes closed. The room was lit with scented candles, so the light wasn't harsh. I was slowly pushing water around, making imitation wave sounds that I liked. I was so into it I had no clue

I wasn't still alone until I felt a hand on my shoulder. I jumped, and my eyelids flew open. Alistair was standing there smiling down at me. I gulped at the sight of him. He was naked. The tub placed me at the perfect height, so I was staring right at his cock. Even soft, he was impressive to see. Immediately, all thoughts of tiredness and my aching body fled, and my mind switched to thinking of the delicious things I could do to him and have him do to me.

Before I was able to grasp him, he pushed me forward and stepped into the tub behind me, and then he sat down. Sliding his legs on either side of mine so I was trapped between his, he tugged me back until I was reclining on his chest. I pouted out my lip, even if he wasn't able to see it.

"Stop pouting," he said humorously.

"Who said I was pouting?"

"I know you. You're not done relaxing yet. I'm not letting you get distracted."

"There are other ways to relax. I can think of one or two right now," I said in a sultry voice.

He chuckled, then nibbled his mouth on my ear. "I bet you can, but just stay like you are. I promise if you do, I'll make it more than worth the wait," he whispered.

His gruff voice and that accent made my nipples bead into tight points. Heat flashed through my body. Deciding to see what he meant, I shrugged and forced myself to relax against him more. He picked up my wine glass on the edge of the tub and the bottle next to it. He poured more into it and then raised the glass to my mouth. I took a big sip. It was one of my favorite Maeve ones. I savored the taste on my tongue before swallowing. I hummed in appreciation. He took a drink.

"I've got to admit, I've never been a big wine drinker, but this and a few of the others you make might persuade me to change my ways. I'm more of a Scotch ale or whiskey guy."

"Imagine a Scotsman preferring Scotch ale or whiskey. Who would've ever guessed?" I teased him. I knew what he liked to drink and even the brands. I paid attention to everything he liked over the years. To say I was sort of a creepy stalker wouldn't be an understatement.

He tweaked my nipple, making me moan as he said, "Behave, Ms. Smartass. If you don't, I won't let you have the surprise I have planned."

"What surprise?"

"If I tell you, then it's not a surprise. Tell me what you were thinking about in here. It better not be about today or work."

"I tried not to think of today or work. I was more or less listening to the sound of the water as I moved it around. It's relaxing. And enjoying how the hot water was helping to loosen the knots in my body."

"You love water. You always have. Even when you were little, we had to watch you to be sure you stayed away from the ocean or the pools. It's no wonder you swim like a fish. Are you sure you're not really a mermaid?"

I giggled as I flipped my legs up out of the water. "No tail. I think it's safe to say I'm not, although when I was little, I did like to pretend I was."

"I remember. You had that mermaid tail you'd wear in the water."

"*Dia*, you remember that? I did love that thing."

"Do I remember? You practically slept in it. Where

are these knots you mentioned?"

"They're just scattered all over. When I get stressed or overworked, they hurt," I said with a shrug.

"I don't like to see you in pain."

"I'm fine. Having you in here with me is helping."

We sat there in silence, just enjoying the water. He was slowly pushing it around, making those wavelike noises I loved. I sometimes sat on the beach at home and listened to the waves for hours. I was half-asleep when something cool and wet ran down my shoulder to my chest. I'd closed my eyes, so I had to open them. When I glanced down, I saw red wine running down me, and then his lips and tongue were there lapping my shoulder. The rasp of his tongue, compared to his facial hair, made me shiver.

I twisted so I was halfway facing him. He took a drink from my glass, then lowered his head and kissed me. As he did, wine filled my mouth. I swallowed, and then our tongues greedily twined together. The taste of the wine and him mixed was heady. I moaned as I wiggled the rest of the way around so I was straddling his lap, facing him. The kiss went on, and it was hot.

When he lifted his head, I was wild with need, and all we'd done was kiss. He tipped the glass again, and this time, it ran down my breast and off the tip of my nipple. I gasped because his hands grabbed my ass and lifted me up higher, then he latched onto my wine-soaked nipple and sucked. I whimpered. His tongue was lashing it, in between his teeth gently nibbling on the hard nub. More moisture flooded between my legs. I writhed and bumped into something long and hard. I moaned.

Attempting to get some relief, I rubbed my pussy

against him. The head of his cock bumped against my clit, making me undulate more and faster. My breath was coming out in short gasps. Just that much, and I was close to coming. As he tugged on the nipple he was biting, a hand came up to toy with the other one.

"Stair, don't stop. I'm so close," I begged.

I cried out when he let go of both. Before I could ask why, he lifted me, so I had to stand. When I did, he stood. His gaze was heated as he ran it down my body and then back up. "Out," he ordered.

I hurried to step out of the tub. I went to grab the towel to dry off, but I was grabbed and swung around, then lifted so my ass was on the counter. He jerked my ass to the edge, then fell to his knees. He buried his face between my legs and went to town. I bucked hard as he sucked on my clit and thrashed my barbell with his tongue. I was so sensitive. His hands were raised, and they were working both of my breasts. I sank my hand into the back of his hair. I pressed him closer. He gave a growl of approval and ate me more. It took a couple of minutes tops for him to have me crying out as I came. He lapped up my cum and prolonged my release. When I finally stopped orgasming, he stood.

His mouth crashed down on mine, and he savagely kissed me, sharing my taste with me. I didn't mind, and I kissed him back just as wildly. He lifted me. I wrapped my arms and legs around him so he was able to carry me to the bed. Our wet skin was forgotten. When we got to it, he lowered me but never broke our kiss. By the time he did, I was ready for more. I grabbed his hips and tried to tug him down so I could impale myself on his hard cock. He resisted.

"Stair, *mil*, please, I need you," I pleaded.

"I know, and I need you too, but not yet. Wait," he stated.

I let go and sank back fully onto the mattress. He smiled at me in that sexy way of his, and then I saw him reach under his pillow. When he brought out his hand, it was holding one of my small vibrating dildoes. He held it up.

"Look what I found. So *leanabh*, do you like how this feels?"

I nodded. "Yes, but not as much as I love your cock. There's no comparison, Stair."

He switched it on. Holding it up for a moment, I watched as he lowered it to my clit. The vibration made me gasp. He worked it in circles as he took turns watching it and then my face. I was starting to ramp up again when he suddenly slipped it into my pussy. I moaned. He thrust in and out. As if it wasn't enough to excite me, he began to talk.

"Tell me, *mo ghràdh*, have you ever fucked yourself with this and imagined it was me inside of you."

I nodded. Too many times to count.

"And how often did you do that? Once a month? Weekly? How hard would you come when you did it?"

"I did it all the time. Sometimes, several times a week. I'd always come harder when I thought of you. But that's not all I did to make myself come."

"Oh, really. Do tell." he sped up the thrusts. Wanting him to be as horny as I was, I went for it.

"Oh, I'd fuck myself with this one and even bigger ones and pretend it was you. When I'd come, I'd scream so hard. It felt so good. And when I was really horny and wanting you even more desperately, I'd slick one of them up with lube, then work it into my ass and fuck it pretending it was you. *Dia*, it felt so good. The burn, then the intense pleasure of it. I want to know what it feels like for real. Will you show me one day?"

This time, he was the one to moan. His thrusts with the vibrator were frantic. I tipped over the edge into bliss. I moaned and whimpered as I thrashed. He held me down and had his gaze glued to my pussy as I came. I was so limp when I was done. It was crazy. Next thing I knew, he pulled the vibrator out of me, tossed it on the bed then he was thrusting his cock into my pussy in a single hard stroke. He was way bigger than the vibrator, and I instantly tightened down on him.

"Fuck, yes, so tight. That's it. Give me that pussy. It's mine," he uttered as he slammed into me.

Watching me come and my talk must've really turned him on. He hadn't ever been this wild before. In a flash, my legs were shoved up nearly to my shoulders. He pounded my pussy as he ground his pelvis against my clit. The feel of his metal piercings so deliciously rubbing inside of me was incredible. He hit my G-spot every time he thrust. When his head came down, and he latched onto a nipple, I screamed, and more wetness came sliding out. I was already close to coming again.

I ran my nails down his chest, which made him groan and, unbelievably, thrust faster. Three, maybe four strokes more, and I was coming again. I moaned long and hard as I did, but if I thought he would come with me, I was wrong. When I was done, he was still hard when he pulled out. He stroked his hand up and down his wet length, then moved me around until his cock was by my head. He tapped my lips with the head. I could smell both of us. It made me even hornier, which after two orgasms was incredible.

"Suck me," he pleaded.

Slowly sticking my tongue out, I swiped the head and then opened my mouth to take him inside. Our combined flavor burst on my tongue. I eagerly took him deeper. I was just getting set into a nice rhythm to bring him to completion with my mouth when he pulled out.

"No!" I cried.

"Turn this way," he uttered as he moved me to the end of the bed to face the foot of it. Then I heard a snap, and glancing over my shoulder, I saw he had a tube of lube. My heart jumped. Did this mean what I hoped it did? He slicked lube up and down his length, adding to my cream on him as he stared at me. His gaze was so feral.

"You wanted to know what it feels like. Do you still want to? Do you want me to put my cock in that tight little asshole of yours and fuck it until you can't stand it and come taking me with you, so I can fill your ass with my cum? Do you?"

"Yes, *Dia*, yes!" I pleaded.

"Good. Now, look at the TV."

I was confused. Why would he want me to look at a blank screen? He gestured toward it, so I did as he asked. A second or two later, it came on, and when it did, I gasped. We were on the screen. The angle was one which showed us so I could see him kneeling behind me and had a clear view of my ass and his cock. As I watched, he spread my ass cheeks. The image on the television showed him doing it.

"I want you to reach back here and hold these cheeks open for me."

I flattened my chest to the mattress and did as he

asked. It was weird but cool to do something and get to see it on the screen. As I held myself open, he grabbed the base of his cock and pressed the head to my asshole. I knew enough to breathe and press out. Slowly, he pushed inside. Jesus, his cock was so much bigger than my dildoes or any cock I'd ever had in there. The one guy I'd been with who was into anal hadn't been nearly his size. It hurt and burned, but I knew the reward would be worth it. I just had to get past this part.

The sight of his cock sinking into my ass was hot, so damn hot to watch. He groaned. "Look at that. Fuck, that's sexy. Watch your little hole take my cock, *leanabh*. Watch how it's stretching to take me. Does it burn?"

"Y-yes," I stuttered.

"Is it too much? Do you want me to stop?" he paused as he asked.

"No! Please, no."

He grinned, then resumed working himself inside. He took it slow and used short back-and-forth thrusts to work himself deeper and deeper. Watching him on the television made me slicker. My cum was sliding down my thighs. When he was fully seated, I was ready to lose my mind. The burn had been intense, but it was easing, and the need to have him fuck me deep and hard was mounting. I wiggled my hips as I squeezed my inner muscles.

He moaned, "Christ, don't."

I inched away from him and then pushed back on him. We both groaned. His hands gripped my hips tightly. "If you do that again, I'm gonna fuck your ass hard until you're raw. I'm barely hanging on. You have no idea how good you feel, Ais," he snarled.

In answer, I did it again. He let out a howl like an

animal, and then he pulled back and slammed his whole length back inside. I screamed. I let go of my cheeks so I could fist the bedding. He used his hands to spread them again. My eyes were glued to the television as he fucked me. The sight of us in our very own porno was incredible and so damn fantastic.

His face was twisted into a snarl as he pounded in and out of me. The slap of our skin coming together, our loud breathing, and muttered words of praise along with curses made me wilder. I began to meet his thrusts by pushing back.

"Jesus, oh fuck it's too good. Too much. Fuck, yes, don't stop. Come for me. I need to feel this sweet ass milking me dry, Ais. Make me come," he half pleaded and half ordered. I was so close all I could do was nod.

We rutted like wild animals, for I don't know how long before I lost it. I clamped down on him and came. As I screamed and bucked as I tried to breathe, he let out a loud bellow and began to jerk inside of me as he pumped his warm cum into my ass. I whimpered brokenly. I knew I'd never be the same. When I stopped coming, he was slumped over my back.

Slowly, he sat up. "Look at the TV," he said hoarsely.

I did as he asked and saw him pull out his shrinking cock. When he was free, I missed him. He kept my cheeks spread. I wondered why then got my answer when moments later, his cum came oozing out.

"Look at that. So beautiful. Are you alright?"

"I think so. My brain isn't working," I whispered.

He laughed, and then the screen went dark. He flopped down next to me and eased me into his arms. He gave me a tender kiss. "Ais, was that too much? Should I have told you about the cameras? I thought it would be a fun surprise but was it too much?

"That was amazing. Stair. We starred in our very own porn movie."

He smiled. "And I recorded it in case we ever wanna watch it again. It's so goddamn hot watching you during sex. I've never wanted to film it until you. If you don't want to keep it, I'll erase it, and we won't ever have to do it again. I just wanted you to see what I see."

"Keep it. I loved it."

"Good. Now, rest for a few minutes, and then I'll take us to get cleaned up. I think this is the beginning of a long night."

I moaned, but not in protest. I couldn't wait.

Alistair: Chapter 11

I knew the confrontation with Brynes would have Darragh and the others sending out more men to watch over her. If they hadn't insisted, I would've. I wasn't taking any chances with her. I was still burning with the need to beat him some more for what he said, especially calling her a whore. She was far from one. His insults to me I couldn't care less about.

Knowing we had to wait for more reinforcements and that she was stressing, I'd come up with the surprise last night using the cameras. I was so lucky and thrilled she'd loved it as much as I did. She was my match in every way. Sex with her was out of this world and nothing close to what I had with the women I used for sexual relief in the past. I knew I'd never grow tired or bored. She'd keep me on my toes for the rest of our lives.

Aisling refused to work from the house. She said she wasn't gonna allow Brynes to run her off from her winery. Since I figured he wouldn't strike this soon, nor anywhere it would be easy to know it was him or his men, I agreed we'd go to her office there. We'd been here a couple of hours so far. I let her work while I roamed the building and then the grounds more to see where we could tighten security.

With people in and out all day, it was hard to do. She not only had her employees, but there were also people coming and going, taking tours, and tasting wine. All of them might be a potential threat. There were cameras all over, but I saw a few places where we needed to add some. Thankfully, her office was set up so that if there were threats, it would lock down and make it almost like a panic room. I think every one of the family's businesses where they had an office was set up the same.

I prowled the perimeter and buildings while Creed, Reggie, and Dario were watching over her. I needed to be ready when her family got here. Yes, as expected, there were some coming. I got the message not long ago. I decided not to tell her. It would only make her more nervous, and she needed to concentrate on work. It wasn't as if she'd be able to talk them out of coming if she knew. They were on the plane before they even told me, not that it was unexpected. I wondered who was coming.

Glancing at my watch, I saw they should be here anytime. After making my last inspection, I headed back to the office. I wanted to be with her when they arrived. Entering the building, I saw Reggie and Dario were stationed outside her door, which meant Creed was inside with her. I gave them a nod, and they acknowledged it with identical chin lifts.

Knowing Aisling would be so involved with her work that she hadn't thought of lunch, I went to find Carrie. She would know the best places to order food from, which could be delivered out here. I found her in the copy room, as I called it. She jumped when she saw me.

"Sorry, I didn't mean to scare you. I have a bad habit of sneaking up on people," I told her with a smile.

She gave me a small smile back. "Yes, you do. I didn't hear you. Can I help you?"

"Yeah, you can. I want to order lunch, but I have no clue which places are good or who delivers. I thought you might."

"There are a few places we usually order from. I can get you a menu if you'd like, and then I can place an order for you."

"Why don't you decide? I want to order for everyone and some extras. Give me a second, and I'll give you a head count to add to all of you." As she patiently waited, I texted Aidan. I knew he was coming. It didn't take but a minute to get his reply. I shook my head. He said to expect fifteen. God, Aisling was gonna lose it. I didn't know how many were family versus guards.

"Make it twenty-five plus all the employees. Here's my card to pay for it," I went to take out my wallet.

"Your card isn't necessary, Mr. Graeme. We have a company account with all of them. I'll charge it to that. I assume it's work-related and not for pleasure."

"Yes and no. Can you have it here, say within an hour, hour-and-a-half?"

"I can. No food dislikes or allergies before I order?"

"Not that I can think of. This crew is pretty open to food. As long as it's good, they'll be happy."

"Then I'll get right on it."

"Thanks, Carrie, and please, call me Alistair."

"Okay, I'll let you know when it gets here, Alistair," she said with a bigger smile on her face. As she hurried off to her desk, I went over to the guys.

"Anything?" I asked, although I knew the answer

was no. If there had been, I would've been the first to know.

"It's been quiet. A couple of visitors wanted to speak to her, but they were told she was in a meeting. Seems they wanted to meet the woman behind this. Personally, I think they just wanted to meet an O'Sheeran so they could brag about it. You know how they are," Reggie said with a roll of his eyes.

It was true. People acted as if they were celebrities, and it irritated the family to no end. I had Marco, Remi, and Zeke stationed throughout the winery grounds in case something would pop off. They were our early warning system. At least we didn't have any paparazzi bugging the shit out of us. They were the worst, in my opinion.

"Aidan and some others will be here soon," I informed them.

"Does she know that?" Dario asked as he raised his brow.

"No, and I'm not telling her. She'll only get worked up. When they get here, show them in. Oh, and lunch will be coming in about an hour or so."

"Hopefully, you're still alive to enjoy it after she finds out you knew and didn't say anything," he said with a grin.

"Hey, why do you think I carry weapons and have been extensively trained?" I joked.

He and Reggie both laughed and shook their heads. They knew exactly how well-trained I was. Slapping them on the shoulder, I knocked on her office door. A few seconds later, Creed opened it. I walked in after acknowledging him. She was at her desk, staring intently at something on her laptop screen. She didn't look up, and I didn't disturb her.

"I'll stay with her," I whispered to Creed.

"I'll be outside if you need me," he said before leaving.

Walking to the couch, I sat down to wait for her to get done with whatever she was doing. While she worked, I scrolled through emails on my phone. I had access to encrypted information. Even if I wasn't actively working on a Hounds assignment, as the leader, I needed to keep up on everything we had going and any potential new cases. My people had orders to keep me in the loop on everything.

I was studying a new request we just got today when I heard the creak of a chair and her footsteps coming toward me. Closing out the window, I raised my head and smiled at her. No matter how many times I saw her, she always took my breath away. She had outer beauty, yes, but there was so much more to her. Inside, she was even more beautiful, in my opinion. As she sat next to me, I encircled her shoulders and hugged her.

"How's it going? Anything exciting?" I asked.

"Right now, not much other than reading through what my lead viticulturist has been doing to the new grapes we've been growing to make the new wines. I think we need to make a few tweaks to what we're doing, and I suggested those to him."

"Have I told you how proud I am of you?"

"Proud of me for what?"

"The passion you have for the winery and the hard work you not only put into educating yourself on winemaking but also the work you continue to do. You could sit back and leave things as they are, but you don't. You keep improving things. These awards you've mentioned will be well deserved."

"Thank you. I do love it. I was surprised at first by how much I did. Now, it's become a passion. What about you? Isn't your work with the Hounds a passion for you? I know you do a wonderful job. The number of people you help every year attests to that."

"It is a passion for me, and I've never wanted to do anything else. Everyone assumes I did it because my *athair*, dad, did, but that's not why. Sure, I was proud of him, and in many ways, I wanted to be an upstanding man like him. However, it was what I saw in those they helped and protected that really made me want to do it. I endured all the training and those years in the special unit to ensure I could do my best for them. I wouldn't know what to do if I wasn't a Hound."

"No matter what you do, I know you'd be excellent at it, but I think the Hounds is your spot. I'm so proud of the things you do with them."

"Oh, you are, are you? You deserve a reward for saying that," I said with a low growl as I hauled her closer and then kissed her.

Kissing her never grew old, either. I'd waited too many years for her to pass up the opportunity. I felt starved for her kisses and took every chance I got to get more. Her tongue twined with mine. Things grew heated, and my cock began to stiffen. I was running my hand up her thigh to slip under her skirt to see if she was wet when there was a knock at the door. She whimpered as I lifted my mouth away from hers. I put my hand back on her knee.

"Yeah, what is it?" I called out. My voice was gruff with my need.

The door opened, and Creed stuck his head inside.

I knew, by his blank expression, that the cavalry had arrived. "You have people here who are anxious to see you both."

"Who is it?" she asked.

Before he was able to answer her, he was tapped on the shoulder. He moved back and swung the door open wider. In strolled the troops, and in the lead was Aidan. In addition to him, there was his bodyguard Gael, Shane with Niall, Rian with Reign, Ciaran with Daniel, Rory with Fionn, and Tiernan with Milo. In addition to her family and their personal guards, they brought Kendric and Eamon, two of their enforcers, and Cashel and Vander, who were foot soldiers like Reggie and Dario. They filled her huge office. Her eyes widened as she took them all in. After checking them over, she turned to look at me.

"You knew they were coming, didn't you?" She uttered suspiciously.

I didn't lie. "I did, and I didn't tell you because I knew you'd stress over it. They didn't tell me until after they were in the air, though. *Leanabh,* you had to know it was happening."

"I'll talk to you later about the stressing me part. As for them coming, I did know, but this is ridiculous. Why does it take all of them? It's not like Chris is gonna put out a hit on me!" she protested.

"How the hell do you know he won't? Just because we've been at peace with his family for years doesn't mean they haven't been secretly waiting for something to give them a reason to come after us," Aidan argued.

She opened her mouth to argue back, but he cut her off by lifting her to her feet and hugging her. This set off a round of her cousins and brothers hugging her and the men greeting her and me. I shook hands with her family and guards. Once that was out of the way, the discussion resumed.

"He'd be stupid to do it over something like this, Aidan. I doubt his whole family will back him doing it even if he was inclined to. We still have more muscle and power than them. They know what happened with 'you know who.' I don't see him being suicidal."

"Hurt pride and unrequited feelings can drive a person to do a lot of things they might not normally do," I warned her.

"Like what?" she asked.

"We rescue people who've been kidnapped at times. I admit, there were more than a few times I was so tied in knots over you and how I feel I thought briefly of kidnapping you and seeing if I could get you to admit you had feelings for me or they could grow," I admitted.

"What!? You're joking," she said in shock.

"No, he's not. I can't believe you didn't see how in love with you he was all these years. I swear we wanted to kidnap you both and lock you in a remote cabin until you both came to your senses and told each other. It damn near killed us," Tiernan grumbled.

"Hell yeah, too bad *Daid* and *Mam* vetoed it," Shane added.

"You're all crazy. Okay, enough about me and Alistair. Are you all planning to stay for a bit, or what? And when you leave, who is being left behind to be bored to death watching me?"

"We thought we'd stay a few days and see what happens. It'll do Chris good to see you have family here. If he wants to come back and start shit, we'll be here. When we go back, if things are still up in the air, Kendric, Eamon, Vander, and Cashel will likely stay. If they're needed elsewhere, then we'll bring on more Aegis security. Alistair said you already have three here. How're they doing?" Aidan asked.

"There hasn't been anything for them to do other than help me check for security issues and where things can be shored up, but they seem disciplined and know their stuff. I've been quizzing them," I explained.

"Of course you have. I swear, we'll have to pay them extra for putting up with him," Rian said as he smirked at me.

"You're just jealous I'm so much better at it than you. Don't be. One day, when you're a hundred, you'll be half as good as me," I needled him.

"Fuck you, Alistair. I think we need to have a long talk with Aisling and get her to change her mind about you."

"And you can disappear," I shot back.

This got us all razzing each other, which was not only fun but also eased her tension when she joined in. The others stood there, either grinning or adding their comments, too. It wasn't until we were interrupted by the buzzing of her office phone a good while later that we stopped. She went to answer it with a grin on her face, which meant we eased her ruffled feathers.

When she was done, she got our attention. "It seems lunch is being served in the employee lounge. Let's go eat before you guys turn even more feral." They mockingly growled at her. I let Ciaran lead her out while I brought up the rear with Aidan and Gael.

"She doesn't think he'll do shit, but I'm not convinced," Aidan whispered to me.

"I'm not either. The shit he said might not sound

horrendous, but I saw his face. He's not just letting this go. Whether he causes trouble or whatever, he'll do something. If he harms her in any way, even emotionally, his ass is mine," I told him.

"You may have to flip coins with us to get the privilege. We'll see," he smirked.

I shoved him, and we instigated each other all the way to the break room.

◆◆◆

Aisling was exhausted. I could tell. Having to deal with part of her family and the ones they brought with them was a lot. After lunch, we'd let her get back to work while I showed the guys what I planned to shore up, and we talked more about Brynes. It still worried me that Cody hadn't been able to discover a credible threat against either family to explain the car slamming into them. There were always vague ones out there. They never stopped. We should be eliminating threats, not adding them. The only problem was, I didn't see how she could've broken the news to him about us without causing the rift. It was now just a matter of finding out how big it was.

The house wasn't big enough to accommodate everyone, so the foot soldiers and enforcers were at a nearby hotel when they weren't actively on patrol and guard duty. The family members and their bodyguards were divided. Since the house had me and Creed and a state-of-the-art security system, and the O'Sheeran men were all highly trained themselves, their guards were at the hotel as well while they stayed with us. It wasn't ideal, but it would work.

I hoped having them in the house wouldn't cause

more stress on Aisling. She needed to be able to relax, and one of the ways I planned to help her do that was through sex. If they started to interfere in our intimacy, I'd personally escort their asses to the hotel as well. When I informed her of this, she laughed and said she might lie just to see me do it.

After dinner and time hanging out together, she and I were now alone and curled up together in bed. We had the fireplace going, and we were talking. I was amazed at how much enjoyment just holding her and talking gave me. We didn't need to be having sex or anything. We were discussing what was on her agenda for tomorrow. I discovered she had two meetings. One at the winery and another in San Diego. Both were with potential new distributors. She was excited because both were lucrative accounts if she was able to win them.

"Is there anything special you know they're wanting?"

"They tend to be rather picky about who they allow in their establishments. They both have several high-end restaurants and tend to stick to wines from Napa Valley or Italy. One of them is a wine snob, as I call it. They think only wines from those two areas and well-known names are the only ones who make great wines. To get them to even sell one of Maeve's would be a major win. I've been preparing for these meetings for a while. I was supposed to do them the last time I was here. They weren't thrilled to reschedule."

"*Mo ghràdh*, you were hurt in a wreck and had major surgery. You could've very easily died and was in critical condition. What the fuck did they expect?" I asked in outrage.

"To them, it means nothing. A lot of these companies are heartless. As much as I want their business for a variety of reasons, mainly because it opens the door for others like them to consider us, I'm not holding my breath. However, I owe it to the family and our employees to pursue every lead, no matter how unlikely it may be."

"I love how much you care for others. I can't wait to get a look at these clowns."

"I doubt you'll meet them. It's not like you can go in with me."

"Is Creed?"

"Yeah, they know I always travel with one guard, and it was negotiated ahead of time."

"Well, tomorrow, I'll take Creed's place in the room, and he can stay outside."

"Honey, there's no need for you to do that. I thought you might take time to explore or do whatever while I was in the San Diego meeting. The one here, I knew you'd find something to do."

"There's a need to make sure you're safe. Would someone be an idiot to come to the winery or into a meeting and harm you? Yes, but not all people are rational. The world is filled with crazies, and with what happened out here last time, you have to forgive me if I can't take the chance. You were never targeted, except here in California. Maybe it's a coincidence, but maybe not. I'll remain silent in the background, but I want to be there. Besides, it'll be my first chance to watch you in real action." I gave her what I hoped were puppy eyes.

She laughed, then shoved me away. "Okay, you can go if you never do that again. I hope our kids never try those on me because if they do, all I'll do is laugh.

You never used those as a kid, did you?"

I chuckled before asking, "Don't you remember my dad?" She nodded yes. "Then you know they would've never worked on him. As for Mom, well, maybe sometimes but not always. Our kids better hope they take after you, or maybe not."

"Why me?"

"Come on, those lethal eyes and your delectable pout. It got to me when you were a kid, and even now, you still make me want to give in to you. They better hope that if they try it, it's not something that may put them at risk. If it does, then hell no."

"So if I were to bat my eyelashes at you, pout, and tell you I'll die if I can't have something right this minute, you won't be able to say no?"

"Does it risk your safety?"

"Well, not really, although it might."

"What is it?"

She leaned closer and slightly over me, and as she did, her hand slid from my chest, down my abdomen, to my cock. We were both in bed naked with only the covers over us. She gripped my cock and slid her hand up and down. All it took was for her to touch me, and I began to harden.

"I want you to make love to me. Make me scream and beg, Stair. I want to come so hard I can't think," she whispered sultrily.

Having no objection to her request, I flipped her onto her back. She let out a squeal as I caught her off guard. "You keep that up, and you'll find yourself in a load of trouble, little girl," I growled.

She pouted out her bottom lip. "But I can't help it, big guy. I hurt, and I need you to make it all better. I know if you give me this big, hard cock, it'll take care of this ache I have."

"Oh, you do. Where exactly is this ache?" I played along.

"I can't tell you. I have to show you. Let me have your hand."

She let go of my cock, which I wanted to protest, but I held back and let her take my hand. She slowly rubbed it along her soft breasts to her belly and then between her legs. She moaned as my fingers delved into her wet folds. She was slick already. I circled her clit, then flicked my nail against one of the metal balls on her barbell. She moaned and pushed herself harder against my fingers. Grasping one ball, I tugged gently on it. Her head went back, and she cried out.

"Ahh, my little girl likes that. I wonder what else she likes? Maybe this," I said before thrusting a finger inside of her. She whimpered loudly. I thrust in and out slowly, and then on each stroke, I increased the speed and the number of fingers until I had three inside of her. She began to ride my hand. I worked her pussy for only a few minutes before she clamped down and came crying my name. I prolonged it as long as I could before pulling my hand free.

I raised my fingers to my mouth and licked them clean. I hummed in appreciation. She was lying there watching me. I flopped onto my back. "Climb up here and ride my face. I want you to cover my face in your sweet nectar. I need a treat."

She shakily got to her knees and then swung her leg over so she was straddling me. I grabbed both ass cheeks and jerked her pussy down on my mouth. I inhaled deeply. I was hard as a post already. It would take self-control to be able to eat her out without coming. I'd have to see how far I got before I had to sink my cock inside of her pussy. The thought of how she strangled me every time I did pushed my control a level closer to zero.

I lapped, sucked, fluttered my tongue, hummed, and even bit her folds and clit over and over, making her gasp and plead. I didn't stop until I pushed her over the edge into a hard orgasm. I eased her down as best as I was able. When I raised her off my face, she had a dazed look in her eyes. Growling, I yanked her down my body and impaled her on my raging cock. She sobbed.

I thought I might have to do all the work, and I was fine with it, but she surprised me. She started out gently riding up and down my length. With each stroke, she picked up speed just a tad more. Soon, she was riding me hard and grinding herself on me over and over. My lower back was tightening in preparation for my orgasm.

"I'm getting close," I warned her.

This set her off, and she rode herself up and down on me frantically as she squeezed her inner muscles over and over. I stood it for maybe a minute, and then I was done. I thrust myself into the root and held her still as I pumped her full. She orgasmed along with me. When we were done coming, she slumped on top of me. I wrapped her in my arms and let myself soften as I whispered to her how much I loved her, and she did the same back. We drifted in a sea of contentment.

We stayed there for a good while before I knew we had to get cleaned up and serious about actual sleep. She needed her rest so she would be on top of her game tomorrow. The first meeting was at ten at the winery, and the other one was at three in San Diego. Depending on the time of day and traffic, it could take us a couple of hours to get there.

"Ais, we need to take another shower, and then you need to sleep."

She whined. "No, let me stay like this. I'll shower in the morning."

"No, now. You won't rest well if you don't." I knew from a prior conversation she wouldn't sleep restfully unless she were freshly showered or bathed. She was never one to like morning bathing. I didn't care one way or the other for myself. I scooped her up and then walked into the bathroom. She didn't say another word of protest as I bathed her.

Aisling: Chapter 12

The first meeting went slightly better than I'd hoped. They did let me show them a tiny bit of our operation before we sat down to discuss what Maeve's Cellars would be able to do for them. Small samples of our current top three wines were tasted. They asked a lot of questions, and I was super relieved that I had all the answers readily available to them. Alistair remained in the background and didn't say a word as promised. I saw the three reps cast him more than a couple of curious looks. I merely introduced him as my security for the day. By the time they left, we had to get on the road to make the meeting in San Diego.

Our actual meeting was in La Jolla, which was actually about a dozen miles from downtown San Diego. It was an affluent area along the coast with not only scenic views but lots of fine dining and seafood restaurants. It would be a boon to get into more of those. There were several residential communities there, as well as various businesses, medical, and educational institutions such as the University of California, San Diego, the Salk Institute, Scripps Research Institute, and Scripps Institution of Oceanography, which was famous.

Since it was work, Alistair, Creed, and Dario went with me while the rest stayed behind to do whatever they wanted. We did make plans for my family to join us later in La Jolla at a favorite spot of mine for dinner. I'd called the owner and made reservations for two parties of eight.

Traffic was intense, as usual. The freeways in California could test the patience of a saint. Florida was bad enough, but this was worse, in my opinion. No way I'd want to live here. What had I been thinking when I entertained the idea of marrying Chris? I would've lost it just due to the traffic. Now the weather was beautiful. We contended with killer humidity in Florida, but it wasn't a major issue here. In Temecula, we were in what was a semi-desert area, so at times in the peak of summer, it was well over a hundred degrees but the heat was dry. Great for growing grapes.

Dario was driving with Creed in front. Alistair and I were in the second row, with Reggie in the third. We took a large SUV so we'd have plenty of room. They didn't want to feel constricted, and no way would Alistair tolerate them in a separate car, not after the wreck. It was no surprise they were armed. What would shock most people was to know I was carrying a gun as well.

The meeting was to be held at the main office of the company I was hoping to do business with. They had restaurants not just in La Jolla but also in other affluent areas of So Cal. They had been around for thirty-five years, and they were more old-school, hence the prejudice toward only Napa Valley and Italian wines.

It was decided on the drive after I showed the guys a map of the building at the house that Reggie and Dario would remain outside on watch. Creed would be in the building but not at the actual meeting, and

Alistair would be with me. After parking the car, we headed inside. Of course, the four of them had their heads on a swivel. I wasn't moseying along obliviously, either. I saw nothing suspicious or alarming. When the three of us entered, the receptionist gave us a bored look, although her lack of interest almost immediately changed to fascination as she checked out Creed and my man. I didn't like other women desiring Alistair, but it was something I had to live with. He was too attractive for women and even men not to notice. As long as they never pursued it, I'd be fine.

I confidently walked up to her as they hung back and scanned the area. I wanted to laugh. They looked intimidating, and the dark sunglasses with their suits screamed bodyguards. A lot of times, our guards made it obvious who they were. Other times, they would work to blend in. It depended on the situation.

"Hello, I'm Aisling O'Sheeran. I have a three o'clock appointment." I told her with a smile.

She was still distracted by the men. It took a second or two for her brain to click back online. I wanted to snap my fingers and tell her to snap out of it, but I behaved. "Oh, um, yes, Ms. O'Sheeran. You're expected. Just have a seat, and I'll let them know you're here."

"Thank you," I told her before walking over to the expensive seating area they had.

I sat, and then Alistair joined me. Creed remained standing. Priceless pieces of art and expensive furniture adorned the entire place as far as the eye could see. They believed in making a statement. Our businesses did as well, but not ostentatiously. There was a fine line between tasteful and vulgar. They were edging into vulgarity.

We were kept waiting for about ten minutes. Something I was expecting. I hadn't told Alistair about the men we were about to meet. I knew he wouldn't like them much. This was merely them showing me how unimportant I was. I doubted if my name weren't O'Sheeran, they would've bothered to meet with me. Even as arrogant as they were, they'd never deny me at least a face-to-face meeting, even if it were only so they could brag they'd met one of the infamous O'Sheerans.

The receptionist was busy on the phone. We were too far away to hear what she was saying, but she kept casting glances our way, so I knew she was talking about us. Finally, she put down the phone and got up. As she came toward us, she swayed her hips. I was wearing high heels, but the six-inch stilettos she was wearing to work in the office were ridiculous. I expected a woman to wear those to a nightclub. I wondered if she hoped they'd catch her a husband.

"Ms. O'Sheeran, come with me. Your friends can stay here," she smiled at them.

"Creed will be happy to stay, but Mr. Graeme comes with me."

She frowned. "This is a private meeting."

"Yes, it is, but I was clear I would have one person with me. Is that going to be a problem?" I raised a brow at her. Sure, I wanted their business, but I wasn't about to be walked all over.

She hesitated a moment, then shook her head. "Of course not, come this way."

We followed her down a short hallway to impressive ornate wooden double doors. She knocked, paused, then opened them before she breezed in, leaving us to follow her. Inside was an executive office combined with a private conference room. Again, everything screamed wealth. There were two older men in suits seated at the conference table. They got to their feet as she glided toward them. I saw the lechers checking her out. Her skirt was way too tight and short, and her top was molded to her upper body, showcasing her breasts.

"Mr. Hayes, Mr. Tillman, Ms. O'Sheeran, and her... guest are here."

I'd done my research on the two men and their company, so I knew them by sight. They gave me a head-to-toe scan, and, like with her, they had lustful expressions. I felt the anger coming off Alistair, but you would never know it if you looked at him. He was passively standing there with his hands folded in front of him.

"Serve the refreshments, Rebecca," Tillman ordered.

She scrambled to the other side of the room to a bar along the wall. While she busied herself there, the introductions were made.

"I'm Henry Tillman, and this is my partner, Sebastian Hayes." As he introduced himself, he held out his hand but to Alistair, not me. Strike two. The first was the look.

I stepped closer, and I took his hand, shaking it firmly. There was a flicker of shock in his gaze. When I let go, I grabbed Hayes's hand, which he'd extended at the same time. "Hello, Mr. Tillman, Mr. Hayes. I'm Aisling O'Sheeran, and this is my associate, Mr. Graeme. Thank you for making the time to meet with me."

They hesitated for a moment, then plastered

polite smiles on their faces.

"Welcome, please have a seat," Hayes interjected.

We took seats across from them. As we did, Rebecca was back with a huge tray. It was filled with wine glasses, a few bottles of wine, and a crystal decanter of whiskey, I guessed. She sat it in the middle of the table and then quietly left, closing the doors behind her. I placed my briefcase on the floor next to my feet and sat back, portraying that I was relaxed, even if it was far from the truth.

"Well, Mr. Graeme, we're not familiar with your role at the O'Sheeran corporation," Tillman stated.

"Mr. Graeme's role isn't part of Maeve's Cellars. At Kin of *Éireann* Inc. I oversee that business."

He waved his hand dismissively. "I know you're the face of it and all that. And I understand why. Having an attractive spokesperson certainly helps a business, but we're interested in speaking to the actual brains behind Maeve's Cellars. This is a business meeting, after all. We thought one of the men would be here, one of your brothers or cousins," he said dismissively.

My ire at him was inching up by the second, the condescending misogynistic prick. I fought to keep my smile on my face.

"Gentlemen, I'm not just the spokesperson for Maeve's. I am the one behind the business. There isn't a decision made that I'm not directly involved in, I assure you. No one in my family knows more about it than me. After all, I went to college specifically to be able to run it and do it knowledgeably."

"If that's true, why is he with you?" Tillman asked. He seemed to be the mouthpiece of the duo. All they were focused on was Alistair. This was quickly going down the drain. At this rate, they'd never hear my pitch. Disappointment and anger filled me.

"I'm here as part of Ms. O'Sheeran's protection detail," Alistair said gruffly.

"Surely she doesn't have to have bodyguards everywhere she goes." Hayes sniffed.

I had a choice. I could continue to let them feel superior and talk down to me in the hopes I might still get a chance with them, or I could bring out the inner lioness and show them who they were talking to. Fuck it, lioness it was.

"Apparently, you haven't ever dealt with those of extreme wealth and stature. I get it. You're a small start-up company. Hopefully, one day, if you grow significantly, you'll be exposed to more people like my family. People with our wealth and notoriety typically don't run around without protection. Everything we do is important in someone's eyes. It's the price we pay for being so successful. Most people we do business with know this and have no issue with our guards. The chance to be associated with Kin of *Éireann* Inc. and my family makes it worth it, let alone the money it makes them. If the fact I'm a woman is a deal breaker, then we'll leave. After all, I have meetings set up with other more prominent restaurant owners in the area."

They exchanged panicked looks. They didn't want to piss off my family, and the mention of other owners made them think of one of their main competitors, Caliari Corporation. They were bigger and had more restaurants. I was in talks to meet with them as well. I went to stand, and this prodded them into action.

"No! No, please stay. We didn't mean anything by

our questions. Naturally, we understand. We were just surprised to find you're the brains behind it. You're so young," Hayes quickly added.

I slowly relaxed back in my chair. "I grew up learning the business. It's true it was started by my Uncle Patrick soon after he met and married my Aunt Maeve. He bought the winery and named it after her. He grew it over the years, but there were so many businesses he, my Uncle Sean, and my *daid* managed. When they had children, we were all taught that one day, we'd work in some capacity for the family. I've always been interested in grapes and the whole winemaking process, so it has become my passion. I took over as soon as I graduated from college, and I've grown it.

"I'm not just here to get you to sell our wines in your restaurants. I'm here to let you know of new ones we have coming, which are going to be award-winning without a doubt. They'll help put Southern California on the map as legitimate winemakers. It's no longer just Napa Valley, Sonoma, and Italy who make outstanding wines, gentlemen. The world has expanded, and real businessmen and women have to adapt and embrace changes in order to stay relevant. I'm here to offer Tillman and Hayes a chance to do that."

I had worked up a softer sales pitch, and this one. I hoped I wouldn't need to use the harder one, but with their attitude, I was happy I'd planned both. At this point, I wasn't sure I even wanted to do business with them. They were the kind of people who rubbed me wrong in a big way.

"We're very interested in staying current and being industry leaders. We'd like to see what you're proposing and hear more about these award-winning wines," Tillman hurried to assure me while his partner nodded his head. Settling in, I pulled out the charts and papers I had in my briefcase, and I went for it.

An hour and a half later, we were shaking hands and walking out of their office. They were overly eager to sell our wines. Before leaving, I turned to them with a patronizing smile. "Gentlemen, I'll think over your offer, and I'll let you know if Maeve's Cellars will sell our wines to your restaurants or not. We have to be selective, you understand, and we don't want to saturate the market all at once. I'll be in touch one way or the other. Thank you for your time."

They stuttered and kissed ass all the way to the elevator. When the doors shut on me, Creed, and Alistair, I sagged against the wall. I jumped when Stair burst out, chuckling.

"Christ, you're a viper when you have to be. The way you dealt with those fuckers was amazing. Creed, have you seen her in warrior-woman mode?"

Creed grinned and nodded. "She's sweet as pie until they piss her off, then the barracuda comes out and watch out. So those assholes riled her up?"

"Oh yeah, they were two misogynistic bastards. I wanted to punch both of them in the mouth. How dare they be so stupid to think that because she's a woman, she's a mere figurehead and doesn't have a brain?" he asked in disgust.

It warmed my insides to hear him say it. I'd felt his unspoken support the whole time, and I knew if it had gotten much worse, he would've been championing me even though I was able to do it myself. The elevator opened, and Reggie and Dario were standing there waiting for us. I took Alistair's hand as we exited.

"Thank you, Stair. I hate it when I have to deal with people like them, but it's par for the course sometimes. I hate that they made me act that way, but it happens. Thank you for being there."

"All I did was sit and watch," he said as he squeezed my hand.

"Yes, but I knew you were supporting me. I could feel it. Now, let's get out of here. The whole building makes me feel claustrophobic. Could you imagine working here every day?"

We all shuddered. As we aimed for the front door, Rebecca came trotting over in her heels. She was gushing all over us, but mainly the guys, now that she had two new victims to flirt with. I held in my laugh as she tried her best to gain their attention and they ignored her. She was sulking when we kept going. Exiting the building, they were back in professional mode. It wasn't far to the parking garage where they had left the car.

Before they let me get in, since it had been out of their sight, they visually scanned it and then took out a small box-shaped thing with buttons. They scanned it along the car, especially the underside. I knew it was to detect bombs. Crazy, I know. They didn't do this all the time, but with the last time I was in Cali still fresh in their heads, they did. I knew it was on Alistair's orders.

Once they deemed it safe, they opened the doors, and we got inside. Back on the road, I directed them to where I wanted them to go. It was getting close to five o'clock, and afternoon rush hour was happening. Using the navigation system for back streets, I directed them through La Jolla. I wanted to show them some of my favorite spots before we joined the others for dinner at six thirty.

No surprise one of those spots was a beach. We parked and listened to the ocean. Even though we had one back home, there were differences in the water in the Atlantic and in the Pacific, no matter what anyone said. The salt smell in the air relaxed me. I could never live long away from water. It didn't need to be the ocean, but some kind of water was a must. In Ireland, at our home, there was a large lake. Thinking about it, I realized all of our properties had water, whether it was a lake, ocean, stream, pool, or fountain.

I was in a good mood again when we pulled up to the valet stand at the restaurant. I saw the others were already there waiting for us. I was looking forward to a fun night with family and friends. Yes, I considered our guards, soldiers, and enforcers friends. We treated them like family. It was the only way to instill loyalty. Entering the restaurant, we were greeted by the owner. He was a sweet older man I'd met and became acquainted with a few years ago. He took pride in his restaurant. I had to admit, part of the initial attraction to it was the name Delaney's, which rightly so screamed Irish to me.

I held out my hands so he could take them. He was a courtly gentleman who always kissed my cheek now that he knew me. He was in his late sixties, I would guess. I'd worked hard to get him to use my first name, but he insisted I do the same.

"Hello, Aisling. You have made an old man very happy. To see your beautiful face is my reward," he said with a smile.

"Ardal, you flirt. You'll make me blush. It's

wonderful to see you too, although I have to warn you, I can't flirt this time. I have someone with me," I pretended to whisper.

His smile grew bigger. "Oh really, well, introduce me to your friends and then this fiend who is trying to steal you away from me."

Everyone laughed, including Alistair. "Everyone, this is Ardal Delaney, the owner of this fabulous establishment, one of my favorite places in California. Ardal, these are three of my brothers–Aidan, Shane, and Tiernan. These are my cousins–Rian, Ciaran, and Rory. These other rather stern guys are our guards and friends–Gael, Niall, Reign, Daniel, Kendric, Fionn, and Milo." I paused when I finished pointing them out.

"It's a pleasure to meet all of you. And I assume this rather large, intimidating man you didn't introduce is my competition."

I laughed. "Ardal, this is Alistair Graeme. Alistair, this is my beau, Ardal."

"I'd say it was a pleasure to meet you, Ardal, but not if you're after my woman," Alistair growled menacingly.

"What!? You're allowing a Scotsman to steal an Irish rose, and you call yourselves Irishmen, for shame. I'll spirit you away when he's not looking," Ardal said first to my family, then conspiratorially to me.

We were all laughing loudly and joking. When we calmed down, he shook hands with Stair and welcomed everyone. Then he showed us to our tables. The ambiance of Delaney's reminded me of the study at our family home. It was lit with lowlights, rich mahogany wood polished to gleam warmly, thick carpet underfoot, and walls painted a deep dark green.

Growing up, I spent hours in the study, just reading and relaxing.

There was no way we didn't attract attention as we were escorted to our tables. Our number was enough to make people stare, but my brothers and cousins were recognized even if I might not have been. The whispered conversations in the room grew louder. Used to it, I ignored it like the rest of my family and the guards did. Ardal beat Alistair to pull out my chair, and the cheeky man gave Alistair a smirk as he did it.

The family sat at one table and the others at the table between us and the door. As the evening passed, we enjoyed not only great conversation, special attention from Ardal, and excellent service but also outstanding food, and they, of course, proudly served Maeve's wines. We were kicked back, and I told my family how the second meeting of the day had gone. They were protesting how the last two potential customers greeted me as we waited for our desserts to come. A great meal wasn't complete without dessert, in my opinion. I always checked out those first to decide what I'd eat for the main course to leave room for it. My family knew I did, and they loved to tease me about it. They asked me why I didn't just eat my dessert first.

I was laughing as I told them how Tillman and Hayes were kissing my ass at the end when Alistair pulled his phone out of his pocket. He glowered when he read it. He glanced over at me.

"What?" I asked in alarm.

"Don't look now. Kendric said that Brynes just walked into the front. He's waiting to be seated."

My happy mood dimmed. Why, of all the places in the world, was he here? He didn't even live close to

La Jolla. Newport Beach had plenty of great restaurants. Was it bad luck, or did he somehow know we were here? The cynic in me was leaning toward the latter, which was egotistical.

Stair grasped my hand in my lap. "*Leanabh*, don't pay any attention to him. He might just be here to eat. It would be stupid of him to make a scene here with all of us. From what Kendric said, he only has Scotty and one other guy with him. Keep talking. Laugh and keep your eyes on me," he said firmly and loud enough for my family to hear. They all gave the appearance of enjoying themselves and being oblivious to Chris. I pushed my uneasiness away and did the same.

I thought we were in the clear when he took a seat with Scotty and the other man and didn't even look over at us. I went back to enjoying myself. It wasn't until after our desserts were served and we were all digging into them that it went wrong. I'd taken my first bite and was savoring it when Chris and Scotty walked up to our table. The other guy hung back. My appetite fled. I knew when I saw his face the evening wasn't ending pleasantly.

He peered intently at Alistair and then at me before he moved on to study the others. "Imagine running into you all here," was his opening line. The slight twist to his lips told me what I wanted to know. He somehow knew we were here. He came on purpose to make a scene or just to irritate me.

"Yeah, what are the odds?" Aidan said back.

"Well, I guess I shouldn't be surprised. After all, I'm the one who brought Aisling here the first time. Remember that, Ais? We had such a good time at dinner and later," he said with a smirk, and innuendo was clear in his tone.

The bastard was trying to imply we had done more than eat. It was true he was the one to bring me here, but that was all. It wasn't unusual for me to go out to dinner with him once in a while when I was in California. His need to try and start something with Alistair was evident. Stair knew it had never been sexual between us, but it would still rankle him. I held my breath, waiting to see what would happen.

Alistair:

Staring at Brynes standing there with that smirk on his face and hearing his insinuation about him and Aisling was pushing me to explode, which I knew was what the smarmy bastard wanted. He wanted a public blow-up with him as the victim and me as the aggressor. Well, I had news for him, but I wouldn't do it. I did get satisfaction seeing the bruise on his jaw where she punched him. I had no doubt he had one on his torso, too.

"Yes, the art gallery exhibit afterward was great. There was some beautiful artwork. If I recall correctly, I bought a piece for my house," Aisling responded back calmly, though her hand was gripping mine tightly under the table.

"Come on, you know what I'm talking about," he taunted.

"Is there a reason you stopped by our table?" Tiernan asked.

"Why wouldn't I? Aren't we friends? I thought friends talked to each other."

"Are we friends? After what you said to Aisling and about my wife and the other wives, I don't think you can claim that," Aidan said with an edge to his voice. He was not happy about Brynes' slumming comments about Karizma and the others. I didn't blame him. He called my woman a whore. I wanted to

CIARAST JAMES

annihilate him.

"Aidan, it was in the heat of the moment. I didn't mean it. I was upset and understandably so."

"Why was it understandable? In the heat of the moment is a cop-out," Shane added.

"Your sister led me to believe she and I were to be married. The next thing I know, I'm kept from seeing her for six weeks, and when I finally see her, she claims she's with him. I merely pointed out he can't give her what I can, nor does he have the same experiences as she does. She's making a mistake, and I hope that with time, I can show her that she is."

I kept my voice low, and I made sure I had a smile on my face as I interjected. I stayed in my chair even. "Brynes, she's mine, and nothing you say or do will change it. She was never yours. She's been mine since she was eighteen. Have some pride, and don't show everyone you're a childish, spoiled brat throwing a tantrum because he didn't get what he wanted. Grow up. Move on. I won't tell you again. Leave us alone."

His expression contorted to one of fury. "Fuck you! You don't tell me what to do. Who are you? Nobody. Some parasite who saw her wealth and somehow tricked her into thinking she loves you. Your friendship with her family is a laugh. I don't understand what hold you have over them to make them agree, but I'll find it, and when I do, I'll smash it." His voice was louder, and people were turning around to stare at us.

A flash of light caught my attention. A quick peek in the direction it came from, which was the front area, I saw paparazzi. Christ, who called them? No doubt someone did. Maybe even Brynes. If he were hoping they'd catch pictures of me or one of the others hitting

224

him, he was gonna be disappointed. When we didn't rise to his bait, his pussy excuse for a bodyguard popped off.

"Mr. Byrnes, don't waste your time on them. They're not worth it. This one especially isn't. The better man will win," he said with a sneer to his lips.

I smiled at them both. "The best man already did. If you're nice, we'll send you an invitation to the wedding."

I knew the instant my words broke the tether on his temper. Rage flashed across his face. His fists balled up, and he lunged in my direction. As he did, I sat there calmly. I could beat his ass into the carpet without getting out of my chair if I wanted. Instead, I sat there, turning the tables on the little prick. He wanted pictures, and he'd get them. Only he'd be seen as the aggressor, not us.

As his fist landed on the side of my face, I heard people gasping all over the restaurant. Aisling cried out in outrage. His so-called guard tried to stop him to no avail. I lashed out with my foot and caught him behind the knee, buckling his leg. As he fell to his knees, I lashed out again with my leg, and my foot took him in the jaw, in the exact place Aisling had hit him. I felt his jaw give.

The beauty of what I did was it was at an angle, and based on the location of our table, no one was on that side of it. My hands were now visible on the table. Other than my companions, no one saw me touch him. He let out a garbled scream of rage as he clutched his dislocated jaw.

"Y'all pay," he gritted out as Scotty helped him to his feet. The other bodyguard had joined him. The paparazzi were going insane, snapping pictures and yelling for comments. We all sat there with perfectly puzzled and shocked expressions as if we had no idea why he was acting the way he was. I saw Ardal wringing his hands.

"Chris, I think you need to go home. You've had too much to drink and don't know what you're saying or doing, buddy. Do you need help getting him out to the car?" Rory asked loudly with feinted concern.

"Fuck you," Scotty spat back as he and guard number two led Chris away.

Once they were gone, we went back to eating as if nothing had happened. Anyone watching would see us as innocent of anything. But we knew he'd declared something tonight, and we'd have to be on our guard even more. He, for sure, wouldn't let it pass, even if we had to wait a while for him to make his move again.

Alistair: Chapter 13

The weekend passed rather quickly. Everyone was on higher alert because of the confirmation with Brynes. The O'Sheerans agreed with my assessment. Something had flipped or broken in him, and he wouldn't rest until he felt his pride had been avenged. Aisling swore she had no idea why he was taking it so hard. Yes, they'd shared some kisses, which I detested knowing, but she said nothing more. She hadn't mentioned to him her idea of a marriage of convenience. She claimed that while they would occasionally go out or attend an event together, sometimes, they didn't speak for months at a time. No late-night calls or texting back and forth.

My personal thought was that he'd been waiting and living his life. He knew that one day, he'd have to marry to carry on the Brynes name and to have heirs for the family. At some point, he must've settled on Aisling as the woman who would be ideal as his wife, and who could blame him? Too bad for him. She belonged to me, and I didn't give up what was mine.

Her family wasn't keen on going back to Florida without her. They tried to talk us into coming back with them and doing the work remotely. They should've known not to waste their breath. She still had several things to do here before she would go home. Admitting defeat, they agreed to go back, but the men they brought would stay and join me, Creed, Reggie, Dario, and the three Aegis employees, when needed, to protect her. She still thought it was overkill, but it was the only way they'd accede to her staying.

We saw them off this morning. She promised them she wouldn't spend a minute longer than she had to in California. I was anticipating our return home. I had plans, and I didn't want to delay. It was bothering me that I didn't have my ring on her finger. There was no need to wait. We'd been waiting for years already. The only reason I hadn't given it to her yet was I wanted to do it in front of her entire family and make it special. Even though I thought I would never have a chance with her, I found and bought her ring several years back. I saw it, and I knew it was meant for her. I prayed when the time came, she'd agree and love it. If not, I'd get her one she did love.

As soon as we saw them off, it was back to the winery to work. I stuck near her. I was actually enjoying myself even if she kept apologizing about boring me. I was learning so much, and I had no idea what really went into creating a wine until this trip. I thought you grew the grapes and processed them, and that was it. Boy, I was wrong. There was a ton of science to it, and Aisling was well-versed in it. Watching her work was incredible for me. I told her to stop apologizing because I wasn't bored at all.

The interest and passion on her face as she talked to her viticulturist were beautiful to see. She was in her element. It reminded me of how much I loved my work with the Hounds. Even though I was here with her, I was still working. In fact, when we went back to her office so she could do more, I excused myself to an empty office to have a conference call with Darragh. The others were watching her and the winery grounds.

When the call went through and the video link opened, I saw not only Darragh but several other O'Sheeran men. I tensed. This was supposed to be a regular meeting to discuss the latest requests we'd received. Usually, there were none of the others unless something big was happening or we were in the later stages of planning, and they needed to be brought into the picture.

The door to the office was shut, and I knew no one would be able to hear us. The office was soundproofed like Aisling's. Sometimes other family members, when visiting, would use it. You could never be too careful who might hear something even if you thought your people were trustworthy.

"I see this is going to be more than a rundown of new requests. Hit me."

"You're right. We'll get to those, but this first part takes precedence. Cody, why don't you tell Alistair what you have?" Darragh asked. That's when I saw Cody come into view on their end. Shit, it had to be bad if he was presenting.

"Hey. Alistair, let me say first it's not anything definitive which you know pisses me off. I'm still trying to track shit down. I've been tearing through Brynes' family, trying to determine if any of the people threatening them might've been responsible for what happened to Aisling. At first, they cooperated by giving us names and other information. However, since the showdowns with you out there, that's been shut down. We've been told in no uncertain terms to fuck off by Christopher Brynes. He's taking his butt hurt to the extreme. Honestly, I hope it is someone after him, and it was a fluke that Aisling was there, and whoever it is, gets his dumb ass," Cody grumbled.

"But you can't be sure," I said with a sigh.

He shook his head. "No, I can't. There's chatter out on the dark web and the sites pertaining to things like that. You just need to know where to look, and I do. I monitor them for talk about the family all the time. While there's always a degree of it no matter what, I haven't seen it increase for either family, nor is there specific talk about a possible hit on them or us. That doesn't mean someone isn't after either party. It's just that they're keeping it in-house and close to the vest. They're not talking or seeking outside help."

"Son of a bitch, it's been almost two months. If it was a strike against either of them, why hasn't whoever tried something not made another attempt? I mean, has Brynes been stepping up his security so much no one can make a play for him? Friday night, he had one extra guard that we saw, and truthfully, he wasn't impressive. We haven't seen anyone suspicious around here, nor has anyone tried to strike out at Aisling," I replied as I thought out loud.

"Exactly. The last thing we want is to relax our vigilance and then have someone make a move against her or any of the family. Right now, it's the women we've stepped security up with, but you know how they can be. They may try to revolt soon," Cian said with a grimace. All six men with wives were on the call. Even the older men weren't pleased looking.

"Aisling may try it, but I already told her when it comes to her safety, I won't be persuaded to let things slide. She can bitch, fight, and anything else she wants, but it won't work. If it means putting her ass under house arrest or tying her up, then so be it," I growled.

This made them all laugh. "Please, if you do either of those to her, film it. We'll play it at your funeral," Aidan teased.

"Shut up. I know how to soothe her ruffled feathers."

"La, la, la, I don't need to hear those details," Cormac said, covering his ears. He grinned as he said it, and Aidan pretended to gag.

"We all agree. No details, or we'll have to kill Alistair. Okay, back to what Cody was saying. The reason we have him on this call isn't only in case you had specific questions for him but we wanted to talk about what we do next," Darragh interjected.

"I hate to add to your workload, Cody, but I don't think in good conscience we can stop trying to determine who and what are threats. If you find out that it was always against the Brynes or that jackass Chris personally, then fuck 'em. It's his problem, in my opinion. You guys might have other thoughts. If we hear nothing about the family or Aisling and there are no new attempts over the next month, then maybe we should think about easing off, but not all at once."

They muttered back and forth before it seemed they settled on an answer. It was Cormac who gave me his thoughts.

"*Mac*, we agree with everything you said. We'll pray we can eliminate it as a threat to her or us, but if not, we won't ease back the security. Do you have any idea how much longer she'll want to stay out there?"

"Another couple of weeks, ideally. She's working to get the meetings she wanted to do in person out of the way. The two she had on Friday were big ones, and she has one more this week with Caliari Corporation. Those were her top three, she told me. Her work with her team at the winery is going great. They're on track, according to her. I gotta say, she's impressive as hell. She knows this business inside and out."

"She does love it and puts her all into it. No complaints on the family end. Okay, we'll keep it as is. You work to help her tie things up as soon as possible. We'll all feel better even if we don't know who they were after if she's here. Anything else before we move onto Hounds' business?" Dar asked.

They all shook their heads no, the same as I did. At his chin lift, the majority left. Most didn't attend these types of calls, so it wasn't a surprise. I saw Cody stayed, which made sense since he led the team that checked into both parties of those we ended up accepting their cases. The other guys left after saying goodbye. It was the three oldest O'Sheeran men who stayed. Hmm, that was interesting. Yes, they still took an interest in the various dealings of the family, even if they were technically retired, but I couldn't recall the last time all three attended a meeting of the Hounds, not at this stage, anyway.

"You have to be wondering why *Daid* and my *uncaili* stayed. It's because of one of the requests we received. It took us all by surprise," Darragh began.

"Alright, tell me."

"It came from someone in the Bragan family," Patrick stated.

Well, that was unexpected. Why would one of the top Irish mafia families in the States ask for outsiders to help them? And with what? "What did they ask us to do?"

"It seems they have a problem with young women and girls in their territory going missing. They think they might have an idea of who's responsible. They're asking for the Hounds' help in eliminating the offending party or the offenders they think are behind it," Sean added.

"Kinda odd. I would assume they have the means to go after the culprits themselves, so why ask for outside help? Has there been a change in the family's strength or dynamics I don't know about?"

"If there's been a change, we haven't heard about it either. The reason I believe they want to go outside is they believe it'll bring a lot of heat down on them if they do it themselves," Darragh said. He exchanged a mysterious look with Cody.

"Enough dancing around, just tell me."

"First, let me say they believe the missing women and girls are being trafficked. If it's true and they're not just runaways or women getting free of a life they don't want, then we should consider how we might be able to help. The tricky part is the ones they believe are behind it. We could be looking at war if it becomes known we had any involvement. Alistair, shit, I'll just say it. According to the contact, they think it's the Byrnes family," Patrick dropped the bomb.

To say I was stunned would be an understatement. In the history of the Hounds, they'd never been asked to go up against any of the Irish families since the O'Sheerans went legit, except for the thing with the Doyles, which was voted on and approved by the five other families. Sure, the Russians or the Italians or others, yes, but not their own.

Secondly, this, on the heels of the current problem with Christopher Brynes and the unknown assailants at the wreck, made it more suspect.

"Are we sure they have no clue we're the ones they're asking for help? It would be a great way to eliminate two bigger families if they got them to fight and kill each other," I stated, not that they didn't know the risks.

"We're ninety-nine percent sure they don't have a clue. It goes without saying Cody and his team will do the background checks as usual. The question is, if he discovers the women and girls are really missing, do we take the job if it reveals the Brynes are involved or any of the other Irish mob families? It's like shitting in your own backyard. As careful as we would be, there's always a risk we'll be discovered," Darragh clarified.

"This could be a time bomb, but regardless of who it is, if those women and girls have been trafficked or something equally awful, we have an obligation to do something about it, even if the Byrnes or others we might know are involved. We know the other families aren't all legal. In the past, they've stayed away from dealing in prostitution. They know to keep their drugs and guns well away from our territories," I muttered aloud.

"They do. The thing is, the Bragans are looking to go entirely legitimate. That's not common knowledge. The head of the family came to Darragh and me not long ago to ask for our help with how they can go about it. We kept it quiet until we could determine if they were on the up and up. This request kinda derailed us from staying quiet. We haven't mentioned it to the whole family, but after this discussion, we will.

There's no love lost between you and Chris, I know. You oversee the Hounds. Your input, if we even bother to go through with the investigation, is what we want," Patrick clarified.

I sat there and took my time thinking over the potential risks of us saying yes. It was true, if it ended up being the Brynes, I wouldn't shed a tear, not after how Chris had been acting. I'd never trusted him. He'd always presented himself as too slick and maybe sly. He thought he could charm any woman out of her clothes, and the fact that he wanted to do it to my woman infuriated me, but I tried to be objective.

We'd have to take every precaution not to expose who we were. None of us wanted outright war, and if it ended up in one, we wouldn't want to risk the Connally and Kilkenny families backing the Brynes. It would make it a tough one to win, not that we had no chance, but casualties on our side would be a given if we went up against them alone. That didn't consider each family's allies in other mob families outside the Irish community or even business associates getting involved. We didn't want to start a widespread mob war.

Finally, I gave them my answer: "I say do the due diligence on both families. If it comes back that the Bragans are legit and right about the disappearances, regardless of whether it's the Brynes behind it or not, we help. If it is Brynes and his family, so be it."

I heard sighs all around. "I hate it, but I agree. I pray to God Chris and his family aren't behind anything heinous like trafficking or forced prostitution," Sean said.

"Another thing we might consider is it may not be the whole family. What if only a select few have gone rogue, so to speak? For me, if they're involved, I'm hoping for it to be that kind of situation. The rest of the family may see the elimination of those members as just," Cormac added with a grimace.

"Me too. Okay, Cody, you know what to do. If you need to bring on more help with the stuff you've got going with determining the targeting of us or them, let me know. We can get help from the Horsemen," Darragh offered.

The Horsemen he was referring to were the Horsemen of Wrath MC. Judge, our go-to tattoo guy, was a part of their club, and they were a bunch of good guys. They were tied to another MC we had a slight connection to in Tennessee through our cousin Donal. It was amazing sometimes how small the world actually could be. You'd think an MC wouldn't have computer help of the kind we needed, but you'd be wrong. We'd discovered they had some of the best in the world. Plus, they fought against things such as this all the time.

"I don't think I need it, but if I find I do, you'll be the first to know. There was another request, right? Do we wanna talk about it too? Or are we just gonna discuss this one today and do the other tomorrow?"

None of us had more to say until we heard what Cody found, so we jumped to the second request. It was more of what we considered a standard one, so it was a go for the background to start. I admit, I zoned a tiny bit as they went over the second one. I couldn't stop thinking of what it would mean if the Brynes were the bad guys and the Bragans the good guys. We'd have to tread extra carefully.

It wasn't long before we were done, and the call

ended. I sat back in my chair and ran through possible scenarios in my head. I jotted down notes on things we'd have to consider and possible safety points. I was so consumed with what I was doing I lost track of time. A brisk knock on the office door was what broke my concentration and made me glance at the clock. I was startled to see it was five o'clock already. Where the hell had the afternoon gone?

"Come in," I hollered.

The door opened, and in walked my woman. She had a tentative smile on her face as she came toward me. I rose up and walked around the desk. I met her halfway, and then I took her in my arms and kissed her. It had been hours since the last one. I was overdue for one. I groaned at her taste. She moaned as we lustily kissed each other. By the time she pulled away, I was ready for more than a kiss. My cock was hard, and the surface of my borrowed desk was looking perfect to lay her out on. She laughed.

"Don't even think about it. The desk is too hard. I hope I'm not disturbing anything important. I wanted to check and see how long you needed to stay behind closed doors. No hurry, I just wanted to know if I should have dinner brought in here or if I can cook at home."

"I'm ready when you are. Just lost track of time. I can work on this tomorrow. If you're at a stopping point, let's head home. I'll help you make dinner."

"You can if you want, or you can watch and keep me company. I'd like to have the team join us if you don't mind. I feel they need home-cooked meals, too, and I like cooking for more than just the two of us."

"*Leanabh*, you can invite whoever you want, as long as they leave later when I want my alone time with you."

She gave me a sexy smile. "I agree with that. Okay, you tie up whatever you're doing here and meet me at my office. I'll tell Carrie we're heading home. And I'll let Creed know so he can inform the others."

"Deal."

One quick peck, then she was gone. I closed out my Word document after saving it, then closed my laptop and packed it in my briefcase. I took a leisurely stroll through the building, just eyeing it before I ended up at her office. Carrie was taking her purse out of her desk.

"Have a good night, Carrie."

"I will, Mr. Graeme."

I gave her a stern look. She smiled. "I mean, I will, Alistair. Make sure Aisling doesn't work tonight. She's been going non-stop all day, and I see the gleam in her eyes. She'll try to work all night if we don't watch her. It's your job away from here to take care of her, and mine is to try to do it when she's here."

"Roger that. I'll make sure."

I saw the grin on Creed's face. He was standing outside Aisling's office door.

"I heard that!" Ais shouted from inside.

"We know. We wanted you to. You work too hard," Carrie called back to her with a grin on her face. "Night boss. See you tomorrow."

"Goodnight, Carrie, drive safe," Aisling called back.

"You too," Carrie called out as she gave us a wave, then left. Reggie and Dario were stationed on either side of the front door. I'd checked on my walkabout to be sure all doors and windows were secure, even though

I knew they'd done the same. When Aisling came waltzing out, I took her arm, and we were off. I was looking forward to chilling at the house.

❧❧❧

The insistent ringing of a phone brought me out of a deep sleep. I bolted upright and reached for mine on the bedside table. As soon as I grabbed it, it registered that the ringing wasn't coming from my phone. It was Aisling's. She fumbled to pick hers up.

"Hello," she said huskily.

Glancing at the clock, I saw it was two in the morning. We'd only gone to sleep a little over an hour ago after a very pleasurable bout of sex, which had worn the both of us out. I scooted closer when she sat up straighter, and I saw fear on her face. I wanted to take the phone away and find out who was calling and what they were saying to put that expression on her face, but I fought it.

"When? How much damage? Do we know how it happened?" she fired off one right after the other.

She flipped off the covers and was on her feet, headed for the closet while she talked. I didn't delay getting my ass up and over to my clothes. Whatever was going on, she obviously wanted to go somewhere, and she wasn't leaving without me. I always kept clothes next to the bed. Habit from my military days. I was almost completely dressed by the time I heard her say goodbye. As soon as she hung up, I started to question her.

"Ais, what's wrong? You mentioned damage."

She came out of the closet with her clothes in hand. I saw they were shaking. I went to her and pulled her close. She buried her face in my chest.

"That was Carrie. Since she's here all the time, she's set up to get alerts if anything happens at the winery. The alarm company called and told her the alarms went off, and police were dispatched. She went to see what was up. She didn't call me because she thought it was a false alarm. They happen from time to time. It wasn't. The winery was on fire. I've gotta get there and see what the damage is and figure out what to do. God, how did this happen, Stair? Do you think it's related to the guys in the car who caused the wreck? If it is, why go for the winery and not here?"

"Shh, I know you want answers, and so do I. Let's get the guys and go. You get dressed, and I'll text them. I promise, no matter what, we'll find the one responsible and make this stop."

She sniffed and nodded, then pulled away to dress. I grabbed my phone and texted the group I created for this trip and the men protecting her. I barely sent the text and slipped on my shoes when my phone began to chime with their responses.

The two of us made a super quick stop in the bathroom, and then we were ready. The guys were all waiting at the front door except Reggie and Vander. Creed saw me scanning their group for them. "Reg and Vander went to get the cars. Anything new?"

"Nothing. We need to get there and see what the hell happened," I told them.

The honk of a car horn told us the cars were here. Making sure Ais was surrounded, we exited the house. Dario brought up the rear. He activated the alarm and locked it up. I hustled her into the first car. Vander was driving it. Creed, Kendric, and Dario got in with us. The rest got in with Reggie. We took the lead. I could feel her whole body practically vibrating with tension. I rubbed her leg. I knew words wouldn't help, so I kept my mouth shut.

It didn't take us long to get there. Before we reached it, we saw smoke in the night air. As we got closer, we saw the police cars and the fire trucks. We were stopped by a cop standing in the middle of the road. He came to the driver's window. Vander lowered it.

"Folks, you need to turn around. This is private property. There's nothing to see."

"I know it's private. I own it. This is my family's winery. I'm Aisling O'Sheeran. These two vehicles are my men. I need to speak to your chief and the fire chief. We're going through," Ais told him firmly.

"Ma'am, I can't just let you pass. I need to see some ID and then check out if you're the actual owner," he argued.

I wasn't in the mood for bullshit right then. I leaned toward the window. "Go get Carrie. She's here and the one they called when the alarms went off. She can verify who we are, but make it quick. We're not sitting here all damn night. Ms. O'Sheeran needs to know what happened and how much damage there is. I guarantee you don't want to piss off her family."

He was young and appeared very unsure and nervous. I'd bet he hadn't been a cop long, and he had no clue how to handle people like us. Well, it was good training. "I-I can't leave my post," he said hesitantly.

"Then get on your radio and call someone over here who can help us," Kendric snapped.

The guy fumbled with his radio. He called for backup. While we waited, he eyed us with suspicion and his hand on his gun. He had no damn clue we were all armed and far more dangerous than he was. An older gentleman with gray hair came striding up with a frown on his face. He was in a police uniform.

"What's the damn problem here, Ramsey?" he snapped.

"Sergeant, this woman claims she owns this winery and wants through, and the men in both cars are with her. I told them I couldn't do it until I verified who they were and got permission. She says her name is Aisling O'Sheeran."

The patrol officer might not have a clue who Ais was, but by the expression on the sergeant's face, he did. He peered into the car. Straightening up, he glared at Ramsey. "Let them through! She's an O'Sheeran, and they own this winery. God, do you live under a rock?"

Turning back to us, he gave her an apology. "I'm sorry, Ms. O'Sheeran, please go ahead. Your manager is in the front parking lot with the fire chief and our chief. If you need anything else, let me know. I'm Sergeant Harris."

"Thank you, sergeant," she said with a smile.

After he stepped back, we took off. Glancing back, I saw him chewing Ramsey out by the looks of it. The parking lot was full of people. The firemen were pouring water on the fire, which, from what I could see, was mostly smoke by now. We parked and got out. As a unit, we moved around the lot to try to find Carrie. After about five minutes, we heard a woman shout, and then we saw her. We rushed over to her. She and Ais hugged each other. The men standing with Carrie were giving us the once-over. When they were done, Carrie introduced us to them. Hearing Aisling's name had them all coming to attention. It was hard to see how much damage there was. I prayed it wasn't extensive enough to shut down the winery. If it were, it would ruin the plans they had for rolling out the new wines. It would crush her. I waited to hear the news.

Aisling: Chapter 14

Watching the smoke rise up from the building made me want to cry. All I could think about was all the hard work that might've just gone up in smoke. Along with tears was anger. I wanted to know if it was an accident or if someone had done it on purpose. If it was on purpose, who and why? Was it dumb kids just out having what they thought was fun, or was it more sinister than that?

After hugging Carrie, I faced the men with her. "Hello, I'm Aisling O'Sheeran. This winery belongs to my family, and I oversee it. Can you tell me what happened and how bad the damage is?"

"Ms. O'Sheeran, I'm Fire Chief Walton. My men are still working to fully extinguish the fire so it won't reignite from a hot spot. Right now, the flames are out, but we still have to be careful. There's water and smoke damage, as you can imagine. We won't know the full extent of the damage until we can inspect and have the fire marshall come out and go through it. The fire seems to have started in the section where the actual wine is made. It might be an electrical issue. Again, we won't know until we can investigate. The fire marshal will do that. Are you thinking it might be intentional?"

"I always think that's a possibility. We're a successful business, and people do things we can't understand all the time. Yes, it may be an unfortunate accident, or it might not. I'd like the names and numbers of the fire inspector, fire marshal, and anyone else involved in the investigation so I can stay on top of them," I said firmly.

"I gave those to your manager. I'm sorry, I wasn't aware anyone in the O'Sheeran family was here or would be taking a direct role in this," he said nervously.

"I'm not here all the time, so yes, Carrie handles things, but I'm a very hands-on person. My family and I don't believe in leaving all the work to our employees. I'd like this to be wrapped up as soon as possible. We're on a deadline and have new wines coming out soon. I don't want to delay those if there's any way possible not to, which means getting this back up and running. It's unfortunate it was in the actual winemaking area rather than an office or other non-essential area."

"It is. Is there anyone you can think of who would benefit from sabotaging your winery?" One of the other men asked out of the blue. Until then, only Walton had spoken while they listened. This one was in plain clothes.

"Excuse me, you are?" I asked.

"I'm Police Chief Evans."

"Chief Evans, if you mean have there been any threats against Maeve's Cellars, then no. It doesn't rule out the possibility someone is angry at us for something we're unaware of and decided to do this. The world is a very crazy place at times," I informed him.

He studied me but didn't utter a word for a solid minute or so. When he did, all he said was, "You've got that right. If you'll be sure to leave all your contact information with me and Chief Walton, we'll be sure you're kept in the loop. Any idea how long you'll be here?"

With this happening, I wasn't sure I'd be able to finish much else off other than the Caliari meeting. "I'm not sure. I have business back in Florida, and it may take me away sooner than I'd like. If that were to occur, Carrie would be the point person, and she could get in contact with me if she needed to. If, for some reason, you need me to return, I could do so."

"Good. Alright, well, there's not much more we can tell you right now. Here's my card." Chief Evans handed me a business card. I made sure to do the same to him and Chief Walton, and I got one of Walton's, too. We didn't hold them up for long. When they went back to work, Carrie gave me a sad smile.

"I'm so sorry, Aisling. When they called and said the fire alarm went off, I thought it was a malfunction. When I got here and saw it wasn't, I almost died. What do you want us to do about work today?"

"Those working in the office and other areas not affected will be working as usual. The advantage of the way we have things set up is that the wine tasting and gift shop, as well as the main office, are separate from this and can remain open. We'll get the information on the damage as fast as we can so we can get it fixed and back on track."

"Do you think it'll derail the rollout of the new wines?"

"I hope not, but I just don't know."

"Are you still going to your meeting today with Caliari Corporation?"

"Absolutely. I can still sell them on our current wines and let them know what is coming. The storage area is separate from the processing area. If someone did this on purpose, they either didn't know what they were firebombing or they didn't care. If it was intentional, they should've done their homework better."

As I hung there talking to her, Alistair had Creed and Dario stay with me while he did a walk around with the other guys. I knew he was searching for evidence the cops might not think of. I had no doubt that when we got back to the house, he'd have Cody bring up all the security footage. I was surprised Chief Evans hadn't asked for it. Maybe he would later. What he wouldn't know was we had public recording and then the more extensive private one. It came in handy if the issue required the family to take care of the matter rather than the cops.

By the time we got back to the house, it was five a.m. My meeting was at noon in Orange County. I was exhausted. Alistair insisted I go back to bed and get some sleep. I tried to argue I had too much to do, but he picked me up and carried my yelling and kicking body to our bedroom, much to the amusement of the guys. I wanted to be mad at him, but deep down, I knew he was right. I was fuzzy-headed, and I needed to be on top of my game to meet with Caliari. He promised he'd update the family. After a passionate kiss, he left me to sleep.

GGG

Sitting down at my meeting with the head of Caliari Corp today was the last thing I wanted to do, but I wasn't about to let anything slide because of an unfortunate setback. I was thankful for Alistair and Carrie. They kept things going while I slept and then did last-minute prep. The ride over here took over two hours, and Stair was great at letting me focus on my notes in the car. He didn't become impatient or feel neglected. When I asked him how it went when he called my family, he told me it went well, and we'd talk through the details after I met with Caliari. He wanted me not to be distracted. He knew how important this business would be to Maeve's if we got them to sign a contract with us.

Like my meeting with Tillman and Hayes, he was the one to go inside with me, and the others took up their spots outside the building and in the outer office. The receptionist slash assistant never blinked an eye at him coming with me, and she was professional and extremely personable. Those were two points in their favor already.

My research revealed nothing but great things about the company and its owner. They had ethical dealings, and no lawsuits or claims against them had ever been substantiated. I wanted their business more than Tillman and Hayes's, and it wasn't just because Caliari was much larger.

We were shown into a tasteful office. A man was waiting for us. He came to his feet, and with a big smile on his face, he hurried over with his hand out. I knew from pictures that this was the owner, Santino Caliari. He was in his forties. He raised the back of my hand to his lips and gave it a brief kiss. I found that a lot of Italian men did that or the cheek kiss.

"Ms. O'Sheeran, I can't thank you enough for agreeing to come all the way over here to meet me. I wanted to come to Maeve's, but my schedule lately has been crazy. I'm Santino Caliari. Please call me Tino. And this must be your bodyguard, I was told to expect. Hello," he said as he dropped my hand to shake

Alistair's.

Tino Caliari was a handsome man with charm for days. I knew he was divorced. While I appreciated his looks and charm, they did nothing for me in comparison to Alistair's. I knew Stair wasn't loving the hand kiss. As he shook Tino's hand, he set him straight. I should've known he would stake a plain claim.

"I'm Alistair Graeme. Yes, for today, I'm Aisling's personal bodyguard, but it's only because I have the privilege of being her boyfriend, although I hate that word. After all, we're not boys, are we?"

"Ah, I see. Good to know. I had no idea she was claimed, although I'm not surprised. I'll admit, her beauty is well known, and the hand kiss was my opening gambit in case she wanted to mix business with pleasure. Sorry. It won't happen again, but you can't blame a guy for trying and hoping," he said easily to both of us, and I heard the sincerity and humor in his voice.

"I accept your apology. She is beautiful and very tempting. Just keep the kisses to her hand, and I'll be fine."

"You're a very lucky man. Please have a seat. We don't need to stand on formality here. Call me Tino. Can I get either of you something to drink?"

He went to a cart beside the small table we'd seated ourselves around. Unlike the other day with Hayes and Tillman, the cart contained no alcohol. Instead, it contained lemonade, iced tea, ice water, and a variety of sodas.

"I'd love some lemonade if you don't mind. And feel free to call me Aisling."

"The same for me, and you can call me Alistair."

Smiling, he poured our drinks and one for himself while asking how the drive was. When we all had drinks in hand, he took his seat and moved the conversation from pleasantries to business.

"I've been doing a lot of research into Maeve's Cellars. I know it's a small part of the Kin of *Éireann* Inc., your family's corporation. I haven't had the honor of having any working relationship with the O'Sheeran family, but everything I've heard says you're serious businessmen and women, and you treat your partnerships and employees fairly. I like that. Can we cut to the chase, as you say?"

"Absolutely," I said.

If he were about to blow me off, I'd rather he do it now than make me spend an hour making a pitch then do it. This way, no one's time was wasted. The only thing that would've been better was if he'd called and told me he wasn't interested and saved me the prep time and drive.

"I'm expanding my key restaurants. In doing so, I want to expand the selection of wines I offer my patrons. My family is from Italy, in case you didn't guess by my name," he chuckled as he said it before continuing. "Naturally, people expect me and my family to be snobs and only want to sell Italian wines or those made in Napa Valley or Sonoma. There's nothing wrong with those wines, but I like to think out of the box and not overlook great wines just because they don't fall into the typical areas. I've tasted just about every single one of yours over the past few weeks. I have to tell you I'm impressed. And the rumor is you're working on a new line of them that are touted to be even better. I want them. What do I need to do to get you to do business with me?"

I was startled at his bluntness but also happy. It made my job much easier. "I'm excited you want to do business with me. I came here expecting to have to fight for you to even consider it. I'm glad you're impressed with the current selection, and yes, we have new ones coming. I have to be honest and tell you I'm not sure how soon, though. I was planning it to be in a few months, but this morning, we had a fire at the winery, and it affected a section of the actual production area. The wine storage wasn't affected. We have plenty to meet the needs of our customers. It's mostly the lab area where we were finalizing the development of the new wines that was impacted. It may delay our release of those."

"I'm sorry to hear that. I hope no one was hurt."

"It was in the middle of the night, so no one was there."

"Well, I guess there's one positive out of it. I hope you'll be able to get your project back on schedule soon, but even with the delay, I still want to talk about my restaurants offering the wines you have and then, when the others become available, to add those."

"I would love that. I can send you more details on what we can offer and our contract for you to study. Then, you can get back to me with any questions. I have to admit, I wasn't expecting you to be this certain and ready to proceed."

"I was very impressed and halfway ready to just pull the trigger on it, but then I had a conversation, and after I did, any lingering what-ifs were cleared away. You were given the thumbs up by a trusted friend. He assured me working with your family would only benefit me and that your family upholds your business deals ethically."

"Really? May I ask who said this?"

"You may. He said to tell you to let Cian know he's waiting for him to come back so he can steal his wife. Giuseppe Bonadio, Pino, as his friends call him, sang your praises. He told me he serves your wines at Luna Etrusca."

I laughed. I knew Pino. He was a good friend of Cian's and somewhat of a playboy, who, when he met Miranda, thought she was just a casual sex partner for Cian, and he wanted to share her with Cian. Suffice it to say he was quickly set straight.

"I do know Pino. How do you know him?"

"His family and mine have been friends in Italy for generations. He told me what he did when he first met Cian's wife. He's still trying to find a way to make up for his assumption. He's mortified."

"Well, yes, he was lucky my cousin didn't remove his head for what he said and assumed. Miranda told us the story when they came back from Italy. She's gotten over it, I promise. She holds no hard feelings."

"Good, I'll let him know. Alistair, I don't mean to be rude and ignore you in the conversation. Tell me, what kind of work do you do? And how did you succeed in capturing this delightful woman?"

"You're not rude at all. I'm merely here to observe and make sure Aisling is safe. I actually work in security. I was a Marine, and it was natural when I got out to continue similar work. I have an aptitude for it. It's a family business, you might say. I grew up with the O'Sheeran boys, so I've known Aisling since she was born. It took me years to win her, but I was very fortunate recently to find out she feels the same way about me as I do her. She's the love of my life."

I knew Stair loved me, but to hear him so easily admit it aloud to another man, especially a stranger, made me want to kiss him. He had no problem admitting he had feelings for me. I knew a lot of men weren't able to talk about their feelings, not even with the person they loved. My family tended to be the exception rather than the rule. I blew him a kiss. He smiled.

"Damn, you two are so sweet. Why can't I find a woman like you? I'm afraid my track record isn't the best. Hence, many ex-girlfriends, an ex-wife, and no children." He sighed mournfully.

"You have to be willing to meet people, even those who may not be in your usual circle of friends and acquaintances. I was lucky I grew up around Alistair, but my oldest brother and my two cousins, who've all recently gotten married, met their wives in the most ordinary places when they weren't even looking. Ashlyn came to ask the family to help with a delicate project, and Darragh took one look and was a goner for her. Miranda worked as a teller in the bank where Cian went to make a deposit. He wasn't the person to typically make deposits. My brother Aidan's wife went to work at Sirens, our nightclub, as a bartender. Some people might be skeptical, but they're all love matches and soulmates, just like Alistair and I are."

The rest of the meeting passed, mostly getting to know each other, and not talking shop. By the time we had to leave so he could make his next meeting, I felt as if I'd known him for years. He insisted we go to dinner soon, and he promised he'd review the contract and the information I would send him tomorrow to get things rolling immediately. I was so excited as we left.

The guys were waiting for us. This time, when we got to the car, they didn't check for a bomb because they left Vander and Cashel to watch the car. It didn't take us long to be on the road back to Temecula. I excitedly called Carrie to let her know the good news. She squealed with happiness. I asked her if she'd talked to the fire chief. She said no, but there were people there on and off all day. When I was done with her call, my joy dimmed a bit. It was time to find out what went down while I was asleep.

"Alistair, what did my family have to say when you told them what happened? Who did you talk to? Darragh?"

"Are you sure you don't want to enjoy your victory a bit longer before getting into the depressing things again?

"I would, but it's not realistic. I'd rather know what I'm facing."

"I spoke to Darragh, all of your brothers, and your *daid*. Suffice it to say they weren't thrilled, and I know they informed the rest of the family within an hour of my getting off my call with them based on the texts I got. They're anxiously waiting to see if there was anything on the security tape. Cody has it and is studying it. They knew of your meeting with Caliari today and didn't want to distract you, so we're to call them when we get home to see if he found anything. They're worried about this being on the heels of your wreck. The question on all our minds is whether the fire is connected or a whole separate thing. They won't be patient long, so I hope the inspectors and such at the fire department don't drag their heels, or they'll have a pack of angry Irishmen on their doorstep."

"*Dia*, please, don't say that. They need to calm down and wait. You have to talk to them. Maybe they'll listen to you. Surely, with you and the guys here, they know I'm safe, and they don't need to call in the cavalry. I swear they act like I'm ten and can't take care of myself."

"It doesn't matter how old you are, not to them or me. You're precious to us. We'll do whatever it takes to keep you safe. Asking us to do otherwise is a waste of time. I did tell them to stay there and let me handle it, at least until we know more. They agreed grudgingly."

Leaning over as far as my seatbelt would allow as he leaned to meet me, I gave him a kiss. He made it an intense one. When we were done, I smiled at him. "Thank you. I swear if they came out here en masse, I'd run and hide. I love them, but they can be a lot to handle. How long do you think they'll behave?"

"Hell, if I know. I'm not a miracle worker, you know."

Creed snorted, then coughed. "That's for damn sure. Not even Jesus himself can hold them back. If they find out this fire was deliberate, they'll have your ass back in Florida in a heartbeat. They won't risk it being a personal attack against you."

"It can't be personal. If it was, why not do it when I was present or come to the house and firebomb it? I think it's just a coincidence, and a bunch of stupid teenagers got bored and thought they'd play with fire. I hope when we find out who they are, they put them in jail and scare them straight."

"We can hope for it to be the case. Just don't be

shocked if it's not. Do we need to stop anywhere before we get back to the house?" Kendric asked.

"Not that I can think of. What about you guys?"

This change in topic diverted our thoughts from the fire. The traffic was a nightmare, so it seemed to take forever to make it back to Temecula. Before heading to the house, I insisted we go by the winery and see how everyone was doing. I wanted to see the damage in the light of day. I knew Alistair wasn't overjoyed with the idea, but he didn't nix it.

Pulling up outside the building made me want to cry. The roof was caved in on one end. We got out, and I immediately headed to the burned section. I had to see it for myself. Alistair went with me, and I was able to look inside, but he wouldn't let me crawl around in there, as he called it. He said it needed to be deemed safe, and I wasn't in the right clothes for it anyway. He wasn't wrong about the latter. Heels and a skirt weren't ideal climbing clothes. I made a mental note to dress in jeans and boots and come back tomorrow to do it if the fire inspector said it was safe.

I found out Alistair had already arranged for someone to come in and tear down the burned section and haul it away and then for another crew to come do the rebuild. All we needed was for the investigation to be over. The insurance company had been called while we were still at the fire this morning, and they'd come out to take pictures during the day. He really had been busy while I slept.

Carrie ended up hearing we were there, and she came over to talk to me and update me on what she'd been working on that day. The press had gotten wind of the fire, and they were hounding her with calls for quotes and interviews. Why, I had no idea. As far as they knew, it was an unfortunate fire. I knew they'd probably be camped out on the road by tomorrow, causing a nuisance. I wasn't happy for it to start, but I guess I was lucky they hadn't known I was in town or that they had other things to do the past few days. Usually, they'd follow me around, trying to get pictures. It was stupid. Who wanted to see me shopping in the grocery store or running errands?

We chatted for a while, and then I told her to wrap up her day and go home. There was nothing we could do about it. She agreed. As we got in the cars, Alistair informed me of something else he'd worked on when I was asleep.

"Aegis will have some of their people discreetly watching the winery tonight in case this was deliberate and someone gets a wild idea to come back and finish what they started. If they do, they'll be in for the surprise of their lives. You don't need to worry about it. I suggest that when we get to the house, we order dinner. No need to cook tonight, and then we'll call your family to see if Cody found anything on the security video. We'll make an early night of it. I know you're still tired, and I know I am. The guys will work shifts as usual, so they'll get sleep, too. Tomorrow will be a fresh day."

"Sounds good to me," I said as I leaned my head on his shoulder. I sat in the middle seat this time so I could be closer to him. He hugged me close. We were quiet for the remainder of the short ride.

Alistair: Chapter 15

Aisling and I sat in front of her laptop, and her entire family was on the screen. My gut tightened. This wasn't a good sign. I was ready to snarl and ask them what the fuck was wrong. They were going through the niceties of greeting each other. I clenched my fist to help me hold my tongue. When I messaged them earlier to set the time to call, they asked us to have Kendric and Creed join the call. That had put me on edge, but this far surpassed it.

"Okay, enough of the chit-chat. I can see Alistair is about to explode, and we don't want that. I know you have to be dying to know why we're all here and why we asked Kendric and Creed to join us," Darragh broke in to say.

"I've got to say, yeah, I'm on edge. What the hell did you guys find?" I said back impatiently. Ais reached over, took my hand, and squeezed it in support, I think.

"We hear ya. Okay, Cody ran through the main tape. It shows three shadowy figures dressed in all black tossing basic Molotov cocktails through a window that they broke, and then they ran. I don't think they expected one of your neighbors out there to have a fire and rescue company, and they responded to it even before the regular fire department. If the culprits used more cocktails or an actual explosive, they would've destroyed the whole building," Dar explained.

"That's what the regular video showed, I presume. Did you send it to the cops? I want to know what the private security cameras showed," I muttered.

"We did have our legal team send it to the police. They won't find anything on it to help them, but they have it. As for the private one, it didn't yield us much more. They kept their faces well covered, and no identifying marks or tattoos were visible. They ran off to the south of the winery along the main road. We believe they had a car waiting a distance away for them. I wish we had an idea who they were, but we don't," he added with disgust.

"Alright, so what's with the clan being gathered if that's all you have to tell us? And I could've easily told Kendric and Creed this," I told them. I tried to keep my impatience out of my tone. They were my bosses, after all.

"He's trying not to cuss and go off. See the vein in his forehead," Rory said.

"Shut it before we let him go off on you. You're right, Alistair, we have more. While the videos didn't show us anything, Cody and his team finally got a lead, I guess you'd call it. Before you get too excited, it doesn't tell us who did it," Cormac hurried to add.

"*Mac galla*, son of a bitch. Okay, what did he find?" I asked.

"He picked up dark web chatter asking for possible help in taking out a winery in California and the bitch running it. The odds of it being another winery are almost zero, especially when you take into consideration the timing of it right after they hit Maeve's. The IP address was masked, but he was able to unmask it. But the person or persons who posted were smart, and they have it bouncing all over the world to different IP addresses. It's gonna take time to unravel them to get to the source, but Cody is confident they'll do it," Darragh explained.

Instead of making me angrier, hearing this settled me because it meant we had a real lead, and we knew whatever was happening was directed at Aisling. Which meant the wreck she was in with Brynes was almost certainly the same people. I knew Cody would work his magic, and when he did, I'd be able to go after those who dared to target the woman I loved. I'd gladly take them apart slowly. A smile spread across my face.

"*Íosa Chíost*, Jesus Christ, I told you he'd go all *craiceáilte*, crazy Scotsman on us," Aidan muttered. The others were all nodding their heads.

"Whoever did this messed with the wrong person. It sounds like a crazy Scotsman is what you need. Is there anything else? Was there any chatter about the rest of the family, or was it all directed toward Ais?" I asked as I continued to smile.

"So far, nothing against the rest of the family, but we're staying on alert in case it changes. If they can't get to her, they may change their target. No clue as to why they chose her rather than one of us. Or why they're including the winery in the mix. This brings us to the last thing," Patrick was the one to interject this. He had a tenseness about his face, and so did the others.

"What's that, *uncail*?" she asked.

"We want you to come home. We know you have work to do, but surely it can be done remotely. We want to see if we separate you from the winery, if they'll stay to attack it, or if they'll shift away from it to you or one of us. With us all here in one area, protecting everyone is easier. And speaking of work, how did the meeting with Caliari go?" Patrick asked.

I wondered if she'd immediately tell them it wasn't happening or if she'd listen to them. Truthfully, as soon as they mentioned the chatter, I wanted to demand we go back to Florida. I held off, knowing she'd be more likely to listen if I didn't bulldoze her. Her family, on the other hand, could demand it, and she would be less likely to automatically deny them. Although if she said no and I believed she was in imminent danger, I'd remove her against her will, and she'd have to get over it.

"First, let me say I didn't even get to go through my spiel on why he should work with us. He'd already made up his mind." She paused after saying it. I wanted to laugh because we both knew the conclusion they'd jump to and their responses.

"What the hell!?"

"He's an idiot. I hope you told him that."

"His goddamn loss."

When their muttering died down, she continued. "Yeah, he was already sold on doing business with Maeve's. He told me to send over the contract and information, and he'd get to work on it right away. Even the possible delay in the rollout of the new wines didn't deter him. He's tasted all our current ones and is impressed. He's in the process of expanding his restaurants. Tino said a friend helped him make his final decision."

"Tino, is it? Sounds like it went really well, and you're a brat for making us think he said no," Tiernan said.

She laughed. "I know, but I've gotta get my kicks

where I can. It was such a good meeting and so relaxed."

"Who's his friend who helped him decide?" Darragh asked.

She grinned. "I was told to tell Cian that Pino is eager for him and Miranda to visit so he can make up for his faux pas with her. Apparently, Pino's family and Tino's have been friends for generations."

Cian chuckled. The others smile. "Pino and Tino, Christ, do you think they were named to rhyme on purpose?" Rory asked.

"I doubt it. Tino's real name is Santino. He even asked where he could find a woman like Ais. She explained he needed to stop looking and hang out in new places like Dar, Cian, and Aidan did. I told him I was lucky to watch mine grow up. Although when he kissed her hand as his way of welcoming her, I thought about taking off his head and shoving it up his ass," I told them with a wink. I knew they were trying to ease tension before we got back into the somber discussion of her coming home. This cracked them up. Even Aisling giggled and rolled her eyes.

"He was quick to apologize when he realized who you were, so you had to give him points for that. I'll be sending over the contract and documents in the morning. While I appreciate you trying to soften the blow by talking business, we need to get back to me coming home."

"Before you say no, please consider it. We know you have work, but with the Caliari and Tillman and Hayes meetings out of the way, is there anything more you have to do where you must meet face-to-face with them? And is there work that only you can do there at the actual winery?" Shane asked quickly.

"I–" she was cut off by Cathal.

"You know we only have safety concerns. And if there's a chance others being near you could make them targets or collateral damage, we know you wouldn't want that."

"I wouldn't want that," she squeezed out before the next one threw in his two cents. The next one came from her dad, so I knew it would impact her more.

"*Muirnín*, I don't want you so far away. Whoever is doing this worries the hell out of me. Your *mam* and I want you here. Please, come home until we take care of this threat."

"*Daid*, if you guys would let me finish, I'd tell you I have no problem coming home. I don't want to endanger anyone else, and those meetings are the big ones I had planned. The rest I can do remotely. All I ask is the winery and offices here have added security not only to protect the winery but also our employees. I won't leave them open to attacks. *Tiarna*, Lord, I expect *Mamó*, *Mam,* and the *aintíni* to pop up any second crying." she joked. Or maybe it wasn't one. I had no doubt they'd do it if they thought she was being stubborn.

"They're in the hall waiting for our signal," Patrick said with a wink.

"*Dia*, my family is too much. Are you sure you want to be an official part of it? I mean, you're an honorary member already, but it's worse being official. You thought they had their noses in your business before, wait," she warned me.

"*Leanabh,* there's no way in the world they can scare me away. You're stuck with me."

"Good," she whispered before she kissed me. As

she did, I heard her brothers and cousins making gagging sounds, calling out for us to stop, and complaining they were blind. I kept kissing her as I flipped them off. I took my time before I let go of her. When I did, I smirked at the screen.

"We'll work on making the arrangements to return in the morning. I'll let you know when to expect us. It may take a day or two to get there. I'll talk to Aegis about having their people stay here. Now, if that's all, I think she needs to get some sleep. Oh, and you can thank me later, guys, for showing you how to properly kiss a woman." I informed them smugly, just to push their buttons.

This earned me boos, hisses, and crude remarks on what I could do to myself. By the time we ended the call, we were all smiling and laughing. I sat there with my arm around her.

"Aisling, all joking aside, I know this is stressing you. All I can say is try not to let it overwhelm you. Focus on getting home and what you need to put in place before we do. I'll help you however I can. This will be over soon."

"I hope so and thank you. I don't know what I'd do without you here."

"You never have to do anything alone."

A final kiss and I led her off to our room. There would be time to worry about the details tomorrow.

૯૬૯૬૯૬

As we drove through the gates of the family compound, my whole body relaxed, catching me sort of by surprise. Until it happened, I had no idea I was so tense. If asked, I would've said I wasn't overly stressed. I guess it was the knowledge she was on home turf, and I had tons of allies and backup to keep her safe, that did it.

It took two days for her to wrap things up in California, so we were free to return. The flight was a smooth one. We brought all the bodyguards and others who worked directly for the family back with us. The winery was left in the capable hands of the Aegis employees. They'd mainly watch the winery with an occasional pass by the house. Since no one was there, it wasn't the priority. In preparation for leaving, we made sure to tell anyone who asked that we were leaving and made sure we were seen putting luggage in the cars taking us to the airport.

There hadn't been any more attempts while we waited. The fire marshal did his inspection, and as we knew it would, the report showed it was deliberate. Plain gasoline had been the accelerant in the Molotov cocktails they launched into the winery window. The cleanup began this morning, and we'll soon know the estimate for rebuilding and the timeframe to complete it.

The car came to a stop in front of her house. I knew we'd only be able to stay long enough to drop off our luggage and maybe change clothes, but then we'd have to head to the main house so her parents could see her as well as anyone else who might be home right now. Later, after work, we'd be mobbed by the whole clan. I'd bet money they had a family dinner planned, too. Even though she'd only been gone ten days, it had to feel longer to them.

Growing up, I'd envied them the size and closeness of their family. For me, it was just me and my parents. They weren't close to their extended family, and I had no siblings, and neither did my parents. We'd been lucky to be included in the O'Sheeran family holidays. I was looking forward to not only continuing those as an actual family member but also having children of my own. I wanted a minimum of three if I could. I hoped Aisling agreed. It was something we needed to talk about. Other than knowing we wanted kids, it was undecided.

We were dropped off first, then the bodyguards who lived in the onsite quarters would be dropped off to get themselves organized and possibly to work. Not all of them lived on the compound, but a majority did. Creed was one of the ones who did, and he insisted on helping me to carry in our luggage. Before leaving, he checked to make sure there was nothing we needed. The more I was around him, the more impressed I was. He took his job seriously while still being friendly. He genuinely cared about what happened to her, but I got no romantic vibe from him. Aisling cared for him, too, and it showed. It was like she had another brother or cousin. Watching them go at each other if they got irritated or just wanted to joke around was fun.

"Thanks, man, appreciate it," I told him before he left.

"My pleasure. Besides, I gotta be sure no one is hiding under her bed to do her in. You know what a pain in the ass she is," he said the last part louder, so she would hear him.

"Dream on. The only one who's a pain in the ass around here is you!" she shouted from the kitchen.

He laughed, then gave me a chin lift before closing the door. She came hurrying into the room.

"Damn it, he got away before I could instigate him

more. I'll get him later."

"I swear you two are like squabbling siblings. Don't you have enough of those?"

"Never enough. Give me fifteen minutes to unpack the luggage and change. No, more like thirty. I gotta see if I need to put in a grocery order. You need to tell me what you want me to get. Oh, and we need to decide where we're gonna stay. I assume at least tonight it'll be here, but going forward, do you want to split our time between your place and mine or have us stay in one or the other?"

As she talked, she walked off, so I followed her. We ended up in her bedroom. The suitcases, including mine, were on the bed. She unzipped them. She scooped up a load of clothes from hers and went into the bathroom to her hamper, where she dumped them. Coming back she opened my suitcase.

"Which ones are dirty in your case? I packed mine with the dirty ones on the right and the still clean ones on the left, so it's ready to go. I planned to wash them before we left, but then time got away from me."

Yeah, most people would be shocked to know she even knew how to wash clothes, let alone that she did it. Her question about mine, as well as what she said about where we'd be staying, required me to say something.

"Ais, slow down. We need to talk about what you said about where we're staying."

"Oh yeah, I guess if you don't plan to stay here, there's no sense in me washing your clothes or putting them away here. Sorry." She went to zip up my bag, but I stopped her. I knew from her body language that she was upset but was working not to show it.

"You have nothing to be sorry about, and I didn't

say I didn't want to stay here. Let's sit a minute and talk." I led her to the chaise in her dressing area. I turned so I was facing her, and I took her hands in mine as we sat.

"I'd love to have my clothes with yours. What we need to decide is whether we should stay here or at my place. I don't like the idea of splitting our time, but if you do, I'll do it for a while. Eventually, we'll have to decide on one or the other. I just hate the idea of being apart from you."

"I don't want us to be apart either, but if you need space, I'm willing to give it to you."

"Why would I need space? I've been dreaming of you being mine for years. I want you with me all the time. My house is decent, but it isn't like yours. It's a place to live, and I'm open to fixing it up, finding a new house, or even building something else if you don't want to live in the compound. Or we can live here in this house."

"Be honest with me, please. Do you hate the thought of living here? If you do, I get it, and I'm willing to move wherever you want. Yes, I love my family and my house, but I want us to have our home, not mine. We can always visit, or we can build something new here if you want," she rambled quickly.

"*A stór*, darling, I truly want whatever will make you happiest, and I'm not just saying that. Do I love your house? Yes, it's great. Do I like the idea of being so close to your family all the time? I don't mind as long as we can lock them out when we want our alone time. The thought of you and our kids being safely behind these walls and having guards around day and night makes me extremely happy. Speaking of kids, we need to talk about those soon, but not this second."

"Are you sure you'd be comfortable and happy to live in this house? What would you do with yours? And yes, we need to talk about kids."

"I'll be happy anywhere as long as I'm with you. Mine I can rent out, sell, or keep to give to one of our kids someday. I have a retreat in the swamp not too far away, which I use when I want to totally disconnect and get away. I plan to keep it, but I don't expect you to ever go there."

"Is it because it's your guy's retreat, and no women are allowed?" she asked with a smile.

"No, I figured you wouldn't want to rough it out in the middle of the swamp."

"Why not? I can rough it. I'm not high maintenance all the time. You've never gone with us when we go back to Ireland. We've gone pretty rough there more than a few times."

"I wasn't insulting you, Ais. I'd be more than happy to show it to you. So, back to which house to live in, I think we've made our decision. We'll stay here in yours, and we'll decide later what to do with mine."

"I'm all for that plan, but I want you to tell me if you want to change or add anything. I know we built these houses when we came of age, but we should've thought about our future spouses and maybe waited to be sure what they wanted. We all assumed whoever we ended up with would want to live on the compound and in these houses. We were self-centered. So far, no one has objected, but it might happen."

"It might, but it'll be those couples' battles. I can't see myself wanting to change much, but if there's anything, I'll let you know."

"Yes, please do that. Now, what was it about kids you wanted to talk about?"

"You want to do it now?" I asked. She nodded. "Okay, I was curious to know how many kids you see us having."

"Why? Do you have a limit in mind?"

"Not a limit, but I do have a minimum, but it all hinges on you since you'll carry them unless we adopt or use a surrogate," I told her.

"Wow, okay, I always have seen myself having more than a couple, to be honest. I think it's because I grew up with four older brothers and all my cousins. Not having a loud tribe would be weird for me, but I'm willing to negotiate. My only firm thing is it has to be more than one. Only children seem so sad to me."

"Personally, for me as an only child, I agree it's sad because I was lonely, and if it weren't for your family being my playmates, it would've been worse. They were like the brothers and sisters I never had at home. Ideally, I'd like at least three kids, but it's up for debate. We can choose to foster or adopt if it helps, though having a couple of natural children would be great if possible."

Her smile made me feel warm inside. "Three would be my minimum, too, but I'm open to more in any capacity."

"Perfect. When you're ready to start working on the first one, let me know. I promise I'll give it my all," I told her with a wink. Then I kept going when her hand scooted up my thigh. "Behave, or I'll say, let's start right now," I warned her. I was so happy she and I agreed on how many to have.

"And why wouldn't I like that?" she asked as she scooted closer.

My heart skipped, then sped up. Was she serious? "Ais, you have no idea how much I want a baby with you. I've waited nine years for you. If I hadn't been such an idiot and just told you when you turned eighteen how I felt, we could have a house full of kids already. The image in my head of you pregnant with my baby is crystal clear to me. I want one now, but I don't want to rush you. I want you to want it as much as I do, and if it means I have to wait, then I will."

"Stair, I waited those same nine years and have the same regrets. I don't want to wait. I'm ready. And it so happens that in a couple of weeks, I'm due to renew my birth control shot. I get it every three months."

"Don't get it. If you're sure, then let nature take its course and don't renew. Who knows, we might be welcoming our first baby in the first couple of months of next year," I said instantly and hopefully.

"Perfect," she whispered as she gave me a heated look, which instantly turned me to thoughts of us practicing for the event.

I growled, and she giggled as I jerked her up onto my lap. She straddled me and pressed herself against my cock, which was beginning to harden just at the thought of being inside of her and impregnating her. I tugged her mouth to mine and kissed her. As we kissed, our hands were busy touching each other. I was in the process of lifting her top over her head when I heard a loud voice call out from inside the house.

"Where the hell are you two? You'd better not be fooling around. You have the folks at the house waiting impatiently to see you. Damn it, I told them not to send me. Put your clothes on and get your asses down here. I'll be in the kitchen. Christ," Declan yelled, and then we heard unintelligible grumbles.

Both of us groaned in frustration. Then, as we looked into each other's eyes, we burst out laughing. It would serve him right if we made him come find us. Sighing, I lowered her top back in place. She stood up and then gently patted the aching bulge in my pants. "I'll make it up to you later, big guy," she told my cock. Her silliness made me laugh harder as I reached out to cup her between her legs.

"Yeah, I'll make it up to you too, sweet kitty cat."

Our laughter rang out as we got ourselves together and then went downstairs. Entering the kitchen, we found him at the island. He gave us suspicious looks. "What's so funny? Please tell me you weren't actually having sex."

"No, but five minutes later and..." I trailed off.

"Shit, that's it. Next time, they can send someone else. Are you two done? If you're not, the family may revolt and storm the house soon."

"We're ready. Let's go before we change our mind, and I drag her back upstairs to ravish her."

"Duh, duh, duh, I can't hear you. Come on," he shouted as he stood up with his ears covered and walked toward the door.

We teased him all the way outside and into the golf cart he'd brought. They had them all over the compound since their houses weren't right up against each other, and Aisling's was at the back of the estate. The quick ride to the main house required him to uncover his ears so he could drive. We got our kicks teasing him the whole way. He was threatening to kill us by the time we made it.

We walked inside without knocking, and as soon

as we entered, I heard the sound of a ton of voices. It sounded like the whole family was there, but surely some were still at work. Although they had moved the headquarters from Jacksonville to St. Augustine just two months ago, so they were now merely miles from home. Checking my watch, I saw it was only four o'clock in the afternoon.

As we entered the kitchen, where all the voices seemed to be coming from, I saw I was wrong. The whole family was there. Thankfully, with the combination of a huge kitchen, a large eat-in area, and a massive island, they were able to fit all of them, even if not everyone could sit. When they saw us, Tiernan called out loudly.

"About time. What took you so long? You weren't fooling around, were you?"

Before I had a chance to say something smartass back, Aisling beat me to it. "Yeah, we were thinking about it. I hope you're happy. We were gonna try for *Daid* and *Mam's* second grandchild, but you people ruined it."

To say she shocked them was an understatement. Hell, she caught me off guard. Not that I cared that she said it. I just hadn't expected her to say anything. The whole room grew so quiet it was eerie. Then, like a switch was thrown, it exploded with their voices all talking at once. As everyone tried to be heard over each other, Cormac and Cyndi came rushing over to us. Cyndi was beaming with excitement, and Cormac was smiling, though I thought he was being cautious.

"I know you were only kidding, but know that when you two are ready, we can't wait. We'll take all the grandbabies you'll give us," her *mam* gushed.

"We will, but only when you're ready. We know you're just getting together and all and have a lot of things to figure out," was Cormac's more cautious response.

I glanced at Aisling, and I raised a brow at her. She knew what I meant, I hoped because she nodded and smiled. I answered them. "We're late because we were talking about where we wanted to live. She offered to move to my house or for us to get another house, but I think staying here in hers is the best idea. I mean, her place is great, and I have no firm attachment to mine, and being behind these walls makes it even better, in my opinion."

"Good, good, you have to think about security and comfort," Cormac said.

The others quieted down when we didn't answer them, and they listened to our conversation. "Then we were talking about how many kids we wanted and how we'd get them," Ais added.

"What do you mean, how you'd get them? Don't tell us we have to have the birds and bees talk with you two. I would've thought you knew the way to get those kids at your age. Don't tell us Alistair has no clue," Rory teased.

I gave him the middle finger. "I have a much better idea than you. In fact, if I recall correctly, your first self-pleasuring session—" I was cut off by him throwing an apple from the counter at my head. I caught it and took a bite as I grinned at him.

"We know the mechanics, thanks. What I meant was if we want them to be all ours naturally or if we might adopt or foster some. We're open to all the above. Then we talked about numbers, which isn't your business," Aisling told him.

"Okay, well, hopefully, it'll be more than one or two. You have to compete with the rest of us," Cian said with a grin as he tenderly and lovingly rubbed Miranda's pregnant belly. She was due in just over two months, and two months after her was Aidan and Karizma's baby.

"No worries, we plan to bring several to the clan. In fact, if we're lucky, we might see the first one next year," I said offhandedly.

Cyndi let out a squeal, and then she threw herself at Ais. Cormac's smile grew as he grabbed me and gave me a hug and back slap. The others were back to talking and shouting over each other. It was pandemonium. It took loud, sharp whistles to get them to calm down. Glancing around, I saw it was Darragh.

"I think we need to have a drink and celebrate this. And in case you haven't guessed it, *Mam* and the other ladies have been working on a feast for dinner tonight. I suggest we see what we can do to help and then stay out of the way when we get our parts done. Alistair, Ais, in case you couldn't tell, you've made the whole family happy. Plus, it means there's no escape for Alistair, even if he wanted to run."

And that was how we were welcomed home and announced our plans for the future—well, at least some of them. I still had to ask her to marry me, but I already had my plans in place for it.

Aisling: Chapter 16

You'd think with the threat hanging over my head, I'd be depressed, scared, and hiding behind the walls of the family compound. Wrong. I was actually super happy and was going about my day much the same as I would any other time. Sure, if I had to leave the compound, which was primarily to go to my office space at the new office in St. Augustine, I would have more than one or two guards with me. Most of the time, one of them was my ever-watchful and ultra-protective man.

The beauty was he didn't try to prevent me from doing my work. If he had a concern, he'd voice it, and we'd discuss it. If the risk were worth it, I'd leave the safety of home. If it weren't, I'd stay and do whatever I could from home. I thought we were doing an excellent job of compromising.

Another thing contributing to my happiness was that he was living with me full-time. It was wonderful to have someone to come home to at the end of the day, to share even small things like making dinner or watching a movie with, to talk about work and mundane things. Then, add the ability to go to bed each night with the one you love, and it was incredible.

The day after we got back from California, he went to his place, packed up the majority of his clothes, and brought them to the house. Over the next two days, he packed up other things he would want to bring later and was sorting through what to leave or get rid of. This was when he wasn't busy working on something he had going with the Hounds.

I wasn't sure what the job was, but it must have been important because I knew my brothers and cousins were spending a lot of time in the Command Center with him, Darragh, and some of the other Hounds. It wasn't often that the whole family was involved, but it did happen on rare occasions. I asked him what it was about, but all he would say was they were still determining if it was valid, and once he had all the information, he'd share. Since the other women had been given the same answer basically, I didn't push, but I was curious, to say the least.

Today, while he was busy with his work, I had to go into the main office. Or I should say, I wanted to go. With several of my cousins and a couple of my brothers going and all their security, I knew I'd be safe. Alistair agreed and sent me off with a kiss. I was happy he was staying behind because I wanted to plan something as a surprise for him, and it was hard to do when he could pop into the house at any moment.

The ride to work was entertaining when I rode with so many of my family and their guards. We were all laughing when we got out of the cars at the office. I grimaced when I saw paparazzi standing out on the main road with their telescopic lenses, taking our pictures. They needed to get a life. No one could possibly be interested in seeing us go in and out of work. If they did, they needed a life or medication.

I didn't waste time getting to work, although I said hello to the staff first. It had been a while since

I'd seen some of them. Most had made the move to the new office, and those who didn't, remained behind to work in the satellite one we left in Jacksonville. We didn't make the move to lose anyone and were happy we didn't. Settling down at my desk, I got busy.

I'd been at it for maybe a few hours when my desk phone rang. We had direct extensions people could call, or they called the main number, and a receptionist directed them to the appropriate person. Since I didn't get a heads-up call first, I guessed this was someone directly calling in. I was trying to think who it could be as I answered it. I was here so rarely it would be pure luck to get me. Those I dealt with regularly knew to call Carrie or had my direct cell phone number.

"Hello, Aisling speaking. How may I help you?" I asked pleasantly.

At first, I heard nothing, then a rasping sound. I was about to hang up, thinking it was an obscene phone caller, when a deep, somewhat mechanical-sounding voice finally spoke.

"Leaving California won't protect you, Aisling. You can run, but you can't hide. You'll pay. Tell your family retribution is at hand. I'll see you burn."

I gasped but had enough sense to say something. "Who is this? What have I or my family done to warrant retribution? You're the one who'll pay if you come near me or my family."

"That wreck should've taken you out. My men missed you. You should've stopped then, but you didn't."

"Stopped what?"

"You know! Don't act innocent. I won't let you ruin it!" the voice yelled. It sounded like a man's voice.

"Ruin what? You're not making any sense."

"It's a matter of family pride," he said before hanging up.

I sat there in shock for a minute or two before I took action. I picked up the phone again and called Darragh. He was here today, and we needed everyone else who was here together.

"Hey, Ais, you're bored already?" he asked pleasantly.

"Darragh, I need the family who's here in the office to meet ASAP."

"Why? What happened?" he barked, all humor gone.

"I had a very disturbing call. It was a man who made threats. I need to tell you guys, and then we can let the rest of the family know after we talk."

"Give me twenty minutes, and then meet me in the main conference room. I'll get the others rounded up."

I didn't bother to answer him, and it wouldn't have done me any good anyway because he'd already hung up. I sat there going over and over what the man said and how he sounded. I tried to recall if his voice was familiar. It was hard to tell with whatever he was doing to disguise it with the mechanical sound. After about fifteen minutes, I gave up.

Standing up on shaky legs, I went for the door. Since I was inside and in a building full of security personnel and measures, Creed hadn't been stationed at my door. A part of me wished he was. He gave me a sense of security, which I guess I took for granted, even though I was able to protect myself. I knew I should've called Alistair, but first, I wanted to let the others here know. The call made me fear I wasn't the only target. As soon as I warned them, I'd let him and those at home know. It would mean Stair either rushing here or me being sent home under heavy guard.

I was the first one in the conference room. It wasn't long before others began to stream in. They were all giving me concerned looks and asking what was up. Luckily, one of the first ones was Darragh, and he told them to wait until everyone was there. Glancing around the room, I counted and saw that all of us who came to the office today were here, but Darragh wasn't starting the meeting. I was about to ask why when Alistair marched through the door. *Daid*, Patrick, and Sean were on his heels. Alistair's eyes bored into mine. Oh shit, he wasn't happy. I had to fight not to sink under the table and hide. I guess I should've known Darragh would call him.

He came around the table and sat in the chair next to me. The others found open seats wherever they could. I bit my lip as I looked at him. He was staring at Dar in front of the room.

"I'm sorry, *mil*. I was going to call you as soon as I told everyone here. They might be at risk being in the building with me," I whispered.

"We'll talk about this later," was all he said, and he didn't bother to look at me when he said it.

My heart sank. Had I truly messed up that much? It wasn't a matter of me trying to hide anything from him. I weighed the primary needs and threats. Sure. I had time to call him, but I had no idea what he was involved in with his work, and it wasn't as if I was in immediate danger. I was in a secure building. What if he was doing something dangerous, and my calling him distracted him to the point he got hurt?

I was about to say more to him, but Darragh called us all to attention. The room was full of not only family members but our security guards and the enforcers. Wow, I must've really scared him. I didn't think I sounded that upset. What if it was all just an overreaction on all our parts?

"Aisling got a phone call not long ago. That's why I asked all of you here. Ais, I called Alistair then I asked Cody to pull up your call. We record all incoming and outgoing calls just in case. Cody, play it so we know what we're dealing with. It worried Ais enough to want us all to talk about it," Dar ordered.

It was surreal to sit there and hear myself talking, and it was upsetting to hear my caller's voice say all those things again. When the recording ended, it was quiet for all of three seconds max, and then they all erupted, talking loudly over each other—a typical conversation in the O'Sheeran family. I wasn't able to focus on what they were saying or asking because all of my attention was on Alistair. His face was taut, and I saw fire in his eyes. He had turned to face me, and one of my hands was now practically crushed by one of his.

"Why the fuck didn't you call me the second you got off the phone with this nut? Why did I have to hear about it from Dar? You got almost the whole family together but didn't think once of me. Am I your goddamn man or not?" he snapped. His hand tightened on mine.

I jerked it hard. He glanced down, and I think he didn't even realize he had a hold of me until I did. He let go. When he looked up at my face again, I fought not to cry. When I got angry, I did one of two things.

I screamed, or I cried. I was in the middle of deciding which one I wanted to do. Deep down, I was freaked out, and all I wanted was for him to hold me, but he was yelling at me and asking stupid questions. Of course, he was my man.

There was no way I wanted to cry in front of my family or the guards. Fuck it. I stood up and skirted his outreached hand, and I went straight up to Dar. He gave me a concerned look. "Thanks for throwing my ass under the bus. You can deal with his butt hurt. Let me know if I should be worried about dying or not," I hissed.

He reared back, stunned. I took the distraction of everyone talking and debating, and I shot for the door. Voices were calling me to come back and asking what was wrong, but I ignored them. I heard Alistair shout my name. I kept going. As soon as I got in the hallway, I tried to think of where to go. I needed to calm down before I could rationally talk to him or anyone. My office wasn't an option. It would be the first place they'd go. Whipping a U-turn, I went for the stairwell just steps away. I'd go downstairs to our private garage. It was secure, and no one would be there. I needed air. Being in there with all of them had gotten claustrophobic.

The stairwell door barely shut before I heard Alistair calling my name. I listened, and his calling my name moved further away. He was headed for my office. Slipping off my heels, I started down the steps. No way was I doing four flights in those. My luck, I'd stumble and fall down all four flights and break my neck. As I kept going, I took deep breaths to calm myself. I knew I'd have to face them and explain myself, but not yet. My heart was racing, and I was having a hard time catching my breath. Was this what a panic attack felt like? I'd never had one before.

Opening the door on the last level, I sucked in the fresh air. This was where we parked our private vehicles. We couldn't leave them on the other floors in the garage. I saw the two limos we came in this morning parked to the left. At the entrance, you had to enter a security code to get in, and there was always someone on duty. Sometimes, if our guards weren't needed inside, they'd hang out down here or with the attendant on duty.

Right now, they were all upstairs except the attendant. I wasn't sure who that was. I hadn't paid attention when we came in this morning. I kept my heels off as I paced. My breathing was becoming more normal, but I was still jumpy. The tears I was afraid to shed had dried up. I knew I wouldn't be able to stay here for long, but I needed to calm down and get a hold of myself. Alistair had upset me, but then I knew I had alarmed him by not telling him. It was never my intention to make him angry or to feel he wasn't important.

Not wanting to talk to anyone, I stayed back by the cars. It took me time to calm down enough to know I had to go back in and apologize for running out. No doubt they were all angry with me by now for leaving. I knew I wouldn't be able to go back up the stairs because the door was locked behind me, so I walked over to the elevator and entered my handprint to open it. As the door slid open, I jumped and cried out as I was almost bowled over by men rushing out of the elevator. They were scowling, but those scowls turned to relief, then to worry in a flash. One of them was Creed. He grabbed my arm and began to hustle me not in the elevator but toward one of the limos.

"What's gotten into you?" I asked as I tried to get loose.

"We've been going crazy trying to find you. We thought someone grabbed you. Stay next to me and do as I say. Call up and let them know we have her. They can try to rein in Alistair," he told Micah, Fallon's personal guard. The other one with him was Nolan, Declan's bodyguard.

"Just take me upstairs. I'll talk to Alistair myself."

"We're evacuating. We're the foreguards sent to make sure the cars are safe. The others are coming," he explained in a rush as he practically dragged me to the limo. Thank goodness I still had my heels off.

They took out the scanners they used to check for bombs. Why would they need those when the cars had been here in the secure garage? As they worked, I was tucked behind a large cement column and told to stay. I didn't argue. They were scaring me. I'd never seen them like this. What I wouldn't give to have my purse with my gun. I didn't even have my phone. I left it in my office when I went to the conference room. I had been more rattled than I thought.

I split my time between watching them and the elevator door. I jumped when the door opened unexpectedly, and out came a large group. I recognized several of my family members, along with a couple of guards. In the front, rocketing ahead of them all was Alistair. He had a spooked expression on his face. I stepped out from behind the column. He zeroed in on me right away, then ran over to me.

Before I was able to apologize for running out, he

had me lifted off the ground in his arms, and his mouth was on mine. He kissed me desperately. I moaned in response and gripped the back of his neck. I had no idea how long we kissed before we stopped and became aware of our audience.

"Don't ever run off like that again, *mo ghràdh*. You scared the hell out of us, out of me. I'm gonna tan that ass of yours," he growled in my ear.

Was it bad of me to look forward to a spanking? Probably in this situation, but I grew wet at the thought. *Not the time or place, Ais, focus,* I chided myself.

"I'm sorry. I was on my way back up when Creed, Nolan, and Micah came out and said everyone was evacuating. They wouldn't say why."

"Let's get everyone in the cars, and then we'll tell you. The employees have all been sent home." He gently herded me toward the limos. The others were all watching us.

"They have? Boy, that was fast."

"How long do you think you've been down here?" Aidan asked as he came up to us. He didn't appear happy.

"I don't know, fifteen minutes or so."

"It's been forty-five minutes. Ais!"

"What!?"

"In the car. Talk later," Darragh barked.

We divided up between the two, and then those guards not riding with us got in the other vehicles. It wasn't unexpected to find Alistair getting in beside me. Into our car climbed Aidan, *Daid*, Darragh, Cathal, Sean, and Patrick.

"I'm so sorry. I know I shouldn't have run off like I did. I got upset, and I let it get to me. I needed time alone. I couldn't breathe, and the garage seemed like a place where I'd be safe and still get air. I lost track of time and had no clue I was gone as long as I was. Can someone tell me why we evacuated? Surely the call didn't warrant this extreme of a response."

"We'll talk about you leaving later. Right now, we have other things to discuss. We didn't leave because of the call. It was what happened right after you got up and left. A package was delivered to the lobby. It was addressed to you. With the security measures in place, no one brought it up to your office. Thank *Dia*. They called security, and they called me," Darragh explained.

"What was in the package?" I asked fearfully. The way they acted and checked over the cars made me wonder if it was a bomb. But if it was, why would the cops let everyone leave? It didn't make sense.

"The security guys scanned it through the x-ray machine, and it didn't show anything resembling a bomb, so we opened it. Inside were pictures and a note. They were pictures of you with your face X'd out and their edges burned. The note said you would be the first to pay and for the rest of us to say goodbye to you," Alistair said hoarsely. I gasped. He hugged me tightly to him.

"Who the hell is this freak? What in the world did we do to make him target us, me? Please tell me the cops are dusting it for prints and DNA. The cameras should've gotten a look at him. Whoever he is, we need to find him and put a stop to his bullshit," I snapped. Instead of feeling scared, I was angry.

"Martin is on the way with his CSI team. Cian stayed with a couple of others to meet him. They'll make sure Cian gets home safely, and if there's anything to identify the sender, they'll find it. We're giving them a copy of the call you got. We felt it was safer to just have everyone go home for the rest of the day. Our worry is having you out in the open. We were searching the whole damn building for you. Why none of us thought to look in the garage, I don't know. You left your phone in your office!" Aidan snapped at me.

"I'm sorry. I didn't even notice I didn't have it with me until I was about to come back up. I'm not stupid enough to go outside where I was exposed. The garage is secure and has solid cinder blocks except for a few small windows, which have bulletproof glass if you recall."

"So! What if someone had gotten inside the building somehow and snatched you? Or got past the guard at the entrance to the garage and grabbed you?" Cathal argued.

They were getting themselves riled up, and there was no need. My *daid* wasn't saying a word. He had his hands resting on his knees, and he was watching me. He was across from me. I reached over and placed my hand on top of his.

"I'm sorry, *Daid*. I never meant to worry any of you. I was upset, and I didn't want to let everyone see me cry. It's not an excuse. It's my explanation for better or worse. I'm glad no one was hurt, and you sent them home. What are we gonna do next? We can't have everyone work from home indefinitely. There are meetings and other stuff we all have."

"We'll talk about it when we get home. We'll figure something out," Patrick answered for them.

"Okay. I wish I knew who was doing this. I thought about it when I was cooling off, and I swear I have no clue who it could be."

"What about Chris?" Cathal asked.

"I might think it is if the caller hadn't said his men should've gotten me when the wreck happened. Chris could've been killed if it was his men. Too risky. And Chris's anger is against me, not the whole family. The caller mentioned my family's retribution is at hand, and he won't let me ruin something that, to him, is a matter of family pride. It can't be Chris."

"I have to agree. It's got nothing to do with Chris. That would make it too easy," Darragh said quietly.

The rest of the ride passed in uneasy silence as we all were lost in our own thoughts. Stair didn't let go of me. I knew when I got home, and the whole clan was together I was in for an ass-chewing, and I deserved it. However, I was more worried about finding out who was responsible for this and eliminating the threat. The last thing I wanted was for them to hurt one of my family members or someone innocently caught in the crossfire.

❦❦❦

We were all gathered at the parents' house in the massive family room. When we made it home, everyone there was anxious and asking questions left and right. *Mam* and the others couldn't stop hugging us in between chewing me out. We held off on having a family meeting until Cian made it home to join us. When he arrived, he said Martin had taken the box back to the station, and he'd let us know if the techs found anything.

Alexis was keeping Khloe busy and watching baby Ronan for us. I still felt awful for worrying so many of them at the office. Alistair had been abnormally quiet. I apologized to him several times and begged him to talk to me. He kept telling me he was fine, but he wasn't. Had my childish behavior made him rethink if I was the one for him? The thought he changed his mind made me sick to my stomach. Surely he wouldn't walk away after one incident, would he?

I was sitting on the floor with my back against the side of the couch, and my arms curled around my legs. I was miserable, and all I wanted to do was go to bed and cry. Stair was standing across the room, talking in hushed tones to Darragh and *Daid*. I caught them casting frowns my way a few times. Finally, I had enough. I scrambled to my feet.

"Alright, just spit it out. I know you're all pissed at me. I get it. Alistair, you won't even talk to me, and the huddle you three are in tells me there's more to come. Do it. Tell me you're done with me. Just say something!" I shouted.

I saw shocked expressions all around me, but I only cared about one person at the moment. His eyes widened, and then he was striding across the room to me. I braced myself for his recriminations and rejection. He stopped less than a foot away. His hands came up to cup my face.

"Why would I be done with you?" he asked softly.

"Because you don't want someone like me to be part of your life. I'm too rash, too hot-headed, and too immature. You realize you made a mistake, and you, my *daid*, and Darragh are trying to figure out how to tell me. Just do it."

"*Chíost*, she's lost her mind," I heard Rory mutter. The others shushed him.

"Don't shush me. She has if she thinks he'll ever not want her," he defended himself.

"For once in his life, Rory is right, *leanabh*. I'll never not want you. Yes, I was upset with you earlier. You scared the hell outta me. The reason I'm talking to your dad and Dar isn't me trying to find a way to tell you I made a mistake. I love you, and I always will. The best day of my life was the one when you finally admitted you love me. I'm trying to decide how to tell you what I think needs to be done next."

Relief flooded me, and my knees weakened. He swept me into his arms and held me to his chest. I snuggled into him and inhaled his comforting scent. "Thank you, *Dia*. I love you too," I whispered to him. He chuckled as he squeezed me.

"Crazy ass woman," he muttered in my ear.

"Alright, why don't you just tell all of us what idea you came up with?" Declan asked my man.

Alistair eased back and went to the corner of one of the couches. He sat down, bringing me down to sit on his lap.

"Until we find whoever is making these threats, I want to take Ais somewhere he and his men can't find her. It appears since he's only targeted her and all contact has been made with her, he either blames her more than the rest, or he's obsessed with her for a reason. That being said, we think she's at the greatest risk. I want her out of sight and safe," Alistair said.

"Okay, so why all the side talking? Take her on vacation. We'll make sure the others are protected," Shane exclaimed.

"It's not fair for me to run and leave everyone else behind," I protested.

"See what I mean," Alistair said to Dar and *Daid*.

"*Cailín leanbh*, baby girl, we can secure the other women and kids. You're the one the most at risk. It's not running. It's being smart. I want you to go with Alistair and let him protect you while we figure out who's behind this and why. Once the threat is neutralized, he'll bring you home. You two can get on with your lives and give me and your *mam* those *gariníonacha*, grandbabies we want," he said with a smile. I had to smile back.

The whole family was watching me, nodding their heads. As much as I hated to leave, the thought of them being in more danger if I stayed decided it for me. I half-turned so I could see Alistair's face. He was watching me closely.

"Alright, where do you want to take me? I'll go."

"You will?"

"I will."

"No matter where I want us to go?"

I hesitated for a moment, wondering if I was walking into a trap, but then I agreed, "No matter where you want to go."

He glanced at Darragh. "We'll get our things together, and I'll take her out of one of the tunnels as soon as it's dark. If he or any of his men are watching, they won't see us. You know how to get a hold of me."

"Wait, where are we going?" I asked.

"It's better if we keep it on a need-to-know basis. I'll tell you when we get to our house."

"Is all this secrecy necessary?"

"Maybe not, but I'd rather do it than not. Trust me?"

"I trust you."

His smile made me happy. We spent the next hour with the family, purposefully not talking about what was going on. I knew as soon as we left, they'd be all over it. When he said it was time to go to the house, everyone hugged and kissed us. As he led me outside, I wondered how long we'd be gone and where I was headed.

Alistair: Chapter 17

"You want me to pack what?" Aisling asked.

We were back at the house, and I was having her get her things out to go in my rucksacks, which I'd pulled out. Where we were going wasn't a place to bring a suitcase or your best luggage, so she was staring at me in confusion.

"I said pack boots and long pants. Make sure to bring jackets and long-sleeved tops too. If you have a hat, bring it. No need to worry about bringing girly stuff or fancy clothes."

"Just where are you taking me, Stair?"

"You said you've roughed it and would again, and you wanted to see my retreat. Well, you're getting your chance."

"You're taking me out in the swamp to hide me. I guess that answers my question of whether I should bring my laptop or anything. I was hoping I'd be able to work wherever we went. Okay, I need to make calls and let Carrie and some others know I'll be unreachable." She went for her cell phone on the bed. I grabbed it before she picked it up.

"No, we can't tell anyone you're leaving. There's no need to call Carrie or anyone else. You'll be able to work. I said it's rough and in the swamp. I didn't say it was without all the amenities. I have a generator, and it'll allow us to work. The satellite phone has an uplink, so anything you need to send can be sent, and it'll be encrypted so no one can trace it. It might not be as easy as you typically have it, but it is doable. It's my retreat, but I've had to work from there at times too. Although I'm hoping you'll take it easy with me. We can spend time just the two of us and get started on that baby we talked about. Or at least get in more practice for the real event," I said with a wink.

She took me by surprise when she laughed and then came sashaying over to me. "Stair, we've already been practicing, remember? Or have you forgotten? If you have, then I need to up my efforts so you won't forget so easily."

I tugged her up against me. "Oh, I haven't forgotten a thing. And we can never do enough practicing, in my opinion."

She answered me by rubbing herself against me. The images in my head of her naked and begging me to take her had me hardening. The feel of her rubbing across my growing cock made me groan. We didn't have time to get distracted right now, but I wished we could. Thankfully, the drive wasn't too terribly far. I promised myself as soon as we got there and settled. I'd strip her bare and have her over and over.

Giving her a quick kiss, I smacked her ass and then pushed her away. "No time for play. Pack, then we gotta leave, and then after we get there and settle, you can seduce me all you want."

She gave me a mock pout but got back to work. I had supplies, even clothing, at the retreat, so I didn't have much to pack. On top of that, I had an arsenal. Darragh, Cormac, and I agreed it was the best place to take her for a couple of reasons. The fact that it wasn't well known and that even someone who knew I was with her couldn't trace it to me was one. The bigger reason was it was set up for an invasion. I'd always planned that if anyone came after me for the work I did, I'd be ready for them. We took every precaution, but there were no guarantees in this life. Anyone coming after her there would be in for the rudest awakening of their lives, and they wouldn't walk away.

Once we were packed, we went into the tunnels through the secret entrance in her house. It was a distance to the exit where a car would be waiting. It would be nondescript and not registered to the family or their guards. When we got to the CC, I found Darragh, her brothers, and *daid* waiting on us. I wasn't surprised.

"What're you guys doing down here?" she asked as she hugged Cormac.

"Just wanted to see you off and be sure you had everything. We'll work on this. I have a feeling this person is going to get sloppy, especially if you drop out of sight. We don't want you to stress yourself silly. Enjoy your time with Alistair. *Dia* knows you won't get peace and quiet around here," he teased her.

I chuckled. "That's for damn sure. What was I thinking, wanting a big family?" I joked.

This earned me punches from her brothers and Dar and then a hug from Cormac while the others hugged her. They had a golf cart waiting. I swear they must own stock in a cart factory. Right before taking off, Darragh softly whispered. "You update her on the Bragans' request. As soon as we know for sure, I'll let you know. Take care of her."

"You know I will."

We waved and then took off. With the cart, it

wasn't long before we were at our exit. The tunnels ran all over the place. If you didn't know the map, you'd be lost, which was a plus. I went first to be sure the way was clear. Seeing nothing out of place, I helped her out and then got the bags to the car. Packing them away, we were off.

We both remained quiet on the drive. I kept watch to ensure we weren't being followed, and she did the same. Sometimes, I forgot she'd had the same training as her brothers and male cousins—all the girls had. She was lethal when needed, but I just hoped she wouldn't ever have to be. That was my job.

The way to my place wasn't accessible. You either had to fly in or take a boat. I parked the car where I kept my boat and transferred the bags to it. She was looking around curiously, but so far, she hadn't run off screaming.

"Ready?" I asked.

"Ready. Show me your hideaway, swamp man," she giggled.

I growled as I helped her into the boat, and we set off. It was dark, so the light on the boat was all we had to navigate by, but I knew my way around this whole area. It didn't take too long to get to my property and tie up to the dock. The wildlife was singing all around us. Walking up to the dark cabin, I scanned for signs of alligators or other wild animals.

Ushering her inside, I lit a lamp and then got ready to get the generator started so we'd have light and other comforts. There were times I didn't bother with it, but I didn't think she'd appreciate it.

"I've got to go out back and start the generator. I'll be back."

"I'm good."

I kept a huge supply of fuel for the generator, and it wasn't too long before I had it going. A quick patrol around the cabin showed no one had been there. I had ways of knowing if anyone had been messing around it. None of them were tripped. There were no trespassing signs all over the place, but that wasn't a deterrent to some.

When I walked back inside, I saw a fire in the fireplace. The fridge was empty, naturally, but there was other canned food in the pantry. Tomorrow, I'd get more food supplies dropped in.

"I see you thought I was kidding about roughing it, or maybe what I call rough is a three-star stay. I meant it. We camped in basic tents or under the stars with no modern conveniences. I can catch fish and clean them, build fires, make temporary shelters, you name it. I'm the ultimate Girl Scout," she said with a grin as she came over to me.

"I see that. I know the guys have done it, but I just didn't see you, Cara, and Shiv doing it. And I sure don't see your moms and Seerie doing it."

"Are you kidding? *Mamó* is an expert. Who do you think taught us a lot of it? And our *mamaí*, moms are expert fire makers and cooks. Did your *daid* teach you all of your skills?"

"He did. He loved to go out and be one with nature. He missed the Highlands, but he knew it was better for his family to be here in the States, so he found ways to get out in nature here. Alright, let me give you the tour."

It wasn't a huge cabin, although unlike most, it had more than one room. This one had a bathroom, a kitchen and living room combo, two bedrooms, and a loft. With the generator on, the water could be pumped inside and heated. Give it time, and we'll be able to take a hot bath.

As I was explaining where things were, she interrupted, "When was the last time you were here?"

"About six months ago, why?"

"It's so clean. There's no dirt, and the bedding seems clean and fresh. I expected it to be musty. Humidity alone would do it."

"I'll let you in on a secret. I have a neighbor out here who keeps an eye on things for me and makes sure it's clean. I might've told him I was planning to come out tonight, and he came and put clean bedding on the main bed."

"I thought no one could know we were leaving or where we were going except a few family members. Do all the guys at home know of this place?"

"Only Darragh and a couple of others know where it is. As for Casper, he doesn't talk to most people. He likes to be left alone. He won't tell anyone. He's spent his whole life exploring and living out here. I asked him once why here and not in the Everglades. He said there were too many drug dealers there for his liking."

She laughed. "I've gotta meet him. Do you think I'll get a chance this time?"

"It's likely. He usually checks in after I arrive to be sure everything is good. I pay him to be the groundskeeper. It helps him have a steady income, and he likes to help out. He'd do it for free, but I won't let him."

"You're just a big softie, aren't you?"

I gave her a menacing look and stalked toward

her. We were standing in the loft. She let out a shriek and took off. I admit, I had fun stalking her through the cabin. I let her think she was getting away until I got her to where I wanted her. The cabin was still chilly, so I waited until we were near the fire, and then I tackled her. I took her gently down to the rug in front of the fireplace. It was made out of black bear fur. It had been killed by some hunter years ago. I found it in a second-hand store and thought it was a shame for something this beautiful to be gathering dust. I personally wouldn't hunt an animal just for its fur, but I'd preserve it. Hunting for food was a different story.

I growled like a bear as I attacked her mouth and then her neck. We were alone, and the need to hold off on making love to her was past. She moaned as I nibbled her ear, then down her neck to the edge of her shirt. She'd put on a flannel shirt and jeans along with boots before we left. Yeah, Aisling O'Sheeran actually owned flannel. Wouldn't the public die to learn that?

"It's time to pay the penalty," I told her.

"What penalty?"

"The one for scaring the hell outta me earlier today at the office. For thinking for a second, I'd be angry enough to give you up. For not calling me as soon as you got that call. And for tempting me at the house when we were getting packed. You've been a naughty girl, and it's time to pay. I promise, in the end, you'll enjoy it, but until I decide you've had enough, don't plan to get any rest."

She gave me a sexy smile as she raised her hands over her head. "Well then, put me in the penalty box, coach. I'm all for seeing how you penile-lize me," she cracked up, laughing at the last bit.

I bit her tit through the fabric. She yelped. I rolled onto my side so I had a hand free and could reach her shirt. I slowly started to unbutton it. She reached down to help. I slapped her hands.

"No. You keep those up there. I won't be rushed."

"But I thought you wanted sex. You were all for it back at the house."

"I was, and I am, but I can control myself. I wonder if you can. Who do you think will break and beg first?" I taunted her. I knew she was competitive, just as I was. A battle of wills would be exciting. In the end, we'd both win.

A gleam of determination came to her eyes. "Bring it on, but so you know, I get to torture you too. I won't help you take off my clothes, but everything else is fair game."

"As long as there's no self-gratification. You can't get yourself off to ease your desire. That would be cheating."

"No self-gratification on either side," she warned. I nodded in agreement. "Deal," she said.

She let me unbutton her all the way before she moved. I was in a pullover. She grabbed the bottom hem and inched it up. I let her get it to my upper chest before I went back to hers. She gave me a glare. I lifted her off the rug far enough to work her shirt off, then lay her back down. She pushed my wandering hands away from her bra and tugged my shirt the rest of the way off.

Back and forth, we alternated, not only removing each other's clothes but teasing with touches, kisses, and bites. By the time we were both naked, I was more than rock hard, and she was slick. I knew it would be tough to hold out, but seeing her laying there with the fire light on her skin and seeing her beautiful body all aroused and ready for mine was tougher than I imagined. I prayed like hell she'd break first. After all, I had my male pride to defend, and this was supposed to be a punishment for what she did.

She took me off guard when she launched herself at me. I let her take me over onto my back. I thought she'd kiss me, but instead she latched onto my nipples and sucked. I don't know about other men, but mine were sensitive. Growing up, getting into fights with the O'Sheeran boys had been hell because they liked to give each other nipple cripplers. I learned early to fight dirty. As I got older, I accidentally discovered they were sensitive, not just to pain. Most women never thought of touching a man there, but Ais wasn't one of them. She'd figured out quickly I was sensitive, and if done right, it turned me on.

I fought not to moan. I let her go at it for a minute or two, and then I went after hers. She wasn't able to keep her moans quiet. It became a game of back and forth. The closer she drove me to lose control and beg, the harder I pushed to have her do it first. We were both panting, groaning, and moaning messes. I had no idea how long we'd been at it, but it seemed like hours. My cock was ready to burst. I was dripping as she stroked it. Her pussy was soaked as I finger fucked her. We were both gritting our teeth to stop ourselves from coming first. Lord knows who would've won if we both didn't add another level to it at the exact same time.

We were on our sides, facing each other. I had no idea what she was about to do until, at the same time that I eased my finger into her asshole, she slipped a wet finger into mine. I reared up in shock. It burned and felt foreign. I was about to tell her no when she shook her head. "Try it. Please."

I thought about it for a few moments, then reluctantly conceded. "Fine, but if I say enough, we're done."

"Swear."

I resumed thrusting in and out of her two holes. She was working my cock with one hand and slowly working her finger on the other in and out of my ass. I was about to tell her to stop when she hit something inside of me, and I jerked and gasped. It was all I could do not to come. She gave me a smirk as she kept stroking the spot. I sped up and rubbed across her G-spot. She moaned long and hard.

"F-fuck, I take it that's my prostrate."

"It is. Do you like it more?"

"Hell yeah, so this is what all the hype is about. Shit, I never knew," I muttered.

"It is. You ready to give up?"

"Nope. Are you?"

"Nope."

I was sweating it as we both increased our torture. In desperation, I rubbed her clit with my thumb as I thrust and kissed her hungrily. She cried out as she came. I thought she'd stop working me when she did, only she didn't. As she came, I followed a few heartbeats later. I pumped my load onto her stomach.

I was panting hard when we both stopped coming. We eased our fingers out and lay there. I took long enough to regain feeling in my legs, and then I got up. She made a protesting sound, but I kept going. When I came back with a wet towel, I cleaned her stomach and then her hand. I washed mine in the bathroom.

You'd think that with as hard as I came, I'd be spent, but I wasn't. My cock was still hard. When she saw it, she moaned. Tossing the towel aside, I flipped her over onto her stomach, jerked up her hips, dropped to my knees, and then thrust inside of her. She wailed and fisted the fur beneath her. I bit her shoulder as I rammed in and out of her. I was wild with the need not only to make her come again and take me with her but to dominate her and fill her with my cum.

"It's too much," she cried out.

"Am I hurting you?" I grunted out.

She hesitated before saying, "No, but it's too much."

I kept pounding. Latching onto her nipples, I tugged and twisted them, causing her to cry out louder, but at the same time, she got wetter.

"No, it's not. I'm gonna keep fucking you until you can't move and you're so full of my cum, you'll leak for days. You'll never think I don't want you or keep me in the dark about a threat again. By the time we leave here, I plan to have my first baby growing inside of you, Ais," I snarled.

She contracted hard around me, and then she was thrusting back to meet mine. "Yes, oh *Dia*, yes. Give me your cock and cum. Fuck me harder. I want your baby, Stair. Give it to me."

I roared as I sped up. My heart was thundering as I literally fucked her into the rug. She was screaming and pleading as I brought us both to the edge then we tipped over into fucking nirvana. I came so hard I couldn't see. She was wringing the cum out of me as she clenched me over and over. By the time we stopped orgasming, we were senseless heaps on the floor. I floated like I was having an out-of-body experience. Something which had never happened to me before.

ᘓᘓᘓ

I listened to Aisling laugh as she talked to Casper. He'd come to check on me as I expected the day after we arrived. That was four days ago, and he was back again. He and Ais had hit it off. He kept telling her she could live with him in his cabin and leave me to rot. Lucky for him, he was seventy, and I wasn't too worried she'd leave me, not after the other night. We'd been in subspace for a long time before we recovered. When we did, I made slow, passionate love to her.

We'd been having sex day and night. We were both determined to get her pregnant. Even if the birth control shot wasn't fully worn off, I was hopeful my sperm was potent enough to still knock her up. A part of me wanted to have my ring on her finger first, but with the stuff going on, I hadn't gotten to ask her like I planned. When we weren't enjoying each other, and not just sex-wise, we were both working. I'd told her about the Bragans' request for the Hounds. Her response wasn't too far off from what I expected.

She was staring at me with her mouth hanging open. I saw disbelief written on her face.

"Stair, there's no way Chris is behind this. I admit he can be an asshole and insensitive, and I'm mad at him for the way he's acting about us, but I just don't see him being involved in something so heinous. Are you sure the women and girls have been taken? Could it be that the Bragans are trying to stir things up?"

"Ais, we're looking at all possibilities. You might

think I want Chris to be guilty, but I don't. I don't want anyone we know to be involved in that kind of shit. But if they've been taken and he or someone in his family is behind it, you know what it means. The same goes for the Bragans. We're making no assumptions that they're innocent in this. The one worry we have is that they somehow know the Hounds are tied to your family, which seems impossible, but we're even checking into that, too. Darragh and the dads don't believe they know or are doing it to cause trouble."

"Why not? I don't know them as well as I do Chris's family. They keep more to themselves. What if they want to eliminate the Brynes so they can take over their territory and businesses?" she asked, sounding hopeful.

"The heads of the Bragan family came to Cormac, Darragh, Patrick, and Sean not long ago. They want to go legit like your family. They asked for their help and guidance on how to do it. They want to maintain control of their area and to protect those there while offloading the illegal stuff without opening it up to worse people than them. You know there are much worse mobster families and non-mobster people out there. Ones without any moral code."

She'd been surprised by that revelation, too, but she was still holding out hope that the intel about the Brynes was wrong and that either no one had been taken or someone else was doing it. For her sake, I hoped she was right.

"Hey, are you bringing those drinks? If not, good, that means I can steal her away without a fight," Casper called loudly from the small front porch.

I lifted up the tray of drinks I'd been making and walked outside. I sat it down on the small wooden table I had out there. They were both grinning at me. I narrowed my gaze on him.

"Listen, don't make me have to kill you and leave your body for a gator to eat or a bear to use as a rug."

He scoffed. "Boy, the gators and bears are my friends. I have nothing to worry about. You're the one who should be scared. Are you sure you want to tie yourself to this one for the rest of your life?" he asked her.

"Casper, as much as I'd like to take you up on your sweet offer, I just know I couldn't keep up with you. Besides, he's grown on me over the years."

He smiled. "True, I am a lot of man to handle, so I guess he'll get to keep you. But if you change your mind or he gets out of line, you let me know."

"I will," she told him before kissing him on the cheek. I swear he lit up. He was a crusty old bastard who didn't like many people. Most would call him a recluse. It took me years to get him to talk to me, yet she had him wrapped around her little finger after one visit.

We kicked back and enjoyed our drinks while talking about this and that. She was telling him about her work with the winery. He knew I was in the security business but not the specifics. As much as I trusted him, it was better if he didn't know.

The sun was beginning to go down, and the bugs were coming out. Bugs and Florida were a given no matter the time of day or year. The frogs were starting to serenade each other and us. I was about to ask him if he would stay for dinner when the satellite phone rang. We'd set up a time to check in with the family. This wasn't it. She and I both tensed and exchanged glances.

"Don't you two think you should get that? It's

probably about whoever you're hiding from," he said casually.

"Hiding? We're not hiding?" she said.

"Girlie, I'm old, not stupid. Your man hasn't stopped scanning the area. He's always security conscious, but I saw those new traps and warning systems he's set up since you got here. You're here for more than a retreat or time alone."

"Excuse me," I told him as I answered the call. "Hello."

"You need to get your asses back here ASAP. We know who's behind the attempts and threats to Ais. We'll explain when you get here," Darragh said.

"We'll be there within an hour or so. I have company I'll have to say goodbye to. Or do I need to have her back sooner?"

"That should be fine. We've found out a lot, and it's crazy. As far as we know, the person behind it has no idea where you are. Come in the way you left just to be safe."

"Got it. See you soon."

As I hung up, I saw Casper was on his feet. "Get her outta here. I'll make sure the cabin is shut down and sealed up. Maybe the next time I see ya, you can tell me what this was all about. Take care of her."

He gave me a firm handshake, then a back slap. He hugged Aisling and gave her a kiss on the cheek before she did the same to him. We hurried inside to get our things. In case we had to leave in a rush, we'd kept most of our stuff packed in the rucksacks, which made packing quick and easy. Within ten minutes, we were headed to the boat. Casper stood on the porch, waving at us as we took off.

Later, back at the spot where I parked the car, I stowed the boat, and we loaded it up. The compound wasn't far away, so we were on track to make it within the allotted hour. As we sped toward home, I held her hand and kept my head on a swivel. Just because they didn't think the person after her was nearby or knew where we'd been, I wasn't risking her by not staying alert. As the location of the hidden exit we'd used to leave came into sight, I breathed a sigh of relief. Just a tad farther, and she'd be safe. Then, I'd be free to go on the hunt.

Aisling: Chapter 18

The whole way home, I was on pins and needles, wondering who was behind the threat, wreck, and fire. I was impatient to get there, but at the same time, I hated to leave the cabin. It was so relaxing to be there. I enjoyed meeting and talking with Casper, too. We'd have to go back again soon. The journey back through the tunnel was quick. The cart was where we'd left it, or someone had returned one there.

We went straight to the tunnel, which led to the main house. I had no doubt the family would be gathered in the kitchen or family room. It wasn't late, so no worries about anyone being asleep unless it was Ronan. It was still too early for it to be Khloe's bedtime. As we entered the house, Shane was standing there waiting for us. There was more than one secret door in the house from the tunnels, but this was the centrally located one. The others were mainly in the bedrooms.

"They're all in the kitchen. Come on," was all he said.

We followed him, not that we couldn't guess where they were based on the noise. When we entered, we were both greeted warmly. As usual, there were hugs and kisses before we were allowed to get down to business. Checking out the room, I saw Khloe wasn't there, but Alexis was. I wondered who was with her because *Mamó* was in the room, too, along with Martin,

Cody, and Brayden.

I worked at not getting distracted by the smell of food cooking. There would be time to fill my belly later. A chair was pulled out, and I was gently pushed into it. Alistair remained standing with the rest of the men.

"Okay, we're here. Mind telling us what you found out?" Stair asked, getting straight to the point.

"In a minute. We hate to bring you back so abruptly, but we can't be sure how long we have before they might strike again. Cody and his team found out who was behind what happened to Ais and the fire at Maeve's. Beloved, why don't you tell them the backstory first?" Patrick asked his wife with a tender smile.

I was startled. Why would Maeve be the one to tell us rather than Patrick or one of the other men, even Cody?

Maeve looked tired as she gave us a weak smile. "You're wondering why I'm telling the story. The reason is because this whole thing is all my fault," she said sadly. An automatic denial was on my lips, but I was beaten to it.

"Like hell it is! None of this is your fault, and I don't want to hear you say it again. It's all that bastard's fault," Patrick snapped. The others were all muttering darkly. I felt lost.

"I agree. I can't see this as being your fault, Maeve. Just tell us," Alistair said compassionately. She cleared her throat before starting. Her voice was low as she did.

"Believe it or not, this all started over forty years ago. When I met Patrick, my parents were still alive. The older kids recall my mother being around when they were little..." she paused. It was difficult for her to get whatever this was out.

"I don't remember her, but I do remember you talking about her," I stated, hoping to ease her tension. She gave me a grateful smile and nodded.

"The thing we never told any of you is that the reason she was the only grandparent on my side wasn't because my father was dead." This caused murmurs to break out from us kids. The older adults, of course, weren't surprised.

"The reason we never talked about him is because he wasn't a part of our lives. My father was a cruel, abusive bastard who beat Mom and me. She ran away with me more than once when I was growing up, but he'd always found us and dragged us back. The punishments were terrible when he did. When I turned eighteen, I tried to get her away from him for good a few times, but he always found ways to get her back, and like when I was a kid, the beatings were worse.

"When I brought Patrick to meet my parents, my father showed his true colors. I hadn't said anything about how he was, but Patrick guessed it right away. Suffice it to say, we took Mom with us that day, and he was told never to come near us again. He was frightened enough that we thought he'd do it, and that would be the end of it. Later, we heard he'd relocated to the other side of the country. He never attempted to contact or come near us, so our goal was accomplished. After my mom died, we stopped caring where he was or even if he was alive. That was a mistake."

At this point, Patrick took over because Maeve was too tearful to do it. "What we didn't care to find out and should've done was when he relocated, the son of a bitch ended up marrying a much younger woman. They ended up having a son. From what we've discovered, the son grew to be an abusive man, too. The family Maeve's father married into was a small family with a local winery in California, which, over the years, has grown into a larger, more profitable one. He might've been a bastard, but he had business smarts. He took over the helm of the business since there was no son in their family. The winery has attained some recognition over the past forty years." He paused to let what he'd just said sink in. I knew immediately what happened.

"A winery in California... That's why Maeve's Cellars was targeted. But why wait all these years to come after the family? I assume, based on the story, it's Maeve's half-brother who's behind these attacks. Why does he care now?" I asked.

"Why he cares, we don't know. As for why now, we think it's because Maeve's Cellars is growing and making a bigger name for itself. The rumors about the new wines you're developing and how they'll win awards will impact other smaller wineries. The recognition of putting Temecula even more on the map as a great place to grow wines is a big factor, too. The fact it's run by our family and technically named for and was bought for his sister is too much, we believe." Darragh was the one to add this part.

Silence reigned for a long minute or so before Alistair broke it. "Alright, so we know who, and we can guess at least partially why. How did you figure this out, and where does this leave us? Do we know where he is or anything about his next moves?"

Cody answered him. "It was the IP addresses on the dark web. I finally unraveled them and found out where those messages were originating from. I don't know if he has the smarts to do it or if someone is working for him who does, but he did it the right way. It led me to California and from there to his family winery. He wasn't very smart in sending them from there. He should've used the internet at a coffee shop or someplace that was public, but luckily for us, he didn't. I found out his connection to Maeve when I began to dig into him.

"As for his next moves, the chatter is getting worse and uglier. There's now ranting about how you are ruining his business and must be stopped. He even dropped the hint that a trip to Florida is needed. He hasn't publicly given out your name, but there are people responding they'll help him get rid of his problem. I'm trying to determine if they privately contacted him, but we have to assume at least one did. These aren't decent human beings we're talking about. Unlike the Hounds, they don't care if their targets are innocent or not. It's all about the money."

I knew what he said about the Hounds and others was true. Having to sit and wait for the man and his possible accomplices to make a move would drive me insane, and based on the expressions on Alistair's and the others' faces, they felt the same.

"I know you have a plan or at least the start of one. You got us back here. Why? You could've told us all this over the phone, so I presume there was a reason," I pointed out.

I saw them exchange looks, and then they glanced over at Alistair. It was Darragh who said something. He did it cautiously, I thought. "Alistair, as the head of the Hounds, you know how an operation like this goes. We have a tactical advantage if we make a move before he does. At the moment, he seems to have dropped out of sight. Cody and others are searching to locate him, but there's a chance he's found someone, and they're on the move." He stopped abruptly after saying it.

"You want to use her as bait to bring them out!" Alistair shouted, making me jump. He made a movement toward Dar, but *Daid* stepped in between them.

"*Mac*, none of us want to endanger my daughter. I know you know that. However, Dar has a point. We can't wait for them to attack first. Yes, she's safe behind these walls, but she can't remain here indefinitely. And what's to prevent him if he can't get to her from going after someone else? He might turn his eye to Maeve or one of the other women, or what about Ronan and Khloe? I believe we can do something to bring them out in the open, in a place of our choosing, while still keeping her safe."

I saw the tension in Alistair's body as he stared at my *daid*. I knew it would take a lot of convincing for him to agree. As for me, I saw the rightness of the plan. No way did I want this monster to go after anyone else in my family. This was the best way to ensure it. I got up and walked over to my man. He looked at me, and I saw fear. I placed my hand on his chest as I got closer and stared up at him. His arms wrapped around me.

"Stair, *mil, mo ghràdh, mo neach-dìon,* you know this is the best way." He began to glare again and opened his mouth, but I put my hand over his lips. "I know what you're about to say, but you realize what we have to do. I can't allow someone else to get hurt. It'll destroy me if that happens. I have every confidence in the world that you and my family can ensure my safety while we bring this terrible man and anyone with him to justice. I'm not helpless or weak. I've been through the same training you give all your Hounds, even if I don't practice it every day like you, and they do. You wouldn't hesitate to let my brothers or cousins join you in this. Don't treat me any differently. I can do this."

"*Mo ghràdh, mo shealladh àlainn,* I have no doubts about your capabilities. I made sure you were well-versed in handling yourself. However, there are differences between you and your brothers and cousins."

"The fact I'm a woman," I huffed.

"As much as you hate it, yes, it is part of it. Not because you're weak or any such nonsense. It's because I'm a goddamn primitive when it comes to wanting to protect women and children. It's worse with you, my woman. Add to it, as much as I like and respect your family, they aren't the love of my life and the one I can't live without. If anything were to happen to you, it would kill me, literally. And what if we were unsuccessful in protecting you? Then it wouldn't just be you that I might lose," he said as he placed his hand on my stomach.

Gasps went up around the room. Damn him. He wasn't playing fair. I put my hand over his. As unlikely as it was, since I still had a few days until my shot was to be renewed, I hoped we had created a baby.

"You won't lose me or us if we've been successful. I have no doubt my primitive will be glued to me. There's no way the *Ceannaire Cúirt an Cheartais,* the leader of the Hounds of Justice, won't protect his mate and possible pup to the death. Although if you get a scratch on you, I'll kick your ass," I growled.

"You've really been trying to get pregnant? We

thought you were just kidding. Wow. Okay, I know we're in the middle of something really big and important right now, but this is too. You're trying to knock up our sister. Where's her ring?" Aidan interjected.

I whipped my head around to scowl at him. "Shush. You're not gonna guilt him into asking me to marry him!" I hissed. Not this again.

"Why would it be guilting him? We wanna know. Is he planning to do the honorable thing and marry you? Or is he just gonna defile you and have you two live in sin?" Shane added.

Cathal and Tiernan were nodding their heads in agreement. When I peeked to see what *Daid* was doing, I saw that he was watching Alistair intently with his arms crossed. Dear Lord, this had gone off the rails quickly. We needed to get back on track. Yes, I wanted to marry Stair more than anything, but I needed him to want to marry me just as much and not be pushed into it by my overbearing family.

I peeped a glance back at Alistair. He didn't appear upset, but I wanted him to know I wasn't asking him to propose. "Stair, ignore them. We'll live our lives the way we want."

He gave me such a tender and loving smile that my knees got weak, and I almost melted into a puddle on the floor. He drew me even closer. "*Leanabh*, I told you I love you more than anything. I mean that. And your family isn't capable of making me do anything I don't want to do. They just ruined my moment. I had this whole plan, but with what is coming and their stance, I gotta do this." He scanned them as he said, "I'm marrying your daughter, your sister."

"What if we say no?" Cathal asked. I wanted to

kick him.

Alistair shrugged. "It's a respectful thing for me to ask, but no matter what you say, I'm marrying her. I've waited years for her. She's always been meant to be my wife. The only way this isn't happening is if she says no. No disrespect, Cormac and Cyndi."

When he finished, he went back to staring at me. "So, Aisling O'Sheeran, will you marry me or condemn me to be a bachelor for all eternity?"

Excitement coursed through me, but I had to be sure he was doing it willingly. Despite his speech, what if it was because they put him on the spot? "Alistair Graeme, I would love to marry you, but only if you're absolutely sure this is what you want. Don't let these guys acting a muppet force you to do it. I'll continue to love you no matter if we're married or not, and I'll happily bear your children."

His smile stretched wider. Abruptly, he was kneeling before me on one knee. I heard the other women sigh. I was frozen. Oh, *Dia*, he was doing it. As if his kneeling wasn't enough of a shock, he stunned me even more when he reached into his jeans pocket and brought out a ring box. My heart galloped away, and I was having a hard time catching my breath as he opened the lid.

"I think this shows how serious I am. I was gonna ask your *daid, mam*, and brothers in private for their blessing and show them the ring. It's kinda out of order, but will you marry me? We'll celebrate the way I planned later."

All I could do was nod and hold out a badly shaking hand for him to put the ring on. He slid it into place, and I stood there admiring it. The ring was ornate and unique, but what really caught and held my attention was the center diamond. I fell in love with it instantly. It was shaped like a heart.

"I'm giving you my heart, so I thought it was only appropriate to symbolize it with your ring. Do you like it? Say something." he said softly. I heard the nerves in his tone just a tiny bit. That snapped me out of my trance. I dropped to my knees in front of him and cupped his face.

"Alistair, it's beautiful and perfect. I love it, and I love you. Thank you for making me so happy," I sealed my declaration with a kiss. It was a passionate one, and I took my time. I ignored the guys' groans and mutterings. I knew they were playing around. He returned it with just as much desire. When we finally broke apart, all I wanted was to go to the house and make love.

"Alright, stand up, you two, you're embarrassing us. All this mushy, lovey-dovey stuff. Yuck. Alistair, just so you know, you still have to go through a gauntlet to get our blessing." This came from Rian.

Alistair helped me to my feet as he rose up. He tucked me under his arm. "And exactly what is the gauntlet?"

"We all get into the fighting ring, and you take our best hits or kicks. We have to be sure you can protect her, and you have a teeny tiny taste of what'll happen if you hurt her in any way," Rian explained with a fierce stare.

"No way are you beating on him!" I objected loudly.

"Okay, I'm all for that. Do we do it now or later?" was Alistair's too-calm reply.

"No, you won't!"

"Yes, I will."

We bickered back and forth for several minutes, but he remained adamant. It was *Daid* letting out a loud whistle, which got us to stop. "As much as we love to see how Alistair holds up in the ring, I say we postpone the gauntlet until after we take care of our enemy. We need to plan how we're bringing him out into the open while keeping Aisling protected. That will take some discussion and debate, no doubt, so I propose we all help get dinner on the table. We'll fill our bellies, then get down to plotting."

This seemed to meet everyone's approval, which was how we went from a deeply serious moment to carefree and laughing the next. We all pitched in to finish the meal and get the dining room ready. I discovered that Agatha had been entertaining Khloe. She happily joined us. It wasn't long before the entire family was seated and eating. I made sure to enjoy it. You could never take moments like this for granted. You never knew how many you might get.

Alistair:

We'd talked for hours, laying out our plan. As thoroughly as we vetted it from what we thought was from every angle and ran through every possible scenario, I was still anxious. I was terrified something would go wrong we didn't account for, and she'd get hurt or, worse, killed. If the latter happened, they needed to be sure to end me right then and there and bury us together. I didn't know if I could even stick around long enough to get revenge, but it would likely fall to her family to do it. Aisling seemed confident in the plan and was going about preparing for it as if this was an everyday occurrence for her. She was spending time with her *mam* and the other women at the moment. I was down in the Command Center, rechecking the location and escape routes again.

The sound of footsteps caught my attention. There were more than one pair. Glancing up, I saw a large group of O'Sheerans and some of the guards and enforcers coming toward me. I straightened from where I was hunched over the screens.

"Did something happen?" I asked.

"It did. It's a damn good thing we made our plans when we did. Cody found him. Danvers Kelly is on the move, and he's coming our way. We don't know the exact numbers, but he did get help. By Cody's calculations, they'll be here the day after tomorrow at the latest. We've got to get our spot ready and make it well known where she can be found. We hate that you have to announce your engagement this way," Darragh stated.

We'd decided on a way to bring Danvers out and to where we wanted to confront him. We'd have to be someplace private, so we had minimal chance of collateral damage. But there had to be a reason for the public to know where we were. The family came up with the idea to announce we were going away to celebrate our engagement. It would get a lot of attention in the media. It always did when an O'Sheeran got engaged.

The place we were going to was a beach house the family kept in southern Florida. They used to go there in the summer for family vacations when they didn't have much time to go somewhere further away. I'd gone there several times with them when I was a kid.

"We need to head there no later than this afternoon then to give it time to catch the media's attention," was all I could say in response.

"We know you're not thrilled about this, Alistair, but we've got a super solid plan. Have faith in us and your men," Patrick added.

"I'm trying, but it's still hard. I've waited forever to have her be mine, and I don't want anything to change that."

"We know, and we won't let it. As for the media getting a hold of the news, there are a few of the paparazzi we get along with. I wouldn't call them friends, but they tend to present us in a better light than the others. We'll give them a scoop, and they'll keep their mouths shut about where it came from.

Believe me, when they report it, it'll catch like wildfire. Be thankful the beach house is walled-in and protected from outsiders. We can't prevent them from being outside, but they should be safe. I don't believe Danvers will pass up the opportunity, not when he's been so hot and vocal about stopping her online," Cormac said.

I saw the tension on his face. While all of them were concerned to a degree, he was more so. This was his daughter, his only daughter. She was the apple of his eye, so to speak, even though he loved his sons. Patrick, Sean, and he had been desperate to have a daughter years ago. It had been a crazy coincidence when all of them got one with their fifth child. Once they did, it was the end of any more kids for all of them. They deemed they had a complete family once they got a girl. It was the fact they waited so long, I think, that made them even more protective of the girls.

"I don't believe he'll pass up the opportunity either. All right, everyone should be ready to deploy and be in position. The team will be sent ahead, so they arrive before we do and before the media gets wind of where we're going. We'll arrive later, and no one will be the wiser that we're not there alone other than her personal bodyguard with us. We'll keep it to just Creed being visible. He's expected any time she goes somewhere. It would seem odd if he weren't, and if we add too much visible security, Danvers may not strike. I want this over with so we can get on with living our lives."

"So do we. Alright, let's go find her and get this mission in motion. By tonight, hopefully, the threat will be neutralized," Aidan stated.

"At least this one. Has anyone heard anything

from Brynes? I don't see him not running his mouth still over his butt hurt," I growled.

"No, but then again, he may be involved in other stuff. Cody and his team are still trying to verify everything the Bragans said. Chris will be dealt with one way or the other. If he's innocent in those women's disappearances, then we'll deal with him making waves or saying stuff he shouldn't about Aisling and you. If he's responsible, then he'll be made to disappear, and no one will know where he went. The same for those involved in that reprehensible business," Darragh said with a scowl.

"So be it. We'll concentrate on him after we get Danvers out of our lives. I'm ready. Let's go," I told them confidently. I had an escort as I made my way out of the tunnels and into the house.

Aisling: Chapter 19

I was trying to enjoy being at our beach house. It was one of my favorite spots, and all I had was great memories of it over the years. Our family came here a lot when we were kids. Not so much as adults, and I vowed to continue the tradition with our kids. Thinking of our kids made me scan for Alistair. He'd been like a great big lion since we got here. He prowled the entire house after doing the same outside. I got him inside by telling him it looked suspicious for him to keep walking the perimeter of the property. Besides, we had men hidden strategically along it.

They had orders to let Danvers and his people infiltrate. This would keep the people gathering outside safe. And yes, there were nosy bystanders and paparazzi out there already, and there would be more. The news that Aisling O'Sheeran, one of the notorious mafia family members, had gotten herself engaged exploded in media outlets. The fact they knew next to nothing about Alistair had them in a frenzy. We had no doubt they were frantically digging, trying to find out who he was and how we'd met. They'd find his cover story, which explained he worked as a security consultant but nothing about his actual work. Telling enough of the truth to make it believable was the trick to subterfuge.

Creed had taken himself to the smaller house on the property where guards stayed when they accompanied us. He was giving us privacy. As the hours passed, Alistair grew more tense. I knew I had to get him to relax. All accounts had Danvers not getting to Florida until tomorrow. He was driving across the country rather than flying, which made sense if he was bringing assassins or whatever you wanted to call them with him. I called them killers. They were entirely different from the Hounds.

Going to the front window where he was stealthily peeking out of it, I ran my hand up his back. He pressed into me. The tension in his body was felt under my hands. "Stair, you need to relax. They're miles and miles away. Come for a swim with me."

"Ais, he might've sent men ahead to scope the area."

"He may have, but we'll be alerted if they're sighted. It's dark. No one can see us at the beach. The water is brisk, but it'll do us good."

"Are you sure you want to get submerged in the water? It's probably no more than seventy-some degrees," he warned.

"I know, and I've swam in it much colder than that. I'm putting my foot down. We're going." I grabbed his hand and pulled it.

He resisted, and when I tugged even harder, he laughed. I kept it up until he followed me to our bedroom. I'd made sure to pack a bathing suit and his trunks. I may have a deranged maniac after me, but nothing said I couldn't enjoy stolen moments while we waited for him and his goons to descend. We changed quickly. When I was done, I sent a text to Creed letting him know what we were doing and told him to stay away from the beach unless it was an emergency. I did the same to Kendric. He was with us as well and would pass it along to the men protecting the perimeter. I had more than a swim in mind. Gathering a blanket to take with us along with towels, I took his hand and hauled him outside. It was cooling off, but I didn't mind. We'd soon be warmed up.

When we got to the beach, I spread out the blanket and lay the towels on it. I'd barely finished doing it when I was hoisted off my feet and over his shoulder. I held in my shriek, not wanting to have our people coming running, thinking I was in danger. He swiftly ran to the water. He didn't throw me in, but he walked further and further out into the water. It hit my feet first. It was chilly, but I wouldn't admit it. He kept going until most of me was submerged. It began to feel warmer. Of course, it didn't come to his shoulders. I held onto him. He was staring down at me with a smile on his face, finally.

"You don't need to hold me. I can hang onto you."

"I like holding you. I need to do it, Ais. I'm praying so damn hard this goes off as planned, but there's this fear inside that something will go wrong," he admitted.

"*Mil*, I know. I feel the same. You're all about me being in danger, but if this guy is as bad as we think, he won't hesitate to eliminate anyone between him and me. His hired killers most definitely won't care. I can't stand the thought of anything happening to you or the men, but especially you. You're my soulmate, my heart. It'll kill me if anything were to happen to you."

He hugged me closer. "It won't. I'm a hellhound," he told me a second before he kissed me.

Dia, the man could kiss unlike anyone I'd ever kissed before. He took over not only my mind but my body, too. I eagerly chased his mouth and tongue for more when he teased me by pretending he was about to pull away. He chuckled. I nipped his bottom lip with my teeth as payback. This sent us into a battle. We were not only kissing and twining tongues but licking, sucking, and biting. By the time we took a time out, we were both breathing rather hard. I was turned on. I felt the slickness in my bikini bottoms, and my nipples were pressing against the cups of my top.

He let my legs down but held me up with an arm around my back. I pressed my body against his and let him feel my nipples. As I did, I wiggled a hand down to cup the bulge I knew I'd find in his trunks. He didn't disappoint. His cock was a big hard monster begging for attention. I rubbed my hand up and down his length and gently squeezed it, then his balls. He groaned.

"You're gonna let the beast out if you keep it up," he warned me.

"Oh, I know. It's my goal."

The moon was out, so we had enough light to see each other. I gave him a devilish grin when I said it. He growled, and the next thing I knew, I was hoisted higher. This put his head at the level of my breasts. He used one hand to push a cup aside, then he latched onto my nipple and began to suck and use his teeth. I moaned loudly, not giving a damn if anyone heard me. While he was torturing my tit, he slid the hand away and down. Next, he was working a finger underneath the edge of my bottoms and between my slick pussy lips. I cried out brokenly. The rubbing of his calloused finger over my clit and piercing made me insane. If he did this for even a few minutes, I'd come.

I wasn't able to reach his cock in this position.

I whimpered. This made him let go of my tit. "What's wrong?"

"I can't touch you like this," I complained.

"Good. If you did, I'd be shooting my load in the water. I don't want that. I want to come inside of you."

"I want you to too. Do it."

"I will. Just be patient. First, I want to see you come apart as you come on my fingers. Let me see your face as you get your satisfaction, Ais," he rumbled. His face was taut. He didn't give me a chance to say anything before he was back to attacking my tit and fingering my pussy. When he thrust his fingers inside of me, I wailed. It felt incredible. I was quickly ramping up to an orgasm. The tension in my body was growing fast. I was really close when he stopped sucking and gave me an order.

"Come. Give me all the sweet goodness. I want your pussy good and wet for my cock."

The feel of his fingers thrusting and rubbing over my G-spot and the image of his cock sinking into me was enough to hurdle me over the edge into an orgasm. His mouth took mine to hold in my scream as I climaxed. I bucked and jerked in his arms, and he kissed me until I was boneless. When I slumped in his arms, he let go and pulled his hand free of my bottoms.

He began to walk toward the shore, but I shook my head. "No, do it here. Fuck me here in the water. I can't wait to get to the beach," I begged him.

"You sure?"

"Yes, hurry," I cried. Even after my intense release, I was desperate for him to be inside of me.

"Your wish is my command," he growled.

He moved his arm under the water, and then I

felt the crotch of my bikini bottoms get pulled to the side before I was lowered onto the hard, hot length of him. I moaned the entire time I sank onto him. He was groaning softly as I did. When I was full of him, he moved his hands to both of my hips. I had my hands clutching his biceps and my legs wrapped around his waist.

"Ride me," he commanded.

As I used my legs and arms to raise up, he helped by lifting my hips. I was careful not to go too far. I didn't want to lose him, not even for a second. I was always so deliciously full when he was inside of me. He stretched me so good.

As my speed increased, his breath became louder. I made sure to tease him as I rode him. I did more than bounce up and down. I twisted my hips and flexed my inner Kegel's. He'd moan louder each time I did.

"Fuck! You make me insane, woman. There's nothing in the world better than being buried inside of you. I don't give a damn if it's your very talented mouth, your wet, tight pussy, or that even tighter ass of yours. Shit, I'm close, Ais. So close," he muttered a couple of minutes into our ride.

"I know what you mean. There's nothing I love more than to have your glorious mouth or cock. You make me lose my mind, Stair. Help me. Harder. I want your cum bathing my pussy and womb," I taunted.

This set him off. He slammed me up and down his cock harder and faster. I struggled to keep up. Suddenly, he buried himself to the root, held me there, and growled and grunted as his hot seed filled me. It triggered my own climax. We kissed to stay quiet as we came together. It was perfect bliss. By the time we were done, he staggered to the shore and over to the blanket. He lowered me to it, then fell down next to me. He tugged me into his body and covered me with the towels.

"I love you, Aisling."

"I love you too, Alistair."

We remained there, staring into each other's eyes, and whispering words of love until it got too cold. Then, we grabbed our stuff and went inside.

❦❦❦

I came rearing up in bed. It was dark, and I was disoriented. For a moment, I had no idea where I was, and then it came back to me. As it did, I knew what had woken me up. It was the alarm they'd set up, which would alert us when Danvers or any of his so-called men were spotted. Alistair was already out of bed on his feet and had his phone out. He'd be able to get updates on exactly where they were and an ETA for when to expect them to hit us, as well as the numbers. We'd gone to bed in minimal clothing, so at least I wouldn't be naked if I didn't have time to dress. I jumped out of bed and grabbed my top and pants next to it.

"When, where, and how many?" I asked as I tugged them on.

"Kendric says five to seven minutes out. They see six. No idea yet if one is Danvers. They have three coming from the north and three from the west."

The east side was the ocean, and the south was protected by a huge rocky cliff. You could climb it, but it was dangerous and time-consuming. Some of the men were stationed outside the property and in the surrounding neighborhood to be our advance guard.

Once they let the enemy pass them, they'd come up behind them. The remainder were behind the wall with us. I spent a moment praying that the paparazzi and other bystanders had gotten tired and went home for the night. I shuddered to think what might happen to them if they ran into any of the men coming.

"You need to get into the safe room," he ordered. He was already fully dressed and had strapped on his weapons. I knew it would be useless and a waste of precious time to argue I could help. I'd do as he asked, but if it appeared that he or the others needed help, I wouldn't stay there. I decided to keep that to myself.

"Okay, *mil*, I'm going. Be careful. I love you," I told him. He came over and gave me a deep kiss before letting go of me.

"I will be, and I love you too. Now get in," he said. He went to the wall next to the bed in the master bedroom where we were sleeping and pressed the hidden release. A door opened, and I went inside. As it was closing behind me, I went to a row of monitors we had in there connected to the security system. It would allow me to watch and hear what was happening.

The hardest thing was to sit there watching and waiting. I saw our men and Alistair slithering around the house and grounds. They were on point. While the enforcers and guards were good, Alistair and the Hounds were like ghosts. As inappropriate as it was, watching my man float from spot to spot, all geared up for battle, turned me on. What was wrong with me? I'd never been this sex-crazed in my life.

It wasn't long before I saw other shadowy figures. I knew which were ours by the active infrared, IR, light they had on their shirts. It wasn't visible to the naked eye, but with infrared goggles, they could see each other, and since the security cameras had light IR capabilities, I was able to see them, too. As more and more slunk across the screens, I saw there were more than six, but Alistair and the guys didn't appear surprised, which told me he had been alerted but didn't tell me. I wondered if more came after the initial report or if there had been more the whole time, and he lied so I wouldn't worry. If this were the case, we'd have a talk later. I knew he wanted to protect me, but keeping important information to himself wasn't the way to do it.

I counted a dozen foreign bodies now on the property, and I was dreading there might be even more waiting outside. Just what had Danvers promised these men to do the job? Including Alistair, we had seven men. He assured me when we came, it was more than enough. I didn't doubt they were capable, but it still put it two-to-one for most of them.

I was so involved in watching Alistair mainly creeping up on and disposing of a man that I lost track of paying attention to one of the cameras. It was the one that showed the interior of the house, and it was in the hall leading to the master bedroom. It wasn't until an alarm alerted me that I looked and saw it was the one in the hallway. He'd enabled only that one to alarm, although there were numerous others. He thought they'd be too distracting to me, and he was right. My heart leaped, seeing a dark figure not wearing an IR light creeping stealthily down the hall.

He stopped at each closed door between him and me, opening them cautiously, and checking them out before he would move to the next. Based on the picture on the wall, I knew where he was at. He had two more rooms before the master. I had to make a decision. Checking on the others again, I saw they were all occupied. There was no telling when any of them would realize there was someone in the house. Although there was no way to get into the safe room, even if he knew it was there, he was a threat to them if they came to check on me. My decision was made.

Going to the door, I eased it open only far enough to slip out. Then I sealed it back up. I had my gun out and ready. When the intruder came into this room, he was in for a big surprise. There would be no scared, helpless woman cowering under the bed. I was a damn O'Sheeran, and I didn't cower from anyone.

I tiptoed to the darkest corner. It was well out of the faint light coming through the blinds. I wouldn't trap myself in the closet. I crouched, took aim at the door, and waited. It seemed to take forever before I saw the door easing open slowly. A head peeked around it and then disappeared. It came back again. I concentrated on controlling my breathing. I was happy to see my hands were steady. The door moved inward more, and then the dark figure came inside, crouched lower to the floor. I watched him scan the room and then straighten. As suspected, he went right to the closet. I was waiting because I wanted him close and to be sure of what was behind him. If I shot him in the doorway, I risked hurting anyone behind him in the hall if the bullet went wide or through him. I wouldn't risk it being one of ours or Alistair.

He stepped out of the closet and turned to go toward the bed. I let him. I was curious to see what he'd do if he didn't find me. He kneeled down and looked under the bed. When he didn't find me, he let out a low curse. I figured he'd leave, but to my shock, he went to the wall by the bed and began to feel the wall as if he knew there was a door there to the panic room. How the hell would he know that? No one who was involved in building it would tell. We didn't contract that to outsiders.

The thing with the trigger was it had a well-hidden fingerprint scanner to it. So even if found, if your prints weren't in the system, it wouldn't open for you. I knew when he found this out. He let out a string of swear words.

"Motherfucking son of a bitch!"

I wanted to laugh at the frustration in his voice. Then he began to yell.

"I know you're in there, bitch. You may think you're safe, but I promise you, I'll blow this fucking door off and get you. You're dead. Nothing is saving you."

I'd waited, seen, and heard enough. I eased out of the corner. I stayed low, and I slithered closer. I had a second at the most before he sensed me. I dropped lower before I spoke.

"You're the one who's dead."

He swung to face me and shot. I knew he would, hence me being low. Most people shoot at waist height or higher automatically. The bullet whizzed over my head. I fired back, but I lined up my shot. It took him in the chest. That's when I discovered he was wearing body armor. Fuck. Sure, I had on a vest, too, but I was hoping they wouldn't. Either the others who were shot hadn't, or Alistair and the others were using armor-piercing rounds, which I hadn't put in my gun. If this ever happened again to me, I'd remember.

He doubled over in pain. I knew taking one to the vest knocked the wind out of you and incapacitated you for a few moments. Not wasting them, I raced over to him. He was trying to rise up and shoot me as I did. This time, I went for the head. My shot went true and took him between the eyes. He dropped like a stone.

I was too numb and worried about what was happening outside to let it sink in that I'd killed someone. I pushed it away to deal with it later. Even though I knew he was dead, I did check for a pulse. I hated to touch him, but it was better to be safe than sorry. No pulse. Leaving him there, I went to the closet. My vest was one of the ones used by Alistair and the team, so I knew they'd not mistake me for an enemy, or I hoped not. It wasn't as if I could text them. It might distract them at the wrong time. I grabbed a spare set of goggles I saw Stair put in there when we got here. Slipping them on, I let my eyes adjust to the strange vision. If you'd never worn them, they messed you up, but like other things, I was no stranger to them.

Now that I was out, I didn't want to go back in. What if they ended up needing help? Or more men had joined the first dozen while I was dealing with the asshole in the bedroom? I eased open the bedroom door and started a slow walk down the hallway. I had to check the rooms between the master and the end of the hall just as my assailant had in case someone had come in behind him and was waiting.

I was sweating by the time I made it to the end. Damn, this was nerve-racking work. How did Alistair do it all the time? I kept my finger off the trigger. If you don't, you were just asking to accidentally shoot someone you didn't want to shoot. A slight rustling sound to the left made me freeze. Swinging my head in that direction, I caught the reflection of the IR light. Hoping it was safe to reveal myself and there were no attackers in the room, I stood straighter and turned in his direction. The figure came hurrying over to me. When he got closer, I could see his face. It was Creed. He was scowling fiercely at me.

"What the hell are you doing out of the panic room? Do you want to get yourself killed? Or drive Alistair into a berserker rage?" he hissed as he grabbed my arm.

"I was helping. If you don't think so, go check out the body in the bedroom. He knew about the safe room, Creed. The only reason he didn't get in was because of the fingerprint scanner. How is that possible? And why was I told there were only six attackers, and I saw at least twice that come onto the property?" I snapped back.

He gave me a blank look, telling me they knew there were more than six men. I was gonna kick all their asses when this was over with. I drew back my foot and kicked him in the shin. I put on boots in the safe room as I watched. He sucked in a breath and pulled his leg back.

"Ouch, what the fuck was that for?"

"Being a damn pigheaded man like Stair. Let's stop arguing and go help clean up this mess. Before you try to order me back into the room, it's not happening, and if you try to force me, I'm screaming the whole house down. Tell me the truth. How many came, and how many are left?"

I knew he didn't want to, but technically, he worked for me and not Alistair. He must've remembered this because he sighed and told me after only a couple of seconds of silence.

"There were a total of fifteen. They came in two rounds. Twelve in the first bunch, then the other three. They hung back far enough that the advanced guys never saw them. It wasn't until they came up behind the first group and the one lookout left behind sighted them that we knew. The last I heard, we've killed ten."

"Tell them it's eleven. We need to clear the rest of the house. I don't know if more are in here."

It was kinda dangerous for us to be standing here yapping, and he recognized it. He pushed on his earpiece. "Eleven. Got primary. Clearing the house. Over."

I had no idea what was said back, but the way he flinched made me guess it wasn't good. He tugged me to stand behind him and to his left. "You cover my six. I go in first, and you stay down and to my left. Do not get ahead of me in my field of vision. Got it?"

"I know how this is done. I was trained. Go."

As fast as we could go without giving ourselves away, we worked the first floor. It was empty. Heading up the stairs to where there were more bedrooms, bathrooms, and an office, we crept up the stairs. I was happy they were kept in such good repair. They didn't creak and give us away. We'd cleared the first bedroom when I heard noises coming from the office, which was at the far end of the hallway. Exchanging a puzzled look with Creed, we started in its direction. I knew he didn't want to leave potential enemies at our backs, so we cleared the rooms between us and the office as fast as we were able. When we got to it, we'd found no one in them.

Using hand signals, he counted off before

opening the door. We heard mumbling and swearing coming from inside, but there was no light on. I stayed back and went in low and to the left while Creed went right. When we got inside, I saw there was light from a flashlight. There was a person at the wall where we had a safe. He was busy trying to break into it. Not far from him was another man. They were so into what they were doing they didn't know we were there.

"Have you got that damn thing open yet!? They can't keep them off us forever. I had no goddamn idea she'd have so many men protecting her. Travis must've found the whore in her hidey-hole and killed her ass. He's taking his time getting here. It's been long enough since the shots downstairs," the second man, who was shorter, said.

The one at the safe gave an impatient huff. "Listen, this isn't easy. This is a top-of-the-line safe. It takes finesse and time to do this. I need silence. You're the one who insisted we hit this while we were here. I said we should just get rid of her and go. Yeah, I didn't expect the number of men, but they're no match for my men. You just be ready to pay us what you promised," he warned.

I caught Creed's signal to get down and move further left, so I did it while he did the same to the right. It brought us up behind the two men. I was behind the short one. Holding up three fingers, Creed lowered them to make a fist. As soon as he did, we stood tall, and he called out.

"Put your hands in the air. Do it now, and don't make any sudden moves," he barked.

The men froze. I heard the swift inhalations. I was ready. As far as I could tell, they weren't holding guns, but that didn't mean they didn't have them.

"Do it!" Creed shouted.

Their hands came up. When all four hands were in the air, he flipped up his goggles, and I followed suit. I knew what he was about to do. The lights came on. It was rather blinding, but I kept my eyes squinted on the intruders. They were even more blinded. As our eyesight cleared, as if tied together, we moved in sync over to the two men. I saw the man I was approaching rear back in surprise when he saw my face. He knew who I was, and as I stared at him, I recognized who he was. It was my good luck to catch Danvers Kelly. He'd accompanied his hired assassins, after all.

"You!" he hissed.

"You, I'd like to say it was nice to meet you, Danvers, but then it would be a lie. You were a fool to think you could come after me or my family and not be stopped."

"How do you know who I am and that I was coming after you?"

"Securing him," Creed called to me.

I kept watch on Danvers as Creed holstered his gun, then jerked the other man's hands behind his back and slapped flex restraints on his wrists. When he was secured, searched, and his weapons removed, it was my turn.

"Securing," I called back to Creed. He nodded. As I holstered my gun, Danvers must've felt he could grab me before he would be shot by Creed, or he'd be able to use me as a shield or maybe a hostage because the fool lunged for me. Unfortunately for him, I wasn't an idiot, and I was prepared. When he came flying at me, I automatically drew back my fist and smashed it into his jaw. He dropped like a rock and lay on the floor unmoving. I rolled his deadweight ass onto his stomach and secured his hands behind his back. When I was done, I advanced on the other man, who was watching me wide-eyed. I'd had enough of this shit.

My fist ached a bit, but I wasn't letting them know it. It might ruin my badass bitch status. I got in his face. "If you don't want to end up like your buddy here or way worse, you'd better tell me what you were doing here and what he offered you to do it."

"Lady, I don't snitch. You'll have to ask him."

"You don't snitch. Well, we'll have to see if you stick to that after they get done with you."

"I'm not afraid of your bodyguards," he sneered.

"You might not think you should be, and that's fine because when her man gets in here, he'll put the fear of God in you. Anyone trying to touch a hair on her head is dead, and they likely won't go easily or quickly," Creed told him.

A groan from Danvers diverted my attention back to him. Creed grabbed his prisoner and marched him to a nearby chair. He shoved him in it. As he did, he pressed on his earpiece again. "Two secure in the office. Primary is still safe."

He listened for almost a minute. As he did, he kept busy by picking Danvers off the floor and throwing him into another chair, even though he was still mostly insensible. He was beginning to come around, but he wasn't fully with it. His eyes were still shut. Creed snickered when he got off the radio.

"Damn, you must've given him a helluva pop to the jaw, Aisling. We'll have to start calling you Rocky. Maybe I should let you loose on this idiot," he gestured to Mr. No Snitch.

I chuckled and was about to tell him I'd gladly do it when I was interrupted by the appearance of men in the doorway. The way Creed didn't react, he knew they were coming, but the dog didn't tell me. In the lead was my man, and he wasn't amused. He was glaring and had a savage expression on his face. It was enough to scare me. He marched directly toward me.

"We'll talk later," he growled.

I chose not to say anything. If he wanted to reprimand me, it better be in private. I knew *Daid* and *Mam* strongly disagreed at times, but they kept it between them. We never truly saw them fight, even though we knew it had to happen. He gave me a hard, brief kiss. When he was done, he gave his attention to our prisoners.

The alert one was checking him out. Danvers gave a loud moan, and his eyes fluttered open. They widened when he saw everyone standing there. I knew Alistair recognized him. I watched Danvers' throat bob as he swallowed. There was no way he didn't know he was in deep shit, and there was no way out.

"Your other men are dead. A cleanup crew will be coming to dispose of their remains. No one will know what happened to them. As for you two, I want information, and you'll give it to me," Alistair informed them.

"That one isn't a snitch, according to what he said. I warned him, but he seemed sure he wasn't scared of any of you," I gladly explained.

Stair folded his big arms across his chest and scowled more. "Oh, he's not, well, more fun for us. I promise you before we're done, you'll tell me everything

I want to know. You think you're a bunch of big bad assassins. I beg to differ. You're thugs for hire. You were stupid to ever take this job," he told the lackey.

"Mister, I have no beef with you. It was just a job. I don't have a horse in this race. Let me walk, and you'll never hear or see me again."

"I can't do that. See, then I'd always have to look over my shoulder wondering if you might get stupid again and come after me and mine. I don't live with threats. I eliminate them. It's what makes me the leader of the Hounds of Justice."

Danvers' friend went pale when he heard the Hounds of Justice. It was clear he'd heard of them. His words confirmed it.

"Y-you're a Hound, the head Hound?"

"I am. So you've heard of us."

"Everyone who's anyone in our line of work has heard of the Hounds."

"What's your name?" Alistair asked.

"It's Beck, Josiah Beck."

"Well, Beck, we're not in the same business, not even close. See, the Hounds bring justice to those who deserve it. We don't target innocent people for personal gain, greed, or revenge. This bastard here came after her for no other reason than he's jealous of her success and wants to get one over on a sister he's never met."

Beck looked over at Danvers in disbelief. "You said they stole money and land from you and were responsible for ruining your life and had been threatening you."

"They did. She's ruining my business because her aunt, my half-sister, ruins everything. She drove my dad out of Florida with threats from her mafia family and thought I was gonna let her ruin my family's life work!"

I stared at him open-mouthed. He truly sounded as if he believed what he was saying. The guy was nuts. I stood there waiting to see what Alistair would say or do. I knew he wouldn't let either man live.

Alistair: Chapter 20

I didn't want to spread the mess around and drag Beck and Danvers to the warehouse back home to kill them and then have to dispose of them there. We had a team coming in with a boat under the cover of darkness. They'd clear out the bodies. Another crew would clean everything so it was back to pristine condition and ensure any prints and DNA were cleaned away and spent brass from our guns was picked up and policed, as we called it. In no time, it would be perfect again. We were lucky they used silencers on their weapons, and we'd done the same. The last thing we wanted was to attract the police. Most of the bystanders and paparazzi had left for the night, but you couldn't guarantee that a few stragglers or neighbors hadn't heard anything. Lucky for us, the houses weren't right on top of each other.

It was the cleanup crew who changed my plans. The others we'd killed as we found them. I wanted to take my ire out on one of them, and Danvers was the prime target, but I wouldn't have time to torture him, which had been my plan. After a quick conference with Aisling, I came up with an alternate plan. It was her idea. While we talked, the others were busy rounding up the bodies or watching Beck sweat. Danvers kept muttering under his breath.

Turning to face them, I ignored the flunky and

began to talk to Danvers again. I wanted to hear all the bullshit he had to say, but I knew a couple of people who wanted to hear it more. I placed the secure call. It was picked up quickly. On the other end were Patrick, Sean, Cormac, Darragh, and several other of the O'Sheeran men. I'd had a message sent, telling them that everyone was safe and the threat was contained.

"I wanted you all to have a chance to hear this and to ask questions. First, Danvers, tell us why you think Aisling is to blame for your misfortune or whatever it is?"

"You know why! My bitch of a half-sister put her up to it. She knew our dad had moved on and got a new family, a better one. She was jealous, and to hurt him, she had her rich gangster husband threaten him and buy her a winery in the same area as the one my mom's family owned. They wanted to run us out of business, but Dad was too smart for them. He kept it from happening. So what did Maeve do? She had one of her nieces take over after he died, and somehow, she bribed and fooled people to make them think their winery was way better than ours. They gave her all these kudos and awards for what? Those wines aren't better than ours. It was all pay-offs and threats. I knew if I didn't put a stop to this one and Maeve, my bitch of a sister, would find another way to ruin us."

I saw Patrick and his sons biting their lips, trying not to say anything, but you could tell they were beyond angry. Cormac and Sean were livid, too. I kept going. "Why did you have men go after Aisling with cars? What was your objective, or did you have one?"

"Of course I did! I was gonna kidnap her ass and use her to get them to sell their winery and never step foot in California again, and they'd have to never be in the winemaking business either, no matter where it was in the world. They would've done it, too, if it wasn't for her bodyguard chasing off the guys I hired," he said in disgust.

"Was it this guy and his crew who did it?"

"No, it wasn't us," was Beck's immediate reply.

"No, it was another group. I gave them another chance, and they blew it. They didn't want to after they found out who she was, but I wouldn't pay them if they left the job undone."

"You thought up the fire at the winery," Aisling stated.

He sneered at her. "Yeah, too bad some nosy neighbor put it out so fast. If we'd burned it to the ground, you would've left with your tail between your legs. It was after that I knew I needed new men. Men used to doing the big jobs. It took me a bit, but I thought I'd found them with his crew," he jerked his head toward Beck but gave him a look of contempt.

"You lied to us. You said they were the ones who ruined your life, stole money and land from you, were threatening you, and you needed to get them before they got you. We had no idea of the true story until minutes ago. You went after not only a mafia family but the woman who belongs to the leader of the Hounds of Justice! You're not only crazy but suicidal. I wish I'd never met you!" he yelled.

"Who the fuck are the Hounds of Justice!? Who are they to make you shake in your boots like a pussy?" Danvers snarled.

"We're the men and women who'll hunt for justice to the ends of the earth if we have to. We're the ones you won't know are there until you wake up to find us standing over you. We don't go after innocent men, women, and children. We do our research and only eliminate the scum of the world. You had no idea the O'Sheeran family you accuse of so much is the creators of the Hounds, and I'm the man lucky enough to be appointed their head as well as the man who won this beautiful woman's heart. The woman you came after with the intention to kidnap and now to kill," I snapped back.

"I didn't say I planned to kill her," he protested. I think the reality of who we were and what was to happen was settling in.

"Bullshit! Don't lie now. They're not gonna let us go. He's full of it. He said he wanted her dead and whoever else got in our way. We'd earn a bonus if she died in an extra gruesome way," Beck outed him spitefully. No honor among thieves and killers, I guess.

Protests of anger came through the screen, but it was nothing compared to what I'd let rip out of me. I roared as I grabbed him and threw Danvers across the room. He landed in a heap on the floor. He was no longer tied up, and neither was Beck. I had no fear they'd overpower any of us or run away. If he wanted to fight back, let him.

He was a man still in his prime. From what we knew about him, he was in his early forties. He came bounding to his feet and flew at me. Beck stayed seated. It was a flurry of fists as we went head-to-head. He was no match for me, and that was with me sticking purely to punching and none of the other moves I knew. It wasn't long until he was a bloody heap on the floor. I wanted to keep at him until he was dead, but Aisling's hand on my arm stopped me.

"*Mo gra*, enough for now. *Daid*, do you or my brothers want to ask him anything before we have him disposed of along with the others?"

Her saying *daid* had Danvers lifting his head to look at her and then the monitor screen. We'd called them using a laptop that I sat on a nearby table. "*Daid*, that's rich. You drove mine to the grave while Maeve and her husband lived happily. Patrick, where are you? Where's my useless waste of a sister," he mumbled. He was in no shape to yell.

I figured Patrick would have no problem speaking his mind. What stunned me was when he moved to the front of their group, he wasn't alone. Maeve was with him, tucked under his protective arm. I saw sadness on her face as she saw her brother for the first and last time.

"There you are," he said before he spit at the screen.

"I want you to know something, Danvers, before you die. No one ruined your *daid*. He did that all on his own. Yes, I told him never to come near Maeve or her *mam*, or he'd wish he hadn't. I didn't make him leave Florida. When I bought that winery in Temecula, I had no clue he'd ended up there and had remarried or had anything to do with a winery. Once he left Florida, he was no longer our concern. If we were competing with your winery, it would be the same competition we are to every other one in Temecula and the world. We put in hard work. Period. It wasn't personal," Patrick told him.

"And because of it, I had no idea I had a brother. There was nothing stopping you when you turned eighteen from contacting me. I would've welcomed having a brother, but you chose not to. In fact, I heard you turned into an abusive man just like our *daid* was. Going after those weaker than you or of the opposite sex is cowardly. Aisling took over the winery when she showed a love for it. She's done a tremendous job, and she'll keep it growing. You had no right to try and use her to force us to do anything. And to go after her with the intention of killing her because of this twisted tale you were fed all your life is beyond ridiculous. I'm sorry you never had a chance or knew love, Danvers. If you'd come to me, I would've shown you what true family love was," Maeve told him, getting misty-eyed by the end.

"Our *daid* was a great man! He couldn't help the women in his life. Your whore of a *mam*, you, and my *mam* were all weak and not worthy of him or me. You never stayed in your place," he partially shouted.

I'd heard enough. It was time to end this farce. "Darragh, sirs, it's time for us to go. Our ride is here. We'll be home as soon as we make sure everything is taken care of."

"Do what you need to do, *Mac*. We'll be here," Cormac said.

Patrick had walked off with a weeping Maeve. Aisling shut off the laptop after saying goodbye. She was glaring daggers at Danvers. No one blamed her.

"Alright, let's get these two out to the boat. I'll leave some men here and come back to get you when it's done," I told her.

"No, I want to go too."

Seeing the expression on her face, I knew she was in an arguing mood. "You guys take them to the boat. I'll be there soon." They nodded and hauled both men to their feet, then out of the room. Aisling faced off with me.

"I know what you're about to say, and it's bull. There's no reason I can't go. It's not dangerous."

"It might be. What if we get pulled over by the Coast Guard with a bunch of dead bodies? We'll all be headed to prison for the rest of our lives. I don't want it to happen to you. If I end up behind bars, I need to know you're safe and free and, God willing, raising our child. No, I'm sorry, but no. And I'm not forgetting you disobeyed me and left the safety of the panic room. You were to stay there, Ais."

"I went into the room. The reason I left was you didn't tell me how many men were really there. You lied. I didn't know if one might get by you or sneak up on you. And it was a good thing I did. The guy in the bedroom knew about the wall. I don't know how, but he did. Then we found Danvers and Beck. That's three. As for you getting caught, how do you think it'll make me feel to know you did, and it's all my fault? These men were after me."

We argued back and forth without either of us giving in. Several minutes later, Kendric interrupted us when he knocked on the door. "I hate to interrupt, but we've gotta go if we're doing this. It'll be sunrise soon."

She gave me a determined look, and I gave her the same. We were at a stalemate. I was taken back when Kendric said more. "I get you don't want her to come, and I know she wants to, not because I was listening but because I know her. There is a risk, but it's slight. Aisling, would you stay behind if Alistair stayed, or is it the fact you have to see them all dead that has you insisting on coming with us?"

She started to speak, then paused and thought it over. When she was done, she answered him calmly. "While a part of me would like to see them all gone, it's more I don't want Alistair to go. Why? I don't know. That's not to say I want any of you taking a risk with the Coast Guard, either. I-it's just..." She faded away, and I saw tears.

Taking her in my arms, I saw regret and guilt there. That's when it dawned on me why she was fighting me. She'd killed someone. It was a shock even if you'd been trained to expect it as I was. For her, it had to be twice as traumatic, and she hadn't had a moment to deal with it. She needed me to be with her. I made my choice.

"Kendric, tell my men to go without me. I need to stay with Ais. If they have any questions, let me know. The rest of you don't need to go with them. They can handle this."

"I'll let them know," was all he said before disappearing.

As he did, she dissolved into tears. Murmuring comforting words in her ear, I picked her up and carried her to one of the other bedrooms. The master still needed to be cleaned, and she didn't need a reminder of what occurred there. I curled up on the bed with her in my arms. She sobbed for a long time before she was able to stop. When she did, she gave me an apologetic smile.

"Sorry for turning into a leaky faucet and soaking your shirt. I don't know what came over me. And I apologize for keeping you behind. I know how important your job is, and being with your men is your job."

"My job and men are important to me, but

nothing is more important than you. You watched a man die, and it was at your hand. It takes time to get over it. You can cry on me anytime. And I need to apologize to you for not telling you how many men were coming for us. I just don't want you in danger. As for how the guy knew about the room, we may never know, but it'll be taken into consideration. Before the family vacations here again, we'll be making a new one."

"I'm all for that. How long do you think before we know if they're done and safe?"

"They'll let me know. Soon. For now, why don't you and I rest? If you can take a nap, do it. When they get back, we're heading home."

"I'll try. I wish, in one way, we'd gotten to stay longer, but I need to be home with the family, and I want to check on Maeve. She has to be devastated. He was her brother, even if she never knew him. He made her cry, Stair."

"I know he did, *leanabh*. We'll make sure she has all the support she needs."

The tender kiss she gave me melted my hardened heart. I snuggled her closer and closed my eyes. I wouldn't sleep, but I would rest.

◌◌◌

In the end, it wasn't until late morning that we were on our way home. It wasn't a long flight back. The family swarmed us when we returned. We'd been hugged and kissed and finally settled in the family room together. Maeve wasn't crying, but she did appear sad, and her eyes were still red. She almost cried when Aisling hugged her and whispered in her ear for a long time.

"Alright, we've welcomed them back. It's time to get things on track. We'll give you a break on the fight ring, but we're scheduling it within the next week. I mean, it'll make you look like an asshole after announcing an engagement, and then we have to announce you were too weak to take our initiation and therefore had to give her back but oh well," Shane teased him.

"Hey, you can talk out of your ass all day and night, but there's no giving her back, and I can handle you. Anytime," I challenged back.

I enjoyed the heckling from them, and then the women made me laugh when they sided with me and against their men. We were laughing and enjoying family night, as they called it. They'd brought in pizza and wings. I knew they were comforting Maeve and Aisling. They knew she'd taken a life, and it was weighing on her.

We were sitting there enjoying the food and conversations when Darragh took out his phone. It must have vibrated since I hadn't heard it ring. He read the message, then looked over at me.

"I hate to interrupt the fun, but I need Alistair, *Daid,* and the *uncaili* in the Center for a quick meeting. Cody has an update for us."

I knew what it was about. It had to be about the Bragan and Brynes investigation. The way Aisling was looking at me, she did, too. I would be glad to know one way or another. The Hounds and I should be able to move forward if this was the complete investigation.

Excusing ourselves, we went down to the Center. Since it was officially Hounds' business, the others stayed behind. We'd update them with what they needed to know. Arriving, I found Cody was already there. I swear he crept around like a ninja himself. We didn't waste time. We sat, and he started right in.

"I hated to disrupt your evening, but I knew you'd want to know this right away. I've got information on the Bragan family's request. There is proof the women and girls aren't runaways or their disappearances are false reports. They're missing, and it has been happening for well over a year. It seems to be concentrated in the Bragan territory but not exclusive to them. They have a problem without a doubt," he paused to let us absorb this.

"Any chance the Brynes are responsible like the Bragans accused them?" Sean asked.

Cody sighed as he nodded. "There was reason to suspect them. However, I don't know yet if Christopher Brynes is involved. I can say there are people in his organization and even in the family with suspicious income and activities, which led me to dig, and they appear to be involved. We have enough to warrant going after them. Nothing makes the Bragans appear to be more than concerned, and they're making changes to get out of the illegal activities they've been involved in for years, for decades. I wanted to know what you want me to do. Dig more or go after the ones we know are involved. If we do the latter, we risk not getting them all or the head of it."

Anger and distaste filled me. The thought of anyone being involved in that kind of thing was bad enough, let alone someone we know. I had my thoughts, but the ultimate decision rested with Darragh. All eyes were on him. He took his time before he answered.

"I want to hear your thoughts before I tell you

mine. This is a touchy and personal subject for us. We know Chris and his family as well as the others, even though the Bragans less so."

"I feel we should work on getting more information so we know for sure who all is involved. We don't want any to slip through," Patrick said first.

"I agree," Sean added.

"As much as I want to find those girls and women and prevent others from being taken, the thought of it continuing if we don't get them all at once holds me back from saying go now," Cormac stated. Dar turned his gaze to me.

"Dar, I want to nail Chris's ass to the wall, but if it's not his fault, that's not fair. My personal dislike can't be a factor here. I agree with Cormac about wanting to rescue them and prevent more from being taken, but we all have a great point. We can't risk missing even one person involved. We want to take out the whole dirty bunch. My vote is to wait."

He sagged. "Good. It was mine, too. I want this done, but not before we can ensure it'll be one hundred percent cleaned up. Cody, let the Bragans know the Hounds will take the job, but we're still gathering proof and information. They have to agree to let us do our work without interference, and they can't make a move against anyone. If they do, they'll be on the wrong end of it with us. Bring in as much help as you need to get this done."

"I'm on it. I'll let them know tonight. Thanks, that's all I needed to know. As I get names, I'll let you and Alistair know so you can fill in the others."

"Thanks," we told him. After handshakes all around, he left. I knew none of us wanted to tell the women and the others what we'd learned, but it had to happen. It involved two families they knew, and they'd have to be careful what they said if they had any contact with them, especially the Brynes. It would happen, at least on the social level. They moved in the same circles and supported some of the same charities and such.

"Are you ready?" Darragh asked us. We all nodded before leaving to tell the rest of the family the news. It would bring down the mood. I was ready for a solid run of peace and only good news. I guess it would have to wait a while longer.

Aisling: Epilogue-One Year Later

It was crazy to think what my family had dealt with since this time last year. My issues with Danvers Kelly and his hired goons were the least of it we found. There were worse things out there, and we'd been up close and personal with those. You'd think it meant Alistair and I were the ones in the deep end of it since it involved the Brynes, and we had our issue with Chris. Boy, we had no idea what it would end up involving or who. That whole story was a long one.

It had impacted Tiernan even more than us. Some of it was wonderful since it led to him finding his *anamchara,* and he was happily married with a baby on the way. His joy was so obvious to anyone seeing him with his wife. Their beginning wasn't one any of us had ever imagined in my family, but it was perfect for them. They'd fought hard to make it happen. Who knew his knee-jerk reaction could've lost him his chance at his *anamchara* or the danger that almost took her from him after he did find her?

Thankfully, the family had worked hard to support the Hounds in their work to clean up the sex trafficking ring and to bring home as many children, women, and even some men from that awful existence. We hadn't been able to find them all, and it broke our hearts. They'd worked to make Tiernan's wife safe, too. The Hounds were now on alert for any chatter about this kind of activity, and if they found proof, I knew they'd go after them, too. I wholeheartedly approved of it.

The elimination of members of the Brynes family had hit not only their family and mine hard but also the other Irish families. I wasn't sure if that trust would ever be rebuilt. We were leaving the Bragans and Brynes to heal and the Brynes to rebuild themselves. All families were now alert to signs of this happening in their areas and what to do about it, which was to call the Hounds. They still had no clue the Hounds were connected to us or that my husband was their leader.

Yes, I said husband. After the way our engagement announcement was done and then slightly ruined by Danvers, we'd talked. In the end, we settled for a family-only wedding. We had a blowout reception, but Alistair wasn't one for an over-the-top wedding, and all I wanted was to be his wife. I got the perfect, intimate wedding, and I wore the gown of my dreams. We didn't skimp on the decorations or the food. We had music and the whole nine yards at our reception and danced for hours before he whisked me away for our honeymoon in Ireland.

Of course, I had to agree to spend only half our honeymoon there and the other half in Scotland. It was only fair. I loved seeing his home country. I'd never been there all the times we went to Ireland. I would be back often. And we'd had a more than wonderful honeymoon. By the time we returned, I was pregnant. Our first baby was due any day now. We were thrilled to welcome her. Alistair was overjoyed yet terrified that we were having a daughter. The overprotective primitive had gone over the top with preparations to protect her. *Dia* help her as she grew. He'd better be prepared for her to revolt.

Thinking of our baby made me think of the other newest additions to the clan. Cian and Miranda were still stunned every day by their sweet daughter, Caitlin. We loved to tease them to wait until she got older and see if she stayed that sweet. The bets were she'd be a wild one, so we were already calling her Cat. She wasn't alone. Just two months after her birth, Aidan and Karizma welcomed their son Brannon. Khloe was more in love with him than his parents, and that was saying something since they were crazy about him. He looked so much like my brother, and I had no doubt he'd be as ornery and aggravating as him. Karizma agreed.

Along with the babies and our wedding, things with Maeve's Cellars were better than ever. The winery had been repaired and was back up and running in no time. The new wines were out and a bigger hit than we'd hoped. The buzz about them, the requests to sell our wines, and the awards were rolling in. I'd hired more help to keep up, which would be needed when I had the baby. I'd never give up the winery, but my family with Stair would take priority.

I watched as my loud, obnoxious, opinionated family argued with my husband. They were trying to convince him to go with an Irish name for our daughter, and he kept telling them it was an ancient Scottish one, which wasn't in style, but it would be her name. He loved winding them up. Her name would be Scottish, but it was beautiful and not anything like what he was pretending it was.

I began laughing as all four of my brothers jumped him, and they were wrestling on the floor. They should know he was more than capable of holding his own after the time they got him in the ring. The memory of it still brought a proud smile to my face. He'd stood strong even at the end. They didn't go easy on him, and he took it without a peep. Afterward, when *Mamó* said it was over and he was free to have fun, he'd been happy to beat on most of them except the older men. He stayed respectful of them. Even Darragh wasn't safe. When Alistair was done, there was more than him feeling sore and sporting some bruises the next day.

An unexpected pain shooting from my back to my stomach had me crying out unintentionally. I'd had odd, faint pains all day, but nothing like this. When you were pregnant, you got used to odd pains here and there. Braxton Hicks was the worst, and I'd had a lot of them lately. This one was nothing like those. My loud moan stopped the arguments. Alistair tossed my brothers off him and was over to me in seconds. He kneeled by my chair.

"What is it, *mo ghràdh*? Are you alright?" he asked urgently. His hand went to my stomach, and he rubbed soothingly.

I placed my hand on top of his. I smiled as I told him, "Everything is fine. In fact, it's more than fine. How would you like to meet our daughter today?" Something told me this was the real thing.

If his facial expressions were anything to go by, astonishment swiftly followed anxiety. The next thing I knew, I was airborne in his arms, and he was yelling. I swear, carrying me around was one of his favorite things to do.

"Get the damn car," he yelled.

Pandemonium took over as more than one

person ran for the door. Others were up on their feet in excitement. Alistair was standing there frozen as if he had no clue what to do next.

"I'll go grab your bag from the house and bring it to the hospital. It's still in the front hall closet, right?" Siobhan asked calmly.

"Yes and thank you. Stair, look at me," I ordered. His panicked eyes landed on mine. "Everything is fine. I'm not having her this second. I just think we need to get to the hospital to see if this pain is labor or not. Just think, hopefully, we'll have our daughter in our arms by this time tomorrow."

A slow smile spread across his face. He gave me a tender kiss. When he lifted his head, he growled so the others could hear him. "Let's go welcome Sheena Graeme."

Exclamations of joy over her name were bubbling around us as he whispered to me, "I love you, Aisling Graeme, forever and ever."

"I love you, Alistair Graeme, forever and ever, plus one day."

He laughed and shook his head at my one-upmanship. I'd turned my hidden craving into a lifelong one. Nothing could satisfy me like my Stair.

The End Until Tiernan's Striving
Book 5 of the O'Sheerans